C.M. SPIVEY

from UNDER *the* MOUNTAIN

REUTS PUBLICATIONS

Cover illustration by Jess Taylor, www. jesstaylor.portfoliobox.io
Cover design by Ashley Ruggirello
Interior design by Ashley Ruggirello

Electronic ISBN: 978-1-942111-40-5
Paperback ISBN: 978-1-942111-39-9

REUTS Publications
www.REUTS.com

To the GNs, without whom this book would not exist.

And to Dr. Deborah Vause, who taught me to question what heroism really means.

CAST OF CHARACTERS

Guerline Hevya, *newly appointed Empress of Arido*
Evadine Malise, *her lover and Chief Adviser*

Imperial Council:
Pearce Iszolda, *Lord Treasurer*
Shon Marke, *Lord Justice*
Neren Famm, *Lord Legislator*
Lanyic Eoarn, *Lord Merchant*
Theodor Warren, *Lord Engineer*
Jon Wellsly, *Lord Historian*

The Witches:
Aradia Kavanagh, *Heart of Gwanen Clan*
Jaela, *Hand of Gwanen Clan*

Morgana Kavanagh, *Heart of Adenen Clan*
Aalish, *Hand of Adenen Clan*

Olivia Kavanagh, *Heart of Sitosen Clan*
Tesla, *Hand of Sitosen Clan*

Fiona Kavanagh, *Heart of Thiymen Clan*
Moira Emile, *Hand of Thiymen Clan*
Kanika Asenath, *Memory of Thiymen Clan*

The Guild of Guards:
Bertrand Altec, *High Commander of the North*
Tragar Madacy, *High Commander of the West*
Yana Lot, *High Commander of the South*
Maddox Bolva, *High Commander of the East*
Josen, *Captain of the Palace Guard*
Frida, *palace guard*
Hamish, *palace guard*

Other humans:
Desmond Kavanagh, *son of Olivia*
Undine Wellsly, *Guerline's lady-in-waiting*
Bridget Camlin, *Sitosen deserter and leader of the Del thieves' guild*
Piron, *head priest of the Del Temples of the Shifter Gods*
Derouk Madacy, *governor of Braeden*

Other magical beings:
Aasim of Raeha, *wizard of the Atithi people*
Silas Purvaja, *Queen of the Purvaja dragons*

CHAPTER ONE

GUERLINE HELD THE SMOOTH CERAMIC POULTICE JAR IN HER left hand. Her right held a large scoop of greenish goo, which jiggled and betrayed the shaking she fought to control. She stared at it. Vaguely luminescent, yet transparent enough to show a distorted view of her palm, it waited for her to choose.

Her father moaned, and her gaze listed from her hand to his face. He and her mother were laid out before her, their deflated shapes resting on plain linen sheets. Guerline wondered whose decision it had been to stop sacrificing the Sunese silk to her parents' oozing, wondered if her parents were even aware that their deathbeds had been reduced to roughspun blankets. That cloth was almost worse for the situation than the silk; the linen absorbed all the fluids and odors that hung around her parents in a miasma. In the ten minutes she'd been standing over them, their stench, the smell of rot—sweet, but tangy with metal underneath—had burrowed into her nostrils and permeated her throat.

Her eyes had adjusted to the darkness, and she could see almost every detail of her disease-ridden parents. Pieces of their scalps peeled back from their skulls and piled wetly on the pillows in grotesque halos. Their hands were so deteriorated they were practically bone, laid on their stomachs and surrounded by little pieces of flesh stubbornly clinging to joints. Their noses were gone, sunken back into their skulls. Their eyes had melted away completely. Their lips were falling off, and their tongues lolled.

It had only taken a week for her parents to decompose, and they weren't even dead yet.

No one would speak of it. A flesh-eating curse. Such things were unheard of in the center cities. Magic had all but disappeared in the capital and surrounds, crawling back to the borderlands where the witch-lords guarded the empire from any who made it across the cliffs, the mountains, the forests, and the seas that formed natural defenses around Arido.

Magic's retreat was the reason she had only a poultice at her disposal, rather than the healing powers of a Gwanen witch.

Guerline relented at last and inhaled deeply, blinking past the sting of pungency in the air. The poultice was useless. She knew it, and if her father had his senses at the moment, he'd know it too. He'd slap her and curse her for getting such a fool notion into her head, demand to know why, at nineteen, she couldn't manage not to be a bother. The poultice wouldn't save him. She doubted that even a Gwanen witch could, at this point. Their only hope, if such still existed, was with Thiymen clan, for the emperor and empress were certainly more dead than alive.

The poultice might ease some of their pain, though, and it was this mercy Guerline debated. She had come to their sick-chamber with every intention of being a help to them, as much as she could. Yet her hand would not turn over, would not apply the poultice to her father's flesh. Tears filled her eyes that had nothing to do with the acidic atmosphere in the room. Was her heart so bitter, that she couldn't exceed her parents in decency?

"Guerline, what are you doing here?"

She jerked to attention, silently cursing the smooth-hinged door. Her brother stood a few feet inside the room. Though she stopped herself from taking a step back, she could not stop her knees from buckling; she leaned against the thick mattresses of her parents' bed.

Alcander wore his customary glare as he looked at her, squinting at the jar and goo in her hands. He held a white handkerchief over his mouth and nose; a pitiful attempt, she imagined, to block the smell of death. Like her pitiful attempt to ward off the thing itself with her poultice.

She looked back down at her parents, fear like an icy rock in her stomach. Her father's chest collapsed minutely, an attempt to breathe. Guerline's own chest tightened as she fully comprehended, for the first time, that when her father died, Alcander would be emperor.

Lisyne save us from the reign of Alcander.

Alcander stomped closer. "Well? Answer me!"

"I was just trying to help," Guerline whispered.

He was silent for a moment, then said quietly, "Stupid girl. Can't you see they're beyond help?"

Guerline's stomach turned at the softness of his voice. She tried to stand still as he stalked toward her, boots hissing on the stone. "Mother is . . . but if we could just summon a Gwanen witch—"

"Absolutely not."

She slumped forward, cast her eyes down, and bit her lip, but Alcander stayed where he was. Slowly, she pushed herself away from the bed and stood on her own. Unable to bear the gelatinous texture of the poultice a moment longer—it felt too much like a stag's stomach—she dumped her handful back into the jar, dragged her palm along the rim, and set it down, taking up the small towel she'd brought and wiping her hands.

"Summon the Thiymen witch, then," she said.

"The damned Thiymen witch has no need of a summoning, she will come when she comes," Alcander spat. "Whether I will it or no."

He looked away from her, staring into the dark far corner of the room, and Guerline narrowed her eyes at him. Surely even Alcander, who hated magic, wouldn't prevent the witch from doing her duty. But if he could, if he had that power, *would* he stop the witch from laying their parents' souls to rest? Guerline couldn't fathom why Alcander the favorite, Alcander the firstborn and heir, would deny his parents their final reward, even if it had to come from a witch's hand.

"Their souls must be taken to Ilys," she said.

Alcander sneered at her. "The god-denier still believes in Ilys, does she?"

Guerline's cheeks flamed, but she didn't look away. It was an old argument among the royal family. Her parents and Alcander were all devout followers of the shifter gods, but Guerline . . . she questioned. Both that the gods existed as anything but stories, and whether such gods as were described should even be worshipped; either question was enough to earn her the hatred of her parents and the derision of her brother. Alcander seemed to delight in reminding her that only her value as a political bargaining chip prevented Emperor Johan from turning her over to the Temple for cloistering and flagellation. As if those threats were meant to teach her to love the gods.

"I have never seen Lisyne. I *have* witnessed the power of the witches. If they say Ilys exists, I will trust them," she said.

"You do wrong to rely on the witches, Guerline. They are exalted enough as it is without a member of the royal family setting such a poor example for the rabble. Remember that they were created to *serve* humanity," Alcander said.

"At least *they* are among us," she retorted before she could stop herself.

Alcander rushed her. She tried to twist away from him but tripped on her gown and fell forward. She flung her hands out; one landed on her father's stomach and sank into the sticky mass, tacky to the touch and soft beneath his sopping velvet doublet. She could feel hard lumps within his guts that could have once been bones.

She screamed and pushed back, slipping again and reeling into Alcander's waiting arms. He snapped them shut around her, strong like bands of iron around a barrel. Her fingers went numb with panic and she collapsed, hoping to break his grip with her dead weight. But he was ready for her. He snaked one arm around her waist and used his free hand to grab both of her wrists together.

"Stop your whimpering. Weren't you paying attention?"

Guerline swallowed hard and stopped breathing. Alcander nuzzled in close to her ear, his smooth cheek scraping the stubble on her shaved scalp.

"Father didn't make a sound when you struck him. Do you know what that means?"

She gulped again. Yes, she did. Father was dead.

"I am emperor," Alcander whispered.

He let go of her waist and she spun away from him, ignoring the burn as her wrists twisted in his grip. When she faced him, he stared down at her, his brown face wide and unreadable. For one horrible moment, she thought he might—

He released her.

"Get out," he said.

She hesitated. It wouldn't be the first time he'd let her go only so he could chase her.

"I said, get out. Now!"

She barely resisted the impulse to run.

Alcander contained the urge to seize Guerline's arm as she brushed past him. She must have thought he didn't notice, but he knew she'd been purposefully avoiding him. He wouldn't stand for it. But there would be time to deal with her later.

He walked around the sickbed, hardly breathing, watching his father and mother warily. Both lay utterly still. He went to the windows and ripped the curtains back. Sunlight flooded in. Alcander turned from the window to look at them and gasped at the full horror of their decay.

His stomach churned. Coughing and choking, he ran from the room. The door slammed behind him. He leaned against the cool stone wall and sucked clean air into his lungs.

"Alcander?"

The prince jumped and turned. He smiled when he realized it was only Evadine. She looked pristine in her simple linen dress, with her black hair plaited down her back and her cheeks lightly rouged. She was a welcome vision of health and life after the disgusting scene he'd just witnessed. Her face was passive, but her eyes asked the question: *what happened?*

"My parents are dead," Alcander said.

Evadine dropped to one knee.

"Your Majesty," she said demurely.

Alcander smirked and went over to her, hooking a finger under her chin and guiding her up. He looked into her eyes.

"You need never bow before me, Eva."

She did not respond. Her eyes danced over his face. "You're so ashen, and sweating. Is it that bad?"

His lip curled. "They were living corpses. Impossibly alive even as their bodies disintegrated. But they are dead now, and that's all that matters."

"Thiymen will pay," Evadine said.

Alcander scowled at the dullness of her voice. She said she supported his cause—he certainly believed the reasons she gave for her begrudging support—but he was not yet sure her commitment was genuine. "Yes. Yes, they will. If only we could prove it was them."

"We don't need proof. All we need to do is show the people what happened to your parents. They will know as surely as we do that the disease came from the coven of death," Eva said.

"You know I can't do that. It would deeply dishonor my parents to show their subjects how repulsive they have become."

She pursed her lips. "None of it would fall back on them or their legacy, Alcander. The people will blame Thiymen, as they should. They will be outraged . . . and we will have the momentum we need."

Alcander clenched his teeth and stood silently. He knew she spoke the truth, but he couldn't allow his parents to be seen by more people than necessary. The emperor and empress had been proud and healthy a week ago, and now they were utterly destroyed. He was of the same flesh and blood. The people may very well declare that he possessed the same susceptibility to evil magic and depose him. They had done it time and again throughout history. The people of Arido could not be trusted to stand with him if they knew the truth.

"Alcander?"

"Do not ask me again." He walked away.

"Where are you going?" Eva called after him.

"To the Vale. Go and inform the council of my parents' death, and get everything ready for the washing and the watch. The witch will come soon."

"What shall we do when she does?"

He stopped and sighed, and looked back at her over his shoulder. "Nothing. We can do nothing. Yet."

While he waited for his horse to be saddled, he went to the fountain in the square, just outside the palace gates, and splashed cool water on his face. It refreshed him and relieved some of his nausea. A stable boy came out and handed Alcander his reins. The prince mounted his horse and rode off toward the Orchid Vale, the forest on the edge of the capital city of Del.

It was almost an hour's brisk ride from the First Neighborhood, where the palace was situated. Luckily it was midday, and since it was coming on summer, many people were spending the next few hours indoors. Lake Duveau kept the city from becoming blistering hot, like some of the Southwest, but its effect didn't entirely keep Del from getting uncomfortable under the high sun. Alcander was grateful for his timing, though sweat streamed down him as he rode; his path was clear the whole way.

He slowed when he arrived at the tree line, and then halted. Dismounting, he led his horse to the Stone River that ran through the center of the Vale. He slipped its bridle off and let it drink, then stripped himself of his clothing and waded into the river. The water was still cold, flush with snowmelt from the Zaide Mountains and shaded by the tall trees. Alcander dunked his head under a few times, whipped his braids back from his face, and climbed out of the river. He sprawled on the bank to dry, feeling cleansed of the grossness he'd felt at his parents' sickbed—their deathbed.

The bodies would have to be burned. Such a blight of the flesh must not be put into the earth. Burning was a dishonor, but he was sure his devout parents would have agreed to it if they had had time to discuss it with him. The trick would be convincing the council, and keeping it from the public. The funeral procession would be closed-casket, unusual but not unheard of. The watch, though . . . he hardly wanted to allow the witch to gloat over the ruination of his parents' bodies. Could a Thiymen witch collect a soul through a coffin? Would she even come for his parents' souls? And what would he do if she did? He was a skilled swordsman, but weapons were no match for magic.

He detested Thiymen clan all the more for his dependence on them. Only a Thiymen witch could take his parents' souls to Ilys, the place of rest they deserved—yet how could he give her care of their souls when he knew that her clan had murdered them? To confront a witch without a plan was certain death. His hands were tied. The watch must take place.

His horse looked up and snorted. Alcander raised himself onto his elbows.

"What is it?" he asked.

The horse's eyes were wide and white all the way around. It trotted nervously back and forth. Alcander stood up and listened intently, but he couldn't hear anything over the horse's stamping and snorting.

"Will you shut up?" he snapped at it.

The horse screamed, reared, and ran, breaking through the underbrush in its haste to get away from whatever it had sensed.

"Hey! Come back here!" Alcander yelled, running a few steps after it.

He could still hear it screaming, but it was long gone. Alcander scowled and gathered his clothing, grumbling about stupid animals and the long walk back to the palace. He pulled his trousers on and laced them up, and had started to pull his shirt over his head when he shivered violently. Had it gotten colder in the forest? He looked up; the summer sun was still shining through the trees as it had been before. He shook his head and laughed. He was not usually prone to paranoia, but the eeriness of his parents' deaths had clearly followed him to the forest—and cost him his horse! He stood still and listened as hard as he could, wishing he had the beast's ears or sense of smell.

Goosebumps rose on his arms and he looked down. Though he neither heard nor smelled a thing, he felt it approach him from behind. His breath came shallow and rapid, and his heart raced in his chest despite his attempts to stay calm. Slowly, cautiously, he turned around.

The creature's head was mostly visible skull, with dry-looking musculature around the jaw and ears just barely hanging on. The body seemed oddly mismatched, thick about the torso and hips but stunted in the legs, with a long tail that looked more like a dog's than a cat's. The fur was patchy and dingy, and the uncovered flesh was the same sickly green color his parents' skin had been in their final hours.

But all the oddity of the hell-cat's form did nothing to detract from the evil in its glowing yellow eyes, nor the sharpness of its dripping fangs.

Alcander's hands went to his hips, but his sword was on his saddle.

"L-Lisyne, Mother Wolf and protector of us all," he whispered, eyes wide as he stared at the devil-cat. "Take my form and shield me from evil—"

The devil-cat took a step forward and Alcander shrieked. He jumped backward and fell over a rock. The cat circled him. He was paralyzed; training urged him to find a weapon, but fear wouldn't let him take his eyes off the predator. He felt along the ground with his trembling hands. The cat crept on top of him. Its stench was overwhelming; he couldn't breathe. His vision darkened, and when it returned, the hell-beast was nose-to-nose with him.

"Back! Stay back!" he wailed. He beat it about the face with his hands and elbows. Blood streamed down his arms from the scratches made by the rough old skull. He ceased his attack when he saw the blood, and screamed anew, looking back and forth between his arms and the cat's now bloodstained head.

The cat, for its part, seemed intrigued. It sniffed at Alcander's bloody arm and tentatively licked it with a swollen purple tongue. Alcander watched it, lips trembling and tears streaming down his face. The cat looked down at him, its eyes bright.

"Lisyne! Seryne! Oh please, let me be saved," Alcander whispered.

"Saved?" said a voice.

A face appeared above the devil-cat—a pale blonde girl with blood-red lips. She grinned.

"Alcander. You have been chosen."

Her black eyes sparkled. Alcander screamed. The cat closed its jaws on his throat, and the clearing fell silent.

Guerline woke to shouts in the hall outside her chambers. After her encounter with Alcander, she'd rushed back to her rooms and shut herself in. It had taken ten minutes to scrub the poultice and gore from her shaking hands, and when she was finished, she'd collapsed into a chair in her parlor and sobbed herself into a fitful sleep.

Someone pounded on her door, and she lifted her heavy head to squint at its black expanse. She swung her gaze toward the large window opposite her. Evening had fallen. She'd been asleep nearly all day.

The pounding on her door resumed.

"Princess Guerline! Your Highness! Please, please open the door!"

Still groggy, she tumbled out of her chair, nearly falling as her legs came clumsily back to life.

"Let me help you," said a soft voice to her left.

Tender hands slipped around her waist and under her left forearm, taking her weight. Guerline halted and looked down at her left wrist. A slim white hand held her there, translucent-looking against her dark brown skin. She followed the white skin to a black-clad wrist, up the arm, and looked into the face of a young woman with dark eyes, dawn-gold hair, and blood-red lips. The woman smiled at her.

"Good evening, Guerline," she said.

Guerline scrutinized the woman, furrowing her brow and staring into eyes that were nearly black in the twilight. There was something familiar in her steady expression, and even in the pressure of her hands. Guerline drew a shallow breath, tried to look away, and found she couldn't. She wet her lips.

"Am I dreaming, or have I died, and you are my Thiymen witch?" Guerline asked.

The woman—more a girl, really—laughed. Guerline gasped; it was as if a window had just been opened in a stuffy room.

"I wondered myself, before I arrived. But I think I won't be taking you to any underworld yet."

Guerline nodded, absently gazing about her twilit room. "A dream, then."

Pounding on the door.

The girl laughed again. "If it helps you to think of it that way, then by all means."

Guerline shook the last of the sleep-fog from her head and turned back to the girl, but she was gone. Guerline wavered slightly where she stood and held her breath, waiting for some sign that she was truly awake.

"Break it open. We must find her!"

She cursed and ran for the door, stumbling on her long skirts. Dream or no, she couldn't risk losing a locking door. She flung the bolt back and pulled the door wide, stepping out of the way in case the shouts of "Hold, hold!" didn't stop whatever battering ram they'd been preparing to use.

In rushed Lord Engineer Theodor Warren; Josen, the Captain of the Palace Guard; and Hartt Lana, her father's—Alcander's—Chief Adviser. All three men were flushed of face and breathing heavily, staring at her with wide eyes. She could guess that Hartt and Josen were here on the occasion of her parents' deaths, though why they looked so panicked she couldn't tell. Surely they hadn't just found out; it had been hours. Lord Warren's presence she couldn't account for at all, but the tender way he looked at her provided some hint.

"What on earth is going on?" she asked.

"Your Highness. You must have heard that your parents died early this afternoon," Hartt said softly. His voice was raspy, and Guerline wondered if he'd been crying. Her father had been a hard man who allowed very few into his close confidence. But Hartt, who had a decidedly softer touch than Emperor Johan Hevya, had occupied that position her entire life and then some. If anyone loved her father, it was him.

She nodded. "Yes."

None of the men offered anything further. Guerline raised her eyebrows. At last, Lord Warren stepped around Josen and reached out a hand.

"Permit me, Your Highness?" he asked.

She placed her hand slowly into his, her breath coming short with apprehension. Such serious countenances couldn't simply be for her parents, could they? Toward her, her father was always dismissive at best, her mother spiteful; but as rulers, they were all aloof benevolence—not too distant, just removed enough and fair enough to give the illusion of compassion. She had to admit that the rest of the empire loved her parents much better than she did.

Lord Warren led her to a settee and they both sat. He didn't let go of her hand for a moment, staring at it in his. Then he jerked it back and sat up straight. He looked her full in the face, but still he was silent. Whatever he meant to tell her must have been very dreadful indeed. He'd never been so formal or awkward with her before.

"Theodor." She reached for his hand again.

"Your brother is dead," he blurted.

Her heart stopped. She swallowed, with difficulty, and narrowed her eyes at Lord Warren. Her throat suddenly seemed like sandpaper. "What?"

"He went riding this afternoon. When his horse came back without him, I sent men out to look for him," Josen said.

"They . . . recovered his arm from the Orchid Vale," Lord Warren continued.

Guerline inhaled sharply. "His arm. His *arm*?"

Lord Warren squeezed her hand. His blue eyes shone like sapphires. Guerline focused on them and tried to tamp down the inappropriate, giddy relief threatening to burst out of her.

"It appears to have been an animal attack. Some panther or wildcat," he said.

She coached herself to breathe. Alcander dead. She hadn't wished for it. She'd only ever hoped to get far, far away from him. But her fear of him uncurled itself from around her heart and fluttered in her chest like a swarm of butterflies. She was not, truly, happy to hear that Alcander was dead. Yet neither was she sad.

"Are you all right?" Lord Warren asked.

Guerline took a deep, shuddering breath, trying to fill to the bottom of her lungs. "Yes. I'm fine. I'll be fine."

"We'll arrange everything, Your Highness," Hartt said. "You needn't fret."

"Everything?"

"The washing, and the watch," Hartt said.

"And your coronation, of course," Lord Warren said.

Of course. Her coronation. Because, with Alcander dead as well, she was the next in line to rule. The hysterical laughter she'd been fighting broke through, high-pitched and breathy, quickly turning into sobs.

"Josen, fetch Lady Evadine here at once!" Lord Warren said.

She could barely see Hartt and Josen as they bowed and left the room, and she gratefully sank into Theodor's embrace.

CHAPTER TWO

ARIDAN FUNERAL PRACTICES, AS OUTLINED IN THE BOOK OF Skins and by the priests of the shifter gods, were fairly straightforward. Yet there was an uncertain silence in the air as Guerline, Evadine, and the imperial council stood gathered in the washing chamber. Johan and Maribel had been gingerly transported from their deathbed down to the palace's Temple, shielded by a thick line of guards who kept out the mourners attempting to gather—a recommendation from Eva, who announced it had been Alcander's wish that Johan and Maribel's corpses not be exposed to the general public, in honor of their memory. Guerline had been more than happy to abide by that desire. The fewer people who were forced to take in the abominable sight, the better.

The first step of an Aridan funeral was the washing. The body was cleansed with pure water and doused with perfumed oils, then dressed in their finest clothing and laid out for the watch. The honor of preparing the departed went to their closest relatives, and so Guerline's attendants stood slightly behind her, waiting. But how could she wash her parents' flesh when it was sure to disintegrate under the first pour from the jug? Their bodies lay on a single litter, braced on a pair of rectangular stone washing pools, each big enough for a large man to be laid in fully. The corpses, too, waited for her to begin.

The silence became awkward, and still Guerline did not know what to do. She shivered in the plain linen shift she wore and tried to still the panic fluttering in her mind.

"The princess is overwhelmed with grief. My lords, I beg you, go into the Temple and support her from there," Evadine said. Her clear, sharp voice almost seemed to shatter the empty air, and a rush of relieved sighs filled the vacuum. The councilors shuffled out into the main Temple, some of them patting Guerline's shoulder as they passed. Once she was alone with Eva and the corpses, Guerline hung her head, expelling a stale breath.

"There," Eva said warmly. She swept in front of Guerline and put a hand on her cheek, forcing Guerline to look into her smiling grey eyes. "Now, let's solve this puzzle."

Gratitude lightened Guerline's heart, which pounded in her chest as she gazed up at Evadine. "Thank you, my friend. I could barely breathe with all those people in here, let alone think."

"There was no point to them being here, biting their tongues for fear of looking stupid. They just needed an excuse to leave," Eva said. She shifted to Guerline's side, her arm around the princess's shoulders. Guerline focused on the comforting pressure as they stared down at the rotting corpses.

"It's no less than they deserved," Eva said.

Guerline couldn't bring herself to frown. Instead she said, "We can't lower them into the pools. They'll taint the whole supply, and then Priest Piron will be in a state."

Eva laughed, which broke the spell the corpses seemed to have over them. The two women broke apart and approached Johan and Maribel. Eva bent at the waist to peer down at them, while Guerline bent at her knees and lowered herself slowly into a squat, bracing on the edge of the wash pool. The smell was as bad as it had been yesterday, but somehow it wasn't as offensive to Guerline now. Now, at least, her parents were dead and ought to smell like rot.

"Must we wash them at all? Must we even bother?" she said after a minute of silent pondering that led her in circles.

"The procedure is clear. . . ." Eva frowned. "We should at least make an attempt. What if we don't, and the witch refuses their souls?"

"If I were a Thiymen witch, I wouldn't care how clean a body was on the outside," Guerline said. "They can see how clean one is on the inside."

Evadine was quiet. After a moment, she said, "The way they are now, we'll be washing them on the inside too."

Guerline laughed, then clapped a hand over her mouth and looked up at Eva. Eva stared back at her with wide eyes, the corners of her mouth twitching. The two of them were bent over rotting corpses only a day dead, debating how to wash disintegrating flesh in order to make it *pure* and *clean* for death-witches who, at the handful of watches Guerline had been to, had never spared a second glance for the condition of the corpse. And this did not even begin to cover the strangest of the funerary decisions she was now required to make—that honor went to the single arm recovered from her brother, wrapped and laid at the foot of her parents' bodies. Was she to wash *that* too? Was Alcander's soul in his arm?

Her gaze fell on the abandoned arm, its cloth wrapping speckled with fluids. The guards had searched the Vale for the rest of him, but there was naught but blood to be found, and it could only be assumed that he had been eaten whole by some beast. Why it left his arm behind was a mystery—perhaps it was frightened off, or perhaps it was too gorged on the rest of him. Theodor Warren had offered to simply have it disposed of . . . but it gave Guerline a terrible kind of satisfaction to gaze before her and see proof that her family was all dead.

A shadow caught her eye; she looked up and saw, standing across from her, the pale blonde girl from yesterday. She too stared at the arrayed remains of the Hevya family, her brow furrowed in an expression Guerline couldn't place. Guerline rose, her mind scrambling to read the girl's face, as though she could see there a sign of how to proceed—but before she landed on a coherent thought, the girl lifted her eyes to Guerline's. Guerline blinked, and she was gone.

"Lina?" Eva said.

"Call for a scrub-basin or two, and a scraper of some kind," Guerline said, an idea coming to her. The litter fabric was thin, soft, and sopping with decomposition;

the floor underneath the corpses already puddled with juices. "We'll rinse them on the litter. Hopefully the loosest flesh will strain away, and what remains will hold until the witch comes."

Eva nodded and went to the door of the washing chamber, whispered the order to someone else, then came back to Guerline and took her hand. They waited in a silence that was somehow comfortable despite the presence of the bodies. Guerline's gaze kept drifting to where the girl had appeared. When she woke this morning, Guerline had written off the vague memory of a figure as part of her stressful dreaming. Yet, she had recognized the girl instantly—

Evadine shifted her hand and intertwined their fingers. All thoughts of strange, pale girls were flushed away by the sudden pounding of Guerline's heart. *It's innocent*, Guerline tried to tell herself, while Eva's thumb lightly stroked her hand. Eva had been her friend and companion for years, almost as long as either of them could remember, and there were few enough boundaries between them.

There would be fewer still, if I had my way.

She held perfectly still lest some movement inspire Eva to draw away. As it had countless times in the past year, Guerline's mind spun with a heady rush of questions, fantasies, and insecurities, all triggered by Eva's closeness. The past few months, especially, Guerline had lived in a frantic stasis, her body shrinking from everyone but opening to Eva, only to shrink again before the other woman might notice. Moderating her caresses was a battle of wills, her desire begging her to draw Eva close, while her fear stymied any such attempt.

Relationships between those of the same gender were common in Arido. Guerline's fear arose not from the threat of social censure, but from her father's insistence that she be considered eligible marriage material by various foreign courts. Certain of the empire's sovereign neighbors believed such a relationship . . . unclean. Others believed that *any* relationship outside a sanctified marriage was tainted. So when Guerline sensed the change in her feelings for Eva, she panicked. Johan had warned her what would happen to any lover she might take, regardless of gender.

But now, he was gone, and she could decide for herself. Nothing stood in her way but her own fear that Eva would not return her love. Guerline squeezed Eva's hand, and Eva smiled at her. Her grey eyes shone bright against her golden skin.

"Eva . . ." Guerline said.

There was a knock on the door, and Guerline cursed under her breath—she could have sworn Eva did too. Guerline extricated her hand and went to the door.

"Good," she said, when she saw the servants with the basins she had asked for. Her cheeks felt warm. She hoped the blush wasn't noticeable.

She bade the servants enter and directed them to set the basins under the litter where her dead parents rested. The basins—large metal ones for laundry—filled the space under the corpses nicely. When the servants had gone again, Guerline sighed and took up the laundry bat they'd brought her to serve as a scraping tool. Evadine took up one of the carved clay jugs from a shelf on the wall and filled it with water from the pool. Her movements were so elegant, she almost looked like the water dancers that performed on the lake on High Summer's Night. Eva straightened and lifted her gaze to Guerline's; Guerline quickly looked down at her parents instead.

They oozed.

"Shall we?" Guerline asked. Eva nodded. Guerline returned the gesture and said, as one last offering to her devout parents, "Lisyne, Great Wolf, Mother of Arido, though I wash this my father, this my mother, of their earthly odors, I beg you will remember their skins. Remember their scents. Their forms are yours and yours alone, from this moment on."

Eva hefted the jug, and then paused. "Not your brother too?"

Guerline glanced at Alcander's arm. "Let it be an experiment. See if the witch comes for un-cleansed flesh."

Evadine gave a huff that was almost a laugh and splashed water onto Johan and Maribel. The water sloshed among the soft bones and jellied organs for a few seconds, then pinged, yellow with bile, into the basin below. Guerline, her lip curling, used the edge of the laundry bat to drag the pooled liquid through the cloth.

"Disgusting," Guerline muttered. Eva laughed.

After the longest hour of their lives, the two women summoned the rest of the council to assist with the dressing of the corpses. Though they'd opened the chamber's vents, the pungent smell of rot mixed with the sweet perfumes and astringent oils made the air feel thick. Guerline found she didn't mind; it certainly motivated the councilors to dress the deceased quickly, which was easy since she'd decided to use only the outer robes. Attempting to dress them fully would only have made them fall completely apart, and no one wanted that.

The councilors used a fresh litter to transfer Johan and Maribel into the Temple's main room. The sanctuary was circular, and the floor was covered in soft animal pelts of all kinds, meant to represent the breadth of the shifter gods' personas. The plentiful benches formed concentric half circles, starting at the back of the room. The far wall featured statues of the three gods in their human forms. The farthest to the left was Tirosyne, the Jolly Tiger. He was depicted as large and broad, with abundant hair and beard. The farthest to the right was Seryne, the Lucky Fox. She was small and spritely. In the center was Lisyne, the Great Wolf, Mother of Arido. According to the Book of Skins, it was she who had created the world and populated it with humans, then made the witches to protect them. She was tall and straight-backed, stern and proud. A giant wolf stood behind her.

A plinth had been erected in front of the shifter gods, and upon this her parents were laid. Bare-footed, as was required in the Temple, Guerline stepped from soft fur to coarse hide until she reached the first bench. She and Eva sat together, and the councilors arrayed themselves behind her. The watch began.

Watches never took long—Guerline had never heard of one that lasted more than two hours. The magic of Thiymen clan somehow alerted them whenever a human died, and they came swiftly.

Tiredness plucked at her, attempting to pull her spine out of its straight alignment and curve her into herself like an old woman, barely strong enough to hold herself up. She resisted it, breathing deep into her chest and using each inflation of her lungs to reassert her posture. Beside her, Eva was tall and still and somber.

The chamber was silent, but this time the silence was tinged with fear instead of awkwardness. They all knew who was coming—only one witch of Thiymen was exalted enough to escort the souls of royalty.

Fiona Kavanagh. The Heart of Thiymen.

And the most hated witch in Arido. She was synonymous with death, and as such, was the focus of human fear. The Book of Skins spoke of rebirth through Mother Lisyne, yet the people of Arido clung to the life they knew. Fiona, and the witches who served her, represented the end of that life. It was not hard to understand why she was hated, but Guerline pitied her, even as anxiety rose at the thought of seeing her face to face.

Would she come? As Heart of Thiymen, it was her duty to collect the souls of the emperor, empress, and the heir, but Fiona had not been seen outside her Citadel— as far as Guerline knew—in twenty-five years; not since Guerline's grandmother had died. That, at least, was a matter of record.

It was said that Fiona was terrible to look upon, swathed in black but bleached bone-white in every part of her flesh from trafficking so much in dead magic.

Guerline barely had time to conjure up an image of the infamous witch before the air went winter-cold. Everyone in the room sat up straighter, and all eyes snapped to the bodies before them. There was a sharp crack, like a whip snapping. A bright purple light appeared in a vertical line behind the corpses. Two hands appeared out of thin air and pushed the light apart like a curtain. Out stepped a tall woman. Fiona.

She was thin, almost a skeleton herself, and wore a long black robe. Her head was covered by a large hood; she reached up with black-gloved hands and pushed it back, revealing a hollow-cheeked face. Her skin was smooth, as was her hair, which hung straight from her scalp. She was indeed white as bone, in all things except her eyes and lips—these were both as black as her clothing.

Those black eyes found Guerline's, and they were flat and solid, like stone. Guerline's blood went cold, but she rose anyway and strove not to shake.

"My condolences on your loss, Your Highness," Fiona said. Her voice was barely more than a whisper. Guerline managed a jerky nod in return.

Fiona continued, "Who is responsible for this man and this woman?" This time, her voice was strong, filling the sanctuary and making Guerline jump. She was surprised, not just by Fiona's change in tone, but what it implied—had the Heart of Death truly meant to offer her some private comfort? That hardly seemed to match the folk-descriptions of her.

"Guerline," Eva whispered sharply.

"I am," Guerline said, fulfilling the script.

Fiona's mouth twitched. "And do you send them into the care of Thiymen clan, to be taken to the realm of the underworld in which they may receive their appropriate peace or punishment, as determined by the Judges?"

Guerline nodded. "I do."

"Then I, Fiona of Thiymen, promise to deliver their souls safely thence," the witch said.

Guerline nodded again and stepped back. Fiona leaned first over Johan's body, then Maribel's, and put her hands on their chests. She didn't seem to mind the condition of the flesh, though of course, they had perfumed it, hadn't they?

Slowly, Fiona drew her hands up. The bodies glowed with blue light, and as Fiona lifted her hands, the lights rose and took on the likeness of Johan and Maribel respectively. None of the onlookers so much as breathed. Fiona stepped back and righted the souls so that their feet were on the floor. They opened their ghostly eyes and looked at her. Guerline held her breath, but the souls had eyes only for their witch escort.

She could have sworn Fiona smiled as she lifted her hood and turned her back to the mourners. She held a gloved hand out to each soul. They took her offered hands, and she led them through the curtain of purple light. Another crack split the silence, and suddenly, both witch and souls were gone.

Alcander's arm remained, untouched and unacknowledged.

The mourners released their breath with one collective sigh. Guerline blinked a few times until she no longer saw spots of light, then turned to the councilors seated behind her. She took a deep breath, in no hurry to speak as she gazed at those familiar faces, still marveling that she had just been mere feet from one of the most powerful figures in Arido—indeed, marveling that *she* was now also considered one of those figures.

That thought sent a chill down her spine. She found Eva's eyes, and they smiled at each other; she took comfort from that and used it to fuel what she had to say next.

"Burn the bodies," she said. And she walked out of the chamber, leaving Eva to enforce the dishonor, as planned.

Guerline screamed and vaulted forward in her bed, gasping, struggling against shadows so black they made the darkness of her room seem like daylight, pushing until her hands met warm resistance. Slowly, she became aware of the sound of Eva's voice, humming in the dark. She felt the mattress shift under her and realized that Eva had joined her on the bed. She hadn't even known her friend was in the room.

"Eva, what—"

"It's all right, Lina, I'm here," Eva said. "Do you want me to light a lamp?"

Guerline stared, unseeing, though even as she breathed, her eyes began to discern familiar shapes in the night-washed room. One breath, then another, each one deeper than the last. She found herself shaking her head, though she knew Eva couldn't see it. She swallowed, the motion painful, and found her hoarse voice. "No, no lamp. I thought . . . you promised you'd sleep in your own room tonight."

Eva's chuckle was almost like a caress. "I lied."

Guerline managed a sigh that was more grateful than exasperated. It had been two weeks since the rest of the royal family died, and she was not holding up well. She had barely gotten any sleep thanks to a plague of nightmares—her parents' rotted faces, blood dripping on her face from Alcander's stump of a shoulder—and her days were filled to the brim with invitations from the First Families desperate to gauge the strength of their new empress.

Thus far, she had refused them all, taking full advantage of the mourning traditions set in place by the Temple of the Shifter Gods. Her time was almost up, though. She would soon have to rejoin the world—as its leader, not merely its sometime observer. She reached for Eva and was immediately comforted by the other woman's embrace.

"Wait," she said. Eva froze. "If you're going to stay, you may as well get comfortable."

That earned her another small laugh from Eva. Guerline watched her silhouette as she stood and removed her linen overdress, leaving only a sheer chemise that Guerline remembered rather than saw. Eva climbed back onto the bed, slipping under the covers this time, and returned to Guerline's side. Guerline curled up against her, settling comfortably against the taller woman's torso. Eva's hand found a resting place on Guerline's cheek, and her thumb moved slowly back and forth over her skin.

"Was it like the others?" Eva asked.

"Yes," Guerline replied.

The nightmares followed the same pattern, taking some of her worst memories and exaggerating them, forming a horrible pageant of her life. First would be the time Alcander had locked her in the sewing room, except the fabric was water and it slowly drowned her. Next she'd relive the night she saved a starving dog from a stable hand, only this time, there were no guards to hear her cry. And then, invariably, inevitably, the night just three weeks ago when Alcander had come to her chamber—

She stiffened and glanced instinctively at the knife on the bedside table behind her.

"Shh," Eva said, as if she'd known what was going through Guerline's mind. She pressed her lips to Guerline's brow once, then again, soft kisses soothing the panic welling up inside Guerline. "I'm here. I'll always be here, from now on. Sleep."

The pervasive exhaustion of the past two weeks tugged at her, and Eva's words made Guerline feel safe enough to give into them. Perhaps she could steal just a few moments of restful sleep before the cycle began again. Moved and feeling brave, she kissed Eva's neck and closed her eyes.

She smelled bitter smoke, and opened her eyes—all she could scent was Eva's lingering perfume. She shut her eyes again and gave way to sleep, but not to rest. The nightmare picked up where it had left off, with her brother murdering her in the cleanest way possible, his body a weapon to crush her without breaking a single bone.

CHAPTER THREE

THE CAVES WERE PITCH BLACK, BUT THE DARKNESS DIDN'T deter the Heart of Thiymen. She could find her way through a more total darkness than the natural world could ever provide. Her stride into the bowels of the Zaide Mountains was as firm as ever, as slow and determined as the steady approach of death.

Kanika Asenath walked slightly behind her mistress, watching the back of Fiona's white-haired head carefully.

"Fiona, please. I beg you, leave this to the Guard," she said. "Moira lives to do her duty for you, and I know she will not want to be deprived of the privilege—"

"Moira will do what I ask, even if I ask her to step aside," Fiona said, her voice low and resonant. "And that is what I must do now. This thing is too strong, too strange for them."

They had all noticed the weakness in the barrier between the world of the living and the world of the dead. Each time a Thiymen witch crossed the boundary, it was torn, but the rules of repair were extremely firm. Any witch who didn't immediately close her gap was severely punished. Lately, the Guard had noticed several sloppy gaps, tears which had clearly been made by no Thiymen witch; they were wobbly, indefinite, unwarded, and vulnerable. Someone from another clan was doing dark magic and not cleaning up after themselves. All the extra gaps were weakening the ancient separation of worlds faster than the Guard could repair it—and *something* was pushing through, aiding this decline from the other side.

They were all anxious. If the boundary were to suffer a severe tear, or—Lisyne forbid—fall completely, all the unnatural darkness of the underworld would be unleashed upon them.

When Kanika and Fiona reached the great cavern, the seven witches of the Guard were standing in front of the massive sheet of black rock that served as a physical door between the two planes. Such a door was not necessary to travel between the worlds, but it was the place where the boundary was thinnest, which meant that Fiona wouldn't have as much miasma to push through to get to the other side.

"Fiona!"

Moira's voice echoed sharply in the cavern. As the Hand of Thiymen and Fiona's second in command, Moira had served as Captain of the Guard for three hundred years.

Her skin was pale and her hair was grey, which showed how much time she spent on the boundary; color meant life, and Moira was virtually colorless.

"Fiona, I really must protest," Moira said. "There are seven of us. Let us seal the gate. It is much safer."

Fiona replied calmly. "Moira, you know I trust in your experience and judgment, but you must also know that this is beyond you."

Moira stood rigid, her expression stony. She did not dispute Fiona's words. Everyone understood that Fiona's power was greater, greater even than the full power of the Guard. But that was what made Fiona's involvement so dangerous; she would die younger than they would. She had become so powerful so young—it was certain. She could exhaust herself in this effort. Fiona knew this too, but she was immovable, as always. Moira glanced at Kanika, and Kanika frowned. Fiona had only gotten more stubborn in the two months since the deaths of the emperor, empress, and crown prince. More stubborn . . . and more secretive. Fiona had gone to collect the souls of the departed monarchs, but she had barely mentioned the lost soul of Prince Alcander. She'd only said that she would handle it, and that neither Moira nor Kanika were to involve themselves.

"At least let us support you, Fiona. Let us stand with you," Moira said helplessly.

"This I will allow," she said. "You may form a reserve line behind me."

"A reserve line? Fiona, no. Let us share our power—"

"No. I must have total concentration, and you will distract me," the Thiymen leader said.

Kanika's frown deepened. Fiona's voice was not one to ever be called comforting, but the edge in her tone was more pronounced than usual. Her jaw twitched, just under her ear, and her fists were clenched at her sides. Her face was as impassive as ever, but now that Kanika had perceived it, she was nearly knocked down by her leader's anxiety.

Was Fiona . . . afraid?

Moira nodded and stepped aside to let Fiona pass. The Thiymen leader walked right up to the wall, something that still would have made Kanika flinch. The Guard fell in behind her. Kanika positioned herself in a corner where she could see Fiona and watched; she was the Memory of the Clan and would make a record of this later.

Fiona studied the wall carefully, her white brow furrowed. She flicked back her black sleeves and in a slow, deliberate motion, put her hands on the rippled stone, her long white fingers splayed. For several moments, she remained still, her dark eyes fixed on something beyond. Her fingers twitched slightly every now and then as she manipulated the magical curtain that hung past the rock. All was silent, unnaturally still.

Fiona froze, her eyes wide with shock. She shuddered and began to sink to the ground. Her frame shook as she pushed back against the force of her unseen enemy. Kanika was close enough to hear Fiona's bones cracking, and she winced. The Guard cried out as one and ran forward.

"Stay back!" Fiona shouted.

They halted immediately. She regained her position, spreading her feet.

Kanika's gut twisted with panic as she watched. Fiona leaned into the wall, almost nose to nose with it. Her thin mouth curled slowly up into a scowl of frustration, then a grimace of pain. She dug her fingers into the thick rock to grapple physically with whatever was on the other side. Slowly, her fingers bent into a grotesque, claw-like shape. Fiona screamed in fury as she pushed whatever it was back, forcing it further into the underworld. Kanika and the Guard could only watch helplessly.

At last, she gave an unearthly shriek and slammed her hands flat against the wall. A shockwave rippled through the black rock. Fiona's hands fell heavily to her sides. She swayed, trembling before the great barrier. Immediately, the other witches in the cave ran to her and caught her.

"My lady? Fiona!" Kanika cradled Fiona's unresponsive head.

"She lives," Moira said, crouching on the other side of their fallen leader.

"What was it, Moira-lami?" asked Sempra, another of the Guard. The newest, Kanika remembered; her skin was the color of a tree's inner bark.

Moira met Kanika's eyes, glanced at Sempra, then looked down at Fiona once more. "Believe it or not, child, even I do not know all the secrets of the world under the mountain, nor every thing that resides there," she said. "I daresay there's but one who does."

Kanika brushed a pale strand of hair from Fiona's white brow. Her eyelids fluttered. "Quickly," Kanika said, "let's take her back to her room. Before anyone else sees."

"Sempra, get her legs," Moira said. As she and Kanika hefted Fiona, she said to the remaining witches, "Observe and repair now, as quickly as you can."

Kanika, Moira, and Sempra carried their leader back to her room by the secret way. There would be panic if the Citadel saw her. Fiona was harsh, but precious to those who served her in Thiymen clan; for many, she had been the first to treat their skills as a noble calling instead of a curse. It was sometimes difficult to hold on to the high purpose the clan served when humans flinched at the sight, or even at the mention, of a Thiymen witch. To be treated in such a way, after everything a Thiymen witch suffered for the sake of human souls. . . . Kanika threw a glance back down the path, the hateful gate to the world under the mountain as clear in her mind as if she was still standing in front of it.

She remembered distinctly her first visit. It had been on her first night in the Citadel. Fiona had come to her in the middle of the night, coaxed her out of bed, and brought her down into the belly of the mountains. Nine-year-old Kanika had wept to look at it. It was blacker than her own skin, scored with great slashes cut deep into the rock. There were places where it buckled, and there appeared to be the impressions of hands pushing through; in some spots, screaming faces could be discerned. She had tried to look away, but Fiona had seized her small hand.

"Look at it, Asenath. Look, and understand. This is our great charge. This is the boundary between life and death, and we must keep the two from merging. No one else in Arido can do this, and so we must; though it will take our lives, we must protect Arido from evil," she said. "Never forget this moment."

Kanika had looked at the barrier for what seemed like an age before finally turning and burying her face in Fiona's robes, weeping uncontrollably. Fiona had led her silently back to bed, the way she had done with every new Thiymen witch.

"Kanika . . ." Fiona breathed.

"Nearly there, Fiona-lami," Kanika said, smiling at her.

The three of them laid Fiona in her bed and brought herbal teas for her, which she drank silently. Her hands shook and her eyelids fluttered as she struggled to maintain consciousness. Kanika reached out to help her hold the cup, but Fiona waved her assistance away. She set the cup down and leaned back against her headboard, eyes closed. The three witches waited a long while for her to speak, watching anxiously. They burned with curiosity. Kanika folded her hands over her chest, sitting in her usual chair by Fiona's desk, and meditated. Moira tapped her foot, and Sempra paced.

Fiona stirred.

The three witches flew to her bedside and Fiona sat up, looking at them. Her eyes were glazed over, and her brows knit together.

"It sucks at my soul," she said quietly.

"Like crossing the threshold?" Sempra asked.

Fiona paused. "It is the thing that tries to claim us as we pass."

The words settled heavily in the air as the witches took them in. Crossing the threshold between life and death was dangerous for many reasons, chief among them being the possibility of losing one's soul in the passing and being trapped among the dead. There was always something tugging at a witch's soul during a crossing; it was unnatural to be a whole soul and body in the world of the dead. While they had always known and understood this danger, they assumed it was a natural law; they had certainly never thought it was being done by a conscious *thing*.

Kanika's mind raced through the millennium of history she had committed to memory during her youth, the hundreds of years she had lived. If such a force existed, surely some witch had written about it before. But she knew there was no such record. If it was true that there was a thing under the mountain which stole the souls of crossing witches, it would be widespread knowledge. Kanika trusted that Fiona was right, though; so the question was whether this thing was new, or whether it was ancient. She glanced at Fiona's stuffed bookshelves, tucked into a corner of the room, and remembered Moira's words in the cavern. Fiona had never allowed Kanika to read through her papers, which had never seemed strange before. But that there should be no record of something strong enough, and old enough, to threaten witches' passings . . . it seemed too great an omission. If there were records of it, Kanika was sure they'd be among Fiona's private library. Unease prickled along Kanika's neck—she was the Memory. It was her responsibility to know the history of the clan; how could she do that if Fiona kept information from her?

There was no one to ask, either. The previous Memory of the Clan was dead, and if Fiona was keeping secrets already, she'd hardly divulge them if Kanika only asked. Perhaps . . . the Dragon Queen. She was as old as Fiona, as powerful in her own way.

Fiona slid out of her bed, brushing past the dumbfounded witches and drawing Kanika's attention. She went to a thin cabinet by her bookshelf and pulled out a decanter filled with a dark red tonic. She poured a small glass for herself and raised it to her black lips, throwing it back all at once.

"It senses our current weakness," she said. "It knows our disadvantage and positions itself to strike. It has been imprisoned a long time."

"It spoke to you?" Kanika asked.

"Yes," Fiona said after a pause. Kanika raised an eyebrow but didn't press the issue.

"What can we do?" Moira said.

Fiona didn't answer. She stood with her back to them, as immovable as the stone of her walls. Kanika watched her carefully, wondering what she was thinking, what knowledge she had that she would not share with them yet.

"The Gate must be our focus," she said. "Crossings are forbidden, for now. Every witch is to make strengthening the barrier her priority. Make it known."

Moira and Sempra jumped to their feet. They kissed their fists and pressed their flat palms to their hearts, then left the room to spread the mandate.

"Fiona . . ." Kanika began.

"This is all we can do now anyway," Fiona said. "They know it is dangerous, and that is enough. There's no need to cause a panic."

"Thiymen does not panic," Kanika said with a wry smile. "No witch panics."

Fiona turned and walked back to her bed, squeezing Kanika's shoulder as she passed. She took off her heavy black robe, and, wearing only her thin black shift, crept back under the silky bed coverings and closed her eyes. She looked impossibly frail, now that her black eyes were closed.

Looking down at her, Kanika suddenly saw an old, weary woman. Moved, she reached for Fiona's hand.

"Make the record, and send a copy to my sisters," the youngest of the Kavanaghs said.

The door shut behind Kanika Asenath, and immediately afterward, Fiona felt the charge in the air. She did not open her eyes, too weary even to lift the thin lids. The dragon blood always took longer to restore her the longer it had been absent from Silas's veins. Let the creature think she was rude; better that than she should think she was weak.

"You don't fool me, child," said the creature.

Fiona felt the weight as it sat on the edge of the bed, and did not resist when it gathered her up in her arms. The creature's wolf-fur itched Fiona's face, and she could not tell if it was a dead pelt or if the creature had only partially transformed—it definitely had a woman's arms. In the end, it didn't matter; Fiona curled into the warmth and sobbed as she had not done since she was a child. Six hundred years of not weeping spilled out of her.

"It gives me no joy to see you suffer," said the wolf.

"I do not suffer, to do my duty to you cannot be suffering," Fiona replied.

"Your duty to me," the wolf repeated. "You say you do your duty, and yet you told them."

A fang's edge in the wolf's voice. "No," Fiona breathed. "Not truly. But I need. . . . Something must be done. I'm no longer strong enough."

"I know, child; that's why I'm here now," the wolf said. She kissed Fiona's head and laid her down again. The weight and warmth of her bedding was drawn up once more over her shoulders. "Yet, swear again to me . . . swear you will let none speak with it."

"I swear," Fiona said. "Of course."

The wolf was silent, and Fiona wondered if she had gone. She was so tired.

"What did it say this time?" the wolf asked, in a whisper so small Fiona thought it might have been in her head.

She took a shuddering breath. "All it did was scream."

Another long pause, and then the pressure of a hand on her forehead. "Rest," said the wolf, and Fiona slept.

CHAPTER FOUR

THE DAWN WAS PALE WHEN EVADINE WOKE, BUT SHE DIDN'T
need much light to appreciate the woman next to her. She
knew every line of Guerline's body, knew her every sound;
she had dedicated herself to the study and adoration of
Guerline, her own gentle princess. Eva rested her cheek
against the tight curls on Guerline's head, and while she
watched the sun rise through a tall window, she reveled in
the weight of that head sleeping soundly against her chest.

Two months had passed since the deaths of Alcander
and his parents. Despite Guerline's many entreaties, Evadine had yet to resume sleeping in her own room. How
could she, when Guerline continued to wake screaming in

the night? She had vowed to protect Guerline, even from the phantoms in her own head, however she could.

Oh, but it was such a sweet torture to share Lina's bed so chastely. There were so many innocent moments that took Eva's breath away while she lay awake, vigilant for signs of distress from Guerline. Guerline would roll toward her, and her hand would brush Eva's stomach; she would bend her knee just so that it began to nudge Eva's legs apart. Her lips would find a way to press themselves to Eva's chest, and it would be all Eva could do not to wake Guerline with kisses. A beautiful conspiracy had begun to form in Eva's mind, that these moments were not as innocent as she'd thought, that Guerline was sometimes contriving to touch her from the safety of sleep. The thought thrilled and frustrated her.

Her hand floated up and cupped Guerline's cheek, as it so often did. Eva would have sworn, before the Hevya deaths, that Guerline was in love with her. But their greatest impediments, Guerline's father and brother, were two months in the grave, and still they languished in a mire of unspoken words.

Eva sighed. New impediments had presented themselves since the Hevya deaths. Guerline's nightmares left her with little energy, though they were becoming less frequent; and what energy she did accrue seemed quickly claimed by the First and Second Families, those chiefest of nobles who thought they had such claims on Guerline's time. They never would have presumed in such a way with Johan, sending their heralds day in and day out, demanding audiences before their new empress was even crowned. It was madness, and more, it was rude. Eva took great pleasure in sending them away, especially since Guerline had appointed her Chief Adviser.

"I'd rather be your consort, though," Eva whispered into Guerline's hair.

It wasn't long before the sun blazed through the room. Tomorrow was High Summer's Day, the longest day of the year; an auspicious day for Guerline's coronation, and the reminders of other new impediments to their relationship. Though Guerline would be empress and no longer subject to her father's whims, she would have the responsibility of keeping peace, or establishing it . . . perhaps through a marriage with one of their sovereign neighbors. At least this time, Guerline's husband or wife would come here, to Del, and Eva would not lose her—but that hardly took the sting out of the knowledge that a marriage between Guerline and Eva was, to say the least, politically unwise.

Eva's appointment to Chief Adviser last week had caused a surprising amount of consternation among the First Families. Suddenly, all that mattered was her low birth, that she was the daughter of an ambitious marsh merchant from the peninsula waterways to the south. Her father, whose face she could no longer recall, had gotten over his head in some deal with the imperial household. Eva, then very young, had been given in payment as a companion to the toddler princess.

Despite the method of Eva's placement in the household—a practice outlawed not two years later—she and Guerline had been inseparable ever since. Eva slipped an arm around the still sleeping Guerline's shoulders and held her tight. Guerline was Eva's family, her only love, no matter what else may happen. For all her unsatisfied desires, Eva's greatest wish was to stay with Guerline always.

Guerline had said as much in response to the Families criticizing her choice. "The Chief Adviser's function," she had said, "is to be my right hand, my champion and my guide, to speak with my voice when I'm unable. Who among you could I trust more for this than my best friend of fifteen years?"

Eva had struggled so hard not to laugh at their faces, and she and Guerline had retreated from the luncheon where the announcement was made as quickly as possible. That had been the way of things the past two months— Guerline would marshal herself for perhaps half a day's worth of politicking, and then she would need to withdraw. Eva sighed again into Guerline's hair, her ever-present anxieties rising like storm clouds on a bright horizon.

Guerline had always had a kind of quiet strength, though Eva was typically the only one to see it, and perhaps Theodor Warren, since he matched Lina much in temperament. When Eva had first heard of Alcander's death, and realized Guerline would ascend, it was this strength that had immediately formed a vision in her mind of Guerline, soft and beautiful upon a throne, loved like Gentle Fontaine, second empress of Arido, who was still remembered by some as though she were their doting grandmother.

But Fontaine had ruled only ten years. True, this was because she was old when she came to the throne—but history still stood and showed that the Aridan people favored rulers who projected strength. Eva, though she loved Guerline, was not sure her friend was up to the task of leading an empire still pervaded by ancient tribe loyalties, made worse by the witch-lords at the borders.

Eva scowled. The witch-lords . . .

"So bright," Guerline muttered, her voice heavy with sleep.

Eva smiled, her worries forgotten. "Harken ye, the first lady of Arido stirs. We may all now rise from our beds."

Guerline lifted herself up on her elbow enough to squint at Eva, a smirk on her large lips. Her cheek was pressed with indents from the folds of Eva's nightdress, her hair was smushed into several conflicting directions, and her eyes were puffy and shadowed; but none of that changed Eva's opinion that Guerline was the most beautiful woman in Arido. Feeling brave, she slid down from her half-sitting position and rested her head on Guerline's thick arm.

"Now it is my turn to sleep," she said, closing her eyes.

"Eva, don't tell me you . . . have you slept at all these two months?" Lina asked, her voice serious.

Eva opened her eyes, and saw Guerline looking down at her with new alertness and concern. She smiled and said, "The more sleep you get, the more rested I feel."

"You must take care of yourself," Lina said, her eyes drifting the length of Eva's body. Eva's heart raced. Lina continued, "You ought to sleep in your own bed, for one thing."

Eva laughed. "Oh no, I rest far better at your side."

Guerline didn't lose the serious look on her face, her brows pulled up into an expression of concern that frustrated Eva. How could Guerline look at her like that, when she herself was struggling to sleep through the night, when she had such shadows under her eyes? Firm words rose on her tongue, telling Guerline to mind her own health before she showed concern for others. Eva reached up and put her hand on Guerline's cheek, intending to deliver those words with Lina's full attention—but at Eva's touch, Lina gasped just enough to part her lips, and Eva found *herself* distracted.

She looked from Guerline's lips to her eyes, saw them round and bright. Guerline would never initiate, Eva knew that.

She moved her hand to the back of Guerline's head and pulled while simultaneously arching herself up. Their lips met, and it seemed as if time stopped. Eva shut her eyes, content to stay there as long as the universe allowed it. She ventured only to open her mouth against Guerline's already parted lips, but then Guerline's hand was on her back and pressing their bodies together, and Eva kissed her harder. Her body seemed to almost ripple against Guerline's, flexing from head to toe again and again in an attempt to get as close as possible. Their chemises rode up and their bare legs intertwined. Guerline returned the growing eagerness of Eva's kisses and they clutched at each other, at the fine thin fabric that tangled around them. Heat flowered deep in Eva, and she felt the same heat from Guerline when she slipped her leg high between Guerline's legs.

It was that discovery that finally made Eva gasp and break the kiss. She and Guerline stared at each other, faces dark, eyes shining, each of them panting. Guerline had ended up on her back, slightly propped by the abundance of pillows, and Eva lay half on top of her with that one leg gradually spreading Guerline's. Finally, they broke the stare and looked around, each of them taking in this scene. Eva licked her swelling lips. Had Guerline imagined this as often as she had?

Guerline looked up at Eva in what could have been wonder, a smile tugging at the corners of her mouth, and Eva grinned. She kissed Guerline again, gentle and brief this time.

"I love you," Eva said. "I've said it a thousand times, I know, but this time . . ."

"I'm in love with you," Lina said, nodding ever so slightly. Her smile widened, and she tilted her chin up. Eva kissed her, giddiness bubbling in her chest.

When they broke apart, Guerline glanced to the window. There was no denying now; the sun was up, and it was full day. As Eva stared into the bright yellow light, Guerline hooked a hand around the back of her neck and pulled her down, slightly to the side, and started to kiss her neck. Eva closed her eyes and hummed with pleasure.

"How much time do we have?" Guerline asked between kisses.

"I say we stay until they come for us," Eva murmured against Guerline's ear. The other girl shivered, and Eva grinned. She rested her head against Guerline's forehead and slipped a hand below the coverlet, under the chemise that had ridden up and exposed Guerline's hips. She trailed her fingers along the soft rolls of Guerline's stomach, listening with satisfaction to Guerline's breath get shorter and shorter the closer her hand got to the source of that incredibly inviting heat. When she reached it, she paused, her hand hovering over its target, and she kissed Guerline, who groaned impatiently against her mouth.

"Eva, please," Lina said.

And Eva would have obliged immediately, if there had not been a knock on the door. She cursed under her breath and looked at Guerline, who stared at her, eyes wide with indecision even as her hips rocked toward Eva's hand. Then Guerline closed her eyes, whimpered and tilted her chin up, hips arching. Ignoring the knock, hardly able to think of anything but Guerline's need, Eva kissed her and pressed her hand to Guerline's warmth. Guerline cried out and bucked against Eva's hand, and Eva's whole body filled with a powerful heat. She felt transcendent, physically strong and yet somehow also stretched beyond her body, connected to Guerline and even farther, like the universe itself flowed into her and into her fingers, guiding the movements that made Lina moan. Eva kissed her harder, muffling the moans, swallowing them like they were the only food she would ever need again.

"Your Highness, are you all—oh!"

The voice came from within the room with them, and this forced Eva and Guerline reluctantly apart as they turned to face the intruder. It was a young girl with black skin and curly hair wound into a tall up-do. Her overdress was fine embroidered linen and she wore a comb with a dangling charm over the center of her forehead, which marked her as a nobleman's daughter. Her eyes were wide with shock—she couldn't have been more than fifteen. Eva tried and failed to feel ashamed.

"What do you want?" Guerline asked, her voice surprisingly steady, given how her chest still heaved. Eva fought to contain her smirk as she slid out of the bed and into a light dressing gown.

The girl curtsied, stepping her right foot back and bending that knee. "Please, Your Highness, I am Undine, granddaughter of your councilor Lord Historian Wellsly. I'm to be your lady-in-waiting?"

"Oh yes, I remember now," Guerline said. She sighed, and with that exhale went the last of their exertion. Eva held up a second dressing gown and smiled at Guerline as the princess stood from the bed, adjusted her chemise, and turned while Eva guided her arms into the sleeves of the gown and settled it onto her shoulders. "You know Lady Malise, of course?" Guerline added.

"Call me Eva," she said. Normally, Eva stood on more ceremony; but it was only fair, since Undine had caught such an intimate impression of her. The smirk won, pulling up one corner of her mouth.

Undine nodded, her eyes still wide. "Of course, Lady—Eva." She looked back to Guerline. "Your Highness, you are to have your hair done today."

Guerline groaned, but nodded. Undine went to the bedroom door, and Guerline started to follow; then she looked back to Eva.

"I'll be along in a moment," Eva said. "I just need to wash up."

The reaction was instant—Guerline grinned, Undine blushed, and Eva could not help but laugh. Guerline nodded, and she and Undine left, shutting the door behind them. Eva giggled as she went into the small washroom attached to the bedroom. There was a larger room in Guerline's suite for bathing, so this room had only a counter, upon which sat a basin, a towel, a dish of soap flakes, and a tall ewer of water. The ewer rested on a small stone circle which was enchanted to keep it cool, so that the water was refreshing at all times.

Eva poured water into the basin and washed her hands with her eyes closed, reliving the most beautiful morning she had ever experienced. She was not sure what she'd expected when she kissed Guerline, but what had followed had certainly exceeded any fleeting thing she could have envisioned.

Guerline loved her. Guerline wanted her. It was a dream come true.

But even as Guerline's presence had chased away Eva's worries, her absence allowed them to return. There was every chance their dream come true would stay dreamlike: brief and rare. Evadine was not a good marriage prospect, and that was assuming Guerline stayed on the throne long enough to marry. There had been no official session of council since the death of Guerline's parents—since they must legally wait for her coronation—but Eva knew that Lord Engineer Theodor Warren had been speaking already to Guerline of the anti-witch movement. Guerline had of course known about it before, and she and Eva had debated the issue casually on more than one boring night; but now Lina must actually deal with it and the powerful figures on either side.

Yet another new impediment to their relationship. Lina always argued in favor of the witches. Eva, however, was more committed to the opposition than she had previously revealed to her dear friend. Eva dried her hands on the towel and swallowed her anxiety, then went back into the bedroom.

"Don't you see, Eva?"

She staggered backward, looking for the source of the voice. Suddenly *he* was standing in front of her—Alcander. This time, he came to her as if out of a memory, whole and fully clothed, his brown skin flush and healthy. But this was no comfort to her, because the fear she'd felt in that memory came back to her as well, flooding her and paralyzing her with silence as it had on the night not long before he'd died, when he'd worn that tunic and waved that enchantment at her.

It was a magical dagger of defense developed by the witches of Adenen—a small blade that could be kept on one's person, a final protection should other measures fail. It required no skill to use; the blade recognized a target and, when slashed, sent a pulse of magic that was as painful as any true cut.

Eva knew this from personal experience.

"Don't you see, Eva?" Alcander said again, as he had that night. He slashed the blade. This time, no magic pierced her, but Eva cried out instinctively. "Magic is a thing of pain, and it must be *ours* to control! Ours alone!"

Eva clenched her jaw, shut her eyes, and ran across the bedroom to the exit. Nothing stopped her, and when her hand closed around the door handle, she looked over her shoulder at the empty room. She took deep breaths to steady herself again. Memories were preferable to the other visions, the ones where Alcander was dead, blood dripping from his torn left shoulder, his skin bruised and bloated. At least she knew she could escape the memories. Every time she saw the wraith, she expected it to drag her, body and soul, to the underworld.

She opened the door and strode down the hall to Guerline's dressing chamber, and managed to return Guerline's smile when she crossed the threshold. Guerline's brows pinched inward, and Eva longed for a moment alone with her, to reassure her that the somberness monopolizing her face had nothing to do with their glorious morning together. But Guerline was trapped, seated on a tall stool and surrounded by more ladies-in-waiting. Young Undine was directing them, shouting orders and circling them like some hairdresser hawk, watching as they sectioned Guerline's natural hair and began to install false hair in twists.

Undine noticed Eva's entrance and smiled at her. "Would you like to assist, Eva?"

Eva laughed. "It looks like you have all the hands you need. I'm happy to observe."

The young lady-in-waiting nodded and returned to her minions. Eva and Guerline shared bemused looks as, over the next several hours, Guerline's short curly hair was converted into long twists the orange-red color of a setting sun. This was a slightly brighter version of Guerline's natural hair color, and when Eva did finally get up to closely observe the process, she thought the colors very well matched. She knew little of how the magic behind cosmetics functioned, only that it served as practice for the young witches of Gwanen clan and provided Aridans with many colorful and rejuvenating creams with which to paint their faces, as well as hair modifications such as the kind now being inflicted upon Guerline.

"Remind me why we thought this would be a good idea?" Guerline muttered.

"You've had the same hairstyle for ten years," Eva said. "You remember? Ever since I ruined your hair."

Guerline smirked. "How could I forget? You were so distraught."

Eva sighed and rolled her eyes at the memory. Maribel Hevya had told Eva that, as the princess's companion, it would be her responsibility to maintain the princess's hair. Eva had not the slightest idea, however, how to work with hair like Guerline's. Her own hair was smooth and straight, could not hold a curl if it was threatened. Though she'd tried to do as she was told, knowing that she'd be sent away if she failed, it had been a disaster. Guerline had never seen her own hair being done, only felt it, and could only direct Eva so much. Eva's aggressive child-pride precluded her from asking for help from the maids—who, anyway, averted their eyes whenever Eva glanced toward them. Undoubtedly Maribel had told them *not* to help.

Guerline's hair—and Eva's position—was saved only when Guerline begged the help of none other than Undine's mother, Yaella, who had done Guerline's hair in the style she herself wore and taught them how to do it. Ever since then, Guerline's only hair routine had been for Eva to shave the sides of her head while Guerline herself conditioned and twisted the tight curls on top.

Watching Undine transform Guerline now, Eva was grateful for the new addition to their royal entourage . . . even if she had barged into the bedroom rather rudely.

Guerline's scalp ached. Undine assured her that over the next few hours, she would get used to the new weight of the twists that fell to the middle of her back when pulled away from her face. When swept to one side of her head or the other, they went quite down to her hip.

She had to admit, though, when Undine helped her at last off the stool and led her to the full mirror, that they very much altered her look, and for the better. Perhaps it was simply, as Eva said, because she'd had the same hairstyle for so long—since childhood—but seeing herself with these twists that could fall across her face in a way that reminded her of Eva's silky hair *did* make her look older. More like a woman. More like an empress.

Especially when Undine demonstrated the braids and knots into which she could arrange the twists, which gave her added height and presence. She would need every inch, that much was certain.

The dressing room seemed to blur as Guerline's thoughts flung themselves between memories of all the meetings and luncheons and dinners she'd had, invitations from the no-bility—ostensibly to comfort and congratulate her. Yet each one felt like a test. With few exceptions, the nobility struck her as calculating and self-centered. She supposed they had a right to be so, but she could not help disliking that they now turned their calculations upon her. Aridan history was riddled with usurpations.

Thus far, her simmering panic had been mostly con-tained, or channeled into flashes of aristocratic anger that Eva later praised; but she could not see that attitude lending itself to a long and stable reign.

She hadn't yet determined what *would* facilitate such a reign, but her coronation was still taking place tomorrow.

Someone put their hands on Guerline's shoulders and drew her attention back to the present. She looked into the mirror and saw Eva standing behind her, smiling, her eyes dancing over Guerline's reflection. Undine thanked the other ladies and ushered them out; Guerline boldly took Eva's hands and clutched them in the center of her chest.

Eva smiled wider in response and kissed Guerline's cheek. Even that small gesture sent a tingle down Guerline's spine.

She wanted to go back to that morning and never leave it. Could a witch do that for her, seal her in one perfect moment in time?

"You like the hairstyle, Your Highness?" Undine asked hesitantly.

Eva started to pull away, but Guerline held her hands in place as she looked over at the young lady. "I do, thank you, Undine. And please. No titles, not from you."

Undine gave them a small smile and a brief nod. "Shall I bring up your lunch? I'm sure you're both very hungry."

"Yes, thank you," Guerline said.

The girl curtsied fully and hurried out. Eva watched her go, but Guerline looked back at the mirror, observing the fine line of Eva's long neck. *Forget the coronation, forget this empire*, she thought. *I'd rather kiss her until the end of time.*

"I hope we didn't corrupt the girl too much. She's so young," Eva said.

"She was just surprised," Guerline replied. "You can't blame her. I was a little surprised myself."

Eva slid away from her and took just one hand, intertwining their fingers. She led Guerline out of the dressing room and into her parlor.

"Were you really that surprised?" Eva said quietly. She laughed. "I'm quite the master of myself, then."

"In truth, I was probably too distracted by my own feelings to notice yours," Guerline said. "Isn't that funny?"

"But understandable." They stopped and faced each other, and Eva kissed her. Guerline melted into her closeness. They let go their hands and wrapped their arms around each other. As much as she had enjoyed the frenetic contact earlier, this, she thought, was wonderful in its own way: solid, warm, patient, as if they had all the time in the world to be together, to love each other.

Eva pulled back and said, "What will we do, Lina?"

Guerline knew, from the tightness of Eva's brow, that she was speaking of things Guerline would rather put off considering—but as ever, Eva was right. Undine had seen them together, and though the girl didn't seem like a gossip, Guerline was the empress. Even the most casual of her relationships must be handled with care until her first marriage could be settled. Aridan monarchs were allowed up to three spouses, since marriage was such a useful diplomacy tool, but the order in which those spouses were acquired was one of the delicate political matters Guerline was now faced with.

"I will marry you, Eva," she said.

"Shall I be your first wife, though?" Eva asked. Her expression was wry, but Guerline knew there was no challenge in what she said. Evadine had a talent for asking the necessary questions without arguing, which was one of the reasons Guerline had made her Chief Adviser.

Guerline sighed. "I *want* you to be." If Eva was her first, possibly only, wife, then their children—born of their joined blood by the grace of magic—would be the heirs. Many would be angered by that, given Eva's undistinguished family line, but Guerline struggled to be bothered. She felt, more strongly than she expected, that she didn't care what her noble subjects and sovereign neighbors might think about her preference for Eva, common though her blood might be. If she had come to realize anything over the past two months, though, it was that what she wanted was now only one small part of how she must make decisions.

Eva squeezed her hand, and Guerline nodded to the unspoken words. Eva understood the landscape before them, better even than Guerline did. She had always cared more about the people and the politics Guerline now had charge over.

"Smile now, Lina. Your marriage is a bridge soon to be crossed, but not yet," Eva said. She kissed Guerline's cheek. "Whatever happens, I'm here, I will always be here, and I will always be yours."

"And I will always be yours," Guerline echoed, bringing up their joined hands and kissing Eva's fingers.

Eva smiled, and they separated, seating themselves at Guerline's parlor table just as Undine entered with two servants, one carrying a covered plate in each hand, the other goblets and a pitcher. Undine herself carried a short, wide vase stuffed full with blooming rose heads, which she set down on the table once the servants had deposited their burdens and departed. Guerline smiled at Eva across the flowers, and Undine blushed.

"No one told me that the ladies were—but I thought there ought to be—I thought it would be sweet if—"

"Thank you, Undine, they're lovely," Guerline said.

"They're perfect, Undine," Eva agreed.

Undine nodded, beaming, and poured sweet cider into their goblets with a satisfied smile on her face. When she had finished, she curtsied first to Guerline and then to Eva. Then, she sat herself in a chair by the door and pulled a small book from her pocket.

Eva and Guerline grinned at each other and turned their attention to their food. There was no hurry. Guerline saw to it that there was nothing scheduled on the eve of her coronation, anticipating that, as the hour of the event drew nearer, she would find it more and more difficult to maintain her composure. Eva had assured her they would have the most relaxing day, taking their ease and doing only things that made Guerline happy.

As Eva asked how she would like to spend her afternoon, Guerline could not help smirking.

CHAPTER FIVE

EVA PACED JUST INSIDE THE DOORS OF THE BALLROOM. Even through the heavy wood, she could hear the murmuring of hundreds of people beyond, waiting. For many of them, it would be their first true glimpse of their new empress; and according to Josen, Captain of the Palace Guard, they were, to put it simply, *eager*.

Why shouldn't they be? Guerline was young, mysterious—ignored and sheltered by her family only to be thrust into authority by their gruesome and sudden deaths. Eva's new favorite guard, a young man named Hamish, had told her there were stories going around the Fourth Neighborhood that this was some sort of rags-to-riches tale, that the beautiful princess had been kept shut away and given only the meanest scraps from the wicked emperor and empress, peace for their souls. This narrative had infiltrated the Third and even, Hamish said, the Second Neighborhoods, some citizens of which were now outside the ballroom doors.

How ridiculous could people truly be, and how could they say such things? What did they expect to see? And how could Eva possibly welcome any of them when she knew Guerline was ashen with fear in her chambers?

Or had been, hours ago, when Eva last saw her. Her duty as Chief Adviser, the voice of the empress in her absence, was to give direction to the servants and the councilors and the priest who would oversee the coronation, Piron. Undine had dragged her out of Guerline's dressing room with a strength she would not have expected from the petite teenager. Eva had bristled at being forced to leave Guerline's side, but by the gods of the forest, she would put such a fear into the assembled with her introduction that none would look at Lina as anything other than the strong, dear soul she was.

"Anxious, Evadine-ami?" asked Lord Warren.

Eva tried to keep her face neutral; it was still strange to hear the honorific for council members applied to her name. And it was quite a mouthful. "Not at all, Theodor-ami."

The man nodded and bowed his head, a few strands of brown hair coming loose from the thin black ribbon that bound his hair at his nape. His white skin seemed very pale indeed, and she thought perhaps *he* was the anxious one.

"And how was Guerline when you left her? I mean, Her Majesty?" he asked.

"Still Her Highness," Eva said, with a wry smile which Warren returned. She looked around to make sure no one was near, then lowered her voice. "She . . . was nervous. But rallying."

Warren nodded again, as though that was what he'd expected to hear. Evadine wouldn't have told him anything, except that Guerline was fond of him. He was one of the only councilors who spent much time with her before the deaths of her parents, and he'd been very kind and supportive since then. Eva didn't care much for him and his particular brand of northern conversation, but Guerline needed friends, and he was very clearly disposed to be one.

"Vultures. I hope they'll show the proper respect," Warren said, indicating two councilors lurking in a corner together.

Eva followed his gaze and frowned. Pearce Iszolda, the Lord Treasurer, and Lanyic Eoarn, the Lord Merchant. They had been pestering her for a meeting almost constantly for the past two months. After today, she would no longer be able to put them off. But she had a few more hours yet.

She smirked at Warren and said, "Shall we open the doors? We'll see then who *flocks* together."

Warren nodded gravely—northerners, such taciturn *nodders*. Eva gave the signal to the guards at the doors. They set themselves on the rings and pushed, the heavy metal bands scraping the stone. As the doors opened, the sounds of the crowd swelled. The fleet of guards at the door and at various points along the queue had been given specific instructions, and Eva was pleased that there was no mad rush. Instead, perhaps a dozen or so entered, glittering in the light from the floating Adenen lamps: the First Families.

Warren glanced at her and she thought for a moment that he would offer her his arm, but he seemed to think better of it. She grinned at him, then strode forward to meet the nobles.

"Esteemed families Branwyr, Pental, Croy, Arden, and Masa," she said, bending the knee just slightly. "Welcome."

These five families were the wealthiest in Arido. Each had a home within the First Neighborhood, making them Guerline's own neighbors; but they all had multiple properties. They had their pleasure estates, certainly, like lesser nobles, but these families were First because their duchies were as crucial to the empire's survival as the witch clans. Some of their ancient homesteads were left to the management of sons, as in the case of Lord Branwyr and old Lady Pental. Lord Amiel Croy preferred to manage his own ancestral home, Arido's largest beef ranch, and his displeasure at being required at the coronation was evident—or perhaps he was always that stiff. Lord Arden and Lady Masa left their estates in the hands of trusted servants and rarely left the capital, though each of them for very different reasons.

"Lady Malise, it is a pleasure to see you again," said Sampson Branwyr. Eva gave him a genuine smile and a full curtsy, and one to his son and daughter behind him. Branwyr-vidi's condolences to Guerline at their luncheon had been both sincere and comforting, the only noble to achieve that combination.

Eva exchanged pleasantries with each First Family head, and then handed them off to Lord Warren as the lesser nobles of the Second Neighborhood were allowed in. Some of these she greeted by name, but more were simply shuttled past her in the wake of their better-titled cousins.

She kept her gaze forward so as to catch those she should greet. Some she could not avoid; these were the exceptionally wealthy merchants, those with little to no noble blood but who were yet rich enough to have got hold of one of the estates in the Second Neighborhood. They were very happy to present themselves to the Chief Adviser, and she was very happy to give them as icy a smile as she could muster.

The ballroom was half-filled once the Second Neighborhood had all entered, and as the denizens of the Third came in, Eva retreated to the dais that had been erected at the head of the hall. The Third Neighborhood was home to lesser merchants and tradesmen, and they, unlike the First and Second citizens, had had to queue in the palace yard to get their place in the ballroom, for there was not space for all of them. Eva wouldn't have been surprised if there were even some Fourth Neighborhood citizens mixed in, come early and dressed in their finest—which would be, for most, a clean tunic of good cloth that was brought out barely above once a year, and usually for this, High Summer's Day.

It didn't take long for the hall to fill. The sound of the crowd was amplified by the high ceiling, too much even for the many hanging tapestries to counter. When the doors finally screeched shut, the people at the back appeared to Eva like one solid, many-headed mass. At least there were the First and Second Families, seated on benches that created an airy buffer between the dais and the standing Third Neighborhood people. She tried not to shiver. Eva hated crowds.

She wished she could see Guerline once before the ceremony started . . . but she was trapped here on the dais, while Lina was being ushered into place on the other side of the doors now that everyone was inside. And while they waited, it was Eva's duty to prepare them. She touched the witch-charm on her necklace, activating the dormant magic.

"Welcome, Aridans, to the coronation of your empress!" she cried.

Her voice boomed through the hall, making her own ears ring as silence fell and all eyes turned to her. She drew herself to her full height and stared out at the people, making eye contact where she could.

"There has been a great deal of talk, I think, about the woman we crown today," Eva said. "I've heard some cruel things, some strange things, and many, many foolish things. *Talk* . . . is harmless. But when truth is spoken, the gods of the forest take heed."

She paused for emphasis. "I speak the truth to you now. This woman knows what it means to be cast aside. She knows what it means to be ignored and dismissed. And she has learned, by necessity, to look within herself for strength and support. She has learned to decide what is best without being swayed by outside influence. She knows what is right, because she has seen so much that is wrong."

Another pause, and she did not wipe away the tear that fell from her eye. Those gathered in the hall probably couldn't see it, at any rate. They were silent before her, almost breathless—the echoes of her words died slowly.

"This is a strong woman. A good woman. And as your empress, she will not forget what she has learned," Eva said.

She stepped back to the line of councilors to signal the end of her speech, and deactivated her witch-charm. Applause thundered off the stone, almost covering up the sound of the screeching doors, and Eva allowed herself a small smile of triumph. She did not look down at the nobles who, hopefully, felt her censure of them; instead, she focused on the opening doors slowly revealing Guerline to them. She kept her eyes trained there even as she and the other councilors split to one side of the plinth where the crown and trident—the symbols of Guerline's power—waited.

First in line was Piron, the dark-skinned head priest of the Del Temples, including the palace's own. He wore a great heavy robe of white wolf's fur over the Temple's standard leather tunic, and his brown hair was in a single tight braid to the base of his neck, with the excess pulled forward on either side. The sides of his head were smoothly shaven, reflecting the light as though they'd been oiled.

Behind him were two more priests, in identical tunics and with heads shaven. As they crossed the threshold into the ballroom, they took up a wordless song, splitting into melody and harmony and filling the space with the music.

After the singers came Guerline. Eva grinned, entranced; she could not have looked away for anything. The front portion of Guerline's new red twists had been looped into a beautiful roll that hung over her forehead, and the rest had been braided along the center of her skull, then bound and left to hang loose; one had slipped forward over her shoulder and the rest swung gently as she walked. Her gown was dusky purple silk, beautifully embroidered and winking with thousands of crystals so that she seemed surrounded by starlight as she moved. As gentle and lovely as all that made her appear, though, it was balanced by a metallic waist cincher and a stiff brocade collar that added just enough structure to the ensemble.

Guerline paused at the threshold, and everyone twisted to look at her. Eva heard audible gasps, even from the councilors behind her, and her heart swelled. This woman looked like an empress. She looked broad and solid, strong enough to carry the world, commanding the wide aisle as she stepped forward, even though she was dwarfed by the tall doorway behind her.

Eva felt ashamed she had been worried; Guerline even seemed to carry herself differently, her neck long and her chin parallel to the floor as she walked. Guerline was so short, she usually had to look slightly up. Eva was pleased to see that she wasn't doing that now, and willed her silently to maintain that posture even when the tall priest was ministering the ceremony. She had never seen her friend look so glorious.

The priests mounted the dais and split to the far side, leaving the center open for Guerline and her voluminous gown. The singers continued their song as the princess walked slowly down the aisle, her pace consistent. Eva felt sure she would burst with pride, and with satisfaction at the twitching faces of those nobles who had been so obnoxious when Guerline had granted them private meals. Watching Guerline become an empress even as she walked toward her crown made part of Eva's heart ache, though. *You never wanted this life. . . . We were going to escape, weren't we? Is it too late?*

Guerline made it to the steps of the dais, and Eva held out a hand to her. Their eyes met, and Guerline's stern face broke into a bright smile that Eva could not help returning. Guerline's hand was clammy when she placed it into Eva's, though it took that touch for even her to discern the anxiety in her friend. She squeezed Lina's hand for comfort and held her steady while she joined them above her gathered subjects. With a deep curtsy, Eva released Guerline's hand; Guerline spun to face the hall, her skirt sparkling.

The singers ended their tune, and those assembled broke out once more in roaring applause. Guerline raised her hands to them, and whoops rang out from the Third Neighborhood citizens who perceived she waved to them. Guerline smiled, and though Eva had not thought it possible, the cheering and applause got louder.

They loved her. How could they not? She was a vision, a mysterious and forgotten princess revealed to be a beautiful young woman, wrapped in starlight, with a smile that could make a mountain swoon.

Guerline's waving only brought more cheering, so after what felt like an age, Priest Piron raised his arms and brought silence down. Eva bit her lip to keep from laughing, such was her giddiness. But the coronation had only just begun, and though Eva could see relief in Guerline's face, the true ritual had yet to be performed.

Piron said, "Peace for the soul of His Imperial Majesty, Johan Hevya. Peace for the soul of Her Imperial Majesty, Maribel Hevya. Peace for the soul of His Royal Highness, the Crown Prince Alcander Hevya. Peace for their souls."

"Peace for their souls," echoed the hall.

"Rejoice, people of Arido, that Lisyne our Mother has given us a land in which to thrive," Piron said. His voice was low, rumbling; it was almost as though Eva felt it in her bones, though she saw no witch-charm on his person.

"Rejoice," he continued, "that Lisyne our Mother has given us dominion of the earth, and molded the elements of our protection: Gwanen, Adenen, Sitosen, Thiymen."

"We rejoice," said the hall, emphatic voices balancing the half-hearted ones.

Piron went down the stairs of the dais and held his arms out to each side, splaying his robe like a lizard splays its hood. "Rejoice that the maw of Lisyne will greet our enemies, and that the claw of Lisyne will rend those who would oppose us!" he said.

"We rejoice!" said the hall again.

A few devotees took it up as a chant, and Piron mounted the dais once more with a smirk that made Eva uneasy; but she schooled her features better than the priest, and gave him a neutral face when he glanced over at the councilors. She returned her attention, as he did, to Guerline.

"Rejoice," Piron said, and Eva was sure now that he had a witch-charm to be heard over the chanting, and to marshal them to silence again even while facing away from them. "Rejoice that Lisyne, the Great Wolf, has sent us this, her daughter, to guide us all."

The hall rejoiced again and Eva resisted the powerful urge to roll her eyes. A script like that could undoubtedly go on for hours, and she hoped, for Guerline's sake, that Piron would proceed to the next phase, no matter how enthusiastic the believers at the back of the ballroom were.

Guerline held steady while Piron stared at her and the Third Neighborhood continued to rejoice—did Eva see an attempt at a dance circle?—and at last, Piron turned around. Eva braced herself for him to say "rejoice" again, but luckily, he did not. Instead, he took the crown that was handed to him by one of the singer-priests. This crown was different than the ones Guerline's parents had worn; she'd felt both were too ostentatious, and so they had been relegated to the vaults while this delicate thing was crafted for her. It was a pair of silver combs with smoky white crystals jutting up from it; the combs were bound on one side by a thin silver chain. Eva smiled as Guerline's face lit up—she hadn't seen the completed crown before that moment.

Piron held the combs aloft, where the crystals seemed to absorb the light and glow. As he lowered them, he said, "To wear a crown is no easy thing. As fragile as peace may be, the weight of it is immense." He faced Guerline again. "Guerline of house Hevya, you must stand above us all, to bear with fortitude the power given to you this day. Do you accept this crown?"

"I do," Guerline said. A weight seemed to lift from Eva's own heart as Guerline's voice rang out, clear and steady.

While the hall cheered, Piron placed the combs gingerly into Guerline's braid, one on either side of her head, so that the chain went across her forehead and the crystals spiked just behind the knot of red twists. When he stepped aside to reveal her, crowned, more gasps filled the hall—those simple crystals, with the light in them, reaching for the sky, made Guerline look like a goddess.

Piron, smiling, raised a hand for silence as he returned to the center of the dais. When he received it, he lifted the glittering trident, the light glinting off the three prongs, sharp where the light off the crystals had been soft.

"The trident represents the might of Arido, uncontested in all the world, devastating where it is directed in rage and enlightening where it is directed in compassion," Piron said. Again, he faced Guerline. "Guerline of house Hevya, you must stand before us all, to direct in good conscience the power given to you this day. Do you accept this trident?"

Guerline took a deep breath and said again, "I do."

He handed the trident to her, and she took it in both hands. The priest stepped aside. Guerline looked out over the crowd, holding the trident at an angle in front of her, shoulders back and her face serious.

"On this day, with all of you to witness, I vow that I will defend and honor all the people of Arido, that my every action as your empress will be made with the sincere intent of bettering your lives," she said. "I vow that I will do so out of love, for this land and for my subjects, from now until my death."

Piron slipped off his great robe and held it high, and then walked in a circle around Guerline, intoning: "Lisyne, Great Wolf, O Mother of Arido, take her form and shield her from evil."

The singer-priests echoed the recitative while Piron lowered the robe onto Guerline's shoulders, symbolizing Lisyne's protection of her, just as the crown and trident symbolized Guerline's protection and defense of Arido. Evadine held her breath. It was almost over.

"Good people of Arido, rejoice! I declare you are in the presence of Her Imperial Majesty, Guerline the first of House Hevya, Ruler of Arido, Keeper of the Altecs and the Lansing and the Loti, Commander of Magic, Mother of the Realm!" Piron roared.

Eva's hands soon numbed with clapping, but she did not stop; nor did anyone in the hall, who clapped and cheered as though it was the first time they had been called upon to do so that day. Guerline's face cracked into a wide, giddy grin. She waved once, then looked over at Eva. It was as though Eva had been struck by lightning—she felt electrified and desperate to get out of that crowded, roaring hall. She went to Guerline's side and took her hand, which Lina squeezed tightly.

Eva escorted Guerline off the dais and down the aisle, setting an excruciatingly slow pace that Guerline luckily kept to; they walked out of the ballroom and down the hall, until they reached the Sitosen lift that would carry them high into the palace's upper levels, back to Guerline's tower chambers.

"It's over," Guerline said, again and again, as they hovered near the doors of the lift. Somehow, they had outpaced the councilors and priests that had followed them out, and were now coming toward them.

"Yes, Lina, it's over," Eva said.

She pulled Guerline into her arms, and Lina returned the embrace with enthusiasm, holding Eva tight against her. Eva didn't mind at all; she could feel the trembling in Guerline's hands against her back, like she too was alive with a current that demanded motion. Eva looked back down the hall at the approaching councilors. There would be feasting the rest of the day on the shores of Lake Duveau, the High Summer's Day festival, at which Guerline must make an appearance.

But not yet.

Eva waved a hand at the Sitosen lift and the doors opened to them; before Lina could protest, Eva pulled her into the lift and selected the track to Guerline's floor. Finally, she looked at Guerline, the first time she'd been able to see her up close since that morning. The ladies-in-waiting had dusted some sparkling powder over her cheekbones and shoulders; the impression was that even Lina's skin held starlight. The effect was stunning, and Eva was almost loathe to touch Guerline's face for fear of smudging the powder—almost. She took Guerline's head in her hands and kissed her, softly, gently; she felt her fingers tingle, as if coming back to life after long hours in the cold.

When she leaned back, Guerline smiled at her, her brows raised with hope. "Are we not going to the festival yet?"

"No," Eva said, smirking. "I thought we could celebrate privately first."

Guerline laughed and tilted her chin up for another kiss. Before Eva could oblige her, the lift doors opened. They grinned at each other and hurried down the hall, all the way to Lina's bedchamber.

Desmond Kavanagh winced as the cart hit another stone and sent him flying from his seat once more. He landed with a dull thud and a sharp pain in his tailbone. His escort, a trader named Malcolm, laughed at his groan.

"Ye'd not have such a time if ye'd just get some meat on yer bones!" Malcolm said.

"It's not a question of meat," Desmond said, a tad irritably.

"Well, best get used to it, witch-son," the old trader said. "The Moor Road's the best kept of all the Diamond Roads."

This, Desmond knew, was false. The Moor Road, which connected the north and west of Arido, was in fact the second worst kept road in the Outer Diamond, the roads that connected the four points of the compass. However, Malcolm had only ever traveled the Moor Road, so Desmond did not challenge his assertion.

Desmond had been traveling the country at the behest of his mother since he was a lad of sixteen, touring the central cities where magic was shockingly uncommon. The four witch clans of Arido had kept the country safe from war and natural disaster for one thousand years; but, like his mother said, humans were short-lived and small-minded. For the past nine years, it had been Desmond's job to keep the clans relevant and to humanize the distant Kavanagh sisters.

The Kavanagh sisters—his mother and aunts—were the leaders of the clans. Aradia, the eldest, ruled Gwanen, the coven of life in the south. Morgana held Adenen, coven of strength in the west. His mother was Olivia of Sitosen, coven of wisdom in the north; and Fiona, the youngest, ruled Thiymen, the coven of death in the east. Over the course of their six hundred year reign, the humans had drifted out of the middle plains and condensed themselves either on the borders, close to the clans and the magic, or in the center, where magic only ever came up in discussions of politics. The last few decades, especially, had seen a rise in such discussions, and in the capital of Del, the politicians rarely argued in magic's favor.

Troubled by the disconnect, Olivia had sent her only child—a boy, at that—out into the world to bridge the gap. As far as Desmond knew, he was the only boy-child to ever be kept and raised by a witch mother. Only women could be witches, so if a witch's child grew into a boy, she usually relinquished parental rights to the father or the family that fostered him, even if he had not yet reached the testing age of nine; she would do the same for a girl who showed no signs of magic at her testing. No one was certain why Olivia had kept Desmond, or even who his father was—but his mother was notoriously taciturn and kept silent on the subject.

"How far are we from Olsrec, Malcolm?" Desmond called down.

The old man laughed. "Well now, someone hasn't been paying attention. Look, ye fool, it's right over the next hill."

Desmond grinned sheepishly. "Right you are."

Olsrec was roughly halfway along the Moor Road, and its people often couldn't decide if they were northerners or westerners. They combined the northern penchant for engineering with the western fondness for metallurgy and blacksmithing. And unlike the rest of the country, even the lowliest of the town's buildings were constructed with metal frames. One man, whom Desmond had spoken with at length on his last trip to the west, was experimenting with spinning a metal thread which he claimed would be stronger and more durable than any rope yet made. Desmond couldn't wait to see if he'd succeeded.

Desmond and Malcolm pulled into the center of the city, and there the youth dismounted the cart. He slung his pack over one shoulder, faced Malcolm, and offered him a traditional northern salute by kissing his fist and raising it to the other man. Malcolm, who couldn't remember if he was from the north or the west, kissed his fist, raised it to Desmond, and then crossed his arm over his chest. Desmond laughed.

"My thanks, Malcolm. It was a pleasant journey, as always."

"No thanks necessary, milord. Always happy to lend a hand to the witch-son." He waved and walked away, leading his horse and cart to the trade district.

Desmond strolled to a building on the north side of the town square. It was the Hammermill, his inn of choice in Olsrec: a four-story building of metal and stone, with wooden floors and great black chimneys. It was known for its innkeeper as much as for its food or accommodations. Harval Pentok was harsh, firm, and arrogant, but if a traveler could endure him, they were treated to the best food in Achazia Valley. Desmond had won favor with him by "noticing" that the innkeeper's surname was a far-removed branch of the ancient and mighty Pent family, from whom Arido's first emperor, Lukas I, had come. In fact, Desmond was one of the only people Harval ever appeared happy to see.

Sure enough, when Desmond walked into the tavern floor of the Hammermill, Harval's short, stout frame immediately approached him. He was a broad old man whose muscles had, for the most part, gone slack with age. His skin was brown and leathery; before he was an innkeeper, he had been a carpenter and stone mason. He had worked on most of the buildings in Olsrec, including his own inn. His wide grin afforded Desmond a chance to admire the old man's teeth, which were still white and almost entirely intact. This was quite the feat, since Harval's notion of entertainment was seeing what he could break with them. He'd even gone so far as to try stone and metal, and likened his teeth to both hammers and millstones, which was how he'd come up with the inn's name.

"Young Master Kavanagh! A pleasure to see you. Are you here for dinner or lodgings?" the man inquired.

Desmond shook his hand. "Master Pentok. I seek both, if I may be so bold."

Harval chuckled. "Boldness is a virtue, boy, never beg pardon for it! And how long will you be with us?"

"A few days, perhaps a week. I'm at leisure, on a casual visit to see my aunt at Adenen," Desmond replied.

Harval nodded politely and reached up to take Desmond's pack from his shoulder. Desmond stooped to one side to help him slide it off.

"We'll put you up in your usual room," the innkeeper said. "Take your ease anywhere in the dining room, and Darran will have a meal out for you."

"Thank you," Desmond said.

Harval disappeared up a set of stairs at the back of the room, and Desmond turned to his right, where tables of various shapes and sizes were arranged. He chose a small round table in the middle. There were a handful of other people sitting around him, drinking and eating. The crowd was smaller than usual, but it was too early for supper yet. Most of the guests were likely out about their business.

He nodded briefly to the other patrons and leaned back in his chair, stretching. He infinitely preferred riding a horse to riding in a cart. It just felt more natural. Aunt Morgana had taught him to ride his first summer with her, when he was a boy. She'd given him his first horse, after determining that he was a worthy enough rider to own an Adenen mount. The western clan dealt primarily in war-magic, forging, and horsemanship, and Adenen horses were the best in the empire.

His first horse had been a mare named Seria, after Desmond's grandmother. It was a way for Morgana to honor her mother, who'd died some five hundred years ago, long before she should have; but despite her good intentions, the name seemed to carry the woman's ill fate to the horse. Eight years of constant travel wore Seria down, and she died a month past at Sitosen Castle while Desmond visited with his mother. Desmond was very sorry to lose her; truth be told, he probably killed the creature with his bulk. He stood a head and a half over most men, and his shoulders were very broad. His densely-built body was not the lightest of burdens for a small, pretty mare. He had already determined that it was time to retire Seria and choose a new horse when the shifter gods claimed her. The priests of Javan performed a very nice sending off for the mare, for which Desmond had been grateful, even if he knew the truth.

That was how Desmond had ended up taking a cart to Olsrec instead of riding his horse, and that was how he'd gotten such a nasty pain in his back. He turned to the side in his chair and hung his body over his knees, gripping his ankles to stretch the kink out of those lower muscles. He exhaled.

"Are you goin' to vomit?"

Desmond jerked upward at the voice, hitting his hand on the table and cracking his back in the process. He winced at the pain in his hand but smiled at the relief in his spine, and grinned up at the girl standing over him. Like her father, Darran Pentok was short and solidly built. Unlike her father, Darran was very pleasingly proportioned. She had a small, wry smile, a twinkle in her eye, and the loveliest curly red hair Desmond had ever seen. She was smirking at him now, holding a plate and a mug of ale for him.

"You'll be glad to know I'm not," he said.

"What were you doin', then?" She set the food on the table.

Desmond winked. "I was stretching, just stretching. I had to ride a cart down from Javan, you see. Beastly uncomfortable things."

"You poor soul," Darran said, without a hint of real sympathy. "Is there anything else I can get for you right now?"

"You can give me a real smile."

Darran grinned wide then. She reached down and tugged the end of Desmond's long blonde braid, which had fallen over his shoulder during his stretch.

"Don't you start that now, witch-son," she said. "My sister's a witch, you know. I could write her to tell Morganalami that her nephew's a lecher, and then you'd be in for it."

"I doubt it. Aunt Morgana's more lecherous than I am."

Darran snorted and flicked Desmond's ear lightly. He grinned at her while she shook her head at him.

"There is something you can help me with, though. I need to get a message to Marga. Can you do that for me?" he asked.

"Aye, I can. What shall I say to her?"

"Tell her I'm in the market for a new mount, and that I would like to meet with her at her earliest convenience," Desmond said.

"You're so polite when it's witches you're talking to," Darran observed. She was teasing, but there may have been an edge of real annoyance about her voice and the corners of her mouth. Desmond smiled apologetically.

"I'm only impolite to you because your beauty makes me forget all my manners," he said.

"Oh, you silly man!" Darran laughed.

She fluttered her apron in his face and bustled off to send his message. Desmond thought he perceived a distinct effort on her part not to turn around and look at him again. He chuckled. Darran was really a sweet girl, and very sharp; but there were many such girls in the empire. He couldn't be expected to marry all of them, could he? So instead, he just watched her leave the room, pulled his plate toward him, and began to eat.

CHAPTER SIX

THERE WAS NO WAY SHE COULD DO THIS.

Yesterday, the coronation took place. She had been officially declared Her Imperial Majesty, Empress Guerline I of House Hevya, Ruler of Arido, Keeper of the Altecs and the Lansing and the Loti, Commander of Magic, Mother of the Realm. She'd trembled as the priest set the crown-combs in her hair, and her hand shook when she grasped the trident. Priest Piron had tried to smile reassuringly, but his occupation was so easy that he could not possibly have sympathized with her. If he didn't know the answer to a question, he could simply claim that the ways of the shifter gods were unknowable and ever changing. Guerline didn't have that luxury. The country belonged to her, and she couldn't foist its care off onto supernatural fantasies.

It probably won't help me to think blasphemous thoughts at the altar. She sat at the first of the curved benches in the palace Temple's sanctuary, exactly where she had waited for Fiona Kavanagh to claim her parents' souls. At least that had been a thorough distraction from the statues of the gods. Now, there was no buffer between her and them.

Guerline had once been frightened of the statues, Lisyne's especially. The eyes of the statues were carved out, leaving empty, dead negative space. In a phenomenon she had never understood, the perfectly stationary eyes always seemed to follow her, no matter where she was in the temple. When she had complained of this to the priest, he'd told her that of course the gods were watching her. They were protecting the little princess. Guerline had not felt so much protected as hunted.

It was difficult to pinpoint when she had stopped believing in the gods. Perhaps it had begun when Jon Wellsly, Lord Historian, had given her books on the major religions of the neighboring kingdoms. Alcander had scorned such study, calling those gods and holy texts nothing but folktales. He'd had no answer for why his criticisms could not also be applied to the Book of Skins, but her question had earned her first slap from him, and when he told their parents, she had been separated from Eva for a week. Perhaps it was that response, more than anything, that had pushed her away from such a creed.

The Book of Skins did say that humans had souls, and she of course knew that to be true. But she did not see any great difference between the shifter gods and the Thiymen witches, who traveled between worlds and were sometimes strong enough to take the form of animals.

Despite her skepticism, Guerline had never avoided the Temple. This was partly out of a sense of self-preservation, because it appeased her parents that she should go to the temple; but the beauty of the architecture, with the exception of the statues, also gave some comfort to her. She found peace in the ivy and flowers that trellised down the walls, and the sound of the trickling fountain in the center of the sanctuary. It was sweet and solitary, and thanks to the personal altar in his chambers, Alcander had never come here.

The odds of finding a moment alone in the sanctuary had always been good, and Guerline was pleased it was still the case now that she was empress.

Empress.

The word still seemed so foreign to her, even after all the revelry and speech-making and oath-swearing from yesterday's ceremonies. It seemed impossible that the rule of Arido had gone straight from her esteemed father, a twenty-year veteran of the throne, to her, a nineteen-year-old girl whom no one had bothered to teach governance. The full responsibility had struck her early this morning, waking her from the first sound sleep she'd had in weeks. While Eva still slept, Guerline came to the temple, thinking perhaps to find comfort in the gods. Perhaps she would even try to believe, if what Piron said was true and Lisyne truly would protect her. People came to the temple and left seeming happier for it all the time.

No such luck for Guerline. The gods seemed to glare at her disapprovingly, as though they knew she was a fraud and a liar. She looked around the temple for something that wouldn't judge her and noticed a single dead vine hanging on the wall.

She rose from her bench and investigated. The plants in the temple didn't die. They were magically developed by Gwanen clan and were at least one hundred years old. Guerline touched the blackened leaves lightly. The vine snapped and tumbled to the ground. She stared at it, then glanced back at the statues. She wasn't given to superstition and omen-reading, but with the fate of the empire weighing on her shoulders, she decided caution was best.

"Fine," she said aloud. "No need to make a fuss. I'll go."

"Are the gods speaking to you now, Lina?"

Guerline whirled around, arms raised defensively. But it was only Evadine—Alcander was dead. Guerline smiled. Eva stood in the doorway, watching her with a friendly smirk on her beautiful, angular face. Her black hair was piled atop the crown of her head, artfully tumbling about her ears and falling gracefully down her back.

The young empress embraced her. "No, Eva, the gods are not speaking to me. Sometimes I rather wish they would, but I think, in the end, I'm grateful they're not involved. If I had any more advisers, I would be driven mad."

"Arido has already suffered several mad emperors and empresses. You hardly need to add to that list."

Guerline laughed and looped her arm through Evadine's. The two women left the temple and took the short walk to the garden. It was an ornate labyrinth of tiered stone planters, ivy-covered trellises, and trickling fountains. Guerline wandered it constantly and knew it like the back of her hand, but it was so large that she could still pretend she was lost in it. Tall trees brought in from the northern forests surrounded it and blocked the view of the rest of the palace. It made one feel that the garden was somehow removed from the city. The fact that she took pleasure in this idea made Guerline feel a little sad, and she stopped and sat down on a stone bench.

"What is it, Lina?"

"Oh, nothing. I'm just tired," she said.

Eva arched a brow at her. "You did crawl out of bed at an obscene hour."

Guerline blushed, embarrassed, and cast her eyes down. It was then that she noticed that Evadine was wearing a new dress, and a very fine one at that. It was a two-piece summer dress. The underneath was a long-sleeved shift made with layers of a sheer, floaty material. It was a light cream color, cool against Eva's warm skin, and the seams were all embroidered with a delicate gold design. The overdress was a simple sleeveless robe of heavy purple silk, bound at the waist by a wide gold belt inlaid with silver. It was the latest in courtly fashion, and very different from the plain linen dresses Eva had always worn.

Eva seemed to sense Guerline's scrutiny, and smoothed down the silk over her hips. The style of the dress made her appear even thinner and taller than she was, though, in Guerline's opinion, she hardly needed to employ optical illusions with her clothes. The design was really meant for someone more like Guerline, who was shorter than Eva and much fuller figured.

But it flattered her friend very well indeed, and as she took it in, Guerline felt heat bloom within her. Her gaze fixed on the open front of the overdress, which exposed the sheer underdress in a line that ran the length of Evadine's torso.

Eva laughed softly. "You stare without making a comment. Don't you like it?"

"I do!" Guerline said quickly. She stood and laid her hands on Eva's hips, careful not to touch the metal belt and leave fingerprints on it. Tilting her chin up, she asked, "Whatever is it for?"

Eva kissed her forehead. "My new station. The dressmakers finished it and a few others today."

Guerline nodded and smiled up at her. "It's perfect. In fact, I think the first task I'll ask of you, as your empress, will be to provide me with a suitable wardrobe, so I'll be as lovely as you. You know I'm hopelessly indifferent to such things."

Evadine flushed and glanced away. "Lina, you don't need . . . you've always been . . ."

She looked back up at Guerline, her grey eyes stormy with an expression that sent a bolt of electricity down Guerline's spine. Breath caught in her throat. Unwilling to wrinkle the fine fabric, she released Eva's hips and took her hands instead, holding them tightly, burning with an energy she could hardly describe or process. It had only been a few days, and this new dynamic merely tilted the confusion and anxiety surrounding her feelings for Eva, rather than alleviating it. They couldn't resist each other, now that they had begun. But for her vision of a life together to become reality, so many separate parts had to align.

Still, it was a joy to even be confused about the real possibility that she could marry Evadine. She'd always thought—they both had always thought—that Eva would be married to Alcander. For years he had pursued her, sent her little notes and arranged apparently spontaneous walks and meetings, and often used Guerline to create these opportunities. She'd never believed her brother to be sincere, especially not after . . . but she'd never been brave enough to voice those concerns with Eva.

Movement behind Eva caught Guerline's eye and she glanced past her friend to look at it. It was a sallow-skinned wraith—Alcander. He stared down at her, eyes like flint. Blood dripped from his left shoulder. She bit her lip to keep from screaming. The vision wasn't real, she knew that; it was only a holdover from the vivid nightmares she'd endured for the past two months. She blinked and he was gone.

"What is it, Lina?" Eva asked again.

Guerline looked back at her and gave her a small smile. The rush of heat through her body faded, but she took Eva's hand in hers and squeezed. The two women sank onto the stone bench as one, fingers twined together and resting against their touching knees.

"I'll never get through this without you, Eva," Guerline said.

Eva put her other hand on top of their joined ones. "You won't have to."

They sat in silence for a mere minute before they heard a respectful cough. The two women looked up and saw Lord Warren standing there. He'd donned his work belt over his violet-blue tunic, laden down with pouches, drafting tools, and even a roll of paper tucked through it. He wore a magnifying glass on a chain pinned to his tunic; the glass dangled from a hook threaded through the pin.

"Theodor. What is it? I don't want to be disturbed right now," Guerline said.

"Apologies, Guerline-basi, but I have your letters."

Basi. Ruler. She still wasn't used to the honorific attached to her own name—non-heirs didn't get one. "And?"

"And it will take at least an hour to get through them, and you have only two hours before our council meeting."

Guerline sighed. He had a point. Today's was the first council meeting of her reign and she needed to be as prepared as possible; that meant being up-to-date on any correspondence. She turned to Eva with an apologetic grimace.

"Go on. I'll meet you in the chambers," Eva said.

Guerline squeezed her hand and rose from the bench.

"All right, Theodor. To the office of letters," she said.

He offered her his arm, which she took, and they walked out of the garden. Helping her with the mail was not Lord Warren's job, far from it. But he was a good, kind man who wanted her to succeed, and so he seemed to have committed himself to helping her in any small way he could. She was grateful, even if her heart stayed behind on that bench.

Evadine waited until she could no longer hear the click of the empress's steps or the swish of her dress. She sighed and wiped nascent tears from her eyes, flexing the hand that had held Guerline's. Her masochism had overdeveloped since their first morning together—the thrill she felt at every touch was inevitably paired with pain from her certainty that it would not last. No love was strong enough to survive what she meant to do, even if it was for the sake of the one she loved. The bittersweetness of sacrifice only twisted her heart further.

She whirled around and strode from the garden, turning in the opposite direction to the one Guerline had taken. Guerline would be occupied until the council meeting, and Lord Warren would be there with her. He was meddlesome, as most northerners were. They had an insatiable kind of curiosity that led them into everyone else's business, and Lord Warren had taken a particular interest in Guerline since the rest of the royal family died. Eva could only assume that he was positioning himself as a suitor. It probably would have been a good match, and he probably would have been a serviceable emperor—but Eva did not intend to let things get that far.

She went down into the lower level of the palace, just below the surface, above the dungeons. This level was used for storage, and between the guards on the main floor and the guards further down, it was left virtually unprotected. It was the perfect place for clandestine meetings, as Alcander had shown Evadine years ago. Anger flared in her chest, hot and painful, but she tamped it down. If she refused to think about him, perhaps he would stop appearing to her.

She reached a door just slightly ajar and knocked gently in the sequence the conspirators had agreed upon. Then she slipped inside and pulled the door shut behind her.

"I'm the last?" she asked.

"Yes, and it's about time," said Pearce Iszolda. The Lord Treasurer was an old white man who had lived solely in the palace for years, giving up his own house in the Second Neighborhood. He was of a rather paranoid disposition, which Alcander had derided constantly to Eva in private, though he said it did make Pearce a great ally, since he was absolutely terrified of magic and was happy to inform anyone who would listen of the dangers of witchcraft. While many dismissed him in any but matters financial, even ridiculous statements could sow doubt in a reasonable mind, when exposed to them often enough.

"Well, I had an excuse to cultivate, didn't I?" Eva said. Her voice was sharp and her eyes narrowed. "But now we are here, and we must prepare."

"What have you in mind, Lady Malise?" asked the other man in the room. Lanyic Eoarn was the Lord Merchant, a tall, brown-skinned western man who was shrewd and suspicious, just like Eva.

They were Alcander's men, the bedrock of the anti-magic movement in the capital. At the turn of spring, Alcander had begun dragging Eva to his secret gatherings, where she learned that his intentions were to remove the Kavanagh sisters from their positions as Lords Paramount. It seemed absurd at first—the witches had always guarded Arido's borders, they ruled as an extension of the crown, they had their hands in virtually every function of the empire.

But Alcander had silenced her protests with private demonstrations of dangerous pre-made enchantments, like the one with the dagger that never missed its target. The truth was that Alcander hadn't hated magic; he hated the witches because they could use magic at will, and there was no way for him to defend himself against it. He had been, fundamentally, terrified that a witch would someday kill him.

Eva had resisted his ravings as much as she could, but in the end, his *demonstrations* had had their desired effect. If there was anything that scared her more than Alcander had, it was magic, and the ways it could be used against those without it.

Humans like her, like Guerline, were not safe as long as magic existed in the realm.

When Alcander died, she began to receive messages from Lanyic, Pearce, and others of the movement; somehow, her always coming and going with Alcander had led them to believe she was his chosen captain. She ignored them at first, but she knew they wouldn't stop simply because the prince was dead. The problem was that they were all railers and ravers; few enough of them had demonstrated an aptitude for the long strategizing Alcander had envisioned. Only now, it was *Guerline* who would be undermined by their extremism. They needed sound leadership, someone who would plan for true change and not the kind of reactionary chaos that usually led to a headless monarch and bursting jails. So Eva had reluctantly taken up the mantle of the movement.

"We have spent a long time talking about the problems with witches in this country. I have been very pleased by what I hear in the central cities. There is ignorance and annoyance among the humans, and they grow wary of magic," Eva said. "Now that Guerline is crowned, it is time to push for new laws limiting the power of the clans."

"But the empress herself still favors the witches, does she not?" Lanyic said.

Pearce snorted. "Aye, she has eyes on the witch-son."

Eva ignored the lurch in her stomach at his words. "Yes, but Guerline is easily led. If we show her how the witches are crossing lines and breaking laws, she will be convinced that harsher measures are required."

"But they're not breaking laws," Lanyic said.

Eva smiled. "Not yet. But it makes no matter. We will tell her that they are."

"Lie? To Her Majesty?" Pearce asked.

"You lied to her father, didn't you?" Eva snapped.

He shrank back from her and retreated to the corner, pouting, his eyes sullen and averted. Lanyic raised an eyebrow but remained silent. Eva looked from one to the other sternly; then she smiled warmly at them. She reached into her overdress and pulled an envelope out of one of her pockets.

"This is the first step, my lords. I intercepted it when yesterday's letters came in. It is from Governor Derouk in Braeden, and it is proof that the witches *are* beginning to overstep their bounds. Morgana of Adenen has met with foreign wizards and collaborates with them."

"What? Let me see it!" Lanyic lunged for it.

Eva stepped back, holding the letter aloft. "Not yet, Lord Merchant. I will reveal it at today's council meeting. Save your outrage for the empress."

He frowned, but nodded. Blood was already rising in his cheeks, and Eva smiled. He would be very ready for the council meeting. Pearce was staring at the letter, wide-eyed, just as Eva had known he would. Pearce had a special fear of the battle-witch, coming as he did from the soft and spineless South. They were by far the weakest people in Arido, and Eva was very glad, in the end, that she had not been raised among them.

"Now, the council meeting is not for a few hours yet, so take that time to think of all your grievances with the witches. Do not be seen with each other until it is time to meet, but if you should come across Lord Famm, feel free to engage him. He is the most neutral of the remaining council members. We may yet be able to recruit him," Eva said.

"What of Lords Marke and Wellsly?" Lanyic asked.

Eva laughed. "Never mind them. Marke is too devoted to Black Fiona, and Wellsly would have to consult his books. And we know that Warren is Guerline's lapdog, but he is also very observant, so be careful around him. If he scents conspiracy, he will tell her."

"Would she believe him?" Pearce asked.

Eva hesitated. "She would not want to, but she is cautious, and would inquire."

Though Eva was confident that she could predict Guerline's actions well, she did not want to overestimate herself. She had seen a change in the way Guerline acted even in the hours since the coronation, and as proud as it made her, it also chilled her to the bone. It was possible that Guerline was taking to the crown better than either she or Eva had anticipated. That was what Eva feared more than the failure of her henchmen or her subtle plots—because Guerline could be very clever when it was called for, and if she decided that she *did* want to be empress, it would be harder to do what needed to be done.

"So, be careful," she said. "Be discreet."

She tucked the letter away and went back over to the door.

"I will leave first. Each of you wait a time before leaving yourselves, and I will see you in the council chambers."

With that, she opened the door and slipped out before they could see how her hands shook.

Theodor handed her a tri-folded piece of soft paper. "Another invitation, Your Majesty. This one from the Count of Ledessa. I know his estate. Very charming."

Guerline took it and unfolded it, scanning the elegant writing. "I remember this family. They have a son not much older than me. Arron?"

"Yes. Last I saw him, I found him quite amiable, if a bit reserved," Theodor said.

"I've never met him," Guerline said. She folded the letter again and put it in a pile to her right. "Add his estate to the tour list."

Theodor dutifully did so, his quill scratching across the paper in front of him. Guerline looked at him across the desk, and the words that had stuck in the back of her mind for weeks floated forward again. *Run away with me.* She'd contemplated begging Eva, Theodor, Undine— even Renae, her chambermaid. She imagined asking them, and them agreeing. She'd imagined them saying no, and how she would beg them to at least turn a blind eye so she could escape.

"I can't help but notice that many of these invitations come from lords with eligible sons and daughters," she said instead.

Theodor sighed and deposited his quill in its stand. "It is a common theme. The expectation is that you will marry soon."

She frowned. "Whose expectation?"

"Well . . . everyone's. Even among the council," he said, staring at the table instead of looking up at her.

Guerline sighed and leaned back in her chair. If she was honest with herself, she wasn't surprised. It would be a smart move, an easy way to secure support for the bumpy road ahead, whether she married one of her own nobles, or the second child of a foreign monarch. The thought made her laugh aloud. It had once been *her* fate to be uprooted, sent to a strange country to marry someone she'd never met. Now, she would be the one doing the uprooting. Unless she married Eva, which would undoubtedly insult everyone.

Theodor blinked at her, his brow furrowed with the unasked question of what made her laugh.

"And you, Theodor? Would you have me marry immediately?" she asked.

She knew it was a mistake the moment the words left her mouth. A pink flush filled his pale cheeks.

"Never mind. I don't mean to marry with any haste," she said.

"If I may ask, why?"

Guerline stood and paced, trailing her fingers along the cool wall. It maddened her that there were no windows in this room. The palace was so huge there could not possibly be windows in every room, which was a significant flaw in its design as far as Guerline was concerned. Her heart raced and she took deep breaths. Her tongue seemed reluctant to speak, resisting her attempts to open her mouth and form words. But if she could not tell Theodor, her closest friend aside from Eva, and by far the milder of temper, then she would hardly be able to tell anyone else.

Including Eva—she had not yet voiced this concern even to the woman she loved. Somehow, the fact that she loved Eva so much made it harder to admit the way she felt about marriage.

"I do not want to marry because if I do, I will do what I have always done. I will allow myself to fade into the background. I will hide behind my spouse, just as I've hidden behind Eva all these years."

She let out a deep breath and watched Theodor's expression shift from embarrassment to thoughtfulness. It felt good to articulate the feelings she'd been sorting through privately for the past two months, and in earnest over the last few days. Her journals were bursting with many iterations of these thoughts, thoughts she couldn't share with anyone until this moment. They had not settled, and she could not have revealed such a harsh personal evaluation until she felt sure enough of it herself.

Sitting down once more, she reached across the letters and took Theodor's hand. "I'm afraid, Theodor. I don't like this uncertainty. But this is the first time in my life that I don't have someone above me, pushing me down. This is my chance to be strong, to direct myself, and I must at least try it on my own."

Theodor put his hand over hers and gave her a small smile. "Yes, you must. But Lina, marriage does not mean—"

"I know, I know that. But I know myself too, and I know that if I marry the kind of ruling partner I would want without establishing myself first, I would find it far too easy to let them lead," Guerline said.

He squeezed her hand and let go. "Then I will trust your judgment."

Guerline grinned. "Thank you, Theodor, so much. It means a great deal to me."

He smiled back. "You will always have my support."

She nodded, then gestured toward the door. "Why don't you take a rest? I can finish here on my own. There aren't so many left."

He fidgeted, glancing from her to the door and back again. "If you think it's all right . . . I do have some letters of my own to write."

"Of course! Go on. I'll see you at the meeting," Guerline said.

"Yes. Thank you, Your Majesty," Theodor said.

He stood and bowed, then left the room, shutting the door behind him again. Guerline sighed and pinched the bridge of her nose. Her heart calmed in her chest, and as it did, a peaceful stillness settled into her limbs. She rolled her head to the side and closed her eyes. She could almost fall asleep, though she hadn't been tired a moment ago. Her muscles tensed against a gust of chill wind and she opened her eyes with difficulty. It took her a moment to realize she'd opened them at all. The lanterns had all been snuffed, and the room was dark.

A glow rose in front of her, in the seat Theodor had occupied. It was merely an orb at first, but as she squinted at it, it took on the appearance of her rotted father.

Eyes wide, she tried to keep her breathing steady as the ghost turned its empty sockets on her.

"You should be at rest," she whispered.

"How can I be at rest when my empire is in the hands of my fool daughter?" Johan said.

Guerline gulped and fought to keep the familiar tendrils of self-doubt from taking hold. Her father was dead, and taunting her from the grave was the worst he could do. She would not let fear of him rule her anymore; she would speak calmly until this vision ended. She could at least project assurance.

"But the witch. She took you to Ilys."

"The doors to Ilys are shut!"

Wind gusted through the room again, and her father vanished. Someone whispered her name and Guerline spun around in time to catch a glimpse of luminescent, dawn-blonde hair whipping past. Cold oozed down Guerline's spine. She waited, unmoving, to determine whether she was truly alone. After several seconds of silence, she stood slowly. Hands outstretched, she found the wall and walked along it until she reached the first Adenen lamp. Its magical fire, one of the hired household enchantments still common in the center cities, flared up again the moment her fingers touched the glass orb in which it was housed.

She turned back to the desk and screamed. Johan's head sat at the table, staring at her with a gaping mouth, molars visible through the holes in his cheeks where the flesh melted away.

"Your Majesty?"

The guard posted outside the door burst in, holding her short sword ready. The lamps all flared on again, bathing the room in light. There was no sign of Johan, head or body. Guerline leaned against the wall and calmed her breathing.

"Are you all right, Your Majesty?" the guard asked.

"Yes, Frida, I'm fine. Thank you. I'm through here. Go and make sure the council is gathered," Guerline said.

Frida frowned and cast a suspicious glance around the room. "I'm not sure I should leave you, Majesty."

Guerline smiled and put a hand on her armored shoulder. "I appreciate your loyalty, but I really am fine. I only dozed off and had a nightmare. Please, go on. I'll be right behind."

Though she still frowned, Frida bowed, sheathed her sword, and left the room. Guerline sighed and stared at the spot where her father's head had been.

Would she ever stop seeing dead things?

CHAPTER SEVEN

MORGANA KAVANAGH AWOKE TO THE SOUND OF ROARING.

She sat straight up in bed. The sound was distant and low, rumbling like the ocean. Aftershocks. Shouts rang from the courtyard below her window. The Adenen leader jumped out of bed and pulled on a pair of coarse wool trousers and a leather jerkin. She'd barely finished lacing up her boots when Aalish came skidding through the door without even an attempt at a knock.

"Artan," she gasped. "A sandstorm at Artan."

Morgana cursed and pushed past her captain. Artan Forge was the largest forge in the West, situated between Fortress Adenen and the city of Braeden. It had been safe from the unusual sandstorms thus far because of its position further east from the cliffs, and because of the fortifications Morgana had ordered after the storms began. It was the single most important forge in the empire. If it was damaged enough to halt work there, other forges in the region would not be able to pick up the slack.

The battle-witch dashed through the castle, shouting orders for horses to be readied. She sent Aalish to organize a troop of cavalry witches and depart with them as soon as they were able. She predicted a panic, and they would need witchpower to contain the inevitable crowd. *What is it about disaster that makes everyone want to watch?*

Adenen's previous attempts to stop the sandstorms had been woefully uninformed, but this time, Morgana had an advantage. Three wizards from Raeha, the desert country to the west, had come to the fortress two nights ago seeking a conference. Since their magic used wind and sand, Morgana hoped they would be able to help them understand and conquer the damnable storms.

With Aalish busy, Morgana herself went to the guest tower. She knocked, sharply but politely, on Aasim's door before entering. The leader of the wizards sat up slowly, blinking blearily at her. He was bare-chested, his long black hair now taken out of its multi-colored headdress and simply braided, like hers. His skin seemed to possess a warm glow against the cool stone walls of her fortress, even in the dark. She averted her eyes; though she understood the political and magical customs of the Atithi tribes, she was unfamiliar with the wizard's culture in intimate situations such as this.

She quickly squashed such nonsensical thoughts. Was she or was she not Morgana Kavanagh? She could apologize later. Now was the time for action, not courtesy. She went forward and sat on the edge of Aasim's bed, putting her hands on his shoulders and jostling him a bit. He reached up and gently squeezed her wrist.

"Aasim, I know you and your friends are still recovering from your journey, but I need your help," Morgana began, speaking quickly. "There is a sandstorm engulfing our largest forge as we speak. I must go and try to save it. I hope that you and the others will come help us. You know more about these things than we do."

Aasim studied her face, his dark eyes dancing over her expression. She could see the weariness of the journey still in him. She would understand if he said no—he could be thinking about the political danger of the wizards being present, when many westerners blamed the Raehans for the sandstorms to begin with. Morgana wasn't concerned with such things. Her focus now was on saving her forge, and if he didn't answer her soon, she'd have to abandon his help and do what she could alone. She waited, lips parted, for his answer.

Aasim shook his head as if coming out of some reverie. "Yes, of course I will help you."

He took her hand from his shoulder and squeezed it. Morgana laughed in relief and jumped up from the bed. Aasim swung his legs out from under the blanket. She caught herself and looked away in case—well, she didn't know what wizards slept in!—but Aasim chuckled softly and walked past her. He was wearing fine linen pants. Perturbed, she followed him out of the room, trying to scowl her embarrassment away.

"Those won't do well in an exploding forge," she said as he knocked on the doors of his companions.

He smirked at her. "Don't worry. They repel heat."

Morgana scoffed, but had to smile as she left him to rouse Fazl and Daleel.

They met again in the stables, where Morgana waited on her charger. The wizards' pages handed their horses off to their masters, and the four of them set off for Artan. They rode hard and made good time, but long before they arrived they could see the flames leaping from the huge forge. With every lick of fire against the sky, Morgana grew more and more afraid they wouldn't arrive soon enough. The winds gained strength as they approached, buffeting the riders and their horses until it was hard to stay on the road.

Aasim signaled to Morgana and they pulled up. It was difficult to get close enough to hear with their horses prancing, but they locked hands and pulled toward each other.

"This is not just a sandstorm, Morgana!" Aasim shouted. "See how it is concentrated on the forge? It keeps veering back after it passes over, like it is a conscious attack!"

"So what is it?" she roared back.

"An evil wind out of the Wastes! He is old and hateful. All we can hope to do is push him back!"

Morgana looked from Aasim to the forge. The massive barn doors were open at both ends of the building. People ran in all directions, ineptly dousing flames designed to burn hotter than normal with small buckets of water and dirt. Swirling columns of sand struck coals, spitting fire everywhere. Black smoke mixed with the sand-laden winds and made visibility worse. She stroked her throat with a spell to amplify her voice. Aalish and the troop of cavalry witches would try to keep the people back from the destruction.

As she opened her mouth to speak, one of the western furnaces exploded. A fireball rocketed upward and dissipated as it was caught in the cyclonic winds. When Morgana peered over her forearm, she scowled and groaned. The thatch roof was now on fire.

Aasim leaned into her ear. "I need five or six of your witches!"

"You have them!" Morgana said. "Aalish!"

Her voice boomed across the confusion and her captain looked up for the source. Morgana signaled to her. She watched them ride a few feet off and position themselves in a line across the west edge of the moor.

Satisfied that the wizards would do what they could to send this evil wind back to the Wastes, Morgana galloped over to the remaining troop, shouting orders as she thundered through the lingering humans on her massive black horse. The people fell back, fear written in sand and ash on their faces.

"Get the thatch off the roof, pull it all down and throw it into the moor! Start with what's burning!"

The witches conjured long, hooked whips of air and smoke and began ripping the thatched roof apart. The next obstacle: the barn doors. They were creating a wind tunnel that only served to feed the flames.

Morgana rode into the forge itself. "You four, close the barn doors! You three, with me! Put the damn fires out!"

They ran the length of the forge, dousing flames at sixty furnaces. The wind surged violently, as if fighting back. It roared in through the open roof and forced the barn doors open, rushing through with such strength that Morgana was knocked from her horse.

The Old Wind couldn't relight the fires, though, no matter how hard he blustered. Morgana laughed as she got to her feet, dusting sand from her hands. The wind rushed out through the barn doors, making a horrible sucking sound. The barn fell utterly silent. Her laughter died. Suddenly nervous, she ran out the west door toward where the wizards stood, flanked by witches. She staggered out backwards, looking up. She cursed.

The winds were taking humanoid form now, becoming more and more distinct in the sand and smoke until it appeared that two giants grappled above them. At the base of the battle, Aasim, Fazl, and Daleel stood like statues, eyes closed and mouths moving. Their voices were barely audible over the wind, intoning in a sing-song tongue. The witches were gathered around them, their hands on the shoulders of the men. They didn't know the wind magic, so all they could do was lend their power to the wizards.

Morgana put her anxiety aside and studied the match as a warrior. The wizards appeared to control the sand-man. The smoke-man seemed determined to hold his ground over the forge, but Aasim and the others used the sand-man to try and turn him, flip him, pull him westward whatever way they could. The Old Wind had the advantage. All he had to do was stay put. And so far, he was successful in blocking the wizards' attempts to grip him.

She looked for some way to help. She couldn't get to the other side without running right through the battling winds, and she knew better. She needed something that would break the Old Wind's form, distract him, disperse him just long enough for the sand-man to seize him. But what?

The solution came when she spotted the smoldering thatch from the roof. She grinned and visualized a massive magical pitchfork into her hands. She would have to be quick and forceful, or her diversion would be caught in the winds, miss its mark, and hit something—or someone—else.

Morgana thrust the prongs of her pitchfork into a tightly bound thatch roll. She looked back at the battle, watching carefully; when she saw her opening, she heaved with all her might and flung the thatch into the air. It flew heavily on course, blasting through one of Old Wind's arms and momentarily severing it. Before he had a chance to reform, the sand-man had hooked him under his other arm and between his legs and flipped him overhead the same way she'd vaulted the thatch. Old Wind landed with a crash on the moor beyond the wizards, dissipating all at once. The sand-man bounded after him, dispersing himself into a wall that herded the disoriented wind across the moor and over the Latanya Cliffs.

Silence rang in Morgana's ears. She jogged across the moor to Aasim, Aalish, and the others. The wizards came out of their trances and wobbled dangerously, but they were quickly supported by the witches. Morgana herself caught Aasim in her arms; he reluctantly but gratefully leaned his weight on her. She smiled at him and brushed loose strands of hair away from his face as he looked up at her, heavy-lidded.

"Thank you so much, Aasim," she said with feeling. "I look forward to nursing you back to health personally—it won't even begin to make up for what I owe you and your brothers."

He smiled, too weary to speak. She laughed and hoisted him up, then instructed the troop to gather the horses. She'd send the wizards home with an escort. The rest of the witches would stay with the humans and clear the debris so that repairs could begin at first light. She walked toward the forge with Aasim braced on her shoulder.

"Morgana," Aalish said.

She jerked her head toward the town. Governor Derouk Madacy approached with a gaggle of followers all dressed in their evening robes, their finery glinting in the firelight: Braeden's most influential men and women. Morgana frowned. The governor, she noted, was soot-free. He marched toward her with every appearance of wanting to pick a fight.

Aalish silently took Aasim's weight. Morgana eased out from under him and stepped forward slowly to meet Derouk.

Derouk bowed deeply. "Lady Morgana, thank you so much for saving our forge. You arrived in the nick of time."

Morgana nodded to him and his entourage, but did not respond. She was not in the mood to parlay with this snake-faced man. She waited for him to finish his formalities and go on his way; instead, Derouk stared blankly at her.

"You're welcome," she said finally in exasperation. "This forge is important to Adenen as well."

Derouk nodded enthusiastically, but said nothing. Morgana waited another moment or two for him to get to his point. The moments passed in disappointment. She frowned at him.

"Is that all, Derouk? I must leave. There are things that must be tended to," she said sharply. She and her troops were expended, Aasim and the other wizards were all but unconscious with exhaustion, and there was still a cleanup to organize before the sun rose, something she was sure the governor would want to take credit for but couldn't possibly handle himself.

"Of course, of course, and I'll let you get to them. Some of the forge owners and I were just concerned that the, ah, fortifications did not seem to hold against the storm." Derouk graciously ignored the furious twitch of Morgana's lip. "We think it would be best to apply to the capital for other aid."

"Derouk, the fortifications didn't hold because this was not what we fortified against—" Morgana stopped herself and struggled for an even tone. This man didn't know anything about what had attacked them. "We know what it is now, and we'll soon know how better to protect against it. The capital can't help us."

He smiled a tight little smile and dropped his eyes from Morgana's face. That was when he noticed Aasim, his head nodding against Aalish's helm. Derouk's oily expression changed in an instant to one of disgust.

"So it's true; the desert wizards are here?" he said, perhaps louder than necessary. His escort was immediately at attention. Morgana scowled. This was what he'd wanted all along, to argue about the wizards.

"They may very well be the cause of all our troubles, and yet you give them your hospitality? Do they not deal in wind-magic? Is their land not sand-covered?" Derouk continued. He was working himself up now, becoming louder with every word.

The smiths, who had retreated during the battle, were returning to survey the damage; when they heard Derouk shouting that the sand wizards were there, the panic and anger that Morgana had predicted gained a target. The witches moved Fazl and Daleel to the center of their troop, hiding them on their small desert equines behind a wall of warhorses.

Others took up Derouk's shouting, and he himself left off, turning to smile at Morgana with smug triumph on his face. Morgana watched him silently, her own expression calm. She heard cries for her to turn over the wizards to the justice system, calls for them to be prosecuted, all the foolishness of sheep with a cruel and clever shepherd. Aalish hissed sharply, breaking the cloud of anger fogging Morgana's mind.

"Silence!" she bellowed, the amplifying spell reactivated. Silence fell. "Do you think that I would be host to decimators of my forges? Do you?" she said, her voice now deathly quiet. She stepped forward, invading the personal space of those at the front of the mob. She stared long into the eyes of the men before her, longest into Derouk's beady little eyes. Disgusted, she spat on the ground at his feet and mounted her horse. Aalish and another witch hoisted Aasim up into the saddle behind her. She trotted in an arc, eyeing the crowd.

"Think before you speak," she shouted, "or the words will be your last!" She spurred her horse and galloped out with the troop. *Let the humans handle their own cleanup, if they are so quick to distrust us.*

CHAPTER EIGHT

WHEN DESMOND WOKE THE MORNING AFTER HIS ARRIVAL IN Olsrec, he saw a stuffed pastry and a note sitting on his bedside table. The note said one of Marga's assistants would meet him at the inn and escort him to the ranch. That was somewhat unusual. Marga was a very busy woman, and he hadn't expected to hear from her for at least two days, let alone get a meeting with her so soon. He couldn't say he was disappointed, though, so he got out of bed and dressed. He ate the stuffed pastry—full of eggs, bacon, and good cheese—on the way down the stairs, a satisfied smile on his face. No one made stuffed pastries like Darran.

He popped his head into the kitchen, hoping to congratulate her on an excellent breakfast. She didn't appear in a mood to talk, though. She saw him, rolled her eyes, and jerked her head toward the door of the inn. He tried to speak, but she immediately began pounding down dough with a rolling pin. *What on earth have I done to offend her?* he wondered, walking slowly out of the inn. He hadn't even gone to see her last night.

Ah. Perhaps *that* was the problem.

He almost started laughing, but stopped when he realized that his escort was already waiting for him.

"Hello, witch-son," she said.

"Dona," he said warmly, opening his arms wide. "It's been ages!"

Dona embraced him. She was a tall brown-skinned witch from Marga's ranch, and they had been friends since they were young. They were the same age, and met when Dona turned twelve and had come to live at Marga's to further her specialty in horsemanship. Dona was a rough-and-tumble kind of woman; she and Desmond spent much of their teenage years staging huge wrestling matches whenever he visited on the way to Aunt Morgana's. He tried to court her in his sixteenth year, the first year he'd traveled the country on his own; when he tried to kiss her, she'd knocked him down and told him if he ever tried it again, she'd cut off his lips.

That was when Desmond had known they *really* were best friends.

"Look at you!" she cried as she pulled away from him. "You've grown your hair out like a fancy pony! Look at this, you could sit on it," Dona said, holding up the end of his braid.

It was true, his hair hung down past his hips. He hadn't cut it in six or so years. He'd been joked with about it, people asking if he kept his strength in his hair or if he was trying to compensate for something. There was no particular reason for his hair being as long as it was, he could just never be bothered to cut it.

"Are you finally trying to get married? Hoping to attract someone with your pretty golden hair?" Dona asked, running a hand over her own short, abundant black curls.

"Course not, you know I'm still waiting for you," he said, poking her in the ribs.

In answer, she leapt onto his back and wrapped an arm around his throat. With her forearm over his windpipe, it was difficult to speak, but he tried anyway, gasping that he was only joking. She laughed and released him.

"All right, I forgive you. Here, come with me," she said.

Desmond rubbed his neck and rolled his eyes, following her to two horses tied up at a post. She handed him a set of reins.

"Is this my new horse?" Desmond asked, eyeing the animal at the end of them. He was a good size, but seemed a little old.

"No, your new horse waits for you at the ranch. Bruno's just here to get you there."

Desmond nodded, mounted Bruno, and set off after Dona toward the outskirts of town. Marga's ranch was about an hour's ride outside Olsrec, and that was just the nearest point. The farthest stretched almost three hours from the center of town. They kept a moderate pace, trotting down the well-worn path that would take them to the plains.

"So why bring Bruno along, and not just bring me my new horse? Nothing against you, old man," Desmond added to the horse.

"Because it's not just a question of giving him to you," Dona said, laughing. "We have to make sure Keno actually *likes* you before you try to ride him."

"Gods," Desmond said. "She's not giving me some un-broken stallion, is she?"

"Of course not! Keno is just picky about his riders. He's really a gentle soul, and he dislikes a hard hand. He's more the kind of horse you ask to do things, rather than tell," she explained.

Desmond nodded. He joked, but in the end he trusted Marga's instincts in these things. She knew horses better than almost anyone.

"Will I get to see Marga?" he asked.

"Unfortunately, no. She's taken some horses down to Adenen. They lost a few in a big fire at Artan Forge last night."

"Gods. Is everyone all right?"

"Aye, I think so. The Raehan wizards were able to stop the sandstorm."

They rode in silence the rest of the way. Once they got out onto the plains, they raced briefly, but old Bruno was no match whatsoever for Dona's horse, Gorra. Desmond didn't want to tire the old nag unnecessarily, so they took a much more relaxed pace from then on out. There was noth-ing too pressing at the moment; though the news of Artan did unsettle him a little. It was good that he would be with Aunt Morgana soon, to hear about it firsthand. He could guess that the presence of the wizards would cause some trouble for her.

The ranch came into view, and Desmond forgot those somber thoughts. It was beautiful, stretching as far as the eye could see and dotted with barns and fenced rings. Marga's house was in the center of it all, long and low. The front of the house was flat, but the back of it was curved. Tall trees were planted to one corner, and a long walk went from the other corner to the nearest barn. The house looked like a cat curled up on the hillside.

Dona led him along a fence to one of the smaller barns and dismounted. A girl came up to take both horses from them. Dona patted Gorra goodbye and turned to Desmond.

"This way," she said.

He followed her to a nearby pasture where a few horses were grazing peacefully. Dona whistled a five-note tune and a large bay pricked up its ears. She waved it over to where they stood against the fence. It approached and draped its head over the top, allowing Dona to scratch its forelock.

"This is Keno. He's a gelding, five years old, very well-behaved as long as you're polite," Dona said, smiling. "He doesn't stand for rudeness."

Desmond grinned and gave Keno a small bow.

"It's a pleasure to meet you, Master Keno," he said. "I wonder if I might beg the honor of rubbing your nose?"

Keno sniffed Desmond's ear, then stuck his nose into the young man's face. Desmond and Dona both laughed, and Desmond gave Keno's neck a vigorous rub. The horse made a satisfied whickering noise.

"There now! I was fairly confident he'd like you, but you can never be too sure," Dona said.

"I'm incredibly offended that you had any doubts," Desmond said. "Everyone likes me."

Dona rolled her eyes.

"Come on, you. I'll show you his tack."

After inspecting the saddle and bridle, the two got Keno tacked up and took him to a ring for his and Desmond's first ride together. Desmond was well pleased by the time they were finished. Keno was the perfect size for him, and solidly built. He didn't appear to have tired overmuch, despite all the cantering and the gallop they'd taken outside the ring. This was an excellent sign. Stamina was an absolute requirement for any horse of Desmond's. He would have hated to ruin another mount.

"This will be perfect," Desmond said while he rubbed Keno down afterward. "Now I'll have someone to talk to on those long rides between places. Gods, I wish we had a smaller country."

"Ah, but if the country was smaller, we wouldn't be the greatest empire of the Trident," Dona said.

"My dear Dona, with the exception of Raeha, we *are* the Trident. I don't know why we don't just absorb Raeha. It's mostly desert, and the people are nomads anyway. I doubt much would change, except that if they had any serious problems, it wouldn't require diplomats to figure out the terms of our assistance anymore," Desmond said.

"That may well be true for some rulers, but then there are some who would try to take advantage of the Atithi and the other tribes," Dona said.

"I suppose what we really need to do is find the perfect ruler, and then make them immortal."

Dona threw a curry comb at him.

They went up to the house for a light supper and spent the next few hours trading stories of what had happened to them since the last time they saw each other. Dona had turned down yet another suitor by telling him that he wasn't strong enough magically for her, but Desmond knew that the real reason was because she was in love with Yara, one of the other witches who worked on Marga's ranch. Desmond had been tackled by a little blonde pickpocket the last time he was in Del; she pretended that she was being chased by men who were trying to rape her, and had been thrown completely off her game when Desmond offered to find them and kill them for her, then insisted that she stay with him until they were apprehended.

"Your story wins! Your stories always win," Dona said.

"That's because I get out more," Desmond replied. "One of these days, you ought to come visit me."

"Where? You've yet to settle down anywhere." After a moment, she asked more seriously: "Do you think you ever will?"

"Will what? Settle down?" Desmond considered it. "I don't know. I haven't really thought about it. I do like to travel."

"You've been traveling constantly for eight years," Dona said.

"Aye. I suppose that I'll settle down someplace when Mother tells me she doesn't need me to keep the country together anymore."

"Oh, that's what you're doing?" Dona laughed, then turned serious again. "Well, you're doing a piss-poor job of it, then. The governor at Braeden has whipped his supporters into a frenzy against the Commander. He's making it look like the wizards caused the sandstorm, rather than stopped it."

"What did cause it?" Desmond asked.

"A Waste wind, they said," Dona replied.

Desmond frowned. "And I'm willing to bet Derouk didn't let Aunt Morgana get a word in edgewise to explain things. They never do. I should get to her sooner rather than later. I spent four years convincing Derouk to like me. I may be of use."

Dona nodded. She led him back down to the stable and helped him get Keno tacked up again.

"Give Marga my best. I may yet see her at Adenen," Desmond said, and rode off.

It was full dark when he returned to the Hammermill. He stabled Keno and went up to his room, ready for a good night's sleep and an early start tomorrow. He'd taken a bit of a rest from his diplomatic duties over the past several weeks, but it appeared that it was time to start up again.

CHAPTER NINE

GUERLINE STOOD AT THE HEAD OF A RECTANGULAR STONE table, the seven people of her council before her. Eva sat on her right. Beside her were Lord Treasurer Pearce Iszolda, a southerlander, and Lord Merchant Lanyic Eoarn of Olsrec. Lord Historian Jon Wellsly, a longtime friend who had held his position as long as Guerline could remember, sat at the far end of the table facing the young Empress. Theodor, Lord Engineer, sat opposite Lanyic; beside him sat Lord Justice Shon Marke out of Suel in the East. On Guerline's left was Lord Legislator Neren Famm of the southern city Neva.

Silence rang in the air, absolute and piercing. The room accentuated the discomfort. It was cramped, with flat and expressionless stone walls. Far from inducing successful problem-solving, its bleakness was much more likely to drive the councilors mad.

But at that moment—that one moment—Guerline wasn't thinking about the mind-numbingly bare room. Her eyes were fixed on Councilor Iszolda. The scrawny old man jutted his pointed chin forward defiantly. He seemed to be getting angrier the longer she was silent, as though her calm expression was too much for him to accept. She fought to keep her eyes from twitching.

"I understand your concerns, Pearce-ami," she said softly. "Arido does rely heavily on the witches. That is indisputable. What we had better decide, if our discussion must find this topic, is whether or not it is a dangerous reliance."

Evadine jumped up. "Of course it is!" Her voice rang against the stone and overshadowed the last echoes of Guerline's words. "The witches have too much power. The people, in the border cities especially, follow witch-law over ours, to the point of direct disobedience to the crown!"

"That is because our laws are not always practical," said Theodor in his slow, even tone. "The people of Javan cannot be expected to pay four silver per sheet for the crown's paper when Sitosen has taught them to make their own."

"We're discussing witches, not stationary, Lord Warren," Eva snapped.

"Enough," Jon said. "Power has always been shared by the clans and the crown. We need each other. Arido was founded on magic, and she cannot live without it. This is fact."

Johan Hevya stepped out from behind Jon's high-backed chair. Guerline inhaled sharply but managed to stop herself from jumping. The last thing she needed was to appear insane in front of her council. At least her father was not rotted this time, but fully fleshed. His flabby face scowled at Evadine. He'd never much cared for the outspoken young woman while he lived. Only his wife Maribel's intervention, her insistence that Guerline have a companion, had allowed Eva to stay. Eva herself had often speculated that Maribel's support of her was directly inverse to Johan's hatred of her.

"So you propose that we continue to allow the witches to do what they will?" Lanyic said.

Neren leaned forward. "There must be a balance. The middle plains are empty, and now it is either at the border with the clans, or in the center with the crown. The balance has been upset, and it must be restored—"

"Why must it?" Eva stared at him across the table. He looked away.

"What are you saying, Eva?" Jon asked.

"The witches behave like they have equal power with the empress," Eva said. "This is not the case, nor should it have ever been. The Book of Skins says that Lisyne created the witches to protect us."

"Which they do," Guerline said.

Eva turned to her. Some of the edge was gone from her voice as she continued.

"The champion who protects his lady is still her servant. So should the Kavanaghs serve *you*. I know you admire them. You would treat them as equals. You would encourage their delusions of rank. This is very dangerous. They have such a hold on this country that should they ever decide to unseat you, they could do it in the time it takes you to blink." She reached out and took Guerline's hand. "I fear this; for your sake, and for the sake of Arido."

"Your fears are unnecessary, Eva," Neren said. He seemed to have regained his composure. "The Kavanaghs are content with their positions. They desire no more power."

Evadine's gaze snapped to Neren. Guerline looked down at their clasped hands; Eva's grip had tightened.

"Really, Lord Legislator?" Eva asked, her voice hard again. "Aradia, perhaps, is content. That is her nature. Olivia also I believe to lack ambition. She is happy to sit among her dusty tomes until the coming of hell." She addressed the whole table. "But what of Morgana? Morgana has power, and worse: Morgana has weapons and warriors. Our armies have been molded by *her* hands. And Morgana is not my worst fear. What of the Black Sister?"

Silence fell again. Guerline watched each of the councilors blink and squirm. They struggled to conceal their fear and apprehension at the mention of the youngest Kavanagh. How easily they seemed to forget that they had all been at Fiona's mercy not two months ago, when she came to escort the souls of Johan and Maribel to Ilys. She'd stayed not a moment longer than she had to, and seemed to have no interest in any of the humans beyond what was needed for Thiymen's script—she had even, it seemed to Guerline, been a little kind.

"Fiona's nothing but a good little soldier."

That voice—familiar, but Guerline knew it didn't belong to any of the councilors. She glanced around the room. The girl, the pale blonde one from her dreams, stood beside her father's still-present phantom at the far end of the room. The girl smirked at Evadine; after a moment, though, she seemed to feel Guerline's eyes upon her. Her brow furrowed, and she met Guerline's gaze.

"How is it that you see so much?" the girl asked, her voice a soft whisper that echoed in Guerline's ears.

Guerline opened her mouth, though what she might say, she had no idea. Then she winced at the pressure on her hand, which pulled her attention away from the vision. When she looked back, Johan and the girl were gone. Guerline bit her lip to keep from hyperventilating. Visions of her dead parents, her brother; these she could at least attribute to years of abuse at their hands.

But who was this pale girl? Was she even real?

Eva spoke, her voice like a clarion that grounded Guerline once more in the horrible, dull council room; her madness would have to wait. "Yes. Fiona hates us," Eva said. "She would kill us, given the chance. This I am sure of. She would take the Aridan throne for herself. She lusts for power and would use her black magic to overcome us—"

Shon stood. "Enough! I will not hear Fiona-lami spoken of in this way! You will retract your words."

Eva only smiled at him. His face twisted into a scowl.

"Take them back!"

"Stop!" Guerline stood and pulled her hand from Evadine's grip. "Sit down, Lord Marke! I am appalled by this behavior—especially from you, Eva." She glared down at her lover, who looked affronted. "You, my friend, who knows Aridan history so well. Remember that Thiymen has tried to seize power before. The other clans put her down."

She knew what Eva would say if she hadn't just been reprimanded: Fiona was not the leader then. Would Olivia be able to stop Fiona? Would any of her sisters be willing to stop her?

The empress sat down and shut her eyes. Her heart was pounding. Eva's words seemed like they came from a stranger, and Guerline was wholly unprepared to address them. Eva was no great supporter of witches, but she had always seemed to treat them as most in Del did: a distant and immovable part of the Aridan landscape. Guerline flexed her hand under the table and breathed deep, hoping that her councilors couldn't hear the incessant drumming in her chest.

She opened her eyes. "Now. Neren said the balance of Arido has been upset. I do not think it is the balance of power, nor even of population. I believe it is the balance of preference," she said.

"It is as Evadine-ami said. The closer the people are to the clans, the more they favor the Kavanaghs," Lanyic said.

Jon shook his head. "It's not all geographical. It's political. If a citizen is unhappy with our method, they use the witch method and vice versa. Theodor's discussion of stationary was quite close to the mark, really. I think the best course of action would be to invite the Kavanaghs and their captains to a special council to discuss and rectify discrepancies in our laws. We should send a message to the witch-son, and have him arrange it."

"I agree," Guerline said. "Since we can make no further progress on that subject without the witches, I propose we move on to—"

"Wait!" Pearce shrieked. "We have addressed the threat of Thiymen, but what of Adenen? Morgana is not Fiona; her sisters would not suppress *her*. She must be dealt with!"

"And how do you propose we do that?" Shon asked. His upper lip was curled in a disdainful scowl.

"We regulate her. Send a battalion to her fortress and subject it to military rule," Pearce said.

"No, Pearce. We cannot do that. The soldiers will not raise arms against she who trained them," said Jon.

Guerline sympathized with the exasperation in his voice. They were making no progress on the subject of witches, and likely wouldn't until witches were included in the discussion. There was simply no point in continuing. She picked up her quill and scribbled a note on the parchment before her: *invite witch representatives to be councilors.*

"Out of fear!" Pearce's nasal voice carried in the chamber. "They fear her!"

"Out of love, Pearce," Guerline said. "They have her love, and she has theirs. I fear they are more loyal to her than they ever will be to me," she added, smiling crookedly.

"And that is the very danger," Evadine said. "If they had to choose, and could not follow both of you, who would they support?"

Guerline watched Eva carefully. "I cannot answer that. The most I can do is to work with Morgana so that the choice does not come."

"I fear it has come already," Evadine said. She produced a letter from the folds of her overdress. The seal on it, made of red Braeden wax, was broken.

"It is from Derouk Madacy, the governor of Braeden," she said, louder now so the whole table could hear her. She stood. Her expression was smug; Guerline imagined for a moment that she was being taunted, and her heart twinged painfully. She frowned, the skin of her face uncomfortably and unusually tight.

"What does it say, Eva?" asked Jon. His tone sounded indifferent, but his eyes were fixed on Evadine in a more severe expression than Guerline liked to see directed at a friend. The intensity gave her pause. She did not like the thoughts she had in that moment.

Eva turned to him now. She smiled, but it was not a mirthful look.

"The wizards of the Atithi tribe are in Fortress Adenen. Three of them. They have met with Morgana and dined with her. She calls them her brothers."

"This is an outrage!" Lanyic stood and slammed his large hands on the table. Guerline flinched; Evadine did not. Lanyic looked down at the councilors, fury in his eyes. He turned those eyes on Guerline.

"Do you not recall, Majesty, the letters of recent weeks, bemoaning the destruction of forges by violent sandstorms out of the west? Out of Raeha?" he said. "And now, Red Morgana makes pacts with the desert rats! They are the likely cause of Braeden's troubles—"

"*Enough.*" Guerline stood and mimicked him, slapping her palms against the cold stone. Her body quivered, and she pressed her hands harder against the table.

"I inquired into the storms when we first had word of them. Morgana informed me that they originated in the Wastes of Aadi. We discussed the possibility of Raeha's involvement, but she thought it unlikely. Having no reason to suspect them myself, I agreed. The Raehan tribes have always kept to themselves, have been peaceful. There is strange power in the Wastes, independent of wizards and witches—is there not, loremaster?" she asked, turning to Jon. He nodded. Guerline looked at Eva. The other woman didn't answer. Guerline looked down the table once more.

"Morgana assured me that she would keep her eye on the sandstorms, and possibly confer with the wizards of the Atithi should there be need. It appears that the time has come to confer with them. I think this is a wise choice, since they do know much more of wind and sandstorms than we here in Arido," Guerline said pointedly.

"But can you trust in her honesty, Empress?" asked Pearce. His voice whined.

"The witches of Adenen use Braeden's forges as well, Pearce," said Jon. "Do you think Morgana would willingly suffer her forges and workshops to be damaged?"

"More's the point, what could she possibly gain by such a deception?" Guerline asked. "As Eva has already pointed out, if Morgana wanted to usurp me, she could assuredly do so without the subterfuge of blaming Raeha, nor would she need their help."

Shon laughed an agreement with Guerline's words, and Eva sighed. Pearce glared at Jon, who only regarded him with indifference. When Pearce turned his beady eyes back to the parchment in front of him, the older man caught Guerline's eye and winked. She gave him a grateful smile.

"Councilors, the midday bell rang an age ago and we have not rested our minds for hours," she said. "Please take time now to eat and refresh yourselves. We reconvene at the third hour after noon."

Evadine swept up her books and paper and leaned closer to Guerline. The young empress patiently stacked her own notes, waiting for her lover to speak and hoping her words would not belong to the new ideas she seemed to have, ideas that echoed strongly of Alcander.

"Lina, can you not trust me? My only wish is to save you from making a grave mistake," Eva said.

Her hopes were disappointed.

"Eva, I will take my meal alone today," Guerline said.

Evadine didn't speak. The words hung heavily between them. The headache that had been threatening Guerline all morning became pronounced and insistent. Doubt filled her as she stood no more than a foot from the friend who had become so distant in the space of a few hours. To speak as she had with Eva felt wrong, but so did everything the other woman had said in the council. The only thing of which Guerline was sure was that she needed time alone to think.

Finally, Eva turned and left. Guerline watched the far door close behind her. She gasped for breath to quell the sobs that threatened to break out of her chest. She hadn't known what to expect from the council meeting—certainly not a debate about the place of magic in Aridan society. Eva's position had been most shocking to her. Eva had always been uninterested in magic; she'd never seemed so vehemently opposed before. The last thing Guerline wanted was to fight with Eva, her best friend, her dearest love, her one true ally in this strange new life as a monarch; but she also couldn't go along with what Eva said without considering things for herself.

Two servants brought her meal in and set the tray in front of her. One of them cut a tiny piece of the steak off and ate it. The three waited in silence for a few moments; then the taster nodded and both servants backed away. Guerline cut into the steak herself, glad for something to do with her hands. She chewed a bite once, twice, then spat it out when her mouth was flooded with a bitter, too-sweet taste.

The taster dashed forward. "Your Majesty? What's wrong?"

Guerline took a large gulp of her wine and looked down at her plate. The steak, once brown and pink in the middle, was green and oozed yellow fluid.

Someone whimpered. She looked at the servants— both stared at the food with wide eyes. The taster clutched his throat. Even as she took in their fear, she felt a giddy streak of relief. This was real. "Not a word to anyone," she said. "Throw this out immediately."

They scuttled away with the offending meat, clearly only too happy to follow her orders. Guerline waited for a minute or two so she wouldn't meet them again, and then she ran full-tilt to the gardens. She needed to lose herself in living things.

Guerline jerked awake, managing to do so without screaming. Her windows were still dark with night, and she grimaced at them. If she made it till morning, that would be a full week without being woken by the sound of her own hoarse cries. Her reign was off to a fine start.

She rolled to the other side of the bed, but the sheets were fresh and had no trace of Eva's scent on them. The other woman had left the second session of the council in a rush, and Guerline had not seen her since. She had gotten ready for bed alone, and it was now clear that Eva did not intend to join her that night. Eva had moved into the Chief

Adviser's quarters, which were the only other ones on this floor of the high tower, but that meant little when the empress's chambers were a small mansion unto themselves. They were rooms and rooms away from each other, she and Eva. Guerline pulled the pillow Eva had used into her chest, hugging it tightly.

The afterimages of her nightmare faded more quickly than ever, and a smile tugged at her lips as she thought about Eva; but memories of the council meeting flooded her, washing away the fantasies with such a force that it was almost like a sentient warning. Wide awake, Guerline sat up, frowning into the darkness. Evadine was tender with her, but she was also becoming politically extreme—and it mattered because they *were* the lawmakers. They couldn't just love each other; they couldn't be women who had pints with their friends and ranted from barstools about the state of the empire, women who shared a bed and a love and a life. She was empress, and Eva was her Chief Adviser. A political rift between them was the dynamic that had to matter most, despite what they felt for each other.

Tears stung Guerline's eyes; the darkness pressed in on her and she couldn't stand to be in bed another moment. She climbed off the mattress, edged around the room with her hands out until she found her Adenen lamp, tapped the globe to light it, and then made her way out of her chambers. Twice she almost turned through the doors that would lead her into Eva's adjoining chambers, but she resisted. One of them had to be well-rested.

She made her way to the library and strolled through the stacks, not really looking at the books but being comforted by their closeness. The wide open darkness of her bedroom was oddly claustrophobic compared to the tall narrow lanes between bookshelves. She paused and just rested her free hand against the spines besides her. In a way, the books were protection. An escape she would always have access to. A sanctuary, there for when she needed it.

Without looking, she plucked a book from the shelf and carried it to the circle of soft chairs at the end of the row. She settled in, and then looked at the title, which almost made her laugh: it was a volume of nursery songs.

She flipped through them, humming along a bit, until—

"Guerline-basi, what are you doing up so late?"

She looked up and saw Jon Wellsly standing several feet away with his own Adenen lamp and book. His dark black skin glowed warm in the welcoming pink light, and she returned his smile.

"I couldn't sleep," she said.

His smile faltered. "You're not still having nightmares?"

Guerline sighed. Eva had said she'd told a few of the councilors who had been nagging her about the empress's health. Guerline knew that Theodor had been one, and she supposed Jon was the other obvious choice. He had, after all, known her all her life, and had been her unofficial teacher.

She opened her mouth to reassure him that she was fine, but everything that came to mind at first was false. The nightmares weren't getting better. The nightmares weren't going away. "They're not affecting me as badly," she said. But only because they were becoming routine.

She was going numb to them. Perhaps to everything.

Jon sat next to her, set his lamp with hers, and turned to face her. She mirrored him out of habit.

"Will you tell me what the nightmares are about?" he asked.

Her breath caught in her chest. She hadn't told anyone, not even Eva, about the incident that formed the anchor of her nightmares, nor about the week that followed, in which she had been constantly afraid—locking all of her chamber doors, sleeping in the dozens of empty guest rooms so that he wouldn't find her, hiding in the sewing rooms and pantries and any place she could think of that he would never go. She spent two whole days in the palace Temple pretending to pray for her parents, because Alcander had his own altar and never went to the Temple except for formal ceremonies—and because of a fleeting hope that if she pretended newfound piety, he would spare her.

While Alcander lived, telling the truth would have left her not only at his mercy, but the mercy of a court that had been largely indifferent to her. It wasn't hard to imagine how they would turn a blind eye to whatever punishment her brother could have devised for her. She could have counted her predicted defenders on one hand.

And once he was dead . . .

People still talked about him. Her brother, the true heir. If she told the truth now, when Alcander was dead, it would only undermine her. Perhaps even throw suspicion on her for his death, however improbable it seemed. She was known to be sympathetic to the witches, and if someone accused her of colluding with them to take the throne, it would be oil on the fire of the debate surrounding the place of witchcraft.

And yet, something welled up in Guerline's throat as Jon watched her, waiting patiently. What did he expect to hear? The desire to say it out loud grew hot in her chest, to tell *someone* the truth. Up until now, she had avoided acknowledging what happened—though her nightmares forced her to revisit it—because doing so would have made it real, an actual event separate from the horror her mind reproduced. But what if saying it out loud took the horror away? What if making it real would allow her to really put it behind her?

Jon tilted his head and the motion caught her gaze, refocused it on him. The Lord Historian had always been one of the more loving adult figures in Guerline's life. She could tell him. He would believe her.

"The night my parents fell ill, Alcander . . . tried to force himself on me," she said. Her voice was steadier than she thought it would be. "He didn't succeed, but the memory. . . . It's hard to sleep in my bedroom."

Jon frowned and didn't speak for several minutes, during which Guerline stared past his shoulder and silently hummed nursery songs over the mental chant reminding her that she could not take the truth back now.

Finally, he said, "You moved into new rooms, though."

Guerline's eyes widened in disbelief. That was what stuck with him? "It's less about the room, Jon-ami." How could she begin to explain? This was a mistake. "He came after me in a private space, a space that was mine." Her voice started to tremble and her mouth snapped shut. She breathed deeply, nostrils flaring, and tried to diffuse the panic tingling through her.

"Why would he do such a thing, Guerline-basi?" Jon asked, his voice soft with what sounded like legitimate confusion. She couldn't blame him for that, she supposed. She had been so confused when Alcander reached for her and spoke almost as if he was in a dream, talking to some imagined version of her instead of the real thing.

She unclenched her teeth and spoke slowly. "Alcander always found ways to torment me, to punish me for stepping outside the boundaries he established. He enjoyed . . . being more important than me. More . . . powerful."

Jon shook his head. "It doesn't make sense. What benefit would there be to him?"

Guerline opened her mouth to answer, but was stopped by a flare from one of the Adenen lamps that mimicked the burst of anger inside her. She stood, the nursery songbook still clutched tightly in her hand.

"You asked about *my* nightmares, Lord Historian, presumably because you were concerned about me—and now you're only concerned about my dead, abusive brother?" she seethed. "I don't know why he did what he did, nor do I care. I care only that he *hurt* me, and I—I have been trying to recover my sense of safety, I have been trying to protect my trust in others . . ."

She sobbed once and choked the remaining cries down, then picked up her lamp. She tried to bid him goodnight, but no words made it through the block in her throat, so she simply left. He spoke words she couldn't understand through the blood pounding in her ears, and she looked back once. Behind him, she thought she saw the indistinct form of a woman reflecting the magical light, but she blinked and it was gone, and Jon was too far away to see clearly. Guerline returned to her chambers, locking all her doors behind her, and slipped the nursery songbook under her pillow before settling down to an uneasy rest.

CHAPTER TEN

KANIKA TOUCHED DOWN ON THE GRAVELLY FIELD JUST OUTSIDE the city of Jerica, jogging lightly to slow herself down. As she stopped, she turned and shook the last flight out of her black sail, and then wound the strip of silk around her arm to settle it. Once it was calm, she pulled it through her belt and left it hang where she could get to it easily. She didn't know what to expect in the city, and she might have need of a quick getaway. She unhooked the panel of cloth that covered her face while flying and pulled her hood down.

From where she stood, the city looked normal. She raised a hand over her eyes to block the bright grey light filtering through the clouds. The Citadel had a corp of witches—pulsers was the unofficial name for them—who spent their days casting magic out over the country, searching for the dying and monitoring them until it was time to collect the person's soul. The concentration of death was always higher in cities, but never as high as the pulsers had sensed in Jerica that day. Something was killing the entire population.

Fiona had sent Kanika to investigate.

I suppose it's a vote of confidence. At least, she hoped it was that, and not that Fiona suspected her of nosing around the dragon caves waiting for an opportunity to speak with Silas.

She listened carefully, but heard no screaming. At this distance, she could see no mayhem. That worried her. She took off toward the city in a light run and slowed down as she approached the walls. Still no sound. Jerica was not a large city compared with others in Arido, but it was the largest in the East, and it was never, ever silent—especially not at midday.

Kanika called up her magic and whispered a few words. Her body rippled with warmth, like molasses being poured over her skin. A simple invisibility charm. It wouldn't fool a greater demon, but if there was a greater demon in Jerica, she had bigger problems than whether or not it could see her. She stepped back from the wall a few paces, then crouched down and channeled magic into her fingers and toes. With a deep breath in, she launched herself at the wall and climbed it quickly, like an insect, using the magic in her extremities to gain upward leverage on the smooth surface. When she reached the top, she planted her hands flat on the battlement and vaulted over. She landed neatly on her feet with a soft thud.

She waited there, knees bent, to see if anything reacted to her. There was no movement.

The streets were empty of everything: living, dead, human, animal. The doors of some buildings hung open, but were undamaged. Kanika scurried through the alleys of the suburbs as quickly and quietly as she could. She moved instinctively toward the center of the city. When disaster struck, people either stayed in their homes or gathered en masse. The rows of empty homes indicated the latter.

She reached the merchant shops and slowed down. Finally, she heard something. There was a low groaning coming from the other side of these buildings, and a rasping sound like wind through straw. She also heard intermittent gurgling, but that could just have been the fountain in the square. She took a step forward and heard a nice, long squelch. She looked down.

Her boot was squarely on top of a squarish chunk of something green and gooey. With just the slightest of grimaces, Kanika lifted her foot and shook it off. She squatted and looked more closely at the mess. A flat piece of slimy, light-green hide sat on top of a blob that was yellowish-white and gelatinous. It looked like there were pieces of long dark hair in it, but not attached; more like they'd just brushed the goo and gotten caught. She looked up and saw more piles of the stuff heading toward the square, taking the same route between shops she'd been planning on using.

The trail continued into the shadow of a shop's back awning. Kanika peered into the darkness. She could almost make out a silhouette. Her fingertips tingled with magic as she lifted them and summoned a small light in her palm. She took a deep breath—

"Momma?"

Kanika let out her breath in surprise and the light flew off into the sky, carried by her exhalation. She turned in the direction of the voice and spotted a little boy about six years old, with jet black hair down to his shoulders and eyes of such a dark brown they almost looked black, too. His skin was a creamy dark tan, and his body was wiry with the lean muscle of a child who plays rough. He was staring at her now, his big dark eyes calm and steady. She looked back at him. Her heart was in her throat.

"Feoras," she said.

She let her invisibility charm fall and spread her arms wide. Feoras ran to her. He hid his face in her chest and she embraced him tightly, running a hand over his perpetually tangled hair. She hadn't allowed herself to think about the child until that moment; if she'd hoped to find him alive and discovered him dead, it would have been too much to bear.

Feoras was her son by Jerica's best shroud-weaver, a man named Lorand who became a dear friend of Kanika's over a decade ago. Most witches did not share in the raising of their boy-children or the girls who did not become witches, but she had visited Lorand and Feoras a few times throughout the last year, since he declared his name and gender. Though her visits were few, she often sent small gifts down from the Citadel.

"Thank Lisyne you're safe," she said. "Where's your papa?"

"He looks like a corpse, but he is still alive," Feoras said. His voice was muffled against her robes.

Kanika's eyes widened. "What do you mean, child? Is—is that Papa, in the shadows there?"

Feoras nodded and pointed. She summoned up another light in her palm and blew it gently into the shadows.

A man-shaped thing lay on its side, facing away from them. Her stomach clenched as her eyes took it in. His clothes still covered most of his body, but she could tell from the stains on the fabric that his flesh was beginning to rot. One arm was flung awkwardly behind him. The skin was visible from the elbow down, and it was yellowing and mottled with dark green. Darker lines ran under the skin where his blood was turning to sludge. Clumps of dark gold hair littered the ground under his head.

Kanika released Feoras and went over to the man. She turned him gently over onto his back. He inhaled slowly. It was the rasping, gurgling noise she'd heard earlier.

"Lorand? Lorand, it's Kanika. Gods, Lorand, please answer me," she said quietly.

His eyelids opened slowly, as if with great effort. His dark brown eyes were filmy and unfocused, and the sclera was yellowing. He stared up, but not at her face. She wondered if he could even see her.

"Kanika. You've come." His voice rattled in his throat and chilled her to the bone. Feoras sank to his knees.

"What's happened, Lorand?" she asked.

"I don't . . . it happened so quickly. One man . . . his flesh slid off his bones. Then another. More every hour."

He sighed and closed his eyes again. Kanika rested the back of her hand against his forehead. The skin there was hot and dry. She lifted his shirt slowly and peered underneath. Small, oozing sores dotted Lorand's chest. A sob caught in her chest as she gently let the fabric fall.

"They told everyone to get to the square," Feoras said. "Papa fell. I stayed here."

"That was good, child. Well done," Kanika said.

"It was louder before. It's gotten quiet now," the boy said.

Kanika took a deep breath. She smoothed down Lorand's shirt and stood up.

It was a flesh-eating curse. There were only three that she knew of. One was sent in the form of a miasma which settled around the intended target, be it a single person or a building. The miasma disintegrated the skin of those who came in contact with it. The second summoned a parasite, which was delivered into the target's body during the night, by any available orifice. It devoured the target from the inside out, consuming and excreting so that the person decomposed within their own skin. This was particularly gruesome, since the parasite expelled a compound that kept the victim alive and conscious until either the caster released it or the body fell apart.

The third was so rare she had never seen a case of it in her three hundred years of life. There were no records of anyone ever casting it, so the notes in the scrolls maintained that though it was likely a curse, it could also have been just a normal disease. This curse appeared to have no incantation and employed no physical manifestation, like the miasma or the parasite. The body simply rotted in the usual way, only while the person was still alive. Kanika had read about it centuries ago, during her studies as a witch-in-training, but had never seen anything to suggest that it was real.

"Stay here, and stay hidden, Feoras," she said.

The boy nodded and sank down to the floor next to his father. Kanika slipped through his shop and positioned herself under a window. She had assumed the emperor and empress were killed by the parasite, but now . . . she had a sneaking suspicion she was about to prove that the third flesh-eating curse was indeed a curse, and she expected the worst from the caster of such a thing. If the curse required maintenance, the caster would likely be in the square, the epicenter. If the curse was a one-time cast, it was possible that whoever did it was long gone—unless they were particularly sadistic and wanted to watch. She couldn't decide what she'd prefer.

The window afforded her a fairly good view of the whole square. The fountain in the center was virtually hidden from sight by the pile of bodies around it. It looked like people had clambered into the pool and continued to climb on top of each other. What had they been trying to reach? The statue of Lisyne at the top of the fountain? Disaster always brought out faith. The mountain of rotting flesh was mostly still, though there were shifts and ripples every now and then.

Those who hadn't made it to the center were piled in smaller mounds in the rest of the square. It was as though people had just fallen, as Feoras said Lorand had, and stayed where they landed. They'd fallen on top of each other. Some had arms outstretched, like they'd tried to pull themselves forward, but all was still now.

It looked like there were varying stages of decomposition. Some still looked relatively well, but others were missing limbs or chunks of their guts. Her palms began to sweat. She didn't know how many of these people could be saved, if they could be saved at all. The only things she could think to combat the curse with were strong dark-magic repellents.

She had nothing more specific than that. It would have to do—but before she could begin healing, she needed to make sure it was safe.

She went to the door and eased it open. There was a slight creak, but nothing in the square moved. The stillness was eerie. She slid her sword slowly out of its sheath and held it ready. The sooner this was resolved, the better. She moved toward the fountain with cautious steps, avoiding the fallen bodies as best she could.

A crack sounded behind her, like someone snapping a whip. Kanika ducked and part of a wood beam flew where her head had been. She spun around and straightened up in time to block another piece of the beam. Her sword went through it like butter. Holding the blade up and ready once more, she scanned the square for her adversary. Across the way, someone giggled.

"You stuck around, then," Kanika said.

A man appeared in the shattered doorway of one of the shops. He wore a silver tunic buttoned all the way up to his throat and pristine cream-colored pants tucked into shining black boots. He tossed his long black ponytail over his shoulder and walked out toward her. A grin pulled his sharp features even tighter over his skull. Though he looked human, it was clear he wasn't. The whole of his eyes were black.

"Hello, Kanika of Thiymen. Did you volunteer for this?" the man asked.

She wasn't sure what he meant with such a question, so she ignored it.

"Name yourself," she said.

"You are more motherly than others of your kind, so I thought you might come for your son. He is a curious boy.

You may have noticed that his flesh is still whole. Some accident, I'm sure—or something else?"

Kanika kept her face stony and let his words flow straight to the back of her mind, to be dealt with later. She would not allow diversionary tactics. No one was better at keeping her cool than a Thiymen witch. She allowed magic to gather in her limbs, strengthening her body and increasing her response time.

"You're nameless, then. Good. None will remember you when you're gone," she said.

The man-thing grinned at her. His ponytail, high atop his head, pulled his skin back tightly and made him look like a snake.

"You know better, Kanika of Thiymen. I will never, ever be forgotten—and woe unto those who do forget me."

Wind roared up and tore at Kanika's clothes. She redirected magic to her feet, weighting her to the ground so she wasn't flung into the sky. The man-thing rushed at her. She brought her sword down across his chest, but he turned to black smoke on contact and disappeared into the rushing air. The gusts became a smoky tornado, which launched itself into the sky. It disappeared from sight and the wind died down again.

Kanika gasped for air and let her sword tip drop toward the ground. She didn't know what the man-thing was, but she had the distinct feeling that she had gotten off easy. Could that thing have been what Fiona spoke of? But that was impossible—she had sealed it. Nothing could break through one of Fiona's seals.

She started to sheathe her sword, but stopped when she spotted movement in the pile of bodies on the fountain.

She held the sword ready again and inched forward. If the man-thing was a demon, it was possible he had left behind minions to harvest flesh from the slain. The imps were easy enough to kill, as long as their numbers were not too great. She crept up to the base of the pile, stopped, and waited.

Kanika didn't move. Neither did the bodies. She breathed deep. *Maybe I'm just being paranoid. The thing is gone. I must summon the exorcists—*

Something burst out of the pile of bodies and leapt at her. She barely had time to lift her forearm into a block before it hit her. She careened backwards, twisting to protect her neck, and somersaulted to her knees. Coughing, she looked up at what was most definitely not an imp.

It was a corpse like the others, a man, dressed only in trousers. His ashy grey skin was covered with deep purple bruises. He was missing an arm. The splintered bone of his shoulder stuck out several inches from the remaining meat. It was dingy and yellowed already. His throat was missing, and the ends of his wild red-gold hair stuck to the wound. He carried with him a giant black sword. His shriveled lips were pulled back in a manic grimace.

Kanika got to her feet and gripped her sword with both hands. Her eyes never left the puppet.

"Thought you had gotten rid of me, didn't you, witch?" he said.

She didn't respond. Puppets rarely understood where they were, what was happening, or even who they had once been—but that didn't stop them from speaking. Frankly, she was surprised he could, with his throat the way it was. His demon master must have thought it would be amusing to grant him speech.

He stalked forward, holding his huge sword easily with one arm. She bent her knees.

"I shall destroy you and all your kind for what you have done! I have the power. I am no longer afraid."

He lunged forward. Kanika dodged left and swept her sword at his exposed left side as she passed. He twisted away; her sword barely cut him. He looked down at the thin slit in his skin and laughed. Then he charged at her again.

He was faster than any puppet she'd ever encountered. The magic on him was powerful enough to send chills down her spine. It shivered through her bones with every blow she parried. It made her heavily enchanted sword grow hot with panic in her hands. She tried to breathe deep and keep calm. She wore only bracers and a slim leather chest plate. Without her full armor, she was vulnerable. One wrong move could be fatal.

The puppet's belligerent assault made up for lack of skill with sheer relentlessness. All she needed was one clear opening and half a second to cast a fire spell, but no such opportunities were coming. Meanwhile, the puppet continued to laugh.

"Yes! Taste my revenge!"

Kanika summoned magic to her arms and shoved him away with great force.

"I don't know you!" she roared.

The puppet stopped laughing. He paused his attack and stared at her.

"What?" he asked.

"Your retribution is lost on me. I do not know who you are. It's not I who has done this to you, it was the demon!"

He glared. His mouth trembled as he bared his yellow teeth. "You have done this. You must know. You must know me! How could you have done this and not know me?"

He rushed at her. She parried and pushed his sword away from her, but his body came toppling into hers and knocked her down again. He righted himself and put a foot on her chest. With the tip of his sword at her throat, he looked down at her with wide, wild eyes.

"You *will* know me," he said.

He raised his sword. A cracking noise split the silence. He was gone, leaving Kanika heaving on the ground. She rolled over onto her stomach and coughed. Prone on the ground, the danger finally passed, she allowed herself to be deeply afraid.

Movement caught her eye and she turned to look. Feoras stood in the door of Lorand's shop. How long had he been watching? The thing's words came back to her now. There were children among the fallen of Jerica; all had been affected, save for Feoras. She crossed to him and picked him up, squeezing him. He had seen through her invisibility charm too. If her witch blood gave him immunity to magic, so much the better.

"Will you save them, now that the man is gone?" her child asked.

"As many as I can, pebble," she said.

He wrinkled his nose at the nickname but allowed her to put him down. She drew magic to her palm and conjured a small, sparkling black bird, the messenger of choice for her clan.

"There is dark magic that needs cleansing. Send twenty or so exorcists," she said.

The bird glowed brightly, then vaulted off her hand and into the air. She watched it go, then turned and jogged back to Lorand's shop. She knelt next to him. His eyes opened weakly when she touched his forehead. She put her free hand on his chest.

"Don't worry, dear one. I will bring you back to life," she said.

CHAPTER ELEVEN

ARADIA TIED HER LONG RED HAIR BACK WITH A GREEN SCARF and stepped outside. It was a beautiful southern day. The sun was the bright yellow of fresh corn, the breezes carried fresh-smelling sea air, and the gardens of Gwanen Palace were bustling with activity. The eldest Kavanagh, however, was not fooled by the robust appearance of her land. She, like the rest of her clan and the humans who lived and worked at the tip of Tyr Peninsula, knew the beauty they saw was like the rosy cheeks of a consumptive: a sign of illness, not health.

It all started two years ago, in the height of summer. Water was always scarce during that time, so no one noticed any differences until the tide-walkers reviewed their summer gradations. The numbers showed subtle changes, so small they hadn't been alarming at each measurement; the arc they created, however, showed a slow but gradual recession. The high tide was not coming in as high as it once did.

Even this wasn't frightening. Such changes happened over time. The people of the South accommodated, extending piers and docks a few feet. Then the monsoons came, sweeping salt water over the end of the peninsula. The water receded quickly enough, but its retreat continued past the normal tide line. The gradual lowering of the Sea of Dalia over the summer months became too rapid. Docks could not be extended fast enough, and ships couldn't reach port without the risk of running aground. Unloading cargo now required small boats to row out to where the ships anchored, bringing it back and forth in hopelessly small loads. It took days and consumed port manpower.

Aradia had assigned a detail of witches to assist the transportation of goods and the extending of docks, and launched an investigation into the cause of the lowering sea. Her personal attention, however, had quickly been consumed with another problem, this one on land.

Much of the crop had been washed away by flooding. The following harvest was pitifully small, and this season did not show much promise. Aradia was reluctant to admit it, but something was very wrong. The blight—whatever it was—was creeping northward. The crops in Neva, situated on the peninsula's border with the mainland, were beginning to fail as well.

Gwanen's gardens had thus far been unaffected, and Aradia had planted every square inch of them in a final effort to bolster their stores before what appeared to be imminent famine. When her grim-faced captain came to her in the hothouses and asked that she come inspect one of the outdoor gardens, Aradia feared that her initial misgivings had proved true: in over-working the gardens, she sapped them of the magic that protected them.

Aradia followed Jaela over to the garden, where a withered and blackened tomato vine stood out sharply even from a distance. As she approached, she could see the plants around the dead one withering as well, decay radiating out from the point of impact. She gasped; Jaela squeezed her hand.

"This is the first?" she asked.

"Yes. But there are others that aren't far behind. Many of the plants are still young. We're gathering them and moving them to the hothouses. Hopefully we can repot them and the soil we have stored will be good until they mature."

Aradia nodded. She picked her way carefully through the garden and knelt at the edge of the plant. She ran her hands carefully over the dead leaves. They felt strange, with the musty softness of dusty velvet and cobwebs. Her lip curled in disgust. She turned her attention to the soil.

"The soil is black," she murmured. She gathered a handful and turned it over in her hands. It crumbled, becoming finer with every abrasive pass of her fingers, and sifted out of her hands like sand. A small cloud of black dust rose as the dirt hit the ground again. "Black and dry."

"We've tried everything we can think of to re-irrigate," Jaela said. "Hewyna even took a bowl of earth and poured a whole jug of water on it. The water just pooled on top!"

"Did you see how deep it goes?" Aradia asked. Jaela nodded.

"As deep as our instrument, at least five feet."

Aradia pondered this. That meant that it would soon go deeper than all the roots in the gardens. All plants but the trees would starve. She sighed and pressed her hands flat against the dead soil, routing her fingers into it. Closing her eyes, she pushed into the ground with her magic, going straight down. She would see how deep the blight really was.

Jaela was right; it was deeper than five feet. The contamination continued past ten feet, twenty, thirty, and even further. With each foot that passed, Aradia felt colder, heavier. The energy that buzzed within the soil grew weaker and weaker, until there was no movement in the earth at all. Aradia pushed down until she hit dense, dark rock hundreds of feet below the surface. She pulled back at once, ripping her hands from the earth and standing in one smooth motion, dusting the dead soil from her hands viciously.

"This sickness comes from the very core of the earth," she said with a shaking voice. Her eyes met Jaela's. Her own fear reflected back at her.

"Lady Aradia!"

She turned in the direction of the shout. A young witch ran toward them.

"A ship's run aground at Port Feronia," the child gasped. "The sea's down another three feet and it's a big ship—it's the grain shipment from Xian Su."

Aradia's heart sank. Xian Su, a country across the Sea of Dalia to the southeast, was one of Arido's allies and the one with which they did the most trading. Aradia had applied to the Sunese mystics when she realized how serious the South's situation was, and they'd promised to send the Aridans a shipment of much-needed grain. If the ship had run aground, there might be damage to the hull—which meant the grain was at risk.

She began shouting orders. The witches in the gardens stopped what they were doing and followed her, rushing into the castle to get their sails, the green silk sashes they used to fly. Within moments, Aradia and twenty other witches were speeding through the air to the port a few miles down the coast.

The ship was still half a mile from shore, caught on shoals that once wouldn't have been a threat. Every long-boat and rowboat at port clustered around the stranded ship. On board, the crew members rushed to bring all the cargo to the deck. As she circled the ship in the air, Aradia spotted frothing at one spot where water met hull. It was as she'd feared; the ship was flooding. She signaled three witches and pointed the spot out to them. They nodded and flew down to patch the hull. Aradia took the rest and landed on the water, solidifying the surface into a platform which they eased up to the edge of the ship.

"How much is left?" she called up to the captain.

"About a third!" he shouted down to her. Aradia frowned. It would require a huge effort, but they could maintain the water platform under such a load and move it to the closest pier. They would have to. She looked at the sixteen witches with her. They nodded.

"All right, lower the rest down to us! We'll move it all at once. Waterproof the sacks as they come down! Keep the boats close!" A heavy feeling settled in her chest. Witches didn't believe in luck, but the eldest Kavanagh wished in that moment that long-gone Seryne would bring her some of the good to replace the bad that plagued her now.

It took them several agonizing minutes to ease the water platform up to the closest pier. The citizens waiting at the docks swarmed out to them, taking the heavy grain sacks and passing them overhead along the crowd all the way back to shore. Aradia and her witches let the humans move everything. They focused their power on keeping the platform steady.

Finally, the last sack was in safe hands.

Aradia grinned. "All right, it's done! Release!"

As one, the witches cut off the power to the platform and took to the air.

"Well done, sisters, well done! You four, get back to the ship and help them dock! Jaela, with me. The rest of you, return to the palace!" Aradia shouted over the din of the crowd below.

The witches dispersed according to her direction. Aradia and Jaela flew back down to the docks. In the confusion of unloading, Aradia had lost track of the grain, and she wanted to make sure that it had gotten to Governor Kestran Lot. She spotted the orange livery of the Lot family and flew down to them.

Kestran ran over as soon as they touched down. He was a tall, thin man with the dark skin common in the South and a thick head of dark curly hair. His blue eyes stood out against the rest of his coloring, as did his broad, white-toothed grin. He reached out and squeezed first Jaela's hand, then Aradia's, making quick, shallow bows.

"Lady Aradia! Thank you so, so much for arriving so swiftly. You have saved us all," he said, breathy with relief.

Aradia smiled back. "Of course, of course. I am so very glad everything was recovered safely. All the grain is accounted for?"

"Yes, my men are collecting it all now," Kestran said.

The two leaders turned from each other and surveyed the scene with pleasure, watching the orange-clad guards load the grain sacks into carts to be taken to the public silos. It would be inventoried, and rationed appropriately if famine did strike the peninsula. Aradia glanced down, her heart heavy with that thought. Famine was unavoidable, and soon she would have to write to the southern governors and instruct them in the necessary preparations.

Shouts rose up. Aradia hurriedly scanned the crowd, trying to locate the commotion.

Kestran pointed. "There!"

He took off toward the scuffle. Aradia and Jaela followed, moving as quickly as they could through the throng of people who were now gathering to see whatever was going on.

Jaela cursed under her breath. "Milady . . ."

"I know. Stay close, and be ready," Aradia said quietly.

"Get back! Get back, get back!"

The witches broke through the crowd. Kestran and his guards stood in a clearing, blades drawn against a man wildly swinging a short sword. The man was broad and leathery tan, clearly a farmer of some kind. Behind him stood a lad of perhaps fifteen or sixteen, sagging under the weight of a grain sack as big as his own torso. The boy looked afraid, as afraid of his father as he was of the governor's guards.

"Just put the sack down, boy, or hand it over to my men," Kestran said. His gaze was fixed on the boy, his voice low and steady.

"It's our grain, it's owed us! It's owed!" the man said. His eyes were wide.

"This is the crown's grain, sir, sent by our allies," Kestran said. "Whatever debt is owed you, something else must settle it."

Aradia sighed. She'd thought something like this would happen; that was why she'd come back down, to check and make sure that all was well on the ground. This man had undoubtedly heard rumors from the far south, had possibly seen some of his own crops fail, and was trying to ensure his family's survival with this stolen sack of grain. Aradia understood the impulse.

"No! Stop!" Kestran shouted.

A man came up behind the boy and grabbed him by the throat. The new man shouted something almost unintelligible. He may have been calling the man and the boy greedy. The governor's guards tried to move in on the new man, but the first man was still waving his sword with dangerous imprecision. More people were starting to press forward to join the brawl. The boy dropped his sack of grain, which split and spilled the precious food onto the paving stones.

Aradia put a hand to her chest. This had gone on long enough. She made eye contact with Jaela, who nodded.

The witches lifted their hands and chanted quietly. Green light drifted from their palms across the clearing and into the nostrils of the squabblers. Their movements slowed. The first man lowered his sword; the second released the boy. Steadily, they all laid themselves down on the paving stones and went to sleep. The light drifted out of the circle on all sides, making people shake their heads, blink, and sneeze. Aradia pointed at the spilled grain and it floated back into the bag. The seam restitched itself.

Kestran watched them work their magic carefully. When they were finished, and the light disappeared, he signaled for his men to pick up the grain and to seize the first man.

"Do not arrest him. Please, Kestran. He won't remember his folly," Aradia said.

Kestran squinted at her. He sighed and walked over.

"We cannot make every frightened farmer sleep through these troubles," he whispered.

"Force and cruelty will do nothing to comfort them!" she said.

"What would you have me do, Aradia-lami? I can't put them to sleep, I can only put them in dungeons. And you can't fly over the peninsula breaking up quarrels. You must solve this. You must fix it. That is the only way to keep peace."

Aradia smiled, even as her heart sank. He was right. "I will be in touch soon, Kestran. We will get through this."

She nodded to Jaela, and they took off, headed back to Gwanen Palace.

CHAPTER TWELVE

NIGHT HAD FALLEN AN HOUR PAST WHEN A SHARP KNOCK broke Guerline's concentration. The jeweled dagger tumbled from her hand and thudded against the carpeted floor. A quick examination of her fingers showed no cuts; she flexed them, then looked up at the door with trepidation. She'd spent the last half hour staring into the fire and twirling the dagger in her hands, a trick she'd gotten quite good at since Alcander's ominous visit. She was not in the mood for company.

There had been people knocking all day—Undine, Theodor, Jon—ever since the sun was full in the sky that morning, but Guerline had ignored them all. She'd even blocked the door, since Undine and Bartlett, head of the household, each had keys to the room. Perhaps it was childish of her to hide in her rooms, to refuse to engage in her imperial duties . . . but how could she hold a court before her people when she felt so hollow inside?

Eva had not come. Not once; or if she had, she had not spoken, which seemed impossible because Eva had to know Guerline would have admitted her at once. She had made it through last night without screaming aloud, but she had not slept well, and when she'd finally given up and left the bed for the day, it was as if something had been taken from her during those dark hours alone. Some essential aspect of her was absent; Guerline felt sure that whatever it was, it was with Eva.

Yet Guerline could not go to her. That was how it would have been before, when they fought; Guerline was the one to approach and seek to mend, while Eva was too proud to give way even if she was deeply sorry. But that was no longer how it could be. Guerline was the empress now, and *she* must gather a little of that strength to her. Especially in this case, when Eva was. . . . Could such social views be wholly wrong or right?

It was not unwise for Eva and the others to suggest that Guerline take stock of her relationship with the witch leaders, whom she had not even met—they had not come to her coronation. Whatever wisdom was in their caution, though, for Eva to suggest that Fiona Kavanagh was preparing to murder them all? That Morgana Kavanagh, with whom Guerline had corresponded, sought to usurp her? There was no sense to it. She had been crowned. If the witches had wanted to stage a coup—if they had murdered her family, as some whispers had suggested—why, why would they wait until she was legally crowned? Why not strike in the two months when the crown remained formally unclaimed?

And how could Eva claim to love her, and then strike out at her so unexpectedly in front of her *council*?

These thoughts kept Guerline pacing in her rooms, refusing company and food, through the sun's whole journey across the sky from mountain peaks to crumbling cliffs. She felt untethered; she had clung so much to Eva in recent weeks that to be thus cleaved from her left Guerline reeling. She must center herself again, steadily . . . alone. Tears welled in her eyes and she covered her face. How happy she'd been when Eva kissed her, how much joy filled her when they touched! But Guerline was empress, and she was beginning to understand that the love of an empress for her consort could not be what she wanted it to be.

Her visitor knocked again. Whoever it was, they had waited quite a long time; everyone else had given up hours ago. Her curiosity piqued, Guerline rose from her chair, plucked her dagger off the carpet, and crossed to the door. She lifted the latch and pulled it open, then gasped.

Eva stood outside, her new courtly vestments abandoned. She looked as she always had before, wearing a fine but simple linen dress. Her black hair was bound in a single thick braid, and her expression—small smile, eyebrows raised pleadingly in the center—sent a jolt through Guerline, who had been musing all evening on an entirely different look on her friend's face. Guerline stepped back and opened the door wider. Eva's eyes flicked to the dagger hanging loose in Guerline's hand, then back up at her face.

"Lina. Will you . . . come for a walk with me?" she asked.

Guerline took a deep breath, but couldn't keep the waver of a restrained sob out of her voice. "Of course."

She turned and set the dagger on a small table, then slipped out into the hall with Eva, shutting the door behind her. Eva seemed subdued, and though all Guerline wanted to do was throw her arms around her, she held back to wait for a cue. Eva offered Guerline her arm, and the empress took it, at once disappointed and relieved, resting her hand lightly in the firm crook of Eva's elbow. The hall was empty around them, bathed in the warm yellow light of the Adenen lamps along the walls.

They walked for a minute in silence, heading down the stairs from Guerline's tower into the main part of the palace. Eva remained silent, though she sometimes glanced over at Guerline and smiled a very small, contained smile. Guerline felt her heart speed up. Though Eva's expression lacked an air of mischief, this excursion reminded her of the many nights they'd snuck out of their rooms as children to explore the kitchens, the dungeons, even the palace green. They'd pass whole nights in the garden and return to their beds with the dawn. It was always Eva's idea. Guerline would wait, wide-eyed, until Eva knocked and signaled that it was time for her to come out. Her grip on Eva's arm tightened, and the other woman reached over and put her free hand over Guerline's.

"Close your eyes, Lina."

Guerline raised an eyebrow but did as Eva asked. Eva curled her fingers around Guerline's hand and pulled it off her arm, which she then slipped to Guerline's lower back.

"I don't suppose you'll tell me where we're going?" Guerline asked.

Eva only laughed, and after a moment, so did Guerline. With every step, with the familiar press of Eva's hand on her back, her stress melted a little more.

"Not far now," Eva said.

They stopped, and Guerline listened to a scraping on either side of her. Doors? Heavy ones, most likely to the throne room or perhaps—

"Open your eyes!"

The ballroom. Guerline opened her eyes and saw that they were indeed in the ballroom. She hadn't set foot in it since her coronation, though it had long been one of her refuges in the palace. Her parents had only rarely held balls or large events, so it had been largely unused and therefore a perfect hiding spot for Guerline and Evadine. She looked up at Eva, a wide smile stretching her cheeks. Tears pricked her eyes when she saw the matching grin on Eva's face.

Evadine ran over to a long, thin table along the wall and pulled a small glass orb out of her pocket. She lifted it to her mouth and it glowed softly, another bit of pre-made magic. Eva set it down on the table, and music rose from it, quiet at first but steadily getting louder. Guerline pressed a hand to her chest, sighing happily.

Eva turned and walked back to her, holding out a hand. "Dance with me, Lina."

"Always," Guerline replied.

She took Eva's hand in her right and stepped into her arms, placing her left hand on Eva's upper arm. Eva slipped her hand into the middle of Guerline's upper back, and Guerline smiled at the comfortable pressure. She leaned in closer, and Eva rested her cheek against the skin above Guerline's ear, swaying gently side to side to get the beat of the music.

"Are you ready?" Eva asked.

"Yes," Guerline said.

They broke into the three-step pattern of the most common formal Aridan dance, sweeping through the empty ballroom. Eva was a superb leader, having always taken that part in the years of lessons they shared as children. They had been dancing together so long that there was almost no hesitation between Eva's cue and Guerline's response. Guerline could anticipate Eva's patterns from the slightest twitch of her fingers, the barest intake of breath.

"I've missed this so much, Eva," Guerline said.

Eva's hand tightened against her back. "So have I. I . . . I know I've been distant."

Guerline took a deep breath and moved her hand to Eva's shoulder, squeezing just slightly. She wanted to tell Eva it was all right, that it meant the world to her that Eva had brought her here, brought the music, and offered her a dance even after the disastrous council meeting. But her heart was in her throat, putting a stop to any words she might have said in response.

The song faded and the two women spun slowly to a stop. Eva kept her arm around Guerline's waist, and pulled their clasped outstretched hands in to rest against her chest. Guerline could feel Eva's heartbeat, steady behind her ribcage. She looked up into her lover's face and felt dread rising around her, as if she were slowly sinking into cold water. Eva lowered her head until her forehead rested against Guerline's, and they stood silently together like that for several moments.

"Do you remember the first time we came down here to dance by ourselves?" Guerline asked breathlessly. She was desperate to hold on to the beauty of the dance; to somehow get back to how she'd felt days ago, before her terrible realization that she must stand separate from all, even the one she loved most.

Evadine grinned. "The night of Seryne's Feast. They hadn't cleaned up the ribbons yet."

"We spun in them until we'd tied our own ankles together."

"And then we dragged ourselves around the floor pretending to be mermaids for two hours," Eva said. "What silly children we were."

Guerline smiled and leaned back. Her smile faded slightly as she took in Eva's expression, serious and thoughtful, her brow creasing just above the bridge of her nose and her grey eyes dancing over Guerline's face. Guerline narrowed her eyes, studying Evadine's face in response.

"What is it, Eva?" she asked.

"I'm so glad you survived, Lina. For whatever reason, curse or wild beast, all your family died and you survived, and I am *so* glad. I couldn't—Lina, I know we fought yesterday, but you must know that I couldn't bear it if anything happened to you," Eva said.

She let go of Guerline's hand and put her own on either side of Guerline's face. Guerline let her hands settle on Eva's waist and looked up at her, watching tears fill Eva's eyes, mirroring her own.

"I know," Guerline said, the only words she could muster. "Eva, I know. And I love you for it. I don't want to fight again. But we must—"

Eva kissed her on the mouth, briefly, then leaned back and smiled as Guerline stared, wide-eyed, up at her. Guerline licked her lips.

"Eva," she exhaled.

"Shh, Lina. Let's talk policy tomorrow." She kissed Guerline again, longer this time, and Guerline's surprise faded. Her limbs reanimated and she leaned into the contact. She tightened her grip on Eva's waist and sighed against Eva's lips when the other woman moved one hand to the back of her neck. Eva opened her mouth and the kiss deepened, eliciting a moan from both of them. Guerline pulled ever so slightly away and bit her bottom lip.

"Run away with me, Eva," she whispered. Her heart took off at a gallop, unsure that she'd actually said the words out loud until Eva responded.

"Soon."

Eva kissed her again, and Guerline felt wetness on her cheeks. She pulled back and saw tears spilling from Eva's eyes. She opened her mouth, but before she could say a word, Eva snapped her back into the dance frame and whisked her into the pattern. She spun Guerline out, and Guerline inhaled sharply as she whirled, surprise forming a quick hard knot in her chest. Eva pulled her back in and Guerline stumbled into her. Holding Guerline tight against her, Eva spun them both around with increasing speed.

"Eva!" Guerline shouted.

The two of them stopped spinning and stumbled, falling to their knees in a tangle of dresses. Guerline righted herself and reached for Evadine, grasping her lover's hands and pulling her up to sit. She started to chuckle, but stopped when she saw the slack expression on Eva's face.

"What is it? Eva?"

"I see him in my dreams. Alcander. Every night for the past week. He comes to me, all dead-skinned and rotten, his arm missing . . . he says the most terrible things about you," Eva whispered.

Her face scrunched up and tears fell faster from her eyes. Guerline listened, motionless, sure that even her heart had stopped beating. She was not the only one plagued by the dead. Relief and fear warred in her mind. If Eva had nightmare visions of a dead Alcander too, that meant Guerline was not going mad. It meant something far worse. It meant they were haunted. Guerline remembered Fiona's small smile at the watch as she turned away from Guerline—was it possible Fiona was as treacherous as Eva claimed? Was there any source but Thiymen clan for this kind of terrible necromancy?

Or was it simply that they were *both* going mad? Hysterical laughter seemed to fill Guerline's mind. It was impossible to tell whether it was inside or outside her head; Eva, if she heard it, made no reaction to it, weeping into her knees. If Guerline could see visions of Johan and Alcander and blame them on abuse, then so could Eva, in equal measure. Had Arido put two madwomen in charge of the empire?

Eva lifted her grey gaze to Guerline's. "I'm glad he's dead, Lina. I never—he hated you so much!"

Guerline licked her lips and fought to breathe steadily. "It's just a nightmare, Eva. I'm sure."

"It feels so real. He haunts my steps, he worms into my dreams like a parasite, and I *feel* it—" Eva grabbed Guerline by the shoulders. "Yes. It's real, Lina. I don't know how he does it or why, but I want it to stop. It's magic, and it's vile, and we have to put an end to it before he comes to kill you."

Guerline pulled Eva into her arms and held her tightly, squeezing against the rapid, uneven rise and fall of Eva's breath. She focused on her own, inhaling deep into her lungs, and stared with unfocused eyes at the opposite wall of the ballroom. The soft glow of the music glass was visible in her periphery. She narrowed in on it and wished she knew more about magic. All the magic she had contact with was prepared ahead of time by a witch and sold for a human's use—was there a limit on that sort of power? Could a witch trap souls in little orbs like that one, did a human have the ability to sic those souls on others?

Anger and fear quivered in Guerline's limbs; confusion frustrated her racing thoughts. Eva's visions of the dead had only increased her revulsion of magic. Guerline was glad to have an explanation for Eva's increased vehemence, but the question remained—was she right? Was magic too dangerous to be so liberally used? Were the witches *deliberately* using magic against her?

As Evadine calmed in her arms, Guerline watched the glow of the music glass die and remembered her words to Theodor the previous morning. She couldn't run, or hide. She wasn't going mad. Her ghosts were tormenting Evadine too, and they had to be stopped. But Guerline could not write off all magic as quickly as Eva. She had questions that needed answering, and only the witches had those answers.

She leaned back and put a hand on Eva's cheek, looking into the other woman's grey eyes. "We'll set things right, Eva. Whatever that means in the end. And we'll do it together. Yes?"

Eva nodded. Her lips were slightly parted. Guerline glanced down at them, then leaned in and kissed her lover softly.

"Come on," Guerline said. "It's late, and we're not children anymore. Let's go to bed."

She'd meant it innocently, but her heart leapt at the wicked grin Eva gave her.

CHAPTER THIRTEEN

OLIVIA KAVANAGH STOOD IN HER STUDY, STARING AT THE MAP of Arido on the wall. The desk behind her was laden with messages brought over the past few hours. Aradia said that the situation in the south was worse. The receding seas and a new sickness in the soil would cause an unprecedented famine. It was too much to hope that there would not be confusion and anger, or panic.

Morgana's position was becoming serious as well. After witnessing one of the deadly sandstorms, the visiting wizards confirmed Morgana's fears: the wind came from the Wastes. The human governor of Braeden insisted on blaming Raeha and had launched a campaign to turn the cities of the west against Fortress Adenen.

And Fiona . . .

The record of Fiona's seal was terse and formal, like most messages from Thiymen. At the end, however, was a hastily scrawled note, unsigned, that Olivia could only assume was from the Thiymen Memory, Kanika Asenath.

She will kill herself before she asks for help, the younger witch wrote. *This thing is too much for her alone. She needs all of you. Please, do not forsake your sister.*

Olivia read it again, her heart aching. It was true that Fiona did not ask for help, she never had. She could cling to her pride until the disastrous final hour; but Olivia had long feared that the source of Arido's troubles was in the bowels of the east. All the ancient tales gathered by her predecessor, Neria, spoke of a great battle that culminated in the dark mountain range that Fiona now called home. Each tale carried the ominous warning that the consequences of that battle still loomed over the future of Arido. Olivia had tried, several times, to get Fiona to share her notes. Her younger sister had been nearer the underworld, spent more time in it, than any living thing in Arido. Olivia knew she had uncovered most, if not all, of that realm's secrets. But her entreaties had not convinced Fiona to hand over that knowledge to Sitosen, as she should; for though each clan might have its own Memory, Sitosen was the record-keeper of all, human and witch alike.

Why Fiona guarded the underworld so jealously, Olivia couldn't fathom, and now it was haunting her just as her sisters had always said it would. Try as she might to contain it, Fiona would need the help of all her sisters, and soon.

Olivia sat down at her desk and pulled out a blank piece of parchment. She would write to Fiona and offer her support.

She had not put quill to page before there was a sharp knock on her door. Instead of waiting for her permission to enter, whoever it was swung the door open immediately. None of her witches would dare bypass such a simple courtesy except in times of emergency. The witch, a scribe named Sora, breathed too heavily to get any words out; she could only gesture fruitlessly down the stairs. Olivia nodded and strode swiftly past her.

They raced down the tower stairs and burst into the hall. The desks that lined it were no longer occupied by studious, silent witches. Only a few had witches bending over them, flipping feverishly through books. Other witches raced back and forth along the book-lined walls, pulling more volumes and handing them off to the readers. Five or six were gathered around the source of the commotion, in the center of the hall. Sora hesitated as they neared it; Olivia proceeded firmly, but with caution. Sitosen Castle rarely saw such a ruckus, and a heavy feeling of foreboding settled in Olivia's chest.

The witches parted when they realized she was there. Two men, dressed in dark leathers with a pile of weapons and harnesses at their feet, lay unconscious. One was older, around forty; the other was barely twenty. At first glance, the older man seemed to be merely sleeping; but as Olivia knelt and looked closer, she saw that his pale northern skin was *too* pale. He was almost completely white, and his body was still.

Olivia reached out slowly and put one hand on his chest, one on his neck. There was still a pulse, and he was breathing, though both signs of life were almost imperceptible. As she lifted the hand on his chest, it caught a flap of torn leather. She gingerly pulled the flap back. Underneath, a large chunk of the man's stomach was torn away, the edges ragged with an animal's teeth marks. The skin darkened at the edge of the tear to black, curling under like a withering leaf. There was no blood, not even dried stains.

Olivia looked at the witch who sat with the man's head in her lap, dabbing at his forehead and holding one hand over his eyes. The witch met Olivia's gaze and nodded to the unspoken question. He was beyond saving.

She turned her attention to the boy. Like the man, he was corpse-pale, but he wasn't as badly injured. From what Olivia could see, he had only been scratched by whatever had attacked them. The scratches were shallow, and showed the same blackening as the bite mark. The problem with the boy was the fever. He perspired and convulsed, but his skin was cold to the touch—a black magic fever.

"Keep the man stable for as long as you can," Olivia said quietly. "As for the boy, excise the blackened skin and dress the wounds. Keep him warm and hydrated."

The witches moved quickly to fulfill her orders. Olivia went outside. Sora followed her, and the two witches walked quickly and silently.

"They're hunters," the younger witch said after a few moments. "From Javan. Marqa found them near the Gap of Nor. She heard whatever attacked them as it ran away. She said it shrieked like a banshee."

Olivia frowned. Why had they been so deep in the forest? The Gap was on the eastern edge, a canyon formed in the trees by the foothills of the Zaide and Landene Mountains. Javan was more than one hundred miles from the Gap, too far for most hunters. It was possible that the beasts had carried them that far, but there were few creatures from the Gap region that grew large enough to carry two human men such a distance.

"Did the boy say anything?" Olivia asked.

Sora nodded. "He said that there were two of them. They were large like a bear, but looked more like wolves, and their fur was black. The readers pulled all our zoological indexes, but they haven't found anything that matches the description, not even in the palaeozoology books."

Olivia stopped and pulled a long pendant out from under her dress, holding it in her hands. It was a golden compact, four inches in diameter; the owl that was her symbol was carved into the top. Sora inhaled with a sharp hiss and stepped back. Each of the Kavanagh sisters possessed one of the mirrors. It was their fastest means of communication with each other, to be used only in times of serious need.

She clicked open the latch on the compact. The top half was the mirror, and in the bottom half were three compartments, each covered and marked by the symbol of the sisters: the hammer for Morgana, the wreath for Aradia, and the dragon head for Fiona. Olivia popped the cover of the last compartment, revealing a fine black powder. She dipped her little finger into the powder, then closed the compartment and put her finger in her mouth. The powder tasted sulfuric, like dank and rot, and with this on her breath, she exhaled and spoke Fiona's name.

The mirror darkened. When the blackness cleared, Olivia's reflection was gone, replaced by her sister's face. For a moment, Olivia forgot why she'd called. How long had it been since she'd seen Fiona? Surely she hadn't always looked so . . . dead. Kanika Asenath had been right to beg Fiona's sisters for help. She obviously needed it.

"Olivia." Fiona's voice barely hinted at happiness, only recognizable to someone who had known her before she became the leader of the most hated clan in Arido.

"Fiona." Olivia smiled, blinking away tears. She could regret not talking to her sister for so long later. At the moment, they both had a problem which needed to be dealt with. "Two hunters were attacked this morning. I fear that it was the work of hounds."

Fiona's eyes flashed. She recognized, as Olivia had known she would, that they were not talking about normal hounds. There was only one sort of hound that would prompt Olivia to seek Fiona's help.

"Hounds? More than one?"

"The boy said two."

Fiona turned away from the mirror and spoke a few sharp orders to someone Olivia couldn't see.

"I've sent my Captain of the Guard," she said. "She'll be able to tell you for sure if it was hounds. Are the men still alive?"

"The man is almost gone. I believe we can still save the boy. He was only scratched."

Fiona nodded. The venom wasn't as strong in the claws as it was in the teeth.

"Use an ivy poultice on the scratches. Hopefully that will keep him safe until Moira arrives."

Olivia nodded and closed the compact. She exhaled slowly and looked over at Sora. The two witches were silent for a moment; then they turned simultaneously and ran full-out back to the castle. They burst into the hall. Olivia shouted for someone to bring her the ivy poultice and went over to the dying boy. His convulsions were getting weaker. The older man was being kept alive only by magic. The witch's hand, poised over his eyes, trembled. She smiled resolutely at Olivia.

"Tesla, relieve Carulina, please," she said gently to a nearby witch. Tesla nodded and slowly took Carulina's place at the man's head.

Sora came running up with a bowl and set it on the floor next to her. Olivia smelled the ivy as she approached, clean and bright and alive. The other witches had finished cutting away the dead edges of skin. The scratches now were lined by raw, pink, but definitely living, flesh. Olivia turned the boy toward her to start with a scratch on his right side, scooped up a sizable amount of the poultice, and began to dab it onto the wound.

The boy stiffened on contact, whimpering in pain. Ivy was a resurrection plant. Its magic was working to repair the damage the witches couldn't see unaided, fighting against whatever hellish venom remained in the wound. Coming back from the brink of death was not without cost.

She'd finished salving and dressing the scratches when the doors opened. A thin, grey-haired witch was escorted to where the two men lay. The woman was virtually colorless in her hair and flesh; her blue eyes were almost white. Her tunic and leather pants, both black, contrasted greatly against her skin. She wore an iron breastplate, the signature armor of the Thiymen Guard; though it was heavy, it provided better protection against what they fought than steel would. Olivia knew that this was the Hand of Thiymen, Moira Emile, because Fiona had told her that was who she sent; without that advantage, she wouldn't have known. Thiymen witches all looked the same after two hundred years or so. Olivia stood to greet her, wiping her hands on a cloth handed to her.

"Captain Emile," Olivia said, inclining her head slightly. They didn't have time for proper greetings.

Moira returned the nod. "Olivia-lami. These are the men?"

Olivia nodded and stepped aside to let the visiting witch examine the hunters, signaling for water. She watched as the grim-faced captain turned her attention to the boy. It was clear to them all that the man was beyond help. Carulina and Tesla were keeping him alive only so that they could save his soul from the hound and let it pass on to Ilys, the field of the underworld for good souls. No Sitosen witch could have said for sure what his fate would be if the hound dragged his soul into Hell, and the Thiymen witches had never been much for sharing.

"This is a good dress," Moira said, checking the boy's wounds. "The ivy is working. His scratches should heal. It's the fever now that threatens him." She took a sip of the water provided and rolled back the sleeves of her tunic. She pulled off her black gloves, revealing skeletal white hands. "Whatever happens, do not touch him or me."

The witches in the hall stepped back. Moira put her hands out over the boy's body, fingers splayed like a puppeteer, and closed her eyes. Her fingers began to twitch, this way and that, sometimes plucking and brushing at things that the Sitosen witches couldn't see. They could feel a change in the air; it became heavier and colder, and they instinctually drifted closer to each other.

Suddenly, the boy screamed and lurched upward. Moira jumped to her feet and pushed him back down, her eyes still closed, her hands still in the air above him. Whatever she pushed, it was not the boy; it was something beyond the invisible curtain she manipulated with her fingers. Beneath her hands, the boy writhed and screamed in a language that, of the Sitosen witches, only Olivia had heard before. Moira shouted something back in the same harsh language. She braced her left hand flat against the air. With a great shout, she brought her right fist down like a hammer and shattered the fever's hold on the boy.

The chill left the air. Every witch in the hall exhaled in relief when the Thiymen witch opened her eyes. She staggered backwards into Olivia's waiting arms.

The boy's color had returned, and he now appeared to be sleeping peacefully. Four standing witches removed him to the infirmary. Together, Olivia and Moira knelt on either side of the man. Olivia touched Tesla's shoulder gently. The other witch nodded and gently placed the man's head into Olivia's hands.

Moira sized the man up.

"Now," she said, "when I loose his soul from the hound, you must catch it and lift him up. Look for an old path and let him go when you find it. I only hope he is not too frayed to survive."

Olivia nodded, stroking the man's cheek as she twisted her fingers around the dusty anchoring point of his soul.

Her eyes met Moira's. They were ready. Their eyelids fluttered shut.

The hound was in the mountains now. The hunter's soul was clutched in its teeth as it frantically searched for a tear in the curtain. Olivia, tagging along behind Moira, could feel the other witch's satisfaction. Their linked magic allowed Olivia a glimpse at the other witch's thoughts, and she learned that the entire Thiymen clan had been working through the night to inspect and fortify the barrier. It was likely that the tear the hound had come through had long since been repaired. It was trapped in unfamiliar territory.

Moira's projection transformed into a massive black puma as the witches approached the frustrated hell-dog. She leapt nimbly from peak to peak, finding footholds in impossible places and quickly gaining on the hound. She pushed just ahead of the beast and leapt down onto the hound's back. The puma once more became a woman, armed with two short daggers. She placed the daggers on either side of the hound's neck, slicing up and back. The muscles that connected to the lower jaw severed. There was no blood to spill, since the body was dead, but the hound could no longer maintain its grip on the hunter's soul. Olivia swooped down in the form of an owl and caught the drifting soul in her talons. She flew high above the trees and the mountains until she hit a sweet-smelling current of air, one of the old paths to Ilys; there she released the man. She let herself be carried for a moment or two, slowly releasing the magic.

She and Moira returned at the same time, opening their eyes and relaxing their hands. The man was dead now, but his face was restful. The two witches stood. Olivia lifted a hand to order him carried away when Moira's voice stopped her.

"He must be burned," she said.

Olivia hesitated. The Sitosen witches still gathered gave Moira an incredulous look. Cremation was a sign of deep shame; it implied that the body of the deceased was not worthy to rejoin the circle of life by fertilizing the ground with their flesh. Moira, for her part, remained stone-faced, apparently insensitive to this knowledge.

Still, Olivia knew she was right. A blight in the flesh, like the venom in the man's wound, would put a blight in the earth. She nodded to Tesla, who, though seeming unconvinced, acquiesced.

"Shall we still wash him?" Sora asked quietly.

"Yes, of course." Olivia turned to a young witch-in-training, instructing her to take refreshments to Olivia's study for herself and the Thiymen captain. Moira followed her up to the tower.

"The hounds' bodies are made of dead flesh, scavenged from the wild and reformed," Moira explained once they had eaten. "They are more magic than flesh, and it takes years, decades, to gather enough meat. They are made by demons and sent into the living world to hunt for more material. They usually get through by attacking a witch as she passes between worlds and jumping through the gap the witch has made. Hounds cannot tear the curtain themselves."

"Have any of Thiymen been attacked recently?" Olivia asked.

"No. I know you saw my thoughts."

Olivia regarded her silently, tacitly admitting it. The hounds had come through a tear that was left open. Though Olivia had seen this, she could not tell how such a thing had been allowed to happen. She knew how strict the Black Coven was when it came to closing tears in the curtain between life and death. Moira looked grim.

"Someone from outside Thiymen is using black magic," she said, confirming Olivia's suspicions. "The tears from their passings do not include the same wards that ours do, and none of them have been closed properly. It's all we can do to repair them when we can't even tell if we've found them in good time. And there's something else—something aided by this rogue witch's carelessness. It's still trapped, but it can push, and push it does against these tears, ripping them further. My lady Fiona sealed it the day before yesterday, but even her power can only keep it at bay temporarily."

The other witch's face lit for a moment with fury and fear, making Olivia's heart skip a beat, before returning to its impassive Thiymen gaze.

"This thing under the mountain . . . I have never encountered it, and I have been the Hand of Thiymen three hundred years," Moira said, her voice soft. "Yet Fiona did not seem surprised by what she faced."

So I am not the only one Fiona is keeping secrets from, Olivia thought. She felt a chill through the marrow of her bones at the idea that Fiona was hiding some underworld being from not only her sisters, but from her own right hand. But at least there was one way she could help.

"I know who the rogue witches are," she said.

Desmond climbed the stairs to his room at the inn, lugging two large packs of supplies. He'd spent the day doing errands in Olsrec; his intention had been to spread them out over a few days, but he was eager to get to Adenen.

He was surprised, as he approached his door, to see light flickering from beyond it. He opened it slowly. A woman sat on his bed: tall, blonde, clad in a rich blue gown with a silver cloak draped over her shoulders. A light blue sail was folded next to her. She met his eyes, eyes the exact same shade of blue as hers. He let his packs drop to the floor.

"Mother," Desmond said.

She rose and embraced him. She was much thinner than him, merely half his breadth. As he drew back, he saw the new concern etched on a face already written with years. She squeezed his shoulder tightly and sat him down on the bed next to her.

"What is it, Mother? What's happened?"

"The situation has grown very dire, child," Olivia Kavanagh said. "The creatures of the underworld are breaching the living world."

Desmond gasped. "What? But Aunt Fiona—"

Olivia squeezed his hand reassuringly. "She is fine, for now. But she needs our help. I am going now to my sisters, and then we will go to her. You must go to the capital, to Del, immediately and warn the new empress."

"Of course," Desmond said. "Yes, I'll go at once."

"You must speak to her privately. Do not give her this news at court," Olivia cautioned. "It well may be that we will not have to tell the public at all. Fiona has sealed the gate, and her seals are very powerful. It should hold long enough for the rest of us to get there and decide what must be done."

Desmond nodded, considering this new information. He felt sorry for Guerline. She was so young; to have this placed on her mere days after her coronation!

"How have things been getting through?" he asked.

"There are two rogue witches. You will not remember them; I banished them from Sitosen when you were a child. But they too are in Del, and you must find them and stop them. Employ the crown if you must. Use what I've taught you to negate their magic. Their names are Arginine and Alanine Maravilla."

Desmond nodded again, committing the names to memory and planning his journey. With a little magical assistance and his new steed, the ride to Del from Olsrec would take perhaps a full day. Desmond did not have the ability to cast spells himself, but he had powerful natural energy and was able to use talismans and other spelled objects made for him by his family and friends to channel that energy.

Olivia ran a hand over Desmond's hair and kissed his brow.

"Rest brief and deep, my child, and then go to Guerline. She will need your help. I'll give your love to your aunts," she said.

And with that, she was gone. Desmond sighed, blew out his candle, and settled in for a short sleep.

CHAPTER FOURTEEN

GUERLINE HELD HER FIRST COURT THE NEXT DAY, TO AVOID another council meeting. She knew her advisers were clamoring to talk more about the witches behind closed doors, especially given the reports of various disasters and abominations which had rolled in that morning from three points of the country. Only the East remained silent, and some took this as proof of Fiona's responsibility.

Shon, of course, argued that it only meant Fiona had things well in hand. Those from the East certainly had a strange level of loyalty for the Thiymen leader, there was no doubt about that. She remembered again her parents' funeral, the gentle way Fiona had coaxed soul from body. The black witches were frightening in appearance, but their work was neither pleasant nor easy. Arido expected someone to do it. How could they revile those who rose to the occasion?

These thoughts occupied Guerline as subject after subject came with complaints for her to address. To her annoyance, many of them were small matters—like how many goats a sack of potatoes was worth. Guerline told the man that a sack of potatoes was worth perhaps one old goat, since the potatoes would eventually be used up, while a goat could continue to be of use its whole life.

The man was indignant. "But I was planning to slaughter the goats for meat!"

"In that case—one goat, of whatever age the other man please," Guerline said. "Go by the weight. You shall receive one goat of equal weight to your sack of potatoes."

The man looked like he was prepared to protest, but Guerline waved him away.

"Well done, Lina," Evadine said from her position at the empress's right hand. She and the other council members sat upon the dais in line with Guerline. The empress was elevated above them on a platform.

Guerline grinned at Eva. "Meat is denser and more nutritious than potatoes, and then he's also gained a pelt. It's only right that he give more in potatoes than he shall receive in meat."

She leaned over the small table next to her throne, on which stood paper and ink. She dipped the quill and wrote a note to discuss a hierarchy of arbiters with the Lord Justice. It hardly seemed appropriate that Guerline herself should deal with *all* the minor civil disagreements. She'd never be able to get anything else done.

She was about to call an end to open court when the next supplicant entered. He was a tall, thin man with fair skin and coal-black hair worn in a ponytail at the crown of his head. He was very finely dressed in a silver tunic that buttoned all the way up his throat and was laced down the front. He wore ballooning cream-colored breeches made from a cloth that moved easily, tucked into knee-high black boots that shone. He was exceedingly good-looking in a delicate kind of way, with slim features and arched eyebrows. Guerline sat up a little straighter on the throne, intrigued by this man. Next to her, Evadine frowned.

"Your Imperial Majesty," the man said, sweeping into a deep and graceful bow. "My name is Kieran Brynn. I come on behalf of my masters, the royal family of Giarda."

So he was a courtier from the country beyond the Zaide Mountains. That explained his expensive clothing and his light build. The Giardans were willowy people who built their homes in the trees. Guerline received messages of condolences from them after the deaths of her parents and brother, as well as a gift on the occasion of her coronation. She hadn't expected an emissary.

"We bid you welcome, Master Brynn," Guerline said. "Please, feel free to speak."

"Thank you, Your Majesty," he said with another dip of his head. His eyes met hers again, and her heart stuttered; there was something so familiar about his gaze. As they stared at each other, he smiled, and the expression seemed oddly thoughtful. "It is so good," he added, "to finally see Your Majesty in the flesh."

Evadine scoffed, softly so only Guerline would hear, and Guerline shook her head slightly to dislodge the odd sense of intimacy the emissary's words inspired in her. The sensation that she had met him before, that somehow they had shared something important, was so strong—but her mind was all blank as to actual possibilities. She tried to find something to say in response to the emissary's odd comment.

Before she could, he spoke. "My masters send again their congratulations on your ascension and wish you health and success. However, I fear that I come to you now with a very serious matter, which I pray we can resolve rapidly and amiably."

Guerline frowned and leaned forward to hear him better. "Say on."

"Well—the heart of the matter is that dragons have been attacking villages on our westernmost borders," Brynn said with a pained look on his face.

Shouts of shock and anger erupted in the throne room. Her council members stood and began yelling across at each other. The guards rushed the dais, either in defense of the dragons or with offers to go kill them. Guerline could only be grateful that she received supplicants one at a time, or half the kingdom would have also heard this news before she could decide how to handle it.

"Enough!" she said.

Silence descended on the room. She stood on her platform and glared at everyone until they hung their heads. She looked last at Kieran Brynn, who seemed to be smiling the slightest bit. What on earth would make him smile? Was he impressed by her, or by the commotion? She glanced at Evadine, whose mouth was a thin, furious line as she stared at the foreigner.

"That was poorly handled, Master Brynn," Guerline said. "Such news is grave indeed, and ought not be revealed in public forum. But since you have already opened your mouth, say on and explain this further to us."

Brynn dropped briefly to one knee. "Apologies, Your Majesty. Of course, you are right. I do not know all the details of the attacks, but this is what I do know. They began three months ago, when we began to see the dragons more and more frequently. They came progressively closer to the villages."

"If I recall my draconic calendar, that would have been the beginning of their mating season," Evadine remarked. "Though they mate in hundred-year cycles, the Purvaja dragons are also humans, Master Brynn. To mate, they sometimes swoop down upon men and women, take them to secluded places, and then return to their human forms in order to woo their chosen. Eastern women historically reside in the caves for two or three years after their dragon babe is born."

"They have never come to our side of the mountains in my recollection, Chief Adviser," Brynn replied.

Eva glared at him. "All animals seek to expand their species, including humans. It is not unlikely that after several generations, the dragons would look for new partners."

"Well. Regardless, the villagers knew naught of this practice. As livestock disappeared and fields were burnt up, they began to set traps for the dragons; they tried to fight the beasts. It was, of course, futile, and many lives have been lost," Brynn said.

Guerline inhaled sharply. This was significant news, made all the more significant by the fact that she had heard nothing about it. Giarda could go to war with Arido over this if they chose, and much of her own country would be on their side. Very few people outside the East had any love for the Thiymen dragons. Her mind raced for something to say. She lifted her chin and stared down her nose at Brynn.

"Your masters might have sent word sooner. We could have discussed it with the Heart of Thiymen, and stopped it before any blood was shed."

"Fiona? Fiona wouldn't have stopped them!" Pearce shouted, rising from his seat. His eyes were frenzied. "I'll wager she sent them!"

"Don't be so moronic, Lord Iszolda!" Theodor said. "Fiona's no fool. She wouldn't start a war just so the dragons could have more *mates*—"

"What if that's exactly what she wants?" Lanyic cried. "A war! She's trying to start a war!"

"She's doing nothing of the sort!" Shon bellowed. "My lady Fiona is above such political nonsense!"

"Enough!" Guerline shouted again. She strode down into the center of the floor and turned to face her council. Her hands shook. Whether with fear or anger, she wasn't sure. She balled them into fists.

"That's enough, all of you! We will not have our throne room devolve into a common brawling tavern! If you cannot behave with honor and decorum, we shall have you all removed and replaced!"

The promise was clear in her eyes. All of her current councilors, save Eva, had served under her parents, but they'd been of absolutely no use to her so far. The most they'd done was argue about high-stress topics with no apparent interest in deciding on productive solutions, and they found ways to ignore the ones she suggested. Perhaps she was only nineteen, but she was not a child, and whether they liked it or not, she was the empress.

"Get out of here, now. All of you," Guerline said. She pointed at Kieran Brynn. "You will be lodged in the Dragon Wing. We will discuss your problem tomorrow after we have had a chance to broach the subject with Lady Fiona. Escort him, and post a guard at his door."

Two guards from the wall came to flank Brynn, who was looking at Guerline with barely concealed incredulity. The guards reached for his arms, but he twisted away to avoid their touch and marched out. She strode back to the throne. Evadine stood next to it, staying where she was rather than heeding Guerline's order. When Guerline ordered people to leave, Evadine was not usually included in "people." Guerline felt like screaming at Evadine to leave too, but she restrained herself. Her lover seemed less inclined than Guerline to trust the Giardan courtier, and that appealed to the overwhelming desire to slander someone which Guerline was currently experiencing.

Something about Brynn made her inexplicably anxious. When he'd first walked in, she'd thought the flutter in her chest was because he was a handsome man. After his brief address, she felt differently, but couldn't place the strangeness of her reaction to him. By the look on Evadine's face, she was experiencing something similar, and with any luck, they could figure it out together. It would be nice to be in agreement about something again, too, even if that something was a man who made them uncomfortable.

"I don't trust him, Lina," Evadine said quietly as Guerline neared her.

"Nor do I, though I have nothing but my gut reaction as evidence against him," the empress responded. "I just wonder that the Giardan royal family didn't communicate this to us sooner."

"Especially if it's been going on for three months," Eva sneered. "I understand it's a long journey on horseback or ship from Giarda, but there are faster means of communication. The Giardans have magic-workers, and Thiymen has worked with them before."

"Yes . . . about that, Eva. Thank you."

"For what?"

Guerline smiled. "For supporting Thiymen, defending the dragons, not claiming that Fiona's starting a war."

She'd been grateful that Eva hadn't jumped up with the others; that's what she'd been expecting. It had been very satisfying to see Evadine maintain her composure. So it was surprising now to see Eva's face change into a dark scowl, so twisted it was almost unrecognizable.

"In no way do I support Thiymen clan. I believe the East poses the greatest threat to us, and I mean to see it dealt with," Eva snapped.

Guerline was stunned silent. Eva held her gaze with a wild brightness in her grey eyes, and the anxiety brought on by Brynn's presence doubled.

Eva's voice had almost sounded like Alcander's.

She turned from Evadine and sat down upon her throne, her posture rigid and her chin high. Eva came around and knelt in front of her, putting her hands on Guerline's knees, a slight touch that seemed to sap Guerline of all strength. Guerline took them and held them tightly as she slid off her throne and joined Eva on the ground. She searched Eva's face, but she saw no hint of the mania that had been there a moment ago.

"Lina, I'm so sorry, I don't know—I didn't mean it. Lina, please," Eva said.

"What did you mean, Eva?" Guerline whispered.

Silence for a moment, then: "I don't trust the witches. They frighten me. But you were right in the council yesterday. We cannot truly address the problems with magic unless we speak to them. And . . . you said we will make this right, no matter what that means in the end."

Eva lifted her eyes to Guerline's. "I trust you more than anyone or anything else right now. I trust you more than I trust myself."

She looked tired, so much more tired than she had a moment ago. Guerline hooked a hand behind Eva's head and pulled her forward, kissing her gently on the mouth. Eva's lips were cold, and Guerline felt a pang in her heart, like sharp fingernails digging in. She remembered Eva's panic last night when she spoke of seeing Alcander in her dreams. Somehow, Guerline's brother never made it to the underworld, and he was haunting both of them. She was sure of it.

As Guerline kissed Eva, she vowed silently that she would rid them both of his memory, if it was the last thing she did. *And if it's not just his memory, what then? If his soul remains on this plane to torment you, and her . . . ?* The voice didn't sound quite like her own, but the questions were ones Guerline asked herself over and over. She shut her eyes, envisioned the softly smiling Heart of Thiymen. *If Fiona is my enemy, I'll believe this is a true haunting and her doing. But if she is my loyal subject, she will be able to protect us from Alcander's ghost.*

She pulled back and smiled at Eva. "Send a message to Thiymen clan and inform Fiona-lami that I request an audience with her, either here at the palace or through magical communication. Make sure to state that it is a matter of utmost importance." She kissed Eva again. "And then get some rest, please."

They rose as one; then Eva wrapped her arms around Guerline's waist and buried her face in Guerline's neck, stooping from her greater height. Guerline held her tightly for a moment, and then they parted. Eva stepped down from the dais, still holding Guerline's hand, and smiled up at her.

"I don't know how I could have ever doubted you," she said.

Before Guerline could ask what she meant, Eva curtsied and left the room.

Guerline slumped down in her throne and put her head in her hands. This was only . . . the fourth day of her official reign? All she wanted to do was ride far, far away; maybe go hide in Lisyne's Range far in the north, maybe go jump off the Hurdle, hole up in the Wastes. But she couldn't, because she had responsibilities to the empire, and she felt the weight of them already threatening to crush her.

A hand rested on her shoulder and she knew it was her mother's. She could smell the perfume Maribel wore. Strange that her parents came to her more often now they were dead than when they were alive.

She heard the doors open again and leapt from the throne, ready to behead both the intruder and whoever had admitted them. Luckily for all involved, she saw who it was before she spoke. It was a single person, unbelievably tall with a great wide chest. His blonde hair was bound in a messy braid that trailed below his hips, and his arms were open to her.

"Desmond! Oh thank the gods, Desmond!" Guerline cried.

She ran down from the dais and into his embrace. He lifted her in his thick, strong arms and spun her around. When he came to a stop, he went to put her down again, but Guerline had clamped her arms around his neck and was sobbing violently into his shoulder. Desmond cradled her hips to support her weight and rubbed her back with his free hand.

"What's this now, what's this?" he asked. He carried her over to the edge of the dais and sat down, positioning her across his broad lap. "What's the matter, little queen?"

"Stop it! I can't have you condescending to me too!" Guerline snapped.

Desmond laughed. "I'm sorry! I'm sorry. I apologize, Your Majesty. You're right. May I call you Lina? Then we can just talk as friends."

Guerline nodded, her sobs calming. Her cheeks burned with embarrassment at her outburst—the sobbing, the yelling at Desmond. She was just so tired, and her nerves were frayed. She'd meant to show everyone that she was a strong empress, that she was not to be trifled with; sometimes she felt like she was doing that, as she had in the throne room with Brynn and the rest of her council. But then someone like Desmond came along and comforted her like she was a child, called her pet names like "little queen," and it all came undone.

"There now." He smiled down at her with his bright, warm grin. Guerline smiled back and rested her head on his chest.

"Forgive me, Desmond. I didn't intend to jump on you and then yell at you," she said. "I've just had . . . an incredibly stressful time of late."

"I can only imagine. Of course I forgive you, Lina. Will you tell me all about it?"

"Yes. But not now. I've just gotten it all out of my system, and I don't want to start thinking of it again," she said. "I'm so happy you've come to see me, Desmond. No one warned me that when I became empress, I wouldn't be allowed to have friends anymore."

"There are a lot of things no one tells up-and-coming monarchs, I'm sure."

She smiled again and lifted herself out of his lap. This was reminiscent of all the times she and Desmond had just sat and talked whenever he came to visit. There was no expectation that Guerline would rule then, because Alcander was very much alive and willing. Whenever Desmond had finished his business with her parents and brother, he'd come and just spend his free time with her and Eva. She taught him to dance, to make paper flowers, to play one or two tunes on the harp; he taught her about magic and sword-fighting, and about the country, and what to pack when you're on the run.

He cupped her cheek in his large, rough hand. His thumb moved back and forth softly over her skin. Guerline leaned into the contact. She stared at his face, took in all his features: the warm golden skin, the dark blonde hair, the narrow blue eyes. His mother's shade, his father's shape, he'd said once, but to Guerline, those eyes were all his. They were full of his smile, the smile he gave her now. But behind his expression, she could see that something was weighing on him. She sighed. *This is growing up. Nothing stays simple.*

"I'm very happy to see you, Guerline," Desmond said.

"But you have bad news for me," she said.

"Aye, I have bad news for you. I was supposed to be on my way to see my aunt Morgana, but I was very obviously diverted. My mother visited me last night in Olsrec and bade me come to you."

His hand fell into his lap. Her cheek felt cold.

"She's told me that creatures from the world under the mountain are somehow breaking through the curtain between life and death," Desmond said.

Guerline's hand flew to her mouth even as her spirit sank. She really did need to speak to Fiona, at the very least to find out what the witch knew about all the accusations being levied against her. This forced a much more damning light on everything that had been raised already. The Sitosen witches had sent only news of an attack, not one by creatures of black magic. If her councilors found out, she doubted that anything she could say would persuade them to keep silent—they would take their panic to the streets of Del and ruin any hope of peace.

But what if they were right? Her parents dead of a flesh-eating curse. Her brother's murdered soul gone uncollected, tormenting Eva. A blight in the empire's most fertile soil, dragons attacking the nearest kingdom, an old evil wind decimating the forges where Arido's weapons were made. Something was clearly working to cripple Arido and leave it vulnerable . . . and all signs pointed to Thiymen clan.

Her horror must have shown on her face. Desmond reached up and gripped her hand tightly, pulling it back down.

"Listen, Lina. Mother spoke with the Hand of Thiymen. There are two rogue witches from outside Thiymen clan who are responsible for this. They're making tears and not closing them or warding them properly. This is not Thiymen's fault."

Rogue witches? Guerline had never heard of such a thing, though she knew that meant nothing. She had never seen a witch who wasn't from Thiymen, though she knew the other clans had visited the palace a handful of times. She had been kept apart from them; apart from anything, she reflected ruefully, that might have proved useful to her now. She met Desmond's eyes and felt keenly that what she knew of Arido was limited to history texts and whatever Desmond had told her over the years. If he said Thiymen was not at fault . . . she would trust him. Better that, than the possibility that the darkest and most powerful witch in Arido really *was* trying to usurp her.

"I believe you," Guerline said. "But my council won't. They already think Fiona's trying to start a war because her dragons wish to propagate."

"What?" Desmond asked.

"I had a man from the Giardan court come to me today. He said that the dragons have been raiding and attacking on the far side of the Zaide Mountains."

Desmond frowned. "That's not like them at all. Silas doesn't stand for that sort of thing. Did he say when this started?

"Three months ago," she said.

"I was at Thiymen three months ago; I barely saw a dragon at all, let alone flying to Giarda," he muttered. "Something else is going on."

"I've sent word to Fiona that we need to talk," Guerline said. "I want to hear what she has to say."

"That's good. With any luck, we'll be able to resolve this quickly and easily," Desmond replied. "From the sound of it, you need a new council."

His light tone and half-smile showed that he was joking, but Guerline gave him a stony look. "I believe I do. You don't know the half of it. Those who support me are trying to parent me, and those who are at odds with me just ignore me. With perhaps one or two exceptions, I fear that they must all be replaced."

Desmond nodded, his face thoughtful. "That would not be an improper course of action, Guerline. You are the ruler of the empire, and they must obey and respect you. If they don't, then they're not worthy to serve you so closely."

"My parents appointed all of them."

"You are not your parents. I believe that your rule will be quite different, and because of that, you will need a different set of advisers. Besides, politicians really ought to be changed frequently," he said, laughing.

He stopped when he noticed the stricken look on Guerline's face.

"I don't mean emperors and empresses, obviously. As empress, you are above the pettiness of court. That's why you are the arbiter over all of us. But smaller-minded people get attached to titles once they've got them. You've been a royal all your life, and so there's no need to worry about it going to your head. It's already there, so it won't change you."

"Is that meant to encourage me?" Guerline asked.

"Well . . . yes, it is," Desmond said.

Guerline thought a moment, then smiled. She leaned over and wrapped her arms around him again, and was grateful to feel his arms encircle her.

"I am glad you're here," she said.

CHAPTER FIFTEEN

DESMOND FOLLOWED GUERLINE OUT OF THE THRONE ROOM and into a library parlor. The massive fireplace across from the door was empty and gleaming as though it had never seen a flame. It was flanked by floor-to-ceiling bookshelves. In the center of the room was a half-circle sofa covered in plush cushions. Guerline went and sat down in the center of the curve, kicking off her slippers and resting her feet on one of the available ottomans. He settled next to her, positioning himself so that the light from the one window, high above them on a side wall, shone down on her.

Her red-gold hair caught the sunlight perfectly. It had been the first thing he noticed about her, nine years ago when he first came to Del. She was only ten years old then, and he a lad of sixteen, and no one had even bothered to introduce them. Desmond met the emperor, empress, and Prince Alcander in a private audience at which Guerline had not been present. He'd spotted her on his way out. She had been hiding behind one of the columns in the spacious entryway, apparently waiting to see whoever was visiting her parents.

She'd run away when he approached her. "Stop, little redhead!" he'd cried after her, and stop she had.

"What's your name?" he asked. She told him, and then curtsied and scurried away. Desmond turned around to see her brother Alcander standing there watching. Alcander had the same reddish gold hair, but there was no sweetness in his temper.

"My sister," he said, gesturing after Guerline. "She'll never amount to much. She'll probably be shipped overseas or over the mountains when she's married."

After that, Desmond made it a point to seek Guerline out whenever he was in the capital. She was a bright girl, but her parents kept her very isolated. Her only friend, other than Desmond, was a merchant's daughter named Evadine Malise—the new Chief Adviser, as Desmond heard it.

"So, is Lady Malise among the ones who blame my aunt Fiona?" he asked.

He tried to keep his voice light, but Guerline sighed and covered her face with her hands. That was not the reaction he'd expected. Evadine had never been a favorite of his, but she was deeply clever and sensible. Certainly, she wasn't taken in by low-minded fear-mongering, was she?

Guerline dropped her hands into her lap. "She's frightened of the Kavanaghs. Your family. She—you have to understand, Desmond. So many of us have never even *seen* a witch who wasn't from Thiymen, and you know how they look."

"So she does want Fiona gone?"

"She wants all of them gone," Guerline said.

He scoffed and stood up. "Why on earth—how can she? How can any of them? Do they even realize what the clans do for them?"

He paced in front of the sofa, clenching and unclenching his fist. He had to remain calm. Desmond's duty, for nearly ten years, had been to educate the people about the clans. He'd always felt that, by and large, his efforts were successful. And perhaps they were. Perhaps the nobility simply didn't care; perhaps they didn't realize how vulnerable they would be without the witch clans.

Desmond couldn't even begin to imagine an Arido without magic, or without the clans. The country was founded by witches and then handed over to humans. It was by the grace of his great-grandmother, Lirona Kavanagh, that the humans were involved in government at all. But the humans didn't learn that history. They learned that Lisyne the Mother created the humans, and then made the witches to serve and protect them.

Who came up with that version? Desmond wondered. But he knew that answer too. The whole religion of the shifter gods was a story concocted by the Sitosen witches to explain away people's memories of Lisyne, Seryne, and Tirosyne. He doubted that Neria, the previous leader of

Sitosen, had expected her made-up legend would be used as ammunition against her successors.

"Guerline, what exactly is Evadine's concern about the witches?" Desmond asked.

"She believes the Kavanagh sisters have too much autonomy. She thinks they ought to be more beholden to me, and that I shouldn't treat them as equals."

"I see," Desmond said. "And what do you think?"

Guerline glanced into the empty fireplace. "Desmond, please don't get angry."

"I'm not angry!" he said.

She raised an eyebrow at him and he hesitated, then sighed. He was angry. At Evadine and all those who shared her opinion of his family, at himself for failing to prevent this. He was even a little angry at the unreadable expression on Guerline's beautiful face. She'd never looked at him in that calculating way before. It was Evadine's influence staring back at him, he realized. Evadine's suspicion.

"What do you think, Guerline?" he repeated.

She watched him a beat longer before glancing down and back up. "I think the witch clan leaders, whoever they happen to be, are supposed to be the Lords Paramount of their region, and they're supposed to be answerable only to the emperor—or me, in this case. That doesn't mean I ought to treat them like vassals. I'm not worried about the Kavanaghs overthrowing me or any of that nonsense."

Desmond smiled. He went back to the sofa and sat down, reached for Guerline's hand and folded it in his.

"That's good, Lina. Honestly, my mother, my aunts, only have Arido's best interests at heart. And I can honestly say that they prefer you infinitely to your idiot brother, peace for his soul."

She pulled her hand out of his and tilted her head back, then stood and paced in front of the couch just as he had done. Desmond waited. He could tell she was thinking by the way she chewed on her bottom lip and rubbed her thumbs over her fingernails. Despite the seriousness of the conversation, Desmond couldn't help a small smile. He enjoyed cataloging her habits and learning to read her. It made him feel even closer to her, and close to her was all he wanted to be.

Guerline looked at Desmond, and his smile faded as he realized that her thoughts were much less pleasant than his. Her hands now rested against her stomach, fingers tightly interlaced. He could see the whiteness of her knuckles. Desmond rose from his seat and crossed over to her. He sat on the edge of the sofa and took her hands in his, tugging her down to sit next to him.

He looked at her face and saw fear there, simmering quietly. His stomach clenched. He wanted to tell her not to be afraid, to tell her that she was brilliant and perfect and that everyone else could jump off a cliff—but he couldn't. She came to the throne young, and she would spend her entire tenure as empress wondering who to trust and whether she was ever doing the right thing. It had driven rulers mad before. Suddenly, he was afraid too.

"Listen, Lina, I know it will be hard to do what needs to be done, but I promise I will help you. We can talk to her together, if you wish," he said.

Her head snapped up, eyebrows furrowed, a frown pulling the corners of her mouth down. "What are you talking about?"

"If Evadine is spreading vitriol about the witch clans, she needs to be reprimanded," Desmond said.

"And that's your decision to make, is it? You know nothing of what she's said or why!" Guerline snapped.

She broke away from him and walked around to the back side of the sofa. He watched her, keeping very still as he worked to tame the anger he felt. He studied the way she hung her head, red twists slipping past her shoulders and swinging in front of her; the way her hands gripped the cushions; the sound of her slow exhale, a sign that she too was grappling with strong emotions and trying to maintain her calm.

When she finally lifted her head, they both sighed again and offered each other small, tight smiles.

"I'm sorry, Desmond. Eva has taken some extreme positions with regard to the witch clans, that much is true. But she would not be a very good Chief Adviser if we agreed on everything, and I think her skepticism will be useful when we hold council with the witches," she said.

"Hold council with them?" he repeated.

She nodded. "Yes. Actually, I was planning to write to you before you arrived. I want to arrange a meeting between myself and the Kavanaghs, or their representatives, to address some of my nobles' concerns. To . . . get to know them again. According to the schoolmasters, the clans never even come to Del to test girls anymore, not for a century—I didn't even know that wasn't done any longer. They're so distant, it's easy to be afraid of them."

Desmond sighed and sat down on an ottoman. "This is my fault."

"What? No!"

Guerline dashed around the sofa and sat down in front of him, taking his hands in hers. He lifted his gaze to her and searched her face. Whatever frustration she'd had with him earlier was gone; her brown eyes bored into him, bright, with eyebrows raised earnestly, lips slightly parted.

"My duty has been to educate the humans, to help them see the clans' benevolence. I've very obviously failed, at least here in Del!" He looked down.

"You're only one man, Desmond, and the population has grown considerably since you started traveling. It's been nearly ten years; it's simply time to reevaluate. That doesn't mean you've failed," she said.

He switched their grip, holding Guerline's hands instead, and slipped one hand out from between hers to rest it on top, applying gentle pressure and caressing her skin lightly with his thumb. Her flesh was soft; palace flesh, royal flesh. He felt the scrape of his calloused thumb against it, could almost hear it. Underneath his grip, Guerline's hands seemed to have gone very still; yet they quivered with tension, as though she would not quite relax their weight into his hold.

That seemed odd to Desmond. He looked up from their hands and studied her face again, but her expression didn't seem to have changed, except that her mouth was now closed. He reached forward and put a hand on her cheek, starting back toward her ear. Slowly, he let his hand drift along her jaw until his thumb rested on the corner of her mouth. Her utter stillness was unmistakable.

Was it simply nerves? Did she feel the difference he felt, the one he'd been ignoring since he walked into the throne room and saw her? His skin came alive when he touched her, and he hoped, in a deep part of him that clenched at the thought, that it was the same for her.

She pressed her lips together and leaned away from him, standing, stumbling slightly as she tripped past his knee. He followed her movements with his gaze, letting the fingers that had rested on her cheek curl into a loose fist.

"Why don't we go for a walk? The garden has grown up quite a bit since your last visit," she said.

Desmond smiled. The garden wasn't the only one.

At sunset, Desmond pulled himself away from the palace with some difficulty. He was practically intoxicated, giddy with reawakened feelings.

Since his ill-fated attempt to court Dona, Desmond had not formally pursued anyone. This was not to say that he had been chaste. He had been with many witches, all of them hoping to birth daughters to the Kavanagh line, and he had been with his fair share of human girls too. He was as careful as he could be. He avoided taking to bed girls who seemed interested in marriage, and he kept a stock of contraceptive wraps and potions for himself and those ladies not interested in pregnancy. Through these means he had indulged in a very successful romantic life, leaving no broken hearts, only fulfilled desires. These brief and amiable affairs suited his traveling lifestyle better than monogamy.

The last golden light of the sun flashed off a rippled windowpane. Desmond blinked against the unexpected brightness until his eyes readjusted to the purpling hues of evening.

He had forgotten how red Guerline's hair was.

It was like fire in the sunlight. Red hair was fairly rare in Arido, and Desmond was almost certain that he had found all the red-headed girls in the empire. Guerline, though— her hair had these threads of gold through it, blonde woven through the dark red twists. He couldn't believe he'd forgotten that. It had been hard to focus on anything else that afternoon, as they wandered through the palace gardens.

Well. He had been able to focus on *some* other things. Like the way her breasts bounced behind the tight, stiff panel of her bodice, or the curve of her back, or the swishing motion her dress made with every step, the figure-eight movement of her wide hips while she walked. Had she always moved like that? How had he missed it before?

"It's not just that, though," he said to Keno. The gelding flicked an ear back but otherwise kept clip-clopping through the Third Neighborhood. Desmond held the reins loosely in one hand and looked up at the buildings on either side of the street, moonlight and darkness turning everything different shades of blue.

"She's got a good head for this. Ruling, I mean. She's got patience, she's thoughtful. She wants to get as much information as she can before she starts making decisions. It might be mostly out of fear right now, but if she keeps it up, I think it will be a very effective way to govern. What do you think?"

Keno ignored him. Desmond made a face at the back of the horse's head.

"Anyway, she's smart, is what I'm trying to say. I think she'll be all right. She'll do well."

He smiled. He had always been fond of Guerline, since they were both young. Now, he wasn't just fond of her; he admired her, powerfully. He admired her strategy so far, and he especially admired the fact that she was still Guerline. She still loved to dance, still wanted to learn about magic, still played with his hair and smiled her sweet smile at him, still stared at him like she was memorizing his face. She was his dear friend and his empress, all in one.

The spires of the palace were just barely visible over the tops of other buildings when Desmond reined up outside an inexplicably large, ramshackle tavern in Del's Fourth Neighborhood. It was so awkwardly built that the upper floors were lopsided. The second and third floors leaned forward over the street and slightly to the left, practically resting on the neighboring building. The builders had tried to compensate with the fourth floor, which leaned away from the street and hung over the alley behind the tavern. All the windows blazed with light, and the tavern floor roared. After tying Keno to a post, Desmond ducked his head under the wooden sign, which showed nothing but a crudely painted eye, and entered the building.

The back wall was dominated by a tall, thick bar flanked on either side by stairs. The rest of the open room was filled with tables and chairs, many of which were overturned and damaged. Two drunk men wrestled in one corner, their fellows surrounding them in a tight circle to keep the fight contained. A dwarf, two people in long green tunics, and an old man gambled at a table right next to the door. A large group stood in the center of the room, swaying and singing three different verses of the same song simultaneously and loudly.

It was a typical evening at Dagda's Eye.

Desmond carefully made his way to the bar and ordered a pint of beer from the bartender, a short bald man with bushy eyebrows and a suspicious, squinty gaze. He eyed Desmond carefully as he poured the beer into a horn mug. He seemed to accept what he saw, though; he set the mug in front of Desmond and moved on to someone else. Desmond took a big gulp of the beer and wiped the foam out of his mustache with his sleeve. He turned around and leaned against the bar just as a short blonde woman approached him. She stopped in front of him and crossed her arms over her chest.

"Witch-son," she said.

"Deserter," he said.

They stared at each other for a long moment. Desmond cracked a grin first. Someday, he might like to see how long they could hold out, but he wouldn't compromise Bridget's position in the guild by making her break first in front of her fellow thieves. She grinned back at him and they clasped hands.

"Desmond. It's good to see you," she said.

"And you, Bridget. How go things here?"

Her eyelids fluttered, and she looked down. "Brogan be dead."

"Peace for his soul," Desmond said. "Then you are . . ."

"Aye. I lead the guild now."

Desmond lifted his mug to her in salute and smiled. "Congratulations to you, then, however bittersweet the circumstances may be."

She gave him half a smile in return and sat on a barstool next to him. There was a mug of beer in front of her before she reached for it. Her eyes never left Desmond.

"I thank ye. Now you. What brings you back to Del and Dagda's? Must be three years past since you sought us out."

"Oh, I'm here to marry the empress."

"Ha! You ain't the only one, witch-son, the way I hear it," Bridget said.

Desmond raised an eyebrow. "And what do you hear?"

"I hear Lord Warren's made himself available to Empress at all hours of day and night. I hear Lord Warren don't contradict Empress on nothing. I hear Lord Warren be writing heaps of letters to the head of his northern estate."

"You hear a lot," Desmond said.

"I've a lot of ears," she said.

He frowned. "Well. I'm not worried about Lord Warren."

Bridget tossed her blonde braid, a perfect match to Desmond's, over her shoulder and stared at him.

"What are you worried about, then?" she asked.

"Is there somewhere we can talk privately?"

A smirk crept slowly onto Bridget's lips, and Desmond blushed despite himself. She had the most intense stare he'd ever seen this far from a witch palace. Her eyes just seemed to bore right to the heart of a person—which was undoubtedly why she'd risen through the ranks of the thieves' guild so quickly, though she was only about a year older than Desmond himself. Criminal skill was often only half as important as the ability to strike fear into the hearts of one's rivals, and Bridget had both.

It wasn't fear rising in him as she stared him down, though. He hadn't meant to imply anything and Bridget knew it, but that wasn't going to stop her from teasing him. She glanced at a shadowy nook next to one set of stairs.

"This way."

She slid off her barstool and wove through the writhing crowd on the tavern floor. Desmond followed easily. Bridget may have been small enough to duck and weave, but he was large enough that obstacles moved for him.

Between the staircase and the wall was a narrow hallway. It was almost too narrow for Desmond to fit through, but he turned sideways and sidled in. It ended in a staircase going down, into the cellar. Bridget had disappeared into the darkness. Desmond hesitated; then light flared up in the room beneath and the thief queen poked her head over the stairs.

"Come on then, and shut the door behind," she said.

Once Desmond reached the floor of the cellar, he turned around and pulled the door shut above him. As he did, it flashed blue light and he felt the wood shudder. He rolled his eyes and turned to Bridget, who shrugged.

"Secret meetings should stay secret. Warding be one of the only tricks I got left, and it's useful to me," she said.

"You might have more tricks if you'd stayed at Sitosen Castle longer."

"Witching never suited me, Desmond, you know that."

"You were only there three years!"

Bridget laughed. "And that was more than enough."

Desmond grinned back at her and sat down on a barrel. He was too tall to stand up straight down here in the cellar. Seated, he was only just shorter than Bridget.

"No matter. You're not the rogue witch I'm worried about."

Bridget's grin vanished. She put her hands on her hips. "A rogue witch? In Del?"

"Two. The Maravilla twins."

"Damn."

"You remember them?"

"Well enough, though I was but a child. They was my instructors for third cycle. Mean, they was. Superior like. Looked at me like I was a rat. I reckon they weren't fond of my mother," she said. Desmond gave a sympathetic nod. Bridget's mother was Tesla, who had been appointed Hand of Sitosen after the twins were banished. "I ain't surprised they gone rogue. When?"

"They were banished the year you left. They tried to steal Neria's Shield from my mother's study, and she cast them out. They've been quiet ever since, but now Mother believes they are working black magic and damaging the curtain between life and death."

Bridget frowned. She dug her fingers into her hair and massaged her scalp.

"Do you know where they are, Bridget?"

"What, do ye think I know everything that goes on in Del?"

"Yes."

She laughed and sat down on a bench, pulling her legs up and sitting cross-legged.

"I don't know everything, Desmond, but I do know this. I know that we can't get into the old prison tower no more. It's warded strong; ain't no one I know likes to get near to it. Been that way about a year. And I know that the Mongers don't go into the Vale no more. They say it's haunted, say there's evil afoot in the woods. Brigands, scared of ghosts, can you imagine?" She tilted her head to one side. "Might be they're connected. Might be it ain't ghosts scaring Marcus's men."

"The prison tower," Desmond said.

"Aye."

He frowned at the cellar floor. The old prison tower hadn't been used by the crown in one hundred years. It was just outside the palace walls. If the Maravilla twins had taken up residence there, that put them dangerously close to Guerline.

"Get back to your empress, Desmond. I'll go to the tower," Bridget said.

He looked up. "What? No. I'll come with you."

"Empress needs you a good deal more than I do, witchson. Do as I say and move your flat arse!"

Desmond stood up quickly, groaning as he hit his head on the ceiling, and started up the stairs. He stopped just as he lifted the door, looked behind him, and then back at Bridget.

"My arse is not flat!" he said.

Bridget's laughter followed him all the way out of the tavern.

CHAPTER SIXTEEN

IT WAS LONG AFTER DARK WHEN **G**UERLINE SETTLED INTO BED. Dinner, a meal for her and Desmond and Eva together, had begun tense, but eventually they'd shed their new political selves—Guerline, at least, had pretended she was as she had been before, a second-child with no need to spend time thinking of who might be plotting against her. Eva and Desmond had even achieved a sort of stalemate born of their desire to entertain Guerline, as Desmond told stories of his travels and Eva provided wry commentary. The effect had Guerline laughing for hours, long after their food was gone, and she was almost happy. Desmond was, if nothing else, a fine dinner guest. He had brought bad news, but he also managed to make her forget about it, and everything else.

Almost everything. He couldn't do anything about the new tension she felt in his presence. It wasn't constant, but every now and then she'd turn to him and catch a look on his face, one she had not seen often before but which lent new significance to her behavior toward him. She'd found it difficult to stay aware of it during the afternoon they spent alone together. Sometimes, she would forget, fall back into their casual sibling-like rapport, and then he would put his hand on her back a little lower than he used to, press a little harder than he once would have. He touched her bare shoulders over and over again, lingering caresses, his hand hanging against her skin and running across her neck or her chest if she turned.

Remembering those uncomfortable moments chipped away at her relief and relaxation, and tension crept over her again. She took deep breaths and waited for sleep, trying to keep her mind blank.

Eva had come upstairs with her after dinner, and they had spent the sunset in each other's arms—but when the sun was gone and they sought sleep in earnest, Eva could not be still, tossing and turning. Guerline had tried to comfort her, but whatever disturbed Eva had made her irritable. Eventually, she had stormed out; between this and the new awkwardness with Desmond, Guerline actually found herself grateful for a night alone.

She missed the moment when her eyes finally closed, because rather than the blackness of her eyelids, she still saw her own room. It took a moment to understand that she was dreaming. Her mind swam. Her fingers tingled on the edge of numbness. No longer on the bed, she stood in the middle of her chambers. Every object took on a curiously sharp aspect. The hard lines of her furniture glinted like daggers in the red light of the setting sun.

The nightmare was upon her.

Someone pounded on the door. Her brother opened it without waiting for her leave and walked into the room. He shoved the door shut behind him.

They looked very much alike, she and Alcander, except that he was nearly two heads taller than her. They both had red-gold hair and freckled brown skin, and they were both solidly built, though her flesh was soft where his was muscled. Were he not three years older, they might have been twins. He smiled at her.

"Are you ready, Lina?"

Darkness fell around her and the torment began. The part of her that remained horrifyingly lucid during her restless sleep struggled to wake, but was weighed down by the emotions of her dream self and by the questions dropped on her from above like falling stones in an avalanche. Why now, when it had been at least a week since her last nightmare? And why had the pattern ruptured, why was this the first memory in the cycle when it was usually the last?

Her dream self and her lucid self both cried out as her dream self lunged for the knife, the knife that had been a gift from Eva. The beam of hope her dream self always felt as her fingers wrapped around the dagger hilt burned her lucid self—it was an intoxicating wave of triumph and anger, and it called for her to give herself over to it. But lucid Guerline knew how quickly that beam was snuffed out, how easily Alcander knocked the dagger from her hand.

Trapped in the nightmare, weaponless, she trembled and froze and wept as she wondered how to get through it alive, as that word became the only thing she could think, as she shut her eyes and those two syllables became her pounding heartbeat.

a-live, a-live, a-live, alive, alive, alive alive ALIVE

On the night of the incident, Guerline had been saved, ironically, by the news that her parents had been stricken with the flesh-eating curse.

The nightmare did not include that, though. It continued as if Eva and Josen had never decided to summon Guerline as well as Alcander, as if they had not arrived just after the dagger thudded to the floor. The part of Guerline that was lucid tried to pull herself away from the nightmare, thrust herself above the will to stay alive and into the certainty that she *had* survived. She remembered her bedroom door closing as Alcander left with Josen, over and over again, cementing it until the slamming of the door punctuated her mantra.

a-live, SLAM, a-live, SLAM, a-live, SLAM

Lucid Guerline shuddered from the effort. Fear sliced her, but amazingly, the nightmare did not jump back to the beginning of the assault, nor did it proceed without intervention. Alcander left with Josen, and Evadine rushed toward Guerline's bed.

Guerline reached for her, but when their hands met, it was not Eva's skin she touched. The hand in hers was pale as milk, and, with the certainty that she had done this very thing before, she followed the hand up an arm and saw in full the girl who had visited her the night of her family's death, and so many times since then. The girl's eyes widened, and she turned away, pulling her hand out of Guerline's grasp; but Guerline lunged forward and seized the girl's black robe—

Hot, bitter-smelling air sucked the breath from her lungs, and a roaring wind buffeted her with grit. She squinted against the barrage and saw that she stood in a grey desert. The sky was like charcoal above them, swirling with dark fog, and the land around flat as far as she could see. Something crawled over her foot; she jumped back and looked down, and saw that the earth was infested with creeping lizards, small and frantic, running as if from some predator Guerline could not see. Animal cries pierced the wind and sent chills down Guerline's spine.

She looked up again and saw the girl, her white brow lined with an incredulity that was somehow familiar. Her cascade of blonde hair remained still, even as Guerline's unbraided twists were like whips around her.

"You're not meant to be here," the girl said.

"Where are we?" Guerline asked.

"You're no witch," the girl said. Guerline wondered if she had heard the question and chose to ignore it, or whether her voice had been carried away by the winds that did not appear to touch this creature. Her tone was one of mild confusion, and gave Guerline no clues as to who this girl was and where she had been taken. Was *she* a witch? What landscape was this? Was Guerline still dreaming?

"That is true," Guerline replied. "Please, where are we? Who are you?"

The girl stepped in close to Guerline, and the wind died down to nothing, as if the girl was surrounded by a calm within the storm. She resisted the sigh of relief that wanted to escape her chest and kept her eyes on the girl— the pale-skinned, golden-haired creature she forgot often but recognized instantly.

"Who could have predicted this?" the girl whispered, lifting her starlit fingers to Guerline's cheek.

At her touch, an incredible sense of joy, like galloping across verdant fields, overcame Guerline and she could not suppress a gasp. The girl smiled at her, a brilliantly bright smile that chased away the dark grey fog swirling around them.

Guerline awoke as abruptly as she'd fallen asleep. The red light of evening was gone, and her room was black with full night again. Her chest rose and fell with a steadiness that belied her agitation. She sat up and stared into the darkness.

What was that place to which she'd been dragged?

And her nightmare had returned. She could feel her hands trembling against the covers, just as they had the night of the incident. She'd spent the rest of the night assuring Eva that she was fine, though inside, she'd wrestled with whether or not to tell Eva what happened. By morning, all she'd wanted was to pretend it had never happened, because if she acknowledged the danger, she would also be forced to acknowledge that there was nothing to be done. Her parents were alive but unable to speak, and Alcander had become emperor in all but title. The incident was pushed to the back of everyone's minds. Alcander was drawn constantly away by his newfound duties as their parents deteriorated. Though she kept Eva's dagger in the open instead of in the drawer, Guerline had kept silent.

Yet, she knew: if Alcander had not also died, he would have come again.

Rage welled up in her. She got out of bed and rushed to her dressing table. She felt around in the dark until she found it: a glass cat as large as a man's fist, a gift given to her by Alcander for her last birthday. The cat was in a stretching pose, its forelegs flat on the ground, head tucked, spine arched and tail curved like a scythe.

She ran her fingers over it; then she threw it as hard as she could against the wall.

It shattered with a sound like a human scream, and Guerline felt a gust of wind. She walked carefully over to her sole window, but it was closed. Her heart sped up. Something brushed her arm. She spun around to face her door. A sound like laughter rumbled down her body and she froze.

The familiarity of the experience sickened her. She swallowed her fear and spoke up.

"Who's there?"

The door swung open and she screamed. It was Alcander, bare-chested, his skin yellow-grey and his throat dripping red. She saw him clearly in the dark, his image flashing as if illuminated by lightning.

Then the lightning stopped and was replaced by a soft white orb that grew until it was larger than the one who held it. It was not Alcander at all; it was Undine.

She took a step forward and looked down with a hiss when her feet touched the shattered glass.

"Guerline? What happened?"

She walked carefully toward Guerline and put a hand on her arm. Guerline swayed and sat down on the bed, and it was then that she realized her hem was dirty. She brushed a spot of dust, and it came away silty and soft on her fingers.

It was ash. Tears touched the corners of her eyes, though she could not say what she wept for. She blinked them back and flicked her blankets over her lap to hide the hem of her nightgown.

"Only a dream," she said.

CHAPTER SEVENTEEN

DESMOND KNOCKED ON THE LARGE BLACK DOOR THAT LED
to Guerline's private chambers. There was no answer for
a moment, so he knocked again. Guerline herself opened
the door and stepped back, her hands working at the front
of her silk overdress, the open-front sort that Evadine had
been wearing yesterday at dinner. He stared and realized she
was closing it. She must have only just finished her morning
toilette, and alone, by the look of it. Her handmaiden was
nowhere to be seen.

"Did you sleep well?" he asked.

One corner of her mouth lifted in what was not quite
a smile. "How did you find your rooms?"

"Perfect, as always," Desmond laughed. "May I come in?"

"Yes, of course. I'll call for some breakfast—have you eaten yet? And you can tell me more about these rogue witches and what's going on with Thiymen."

Business was the last thing he wanted to discuss, but at least she was inviting him to do it here in her private rooms instead of moving into the council chamber or the throne room. And he really did need to get her up to date on the information he'd learned thus far; if only he weren't still so distracted, imagining her in her undergarments just moments before he came to see her.

Perhaps he could put off the business for a bit longer. He shut the door behind him and followed her into the room, close on her heels. When she turned around, he grabbed her hand and held it tightly between his. She gasped; he wrapped an arm around her waist.

He'd opened his mouth to suggest that they sneak into the kitchens for a snack, like they used to do, when Lord Warren burst through the door.

A glare crossed his face briefly when he saw Desmond standing a mere inch or two from Guerline. Desmond tried hard not to grin. Lord Warren composed himself and bowed hastily.

"Your Majesty. Master Kavanagh. I'm sorry to interrupt, but you must come quickly. Both of you. Something is wrong."

Desmond and Guerline exchanged a quick glance before following Lord Warren out of the room and down the tower steps. The tall northerners quickly outpaced Guerline's short gait. Glancing over his shoulder, Desmond put a hand on the Lord Engineer's arm. They slowed, and Guerline, holding her dress out of the way of her feet, caught up to them.

"What's happening, Theodor?" she asked.

"I'm not sure, Guerline-basi," he said. "All I know is that people are beginning to gather outside the palace gates. And some of them appear to be carrying corpses."

"*What*?" Desmond asked.

"I know. I can't imagine why, but that's what I was told," Lord Warren said. "Hopefully the guards will have more information for us when we get to the front hall."

Guerline stopped abruptly. Desmond spun around and stared at her.

Lord Warren stopped too. "Guerline-basi?"

"Dead things. More dead things, at my doorstep," she whispered.

Desmond walked over and stood directly in front of Guerline. It took several moments for her eyes to focus on him, first on his chest and then on his face. Her eyes narrowed, and she gave the tiniest shake of her head. Then she pushed past him and took off. Without a word, Desmond and Lord Warren followed, after exchanging worried looks. Desmond had noticed Guerline unfocus like that several times during the previous night's dinner, her expression going vacant, and then flickering with fear for the span of a heartbeat before returning to normal. *More dead things?* He gritted his teeth in annoyance with himself. He should have come to the capital as soon as he heard the emperor and empress were stricken. He should have been with her this whole time.

When they arrived, they saw several of the councilors and two dozen or so guards gathered before the door, talking heatedly.

"Guerline!" Evadine said when she spotted them approaching. She hurried over, threw her arms around Guerline, and kissed her on the mouth. Desmond jerked to a stop and watched, shock-like pressure in his skull, as their kiss deepened.

Evadine pulled back and whispered rapidly, "I'm so sorry about last night, Lina—"

"Don't worry, love," Guerline replied, kissing her again, "don't worry, I forgive you." She broke away and strode toward the guards, her hand gripping Evadine's.

"Who can tell me what is going on outside? Josen?" she said.

The Captain of the Palace Guard stepped forward and bowed. Desmond bit the inside of his bottom lip to stifle his scowl and ran up to the rest of them. No wonder Guerline was so willing to be lenient with Evadine.

No wonder she was so stiff under his hands.

"Your Majesty, the gatherings started this morning," Josen said. "At first it was only a few people. They were demanding to see you. We told them that you were not holding court today, and that you would see them tomorrow. They went away from the gate, but a few hours later they came back, and there were more of them. Since then, more and more people have been coming, from all over the city it appears. Some of them are carrying corpses with them."

"Why on earth have they brought corpses? Are they newly dead, or have the people been plundering the catacombs?" Guerline asked.

"We finally sent a few men out to inquire. It appears that all those gathered have recently deceased family members or friends. They've all been holding their watches, but the Thiymen witches have not come."

"What do you mean, they haven't come?" Desmond asked.

Josen nodded to him. "Master Kavanagh. I know only what was told to me. These people have been having their watches, some for nearly a week, but the witches have not come to escort the souls of the dead to Ilys. The people are panicking. They believe that the witches have turned on them and are punishing their loved ones by leaving them trapped in their dead bodies. They are refusing to bury the dead until the witches come to take the souls."

"Oh no," Guerline said. "And they're gathering outside, with the bodies?"

"Yes. There's at least seventy corpses, maybe more," Josen said.

"Have there been that many deaths recently?" asked Lord Warren.

Evadine sneered. "Del is a huge city. There are that many deaths by the hour."

"Desmond, can you think of any reason why Thiymen would not come for the dead?" Guerline asked. He frowned and rummaged in his pockets.

"Fiona is preparing for war! She's about to make her attack!" Pearce Iszolda squealed.

Guerline groaned. "Gods, would you stop it, Pearce? Something must be very, very wrong for the Thiymen witches to abandon their duties. Desmond, could this have anything to do with what you told me? About the damage to the barrier between life and death?"

"Yes, I'm certain it does. I can't think of any other reason why Thiymen would not come for the dead." He pulled out a small compact—a less powerful version of the mirrors his mother and aunts used to communicate in times of emergency.

"Let me try to get in touch with Fiona," he said, and walked a few steps away.

He lifted the lid of the compact and popped open the compartment with Fiona's dragon-head symbol on it. He dipped his little finger in the sulphuric powder and touched it to the mirror in the lid. It rippled as it should, but when it stilled, all it showed was black nothingness where his aunt Fiona's face should have appeared.

"Aunt Fiona?"

There was no response. He wiped the powder off the mirror with a small handkerchief and opened his mother's compartment. Her powder was a light blue the color of the sky and smelled like rain. He dipped his finger into it and touched it to the mirror. The mirror rippled for a long time, and then went back to normal. Desmond frowned. Either the mirror was failing, which it had never done before, or things were far more dire than any of them had suspected. He tried Morgana and Aradia in the same fashion, and neither of them responded to his call. He snapped the compact shut and put it back into his pocket. Olivia, Morgana, and Aradia weren't answering, and Desmond had no idea what Fiona's black mirror meant. Something was very wrong indeed.

"Well?" Guerline asked when she saw him coming back.

"I can't contact any of the Kavanagh sisters," he said. "Something has happened to them, though what, I couldn't say."

"What should we do about the crowd, Your Majesty?" Josen asked. "The longer the Thiymen witches do not appear . . ."

"I know," Guerline said. She turned away, frowning and rubbing her forehead, chewing madly at her bottom lip. "Desmond, can any of the other clans escort the souls?"

"No," Desmond said. "Only Thiymen witches are trained to do that."

"Can the Thiymen witches pull a soul from a body even when it's in the ground?" she asked.

"Yes, as long as it isn't buried too deep."

"Good," Guerline said. She strode toward the doors.

"Where are you going, Your Majesty?" Josen asked.

"We cannot have hundreds of people squatting before the gate with dead bodies in high summer," Guerline said. "People will get sick from it. The bodies must be buried."

Evadine followed her. "But Lina, the people are superstitious when it comes to the rituals of death. They will not want to bury the bodies until the souls are gone, otherwise it will be like burying their loved ones alive."

"I realize this, but is it less of an indignity to allow their loved ones to rot in public? We have no idea when the Thiymen witches will return, and in this heat, the corpses will rot very quickly. This is our best course of action," she said. Her voice wavered, but her jaw clenched. No one argued.

Her councilors trailed after her out the palace doors and down to the gate. Desmond stumbled along behind them, distracted. It was unsettling that he couldn't contact the Lords Paramount for the empress; it was worse that he couldn't contact his mother or his aunts. These were the powerful, untouchable women who had raised him. They were sometimes beyond conventional means of communication, but the mirror was for emergencies, and he knew the sisters always kept them close. Thinking of whatever might be preventing them from answering made him deeply nervous.

Guerline nodded to Josen, and he unlocked the gates. She, Desmond, and Evadine went out into the square, surrounded by a dozen guardsmen who pushed back the gathered people to make a path for Guerline. Desmond saw the brightly colored summer costumes of the First and Second Neighborhoods scattered among the faded ones of the Third and Fourth. The crowd, which had been wailing and calling for Guerline, Lisyne, *anyone*, quieted down as news of her appearance spread. She walked straight to the fountain at the center and climbed up onto it so that she could be better seen.

"Beloved subjects, we understand your confusion and anxiety," she said as loudly as she could. "Please, rest assured that we are making every effort to discover the reasons behind the absence of the Thiymen witches."

Well said, thought Desmond. Such neutral wording would hopefully keep most of the crowd from jumping to the same conclusions as some of the war-mongering councilors.

"In the meantime, to preserve the dignity of those we have lost, we must lay them in the arms of the earth," Guerline said.

He caught himself nodding along. That sounded much more poetic and spiritual, and less like burying them alive. Still, the crowd did not appear happy with the decision. An outcry rose up, but Guerline raised her hands and called for quiet, which she received after only a few moments.

"We know this is not how things are usually done, but this is an unusual circumstance! We have had it on good authority from the other clans that the witches are still able to collect the souls of your loved ones even from under the ground. We promise that every person who has died will make it to Ilys!"

There was silence as the nervous and grief-stricken crowd decided whether or not to trust the words of their young empress. Guerline held her arms open, palms up, and spun slowly to look at every section of the gathering.

"Please, bring those you have lost here to the palace. We will lay them in the ground on the palace green until the witches come to take them home to Ilys," she said.

Desmond held his breath, but her offer to host the corpses seemed to resonate with the crowd. Some of the tension in the atmosphere dispersed, and he exhaled. Though they were still frightened and confused, the people seemed glad to have some semblance of a plan. Those who hadn't brought their deceased began to filter out of the square to retrieve them, and those who had carried the dead to the palace pressed toward the gates. Desmond offered Guerline a hand to get down. She squeezed his fingers far tighter than necessary. He could feel her whole arm shaking, but, from the look on her face when she turned to Josen, he never would have guessed how she trembled.

"Have the guards assist the people. Take the corpses and bury them on the palace green in shallow, separate graves. Get a carpenter and a scribe to make temporary markers for them so we can keep track of everyone."

Josen nodded, and Guerline walked back toward the palace, followed by Desmond and Evadine.

"That was very well handled, Lina," Evadine said, more emphatically than anything Desmond had ever heard her say.

"Thank you, Eva," Guerline said. The smile she gave Evadine was so warm, so full of a love he'd never seen between them before, that it sent a hot wave of jealousy through him. He pushed ahead and joined Josen in opening the gates in the palace wall. Guerline and Evadine slipped through, and Desmond followed them, leaving their escort to guide people into a queue.

They rejoined the rest of the guards and councilors inside the palace wall and crossed the yard in a slow, stately procession up the stairs, through the huge silvery doors and into the front hall. Guerline put a hand on Shon Marke's shoulder.

"Shon, send word immediately to anyone you know in the east that may be able to tell us what's happening there," she said. He nodded and branched off to climb up a set of stairs to the right, up to the rookery where the messenger birds were kept. Guerline turned next to Jon Wellsly. "Jon, please send the criers out with instructions that anyone with dead, for whom the witches have not yet come, should bring their deceased to the palace."

The old man nodded and took a left off the hall. Guerline dismissed everyone but Evadine and Desmond with orders to keep their eyes and ears open for any developments, and then she returned to her tower chambers with her chosen companions in tow. Once the door was shut safely behind them, Guerline sank onto her bed and let out a shaky breath. She looked up at them, her eyes wide with fear.

"What's going on, Desmond?" she asked.

He looked down at her grimly.

"I'll try to contact Fiona again," he said.

CHAPTER EIGHTEEN

FOR DAYS, THE ENTIRE THIYMEN CLAN HAD BEEN WORKING furiously to repair and reinforce the curtain that separated the world under the mountain from the living world above the earth. It was crucial that the two did not mix, and even more crucial that the thing bound under the mountain not be allowed to escape.

But Fiona had not been among her witches as they raced along the barrier. She had been confined to her room; to her bed, most of the time. Her seal had sapped much more of her energy than she'd revealed. To conceal her weakness, she'd ordered that she was not to be disturbed under any circumstances, and any emergency entrances by

Kanika or Moira must be preceded by a knock. That way, she at least had time to sit up in bed and open a book, or perhaps move to a chair, and look less like an invalid.

Now awake, Fiona propped herself up against her pillows and looked around her room. There was so much black. It was black to match the rock, black to match the grave ash from under the mountain; black, just as colorless as a Thiymen witch's skin. It was a strange thing to watch color leave your flesh, your hair, your eyes. Yet this is what happened to Thiymen witches. They were the shortest-lived of all the clans, because they spent their lives slowly giving pieces of themselves to the underworld. And for what? For the protection of people who despised them? Oh, the citizens of Del told all sorts of tales about Thiymen, but how would they feel if Thiymen no longer took care of their dead?

Fiona made bony fists and clutched her blanket tightly until her anger dissipated. She was usually resigned to the ingratitude that Thiymen faced from these young generations of humans, but sustaining such aloofness was difficult. She kept calm by reminding herself that the humans were ignorant, and determined not to be taught. There was little a witch could do to change the mind of someone who was only interested in that which supported the ideas they already had. She chose her battles carefully, passed over the ones she could not win, and focused instead on the ones she could.

She pushed her blanket back and swung her legs over the side of the bed. Putting her feet on the floor, she stood up slowly and allowed the blood to move with greater freedom through her legs again. *I must cross the room and get my tonic*, she thought. She took a few steps; then the door opened without a knock.

"I specifically asked—" She was cut off by a deep, smooth voice.

"You asked the witches. I am no witch," the woman said.

Fiona looked up, and there she stood, broad and black-skinned and strong. Her hair, molded into thick locks, was bound at the nape of her neck. She wore loose black pants and a black tunic that was cinched at the waist with a wide silver belt. The belt, which had an amethyst set in the buckle, was a gift that Fiona had given her many years ago. She looked up from the belt at the woman's face. Her dark brown eyes were fixed on Fiona, eyebrows knit together. The expression she wore was equal parts worry and accusation. Fiona smiled ruefully up at her.

"Silas," she said.

"You are a fool."

"I know. Come, sit with me and explain why I am a fool," she said, gesturing toward the bed. She retraced the few steps she'd taken and swayed. Silas scooped her up and sat down, cradling her in her arms. Fiona was so small compared to her. She'd always been a large woman, but Fiona had never been this emaciated. Food had lost its appeal to her.

"You've grown old, Fiona," Silas said.

"Yes. Even witches must get old," Fiona replied.

Old age and then death happened very quickly for witches. They aged normally until they were fully grown, and then spent centuries in the prime of their adulthood. It was almost as if they spent most of their lives in a kind of stasis, and in order to achieve balance, an aged witch would deteriorate very rapidly.

Fiona was much younger than her sisters, but she had always known that she would be the first to die. Her power had bloomed brighter at a younger age, and her duties had always been more taxing than those of her sisters. Fiona knew death well, and felt her own coming; but she had planned for ten or fifteen more years, at least long enough to train her replacement in the delicacies of leading Thiymen clan. The seal on the gate had robbed her of that time.

"I was about to take my tonic," Fiona said, as if that excused her from dying more quickly than expected.

Silas laughed, a noise that was not mirthful in the least, and took a dagger from the table next to Fiona's bed.

"No, don't," Fiona said, but a look from Silas quelled the words in her throat. There was no use. She would need to stay alive just a little bit longer, to get everything in order and perhaps see her sisters again, and the dragon blood in Silas's veins would sustain her as it had for the last five years. Though she had some stored in her cabinet, it would be more potent and invigorating coming fresh from the source. So she sighed and nodded, gesturing to a cup she also kept on the table.

Silas set the cup on the edge and held her wrist over it. One quick slash sent her dark blood gushing into the cup. She waited until it was almost full, and then touched the edge of the cut with her free hand. Slowly, the blood trickled to a stop and the skin knit itself together again. The woman who was also a dragon lifted the cup from the table and handed it to Fiona.

"Drink, my love," she said.

Fiona drank, and as she did she felt strength flooding into her body. The magic of the Thiymen dragons wasn't as powerful as that of the true dragons; but the true dragons were long gone, and she was grateful for Silas's gift to her.

Silas was the dragon queen, the current leader of the tribe. She had come into power the same time Fiona did; though unlike Fiona, Silas had killed her predecessor in order to gain control. When Fiona heard of the battle, she'd sent for Silas immediately. She had no idea what sort of queen she would be, and the last thing she needed at that time was a fool-headed youth to deal with. Luckily, she'd found the young dragon to be sensible and strong, if a little disapproving at times. They'd quickly established a rapport, and hammered out a new arrangement between the witches and the dragons. Where before the dragons had been slaves, now the dragons were partners. For six hundred years, Fiona and Silas had offered each other love and support. There were few things more valuable to Fiona than the time she spent with Silas. It prepared and refreshed her for everything else she had to do.

Even now, when all she had left to do was die.

As Fiona opened her mouth to tell Silas she was ready for her death, there was a knock on the door. Fiona lurched up from Silas's lap to stand on the floor, pleased to find her vertigo and unsteadiness gone. She felt more like herself again. She pulled her black overdress on with Silas's assistance before calling "Enter!" to whomever was at the door.

It was Kanika. The young witch looked very young indeed, with her rich black hair, honey-brown eyes, and flushed cheeks. One would hardly know her as a Thiymen witch, and in many ways, Fiona was grateful for that. But those thoughts were for an old woman's deathbed. Fiona knew by the wild-eyed look on Kanika's face that it was not time for her to die just yet.

"The gate?" Fiona asked.

"Yes," Kanika gasped. "It's buckled and cracking—the Guard—"

"Move," Fiona said.

Kanika jumped back, and Fiona swept past her, moving as fast as she could. Silas and Kanika followed. Despite her weakness, Fiona managed a considerable pace, and she thanked Silas again for being so good to her.

The Guard stood in a single line in front of the gate, all shouting and straining. The black sheet of rock in front of them groaned in response. Fiona could see it moving; something was trying to get through from the other side. The seven witches of the Guard were almost at their limit, supporting each other but shaking at the knees and sinking slowly to the ground. One witch in the middle of the line had already passed out. She sagged between two of her fellows, who continued to hold her up to keep the line unbroken.

Fiona closed her eyes, and in the blackness, she visualized the flickering core of her power. It crackled with purple light. She lifted her left hand, and when she opened her eyes, that ball of light was in her palm. Kanika and Silas stepped back. Fiona looked at them and nodded. Kanika's lips trembled; Silas just looked down.

She placed her right hand over the core of her magic and twisted her hands so that they were vertically palm to palm in front of her. She twisted her fingers through the outer tendrils of light surrounding the little ball of power and slowly drew her hands away from each other, stretching and lengthening the magic into a large pane. The current gate was crumbling. The quickest fix was to simply make a new gate. Unfortunately, hers would be only temporary. She didn't have the same kind of resources available to her as the original makers of the gate.

Where are you, now when I need you most? Why have you abandoned me?

Her anger at the reclusive shapeshifters, at the wolf herself, made the miniature gate between her hands fire up with sparks of purple light. She turned her hands palms forward and pushed the gate away from her, allowing it to expand even more.

"Guard! Stand down!" she roared.

The Guard immediately broke their line and collapsed. Those who could walk dragged others back from the line. Silas and Kanika ran forward to help them. Fiona glanced down as they carried the witch who had collapsed past her. It was Sempra, the newest addition to the Guard. Fiona felt a pang in her heart, as if it was her fault this thing had come to face them. She knew such a feeling was foolish. That didn't stop her from feeling it; just like all the years of telling herself that her charge was worthy hadn't stopped her from thinking her life had been wasted thinking about death.

But now death had finally come to her, and she did not plan to go on any terms but her own. In a way, she was grateful that the creature had chosen to rear its head now. Because of it, she could spend herself doing the thing she did best: keeping the underworld under the mountain.

She walked forward, the makeshift gate still expanding in front of her. The creature sensed her coming and screamed at her. It doubled its efforts against the old gate, pounding and scratching behind the rock.

"What are you doing, witchling?" Its voice rumbled through the rocky chamber, dark and rasping, Aridan laid over the guttural language of the underworld. "You cannot put me away forever."

Fiona did not respond. Her temporary gate was now as large as the one it needed to reinforce. Her march forward slowed as she met resistance from the force on the other side. It was much stronger now than two days ago; or perhaps she was simply weaker. Though Silas's blood gave her more fortitude than she expected, it wasn't enough to completely restore her. She closed her eyes and gathered what was left of her power in the center of her being. One blast was all she had; one chance to put a stop to this thing until the cavalry arrived.

"You're dying, witchling. Don't be a fool. I can give you eternal life," it purred at her.

Fiona closed her eyes, her face relaxed as she prepared herself.

"You stupid thing. I have no fear of death," she said.

Please come soon, sisters.

She cried out and pushed forward with all her might, running full-tilt at the sheet of black rock. The creature screamed in return, pushing back. Fiona collided with the wall. There was a bright flash of purple. The sounds of the thing screaming faded with the light. Fiona stood where she was, leaning against the rock, breathing heavily. Her fingers trembled and felt hot. She looked down and realized that her hands and wrists were bleeding. The blood flowed freely from cuts made by the jagged rock. She rolled over against

the wall. Everyone ran toward her. She held up her bloody
hands and spread her arms before them in a gesture of reas-
surance and peace.

Fiona smiled and slid down the wall, dead.

"No! No!" Kanika fell to her knees at the feet of Fiona's
corpse and clutched the hem of Fiona's robe. The Guard fell
down with her. Their weeping echoed through the cavern.
Silas knelt and silently gathered her lover's body up in her
arms. She folded Fiona's hands in her lap and wrapped the
many layers of her robes over them, to cover up the blood.
With that out of sight, and the smile still lingering on her
face, Fiona looked almost young again, the way Silas remembered her on the day they'd met: smooth ivory skin,
inky black hair, lovely red lips, and bright, carefree eyes
blue as a deep lake. Now she was pure white, even down to
her eyelashes. Silas was almost surprised that she had bled.

The mourning was interrupted by a growl that turned
into a whine. Silas looked up and saw a giant grey wolf
standing a few yards from them. It was panting heavily, its
tongue lolling, and its eyes were fixed on Fiona.

The sight of the wolf sent the death of her lover home,
and Silas too wept. She clutched Fiona's shoulders as tears
streamed down her dark cheeks.

"You came too late," she said to the wolf. "You came
too late."

The wolf whined again and walked toward them. The
witches drew back.

"Is it really you?" Kanika asked it tentatively.

In response, the wolf only stared at her. Kanika looked
at Silas, who shook her head. The wolf went right to Fiona,
licked her face gently, and then touched its nose to her

chest. Her soul came forth out of her body, a translucent and shimmering blue version of Fiona. The soul ignored her gathered mourners and put a hand on the wolf's snout. A crackling portal to the underworld opened a few feet away, and from it the witches could hear the song of Ilys. The wolf guided Fiona's soul to the portal and lifted her through; then the portal closed and the song was gone.

In the silence, the wolf turned to look at the mourners. *Bury her*, it said.

Then it bounded out of the cavern.

CHAPTER NINETEEN

MORGANA'S SWORD HISSED, GLOWING RED-ORANGE AND shimmering with heat as she swept it through the air. She held it in one hand, the other hand beside the blade, fingers twitching as she manipulated the magic surrounding it. As her fingers moved, the molten metal twisted, changing from a longsword into a curved saber. A few more movements of her hand, and the blade cooled rapidly, holding its new form. When the blade shone silver again, Morgana swung it with considerable force at the sparring dummy she'd animated. The dummy's head flew across the room; she pulled it back with a gesture and reattached it, then drew her hand back to melt the blade again.

The spell was one she'd been working on in her spare time for a while. She'd taken a forging spell which heated the blade without a furnace, designed for smithies on campaigns so that weapons could be repaired on the march, and added the cooling component so that the process was much faster. She'd been practicing her timing: her goal was to make it battle-functional, so that a witch could repair a weapon or armor on the field as quickly as possible. It was no replacement for traditional forging, but it was enough to get through a battle.

Morgana had gotten quite good at the spell, but she still liked to practice because it took her mind off of other worrisome things. Tonight, it was her sisters she was worried about. She at least felt like she was making some progress in the troubles of her region, after the Artan Forge fiasco. She and Aasim had discovered the source of the sandstorms, and while they still had no idea what was making the winds leave the Wastes now, they at least had a better idea of how to protect against them. Her sisters were not quite so lucky. Olivia had underworld creatures getting loose in her forests, and the report of Fiona's latest seal on the gate was unsettling. Poor Aradia was no closer to halting the sea's retreat, and everything else in the South had come to a standstill as people congregated at the ports, both to help bring goods in from stranded boats and to scavenge what they could from the take. Fear was beginning to grip the peninsula, and zealots were bringing it to the capital.

Angrily, Morgana stabbed through the wooden torso of the dummy. She was a savvy politician, but not nearly as patient as Olivia or Aradia. She detested empty talk and the fear-mongering tactics of the human government.

Adenen was already beginning to feel the backlash of the wizards' presence at Artan, in the form of cowardly, anonymous notes and packages with curses and superstitious sachets. They were too afraid to do more, too afraid to actually deny service to Adenen—for now. Governor Derouk had written to Evadine Malise, and the knowledge of Morgana's allegiance with the Atithi wizards was rippling from Del back into the west. Doubt was beginning to gnaw at the people. Morgana had issued a report, explained as well as she could the situation, but humans had difficulty understanding the magic, and the naysayers were much more vocal. Her people were being bombarded with the hatred of fools like Derouk, who had such a narrow understanding of what was going on.

Perhaps she and her sisters kept too much from the Aridans; but would they even listen? The country had little interest in magical affairs. Even when they were directly affected, as with the sandstorms, the people did not say, "why is this happening?" They demanded the problem fixed, without caring to understand what was going on. It was infuriating. What was she supposed to do; what were any of the witches supposed to do?

Morgana severed the dummy's torso with an impassioned yell and a forceful swipe of her saber. As the dummy slid apart and collapsed, she threw her sword down in disgust. It clattered on the stone, echoing in the vastness of the sparring room. She stared at it, chest heaving, as it slowly rolled on its guard to a stop.

Oh, how she wished things could be different. She did not want to battle whatever was lurking in the Zaide Mountains *and* the people of her own country! Something would have to be done. She would speak to her sisters tomorrow; perhaps, if they all went to Del and spoke with the empress, they could quell this dissension and focus on the real threat.

She turned away from the rubble to go up to her rooms—she didn't even know what time it was—but stopped when she saw Aasim standing in the door. He was dressed for sleep, as he had been when she'd roused him the night of the Artan sandstorm: bare-chested, in linen trousers that were tied just below his knees. He was barefoot. The light from the torches burning on either side of the door played across his muscular, golden chest and enhanced the strong features of his face; but despite all the shadows and reliefs that made him look sharp and harsh, she saw softness in his gaze. He was looking at her with concern. She saw the dismembered dummy in her mind again. He must have been watching for some time; he had seen her lose her composure.

"Lady Morgana, are you all right?" he asked. Though they had dispensed with formalities when fighting the sandstorm, he had since been exceedingly proper with her. She had not been so with him, simply because the *sotu* had no individual titles, but she also did not feel the need for the screen of propriety between them.

"Yes, Aasim," she said, smiling wearily. She thought of the dummy again and her smile became wry. "At least, I am as well as I can be, given the circumstances."

He approached her, his bare feet hardly making a sound. She drifted toward him as well, her boots thudding softly with each step.

"We have learned much about the sandstorms," he said. She smiled, appreciating the way he approached the conversation. He was asking, without really asking, what was bothering her.

"Yes," she agreed. "And with time, I think my sisters and I could solve all of the problems plaguing the continent. But I don't think the humans will give us that time."

"And that is what frustrates you," Aasim said. She nodded. He reached out and squeezed her bare shoulder in a comforting way; then he placed his free hand on her other shoulder and pulled her slightly closer. Morgana's lips parted in surprise. Aasim had shown himself to be steady and calm, composed even at Artan. But there was intensity in him now. She felt warmth rise in her, almost as if it came from his warm hands on her skin.

"Morgana, I have no doubts that the humans of your country will not stop you from prevailing against this evil. You are stronger than these debates. You are strong, and . . . lovely." He paused, his grip on her shoulders relaxing. He stroked her cheek with his knuckles. Unconsciously, Morgana ducked her head into the contact. Her hands rose slowly to rest themselves on Aasim's hips.

"And men cannot help but love you," he said softly.

He cupped her cheek with his hand and caressed her with his thumb. She smiled at the tenderness of the touch. She had had human lovers before, as all witches had; but in her experience, the touch of these men had been filled with a strange combination of reverence and incredulity. Aasim's had neither: respect in place of reverence, assurance in place of incredulity, and the warmth of affection. Slowly, she turned and softly kissed his thumb once, twice. She looked back up at him and saw relief wash over his face: the expression of a man whose gamble had paid off. His other hand came up and tangled itself in her hair, cradling the back of her head as his thumb brushed back and forth over her lips. Her hands inched up his body until her fingers met skin and she pressed her hands into him, pulling him closer.

"Aasim," she exhaled.

As if he had been given permission, Aasim leaned down and kissed her. He held her head in both hands, and while his kisses were soft, the tension in his hands betrayed the restraint he was showing. Morgana wrapped her arms around him and pulled him flush against her. His body radiated heat, and his light trousers did nothing to hide his arousal. They broke apart abruptly and stared at each other, breathing shallowly. Then, with the smallest of movements, they turned toward the door and were suddenly in Morgana's chambers.

As they whipped through her door, it slammed shut behind them, carried by the gust their travel created. Eyes locked, Morgana advanced, and Aasim retreated until they were standing at the edge of her bed. Aasim slowly unlaced Morgana's jerkin, kissing her, while she drew her knees up one at a time to remove her boots. When Aasim had pulled the laces free of the last holes, Morgana shrugged out of the jerkin and let it fall to the floor. In the brief pause that followed, she smirked up at Aasim.

He smiled back; then, their arms wrapped tightly around each other, they fell back onto the bed.

In the same moment, there was a loud crash. Morgana and Aasim broke apart abruptly, looking down to see if it was the bed that had broken. But the crashes continued, and they quickly realized it was coming from outside the room. Morgana jumped off the bed and quickly threw on a shirt.

Seconds later, the door crashed open.

"What in the hell is—" Morgana began angrily.

The words died in her throat when she saw who was standing in the door. The giant grey wolf hardly seemed to fit in the doorway. Her gold eyes were fixed on Morgana, her lip curled and teeth bared. The hair on her back was raised, and her ears were laid flat against her head. Morgana stared, eyes wide, and slowly sank to the floor. Aasim had backed up to her headboard, looking terrified himself. They had no creatures like this in Raeha. There were only three creatures like this left in the whole world.

"Please—" Morgana begged.

Her words were cut off by a growl, and the wolf advanced two steps.

You will come now, she said.

She growled again and the room spun.

Olivia sat on a tree stump, staring in disbelief at the massive fox that sat opposite her. It was jet black, and as big as a wolf. Olivia could only imagine how big the wolf must be in comparison—like a horse, a large horse, or bigger. Like a bear.

History is coming alive around me, she thought, feeling slightly faint. Many in the North regarded her as a seer, which she had tolerated; reading runes was a far cry from actually seeing the future, though—one of the myriad distinctions that escaped even her knowledgeable northerners. Now, she felt that she could never again purport to make even the smallest of prophecies. She was an utter failure as an oracle. Otherwise, she would have seen this coming.

Aradia lay on the ground not far off, trailing her fingers through a patch of wildflowers. She seemed peaceful, at least. When she'd been brought by the gigantic tiger curled up behind her, she'd immediately fallen to her knees and kissed the ground. Olivia knew that Aradia must have been reassured to be on living soil again, and she seemed to have forgotten all else for the time being.

Perhaps she is the wise one here, Olivia thought. *Guessing is certainly not giving me any comfort.*

When Olivia left her son in Olsrec, her intention had been to go first to Morgana, and then Aradia, and convince them to go east with her. Kanika's message from Thiymen had concerned her, and the appearance of hounds in her forest had frightened her. Olivia felt certain that Fiona was in trouble she could not handle alone. Their responsibility to help her came from every possible angle. They were sisters, they were partners, they were friends. They had a familial obligation and a political duty.

They had already put off seeing each other for far too long. They could communicate easily enough through magic, but the four sisters rarely traveled. There was often just too much to do at home, but even that was not a justification, with many able-bodied witches at each sister's command. They had all just become so wrapped up in their own worlds that they'd forgotten each other, and the country, as the country had forgotten them.

Oh, my son. I gave you an impossible task. Desmond had made many contacts around Arido in his years of traveling, but his words were only words as long as the Kavanaghs remained locked up behind their remote castle doors. And to have no witches living in the capital! It was no wonder the nobles sought to change the order of things. The current order no longer made sense to them. Olivia wondered if perhaps they were right.

Her reflections were interrupted by a rush of wind. She raised her arms to protect her face. When the wind died down, she saw before her Morgana and the Great Wolf herself. She was indeed massive, and Olivia felt her breath catch in her throat.

"Gods," she said, unbidden in her amazement.

And so they were. Before her were the shifter gods: the wolf Lisyne, the fox Seryne, and the tiger Tirosyne. They really did seem like gods to her in that moment, huge and rippling with power.

But being a witch, Olivia knew the truth. The shifter gods were not gods at all, they were shapeshifters; the last three remaining members of a powerful magical race. The shapeshifters were creatures born completely of magic, springing forth from nature fully grown. They lived long and were born rarely, and before history began, there were dozens of them in the world. They changed forms at will and traveled the wilderness.

When the humans came, the shapeshifters learned the human shape and human ways, and sometimes traveled about with them. The shapeshifters commanded magic at will, and it was this that made the humans call them gods. The three who spent the most time among humans were the three who remained on the altars in the temples, and the three who stood before her now.

Before long, magic came to the humans too, and Lisyne the wolf gathered them up and taught them how to wield it. It was Lisyne who had created the clans and given the witches their purposes.

But that time of peace ended. In her desire to have powerful daughters, Olivia's grandmother Lirona had pursued a shapeshifter named Abram. Her belief was that the child of a shapeshifter would be stronger than the child of a human. Abram rejected her, though, because shapeshifters did not reproduce sexually and he did not understand what she wanted. Lirona was by all accounts too proud, and she became enraged. The witches far outnumbered the shapeshifters by then, so Lirona led them into a battle which history had forgotten. All the shapeshifters were killed except Lisyne, Seryne and Tirosyne, and Lirona went on to found the country of Arido.

All this was taught to young witches when they began their training. They were all led to believe that those shapeshifters who survived went into hiding or eventually died, since they hadn't been heard from in over one thousand years—as far as most were concerned. Olivia watched the wolf stalk around the glen, slowly shrinking, and recalled the night Lisyne had visited her all those years ago. But those few hours were no clearer in Olivia's memory than a dream she might have once had.

When she'd seen those hunters on the floor of her hall, she'd wondered at first if they were a message from Lisyne, one of her odd gifts. Would the wolf be offended to know Olivia thought her given to such displays? *Doubtful.*

Lisyne stretched, groaned, and began to change. Her hair retracted, bones rearranged. The whole process was grotesque and fascinating, and Olivia couldn't help but stare. Despite the complexities of the magic at work, the transformation was very brief and took no more than a few seconds. As Lisyne was changing, Olivia observed currents of hot air surrounding her and wondered at their purpose. It became apparent when the change was complete and the heated air became clothing which fitted itself to Lisyne's body.

The Great Wolf stood now in her favored female human form, which had been reproduced hundreds of times over in temples all over Arido. She was tall and muscled, with short, spiky grey hair the color of her fur. Her eyes remained gold and almond shaped. Her face was clear and bright like the edge of a sword, and showed only a hint of wear despite the fact that Lisyne was over four thousand years old.

She turned and looked down at Aradia, who was still lying on the ground, and gestured toward where Olivia sat. Both Aradia and Morgana moved over to their sister, and Olivia took their hands as they approached. Lisyne walked toward them and stood with her arms crossed, staring at them with stern eyes.

"Fiona is dead," she accused.

The words knocked the air out of Olivia's chest like a physical blow, and she gasped for breath. Aradia cried out and covered her mouth with her hands. Morgana punched and splintered a fallen log.

One sister dead.

"I'm pleased that you all seem so upset," Lisyne sneered at them. "It's almost as if you had no inkling of Fiona's situation."

"We didn't, Lisyne, please—" Aradia began.

"Liar!" growled Lisyne. "Remind them, Olivia."

"The record. We received a copy of the record made when Fiona re-sealed the gate," Olivia said quietly.

"When?" Lisyne prompted.

"Two days ago," Olivia said.

"And what was on the bottom of the record?" Lisyne asked.

"A . . . a message from Fiona's record-keeper." Her voice trembled. "Lisyne, please, I was on my way to Morgana and Aradia when Seryne—"

"I know, you fool!" Lisyne shouted. "It was about time! But it was too little, too late, Olivia. All of you."

She came forward and looked each sister in the eye in turn, mere inches from their faces. The Kavanagh sisters were powerful witches, but they each quailed before Lisyne. There was nothing else they could do—she was the power of nature itself, five times their age and five times their strength.

"Guarding the barrier between the world of life and the world under the mountain was the single most important charge I gave to the witches when I trained the first of your kind," Lisyne said. "But Lirona forgot—no, I cannot say she forgot, because she never knew. I told her of the thing that we bound under the mountain, but it is difficult to understand what you have not seen. Fiona . . . Fiona understood."

She fell into silence and looked into the woods, lost in thought and reverie.

"What is it, Lisyne? The thing under the mountain?" Morgana asked.

Lisyne's gaze snapped back and she stared at Morgana.

"It is the opposite of nature. It is death. It is chaos. It is antithetical to our existence," Lisyne said. "My people trapped it under the mountain when I was young, in a time almost beyond memory. My greatest fear has always been that it will escape, with so few of us left to bind it again. Fiona feared this too. I had hoped that she would come to you all, and that you would place a new seal together . . ."

She trailed off again, but only briefly, and then turned to look at the sisters again. She seemed to grow as she glared down at them. "But you ignored her, you ignored your charge, and it is because of you that she is dead!"

The sisters cowered, but Morgana set her jaw and stood up.

"Lisyne, it's not like Fiona was the only one who was struggling! We've all had disasters to deal with—" she said.

"Oh, I know! I've been watching." Lisyne grew, towering over them. Her nails began to elongate into claws. Behind her, Tirosyne and Seryne stood and growled. "But you are all fools!" she continued. "What do you think the source of your problems was? The oceans, the blights, the storms, the hounds? Idiots. They came from the only place evil has ever come, that festering pit of darkness into which we threw the destroyer! It is the earth's greatest malady!"

"How were we to have known?" Aradia cried.

Lisyne shrank back down to her customary size, which was somehow more menacing than the giant version of her that had just been bearing down on them. She walked over and crouched in front of Aradia.

"When was the last time you saw or spoke to Fiona?" Lisyne asked, almost sweetly.

Olivia remembered calling Fiona when the hounds appeared in her forest. Her skin and hair had been completely white, her lips stained black, her eyes dark. Her face had been hollow and lined. She had looked dead, and Olivia remembered the pang of guilt she'd felt. It had been the first time she'd seen Fiona in twenty-five years, since Desmond was born. That was the last time all the sisters were together.

"Lisyne, please," Aradia begged, weeping.

Lisyne seized Aradia by the jaw and pulled her forward.

"That's how you would have known," Lisyne whispered. "By communicating with your baby sister."

She released Aradia, who fell back against the stump, whimpering. Olivia reached down and rubbed her sister's shoulder.

"What can we do now, Lisyne?" Olivia asked.

Lisyne did not look at her immediately, her amber eyes fixed on some point through the trees, her nostrils flaring. But at last, the shapeshifter's shoulders relaxed, and she faced Olivia. Her expression was neutral, though her eyes burned. Olivia inhaled shallowly. Lisyne in the flesh was so changeable, one moment calm, one moment raging, the next manic. Magic drew itself defensively into Olivia's chest, for what if this was the calm before the storm of another strike?

The wolf looked into the distance again. "Now? Now we must go and seal the creature once more," Lisyne said.

CHAPTER TWENTY

ALANINE MARAVILLA DID A BACKBEND OVER THE ARM OF HER chair, staring at the wall upside-down, hair skimming the rug. "What if we put each of the coils into a lavender soak?"

"Alanine. These are coils of dead *magical energy*. We're not going to revive them with a bleeding lavender soak."

"But we've tried everything else!"

"Shut up. I need to think."

Arginine Maravilla sat at her desk and scowled at the book of spells and rituals open before her. Her twin sister was right. They *had* tried everything, but the dormant energy they'd gathered refused to respond to any approach. Crystals and herbs did nothing to infuse it with life. Chants hadn't sparked it, symbols hadn't channeled it. They couldn't even release it from the braided silken scarves in which it was bound. The witches' fury increased with each failure. This energy was their last hope. It was for this that they had been banished from Sitosen.

Their former sisters were in denial, but the twins knew the truth. Like any earthly resource, magic would eventually run out. It was recycled, but with each cycle that energy became less potent, a little more worthless. Though they were punished for it, the twins wanted to do good for their fellow witches. They were the only ones who understood that the power would disappear, and they were the only ones attempting to do anything about it. Olivia herself had been irritatingly complacent, thinking it would be centuries before magic expired, refusing to listen to Arginine and Alanine's explanations.

It was Olivia's fault, all of it. They would never have needed to steal Neria's Shield if she had listened; if she had supported them when they wanted to call a conference of the clans, to put the efforts of all toward solving this problem. By rights, the twins should never have *had* to attempt black magic on their own. They should have been permitted to work with their Thiymen sisters. But now, they were banished, and any witch who so much as spoke to them would suffer the same fate. None would help them now.

"You were my captains," Olivia had said. "You were second only to me in the coven, and I lorded no privileges over you. Why was it not enough?"

In the present, Arginine remembered their last day at Sitosen Castle and muttered, "Because there is no such thing as enough."

"What?" Alanine asked.

Arginine looked up. "Nothing. Have you found that bonding spell yet?"

"You mean the one written in runes we can't read?"

"Yes, that one."

Alanine rolled her eyes at her twin and went back to the bookshelf. What seemed like a breakthrough was looking more and more like a dead end.

In one of their experiments, they'd opened a tear in the curtain between life and death, and they'd discovered that dead energy wasn't dead at all. It was simply energy displaced from the living world. Magical energy wasn't recycled one hundred percent; the percentage that was sloughed off as waste bonded in the underworld and became whole again. In many ways, it was more potent, more concentrated than living magic. Since that discovery, Arginine and Alanine had worked to understand it, traveling back and forth across the barrier, thrilled by the possibilities.

They'd worked as quickly as they could over the past month to gather and store as much energy as possible, binding the magic to cloth which was then tightly braided and twisted. Dozens of these long coils were stored in their tower. All the twins needed to do was find the best way to make the energy workable again. The only problem was that it resisted use. The energy almost seemed to work against them; its presence had a negative effect on the twins' ability to summon magic, canceling out the active or living energy.

Alanine was anxious. They could be arrested by the clans and brought in front of the jury before their research was complete. It was only a matter of time before the Thiymen Guard noticed their tears; books were a poor substitute for the real training given to the witches of the Black Clan in matters of warding and sealing. Without something conclusive to show the clans, their punishment would be much more severe this time around.

The sisters argued often about their position. To leave Del would appear suspicious, but going into hiding would give them more time to complete their experiments and hopefully furnish them with the evidence which would justify their actions to the clans. Arginine, however, no longer thought a successful proof would be enough to restore their station and solve the energy problem. The Kavanaghs would continue resisting the truth of finite magic, as they had initially, until it was too late.

The only way to save Arido was to destroy the Kavanagh sisters. The extra power in the coils would give the twins the strength to defeat the four most powerful witches in the country . . . if they could only use it.

"This would be so much easier if we could draw the energy out of the coils," Arginine said.

"I think the cloth is the only thing keeping it stable on this plane," Alanine replied. "It's not supposed to be here."

"Stabilizers. Yes. Of course." Arginine flipped through her book to a different section.

"Arginine—"

Arginine ignored her sister. "Something to ground it, keep it from wheeling free. Aha!"

Alanine looked over Arginine's shoulder and grimaced. "That's never going to work."

"Of course it will. Besides, it's the one thing we haven't tried yet."

"But the dragon has to be willing. We can't force it to use its magic."

"Look, Alanine, it's simple." She pointed to the book. "The dragon absorbs the energy and then releases it again, pure and ready to use, back into the world. A living refinery for dead magic."

Alanine raised her eyebrows. "If it's really that simple, why can't we do it ourselves?"

Arginine scowled. "Because we don't have magical fire in our bowels." She jabbed her finger onto the page. "This is dead magic, Alanine. Dragons are magical vultures. They can eat the dead magic. They digest it, clean it up. If they choose to, they can expel the living magic. It's like they vomit it up. And then it's out in the world and good to use. All we have to do is bind it up again as it's spat out."

Alanine crossed her arms. "You're forgetting two important things, Arginine. First, the Purvaja dragons aren't *true* dragons, so we don't even know if they have this ability. Second, we can't just ask them to help us. The Dragon Queen keeps abreast of clan news. She's sure to know who we are. Never mind their rabid loyalty to Fiona. She'd want to get approval for the experiment, and then we'd be finished."

Arginine frowned. She paced around her desk, winding her long blonde hair around her fist. "What if we offered to break the curse?"

"Petra's curse?"

"Yes! We could free them. Make it so they don't have to be dragons."

"What if they *want* to remain dragons? Do the words 'rabid loyalty' mean nothing to you?"

"It was just a thought, Alanine," Arginine snapped. "Let's go to the Vale. I'm tired of staring at these useless books."

Alanine had no argument on that count. The twins strapped on their traveling belts and drew spells of invisibility around themselves, as they always did when moving through the city. There were hordes of people in the streets, which never happened in the First Neighborhood, and only on festival days in the Second. The sisters grasped hands, and together they poured magic into their legs, then leapt onto the rooftops. Unseen, they jumped from roof to roof all the way out of the city, toward the dark green swath of forest to the east.

Empress jumped down from the fountain and scurried along back to the palace. The people in the plaza watched her go, their faces tight and drawn with apprehension. Empress was so sincere and gentle and pretty, and they wanted to believe her. They wanted to know that their loved ones wouldn't suffer the consciousness of being buried in tiny spaces. This wasn't how things were supposed to happen, and everyone was scared. But Empress seemed so sure.

A large-bellied man with a tangled grey beard scowled as he tromped around the plaza. He didn't have any dead to concern himself with, but that didn't stop him from carving out a stake for himself in the conversation. He was not a very politically savvy man, and he knew jack-all about the girl-child who was their empress now. But he'd heard someone at some Third Neighborhood tavern say witches were ruining the country and undermining all of Arido's core values. He wasn't sure what those values were, exactly, but now seemed like a good time to bring up how the witches were to blame.

"This is all the witches' fault," he said gruffly to the nearest person. "I wager they be watching us now in their scry-glasses, laughin' at how scared we are."

The woman shrank away from his voice—and his smell—looking at him warily and raising an arm in a half-formed gesture of defense.

"You don't know that," she said. "Empress said they're missing."

"So?"

"Could be they're hurt."

"Bah! They're *witches*, nothing can hurt them!"

"You'd be surprised," said another voice.

The arguers turned in the direction of the words and immediately dipped their heads when they saw who it was. The woman who addressed them was extremely petite, with white skin and long blonde hair bound up in a multitude of messy braids wound around her head. She wore breeches, tunic, and jerkin, and stood with her feet spread wide and her hands on her hips. Her dark brown eyes caught the light and gave her a quick, clever look. Behind her was a loosely arranged column of similarly-dressed men and women.

"Ho, Bridget," said the large-bellied man.

"Ho, Bridget," people murmured all around them.

Bridget waved their address away and walked right up to the big-bearded man who'd started the argument.

"Listen here, Groff," she said in his ear. "Forget about them witches for now. They don't matter. Whatever's going on, they ain't here. But we are, and the corpses are, and

Empress has given us instructions. You'd all do best to follow those instructions, you hear?" She gestured to the group of men and women she'd brought with her. "And we here're going to make sure everythin' run smooth. Now carry on. Bring your dead. We'll carry them into the green."

People nodded and went back to their dead. Bridget pointed to her tall, sandy-haired second-in-command and waved him closer.

"Aye, Bridget?" he asked.

"Orran. You know what to do," she said. She seized his wrist and looked him in the eye. "Make sure they be *careful*. They'll be right under the guardsmen's noses."

He grinned. "Course they'll be careful. You don't think they could bear disappointing you, do you?"

She smirked back and shoved him off. Still laughing, he gathered their thieves and took them to the entrance to the palace green, where they handily unburdened the mourners of their corpses and the corpses of their burial gems. Bridget hung back at the plaza entrance, chewing on a piece of jerky. People from all walks of life, dead people with treasures they didn't need, everyone too preoccupied to notice a few small children—it was a pickpocket's dream, something to cheer them up. The adults would take the corpses, the kids would get the mourners, and the Thieves' Guild of Del would have themselves a feast that night.

But she had other work to do.

She slipped away from the square and down one of the side roads, ducking and weaving through the crowd. The old prison tower loomed over the buildings surrounding it, its circular, grey stone form contrasting the rectangular homes with their painted facades. The tower was set back from the street, as if to hide itself. A short path provided access. It was private, intimidating, and long forgotten. The thief queen doubted that Arginine and Alanine's neighbors even realized they were there, which was so much the better for them; it wasn't like First Families to suffer outsiders, even if they were witches.

If you're arrogant enough, ain't nothing scares you, Bridget thought. She crouched and ran down the path. The tower had windows only on the first floor, and those were too high and too small to afford much view of the outside. This made it easy to sneak all the way to the door, but she was still wary. One thing she'd learned being a thief: humility could save your life. The moment you overestimated your abilities was the moment you got caught.

She stopped just short of the tower wall and stood still for a moment. She had not been a good witch, though perhaps starting at such a young age had skewed her understanding of her own power. She'd shown signs of power almost from the womb, and as the magicked child of a witch, she had been kept, reared in Sitosen Castle with high expectations on her. She officially claimed her gender early and started her training at a mere three years old, in a class separate from the nine-year-old human-born witches. But those sparks of magic in baby Bridget had proven to be almost all she'd get. Bridget had lagged behind her classmates from the beginning and felt restricted by the rigorous schedule of the Castle. She ran away at six years old and made her way south, but not alone. Her mother, Tesla, had followed her in secret. Tesla made sure she arrived in the capital safely, saw her to people who would take care of her, and left a few spellbooks for her to use when she was older.

One of the things Bridget had learned from those books was how to spot a ward—and get past it. She cupped her hands around her eyes to block out the summer sun and peered at the wall. Magic was visible as light, and it was only the extremely talented witch who could hide that light completely. She squinted, and then she saw it: the tell-tale shimmer of a magic alarm line.

Not many people in Del used such magical alarms, but the ones who did were always the wealthiest and the greediest, the only ones obsessed enough with their gold to brave the witches. There was something familiar about the Maravillas' ward; they'd likely been providing security services to Dellian citizens since their exile. Lucky for Bridget. It would make getting through much easier.

She closed her eyes and held her palms just in front of the ward, then chanted softly. The best way to get through a ward was to make yourself part of it, so she duplicated the parameters of the spell and surrounded her body with them. The ward was simpler than she expected, relatively void of the traps typically employed. The Maravillas didn't expect magical company, it seemed. But the ward was programmed to recognize certain individuals, including none other than Lady Evadine Malise. Bridget raised an eyebrow and filed that away for later exploitation.

Once her ward-suit was finished, she moved carefully up the front stairs. There were no additional spells on the door, another surprise. There were some lock spells that would expire when the caster died—did that mean the twins were dead? It seemed unlikely. Thiymen would have known, and there would have been no reason to suspect the twins of damaging the curtain between worlds. Once a living thing was dead, it could not come back on its own. It had to be brought . . . or sent. Had something sent the twins back?

Bridget shook her head. Her job was not to speculate. She was not a witch any longer. She was just helping her old friend Desmond.

She opened the door and shut it carefully behind her. No explosions; that was a good sign. She kept her ward-suit up, just in case, and surveyed the room—a common area by the look of it, with lounges and tables, a few books scattered about. Stairs going down on the far side of the room, probably down to the kitchen and stores. Stairs immediately to the right of the entranceway, going up. Bridget went up.

The next floor was a bedroom, lined with bookshelves. Two desks also stood in the center, covered with more books, papers, and magical instruments.

"Definitely witches living here, then," Bridget said. She glanced at the books open on one of the desks. It looked more like a journal than a proper book. The lines were uneven, sloping, and the writing varied in size and slant. The pages were yellowed and wrinkled. She couldn't read the words, though whether that was because it was another language or merely poor penmanship, she couldn't tell. Probably both.

A horn blew outside. The sound was muffled by the thick stone walls, but Bridget felt it vibrate in her ears through the ward-suit. That was interesting. It seemed to be a recognized sound, an acceptable one.

Then someone knocked on the door.

Bridget cursed and dove under the bed. Thank Lisyne for ornate bed skirts.

The twins went to their usual clearing in the Orchid Vale and prepared in their usual way; but when they opened the tear to the underworld, something unusual happened.

"Look at this, Alanine," Arginine said.

Her sister got up from the stump where she usually sat and waited. There was a brighter purple light than usual playing over the edges. It jumped back and forth across the opposite sides of the rip, almost as if it was forming some kind of netting over the opening. Arginine stuck her hand through the tear experimentally. She could still pass, but she winced and pulled her hand back.

"It's like little jolts of hot energy," she said. "Fiona's put some kind of new seal on it."

The sisters looked each other in the eye, debating through a series of squints and eyebrow raises whether they should continue their attempt that morning or wait for the seal's energy to die down. A rumble coming from the other side of the rip distracted them. They leaned down. Through the tear, they could see what appeared to be swirling black smoke. As it moved, they caught glimpses of a half-formed face, winking at them from the blackness.

"You are the twins," the thing said. "You are difficult to tell apart, even down to your souls."

The sisters exchanged glances again. They could feel the energy the thing put off raising goosebumps on their limbs and setting their hair on end. They would have to be careful in speaking with it.

"You know us," Alanine said. "Should we not also know you?"

"In time," it said. "I bring you useful tidings."

"Oh?" Arginine raised an eyebrow. Alanine frowned at her harsh tone, but the thing in the underworld only made a high rumbling that sounded like laughter.

"Oh yes," it trilled. "Would you like to hear my news?"

The smoke rolled over onto itself. Arginine got the distinct impression of a fat, diabolical cat dangling cheese in front of a mouse.

"Yes, by all means tell us," she said.

"Then I shall. Fiona is dead!" it replied in a deep, satisfied boom.

Arginine's eyes widened, and she turned to find Alanine looking at her with the same expression. They knew Fiona was old, but her dying was the last thing they had expected. How did this affect their plans? At first, it seemed like a blessing—but was it really? Arginine wasn't so sure. Far from removing an obstacle, it was more likely to alert the other Kavanaghs to the problems Fiona had been dealing with; problems caused by the twins. But, on the other hand—

"The dragons!" Alanine whispered.

"Yes!" Arginine said.

The greatest challenge to enlisting the help of a dragon was the tribe's unswerving loyalty to Fiona. With Fiona gone, their allegiance was ripe for the taking.

The sisters whirled away from the tear and pulled their sails out of the small bags on their belts. They held the fabric out before them and spoke the incantation of flight. They launched into the air, bursting through the trees, and pointed their hands toward the east.

In the clearing below, the tear remained open. Small tendrils of smoke tested the edges.

Arginine and Alanine blasted through the sky. They lay flat on their stomachs, both hands wrapped around one end of their sail and held out in front of them. The yellow fabric of the silk sails fluttered open beneath them. Flying at such speed was painful and took more energy than usual, but they had to reach the East soon or risk losing the opportunity that had been presented to them. They didn't speak—it was impossible to be heard while in flight—but each was fairly sure of the other's thoughts.

The sun arced away from them as they traveled, and it was high in the sky behind them when they approached the Zaide Mountains. They changed course and headed northeast. The Caves of Purvaja were a gaping black hole in the side of the mountains, wide enough for four fully grown dragons to take off in unison and tall enough for them to stand at their full height.

The Maravilla twins pointed their hands at the cave opening. Then, something flashed off to their right. They glanced quickly in that direction, but it was gone. There was another flash to the left; one below; one above. They paused in their flight and hovered there, their sails billowing under them. The moment they did, their ears were assaulted by high keening wails and deep bellowing moans. They winced against the sounds echoing off the rock face.

It was the dragons, they realized. The dragons were out in force, circling and diving at breakneck speeds, hurtling to the ground and then soaring up into the sky again. Some of them were simply flying in shaky circles, hitting rocks and trees jutting up from the mountainside, bursting right through the low clouds. It was as if they weren't paying attention at all to where they were going.

"They're in mourning!" Arginine shouted.

She frowned and glared down at the dragons, who had not noticed them at all. Their grief was making them absolutely worthless. The dragons were clearly unaware of their surroundings, half of them flying with their eyes closed, bumping into each other and crashing into the landscape. The brutes weren't in their right minds, and would do Arginine and Alanine absolutely no good.

The twins felt hot air blown on them from behind. They turned slowly and saw a black dragon of middling size behind them, beating its wings slowly to stay even with them. It had black eyes as well as black scales, and in the sunlight, its whole body appeared to be winking at them. It made a rumbling noise that sounded like familiar laughter.

"You're the one from the tear," Alanine said.

I am, the dragon said, its voice echoing in their minds.

Arginine glowered at it. "Your news was worthless to us. The dragons are useless in this state."

I never said anything about using the dragons now that Fiona's dead, the false dragon said.

Arginine raised an eyebrow, intrigued. She glanced at Alanine. By the expression on her sister's face, she could tell that the gentler half of their pair was disinclined to trust this . . . thing, whoever or whatever it was. But Alanine had always been more cautious, and it was always Arginine's plans that got them what they wanted. Well, most of the time.

"You have something else in mind?" she asked.

The dragon turned its head to the side to look at them with one black eye, winking in the light. The curve of its jaw almost looked like a smirk.

Follow me, the dragon said. It turned and dove toward the mountains. Arginine looked at her sister. Alanine mouthed the word *no*. Arginine shook her head and dove after the dragon-creature. A moment later, Alanine appeared out of the corner of her eye.

They followed the false dragon to Thiymen Citadel, where a similar scene to the one at the caves was occurring. Everywhere on the battlements, black-clad Thiymen witches ran to and fro, wailing and pulling at their hair and clothes. The grief was palpable. Arginine could see with a glance at Alanine that her sister was moved by it, but to Arginine it represented an opportunity. The dragon looked back at them with its winking eyes, and for a moment, Arginine felt a kindred spirit in it.

Banished yellow witches do not belong, the false dragon said.

Understanding its meaning, Arginine and Alanine each waved a free hand from their heads down toward their toes. As they did, their yellow dresses and sails became black, and their fair hair became even whiter. Now they would blend in with the black-dressed, white-haired Thiymen witches, though Arginine wondered if they would have been noticed even in their brightest yellow gowns under the current circumstances.

They touched down on a balcony, and the dragon changed into a young woman dressed in black, with pale blonde hair like that of the twins. It smirked at them with red lips, lifting a slim white finger to make the signal for silence. The twins nodded; the girl-dragon-creature turned away and set off down the halls of the citadel at an alarming pace. Arginine and Alanine strove not to break out into a full-on run to keep up with the thing they were following.

After several minutes of winding through passages, deeper and deeper into the mountain, the Maravillas were well and thoroughly lost. How the Thiymen witches knew their way amongst so many identical tunnels was beyond them. They kept pace with their guide at all costs, feeling sure that if they lost it, it would not come back for them. Occasionally, it flipped its hair and giggled in its strange way, the blood-red lips the only color in its face besides its solid black eyes.

They arrived finally in a massive cavern. At one end was a thick sheet of black rock that seemed to be separate from the rest of the cavern walls. It was blacker than any black the twins had seen before, and it was buckled and rippled as though it had barely survived an earthquake. There were great slashes and hand prints showing through, and the marks of fingernails scratched at its base. Even from thirty feet back, the twins could feel the pull of the underworld coming from the other side. This, they realized, was the gate—the physical seal placed on the world under the mountain.

The thing in girl's form scurried right up to the wall and turned to look at them, leaning against the black rock with a manic grin on its face.

"I'm so glad you've come!" it said in a high, fair voice. It sounded like strange, atonal music and echoed through the cavern. A chill ran down Arginine's spine. Alanine paled beside her.

"Be not afraid. I have brought you here because we can help each other," the thing said. "I will tell you the secret of the energy in the underworld, and how you can harness it. I will also help you overthrow these Kavanagh sisters you so despise."

"And what must we do for you?" Alanine asked quietly.

The thing smiled sweetly at her and spread its arms wide.

"Open the gate," it said.

"What?" Arginine asked. They barely knew how to open tears; to open the gate itself was surely beyond them.

"Oh, it's not as difficult as all that. Why do you think it's so closely guarded? Anyone could open it!" the thing trilled. "All you must do is make a tear. Just like the dozens upon dozens you've already made."

"Just a tear?" Alanine asked.

"Yes. Only it must be close to the wall. I will take care of the rest," it said. "Come close, now."

Arginine and Alanine looked at each other. Again, Alanine pleaded silently for Arginine to say no, but again Arginine shook her head. Yes, this thing was obviously strange, but it had not yet led them astray. It was offering to help them with their goals, and in their position, Arginine thought it would be foolish to turn down such an offer, especially now that the dragons were of no use to them. Their time had run out, and this was their best option.

Arginine walked forward, closer to the wall. After a moment, Alanine followed her. It was difficult to approach. The tugging from the other side felt like claws hooking into their skin, making long, dragging scratches that burned.

But they persevered, and finally stopped a few feet from where the girl-creature was leaning against the gate.

It eyed them hungrily. "Good. That's it. Now, open the tear."

Arginine raised her left hand, and Alanine her right, and together, they focused their energy on a single spot in front of them, marked by their index fingers. Purplish light crackled at their fingertips and they drew a line in the air toward each other, their fingers meeting between them. Where their fingers passed, the purple light separated and exposed the world under the mountain. The tear expanded rapidly, getting wider than any they'd made before. It seemed to be barely in control of itself, and when they connected each end, and the tear was completely open, Arginine and Alanine jumped away.

Behind the tear, the girl-thing seemed to have fused into the black rock that made up the gate. It struggled and groaned and pulled against the imprisonment. Its girlish voice descended into the rumbling tone they'd heard from the first meeting as it strained and made all kinds of unearthly noises.

At the edges of the tear, the purple light flashed; with each flash, there was a corresponding groan in the rock. The creature's roaring got louder as the flashing increased. Arginine and Alanine inched backward warily. Arginine avoided meeting Alanine's eyes. She was sure there would be accusation there.

The purple light cracked like lightning, illuminating the entire cavern. Rock slid on rock with a horrible screeching. The twins blinked furiously through the spots in their eyes. A giant crack split the gate, running diagonally up from where the creature still struggled. It shifted ever so slightly, and larger and larger chunks of rock came falling down from the severance line. They crashed to the floor and shattered, then dissolved into the black smoke that was always visible through the tears.

There was another blast of purple lightning. A second fracture appeared in the black rock, and the entire gate began to tremble. The creature's roaring mixed with the wind rushing around and around the cavern. It pulled insistently at the twins' hair and clothes. They sank to their knees and huddled next to each other as the smoke surrounded them.

With a final, massive boom, the gate to the underworld came tumbling down. The rock turned to black smoke as it fell and was enveloped by the swirling wind racing through the cavern. Arginine and Alanine lifted their heads slightly, squinting to see through the whirlwind. The tear they'd made was pulsing with purple light and something else, something that made their ears ring but made no noise. The rip was expanding, too, becoming large enough to join into the gaping hole left by the collapsed gate. The girl-thing seemed to have disappeared.

Disoriented, the witches tried to stand, supporting each other as well as they could with their mutually shaky limbs. They wrapped scarves over their noses and mouths to avoid inhaling the heavy smoke. The wind was still strong enough to make walking difficult, but they gripped hands tightly and turned toward the exit, pushing against the strong currents of air that held them back.

"My friends, where are you going?" roared the huge, disembodied voice of the creature.

Arginine and Alanine stopped and braced themselves as they looked around. All they could see was smoke; no girl, no dragon, nothing.

"You cannot leave. Remember, I promised to help you," the thing said.

The gate pulsed one more time; the wind died down, and the glowing purple edges dimmed. The next instant, light exploded and the wind rushed them all at once. Arginine and Alanine were blown over and dragged the length of the cavern; before they hit the far wall, the wind banked and carried them back to where the gate had once been. It dumped them to the ground and they landed on hands and knees, coughing and gasping violently as they attempted to regain their breath.

They looked up. A well-dressed and delicately featured young man approached them out of the roiling smoke. He wore a silver tunic that went up to his chin and ballooning, cream-colored trousers tucked into knee-high black boots. His jet black hair was gathered into a ponytail at the crown of his head. He smirked down at them with a wicked twinkle in his black eyes.

"Arginine," he said. "Alanine. I believe that together, the three of us can do great things in this modern world."

Alanine gripped her throat and heaved, her thin frame wracked and convulsing. Arginine coughed and reached for her sister. Her body felt brittle and cold, and she could not seem to get enough air into her lungs. The scarf felt almost too tight around her face. She rubbed Alanine's back haltingly and glared up at the creature, now in the form of a man.

"Who are you?" she demanded raspily. "What do you want?"

"I am the one from under the mountain," the man replied.

He began to laugh hysterically, and as he did, smoke poured from his open mouth. His entire body dissolved into the writhing mass, but Arginine thought she caught a glimpse of those winking, evil eyes.

A moment later, the smoke rushed toward them, and everything went black.

CHAPTER TWENTY-ONE

EVA LOOKED OUT HER WINDOW AND DOWN AT THE ACTIVITY below. Her view overlooked the palace green, and it was usually an idyllic and relaxing sight; the great expanse of unblemished land was covered in grass such a perfect shade of green that it made one wonder how art could ever hope to surpass nature. And now, it was also covered with scurrying human forms digging half-hearted pits into which empty sacks of blood and bone would be unceremoniously dumped. The priests were certainly about, the sun gleaming off their shaved and oiled heads, doing what they could; but there was no avoiding the ugliness of what was happening below.

At last, *at last*, Eva had something undeniable to use against Thiymen clan—blatant dereliction of duty!—and her hands were tied. She clenched those hands into fists. Any moment now, she expected to see black sails whipping toward them across the sky, carrying hordes of ghostly witches come to steal their souls . . . but she kept her silence. To rail against Thiymen now would only upset Guerline's temporary peace, and she couldn't make such a move. Not when all her efforts were to get Guerline as far away from the dangers of magic as she could.

Half of the city's guards had been recruited to dig individual graves for the dozens upon dozens of recently deceased, Thiymen-neglected citizens of Del. Many of the dearly departed's family members assisted, but the work was tedious and time-consuming. The sun blazed through the afternoon sky, roasting the mess below.

Though the enchantments on the stone protected her from the worst of it, Eva could feel the heat in the air. It did nothing to soothe her clammy skin, nor unknot the cold twist of fear in her stomach. It was happening—it was really happening. Soon there would be no way to stop the fall of the Kavanaghs.

Alcander had always been loose of tongue when he was around her, perhaps out of a desire to impress her with his maneuvering. She still remembered the night he'd told her about his discovery of the twin witches hiding in Del, banished from their clan, and how they too despised the Kavanaghs. Those witches, he'd slurred, provided him the final piece of his plan to revolutionize the empire. He would knock the witch clans down a peg by arresting the Kavanaghs and possibly executing them for treason and insubordination, then prevent the witches from selecting new leaders from within their own ranks. It was Alcander's wish to place a human in the position of Lord Paramount for each region, to rule over the witch clans as well as the human towns.

Yet he knew that the witches would not be intimidated merely by legal action. They were too single-mindedly loyal to their leaders for that. The part of his plan that included preventing the witch clans from choosing new leaders, or from seeking vengeance for the Kavanagh sisters, was the truly difficult part. To use military force would be impossible, since the Adenen witches *were* the entire standing army and special forces. There was little enough Alcander could have offered the witches in the way of bribes because of their magical skill, and to try and buy them all off with gold would have bankrupted the empire. Threats were worthless because he had no teeth to bite them with if they didn't listen to his barking. But whatever action he took needed to be swift and irrefutable, because Alcander had hated to think of what would happen if all the witches in the country came raging with their magic on the capital.

After weeks of this contemplation, Alcander had met the Maravilla twins, Arginine and Alanine. They'd offered him the decisive power he needed. It was their own plan to overthrow the Kavanagh sisters, and Alcander had had no qualms about leaving that part of the plan to them. All he'd needed to do was continue his campaign to turn the people against the Kavanaghs.

Evadine stared out her window at the corpses being laid in the earth. She had continued to visit the twins after Alcander's death, claiming, as she had with the councilors, to be continuing the prince's plans. Where Alcander had been jealous of magic, though, Eva truly feared it, and witches who had turned their backs on the laws of the clans were terrifying to her. Still . . . she'd thought it better to have one hand in the snake pit than to not see the snakes at all.

She often wished that she could divulge everything to Guerline; the past two months had been an exercise in self-control. There were so many secrets, her own as well as the ones she'd inherited from Alcander. The lies were like so many juggling knives, and the longer she tossed them, the faster they spun, the closer they came to slicing her flesh. She had so, so delicately sought to sway Alcander's allies toward less aggressive methods, but now? Something had begun, something that was, despite all her efforts, beyond her knowledge.

She tried to recall all the comments from that morning's handling of the Thiymen situation. Desmond Kavanagh was the son of Sitosen; one would think that he'd be able to contact his relations, but for some reason, he had not been able to. What had Guerline asked him? Whether it had something to do with damage to a gate? Yes, that's right—the gate to the underworld.

Eva frowned. She wondered if that had anything to do with the Maravillas' plans to get rid of the Kavanaghs, and if so, what it meant for those plans. Was this a sign of their success? Was it intentional? Or was it a sign of their failure? Eva resolved to find out. She put on her purple silk overdress and summoned her herald.

Due to the crowd, she exited the palace gates surrounded by twelve guards instead of her usual six. The extra protection, however, did absolutely nothing to protect her from the stench of the square. The rankest parts of the city were confined to the Third and Fourth Neighborhoods and rarely contaminated the center, where the palace and noble houses were situated in a wide and carefully monitored green idyll separate from the rest of the city. But after the perfumed air of the palace, even the First Neighborhood seemed squalid.

The filth of the edges had come to the center, following on the heels of both the living and the dead. Some of the mourners were respectable enough, but the ones arriving now were those who came from the Fourth Neighborhood, and they came in droves. The poor died far more frequently than the rich, and though Eva had always known it, this was the first time she had really seen it demonstrated with such . . . poignancy. The family and friends of the recently—and some not-so-recently—deceased flooded into the square, carrying their loved ones' corpses high above the press of the crowd. The guards flagged them in different directions, to different sections of Guerline's makeshift graveyard, while others went through the crowd and recruited the able-bodied who weren't supporting corpses for grave digging.

There were so many of them that Evadine actually began to doubt the extensive palace green would accommodate them all. And what about afterward? Had Guerline considered that yet? Was she intending to leave all these rotting carcasses in these shallow graves, or would she demand they be relocated to their originally planned places of final rest? The animals would get at them before too long if they stayed in these graves, which were more mounds than pits.

Eva held an absolutely pointless handkerchief over her mouth and nose to try and block the stench of putrefaction, bit her lower lip to keep from gagging, and waved her front men on impatiently. They set off, but were quickly blocked by the mass of bodies. Evadine wished the guardsmen had carried their shields like she'd asked. It would have made it so much easier to get through everyone.

She shot her herald a pointed look, and he began to sound his horn with loud, short, insistent blasts. The people in the square looked around and realized that a noblewoman was trying to get through. Most didn't react, still stunned by their grief and anxiety, but others tried to shift and make room for them to pass. The effect was disgustingly minimal. There were simply too many bodies in the square. Eva's frown deepened, and she gestured her front men forward again. This was going to take a long time.

The group had taken maybe another step when something brushed Evadine's head. She reached up to bat it away and realized that it was the arm of one of the dead men held aloft by his mourners. She shrieked and jumped back. The guard nearest to her drew his sword and quickly severed the offending limb, which fell to the cobblestones with a sickening splatter.

The crowd's reaction was immediate. The dead man's bearers cried out in agony at the ruination of his body and reached down to snatch the arm out of the way. The rest of the people in the square backed away in horror and squeezed protectively around their own darling corpses, as though afraid that Evadine and her guards would simply start going around the square and hacking their dearly departed to pieces. In the rush to get away from Evadine the mad butcher, a wide and spacious path appeared before her and her guards.

"That was extremely effective. Well done, Hamish," she said, smiling at him. Hamish, who was young and relatively new to the palace guard, had been staring in shock at the place where the arm had fallen; at Eva's comment and smile, he turned red and looked at his feet.

She caught a glimpse of the dead man's family as she turned forward again, and her relief at having space to move faltered. What would Lina do in such a situation? Kneel with them, comfort them? She doubted that even Guerline could come up with a way to make the severing of their relative's arm seem all right. Eva looked up into the crowd, determined to ignore them, and froze when she saw Alcander standing just outside her circle of guards, staring at her with black eyes. She closed her eyes and took a deep breath. When she opened her eyes again, he was gone.

"Shall we?" she said to her guards.

The tower in which the Maravilla twins had set up house was a former jail tower, kept close to the palace for trial purposes but otherwise separate. The way was still thick with mourners making their way to the palace, but with Eva's herald announcing their coming, the people made their way to the sides of the street.

The little procession stopped in front of the witches' tower. Evadine knocked on the door and waited, as she usually did, for it to open. It didn't. Eva knocked again, to no avail. She huffed impatiently, and experimentally tried the door handle. To her great surprise, it was unlocked.

"Wait here," she said to her entourage, and she stepped over the threshold, closing the door behind her.

It was dark except for a weak glow at the top of the entrance hall's stairs. The tower only had a handful of windows, and only on the first floor, which was not used for prisoners. Eva put a hand on the wall, lifted her skirts with the other, and slowly went up the stairs. The common area on the first floor was dimly lit by sunlight coming in through the two small windows which looked onto the street. The room looked exactly the same as the last time she'd been in it, nothing out of the ordinary. Eva walked to the center and turned slowly in place, taking everything in. She waited, but still no tall, blonde twins came to meet her.

"Hello?" she called. "Arginine? Alanine?"

No answer. *How strange.* She supposed it was feasible that the twins may be out upon some errand or another, but it had never happened before; that is, the twins had always been home whenever she'd called on them. Witches were notorious for keeping to themselves and their castles—or towers, in this case; especially Sitosen witches, which the Maravilla twins had once been. And how odd, that they should not lock their door, either conventionally or by some kind of magic. Thinking of what might have happened made the hair on Evadine's neck stand on end.

A moment or two more of waiting continued not to yield the twins, so Eva ventured to explore. On all of her previous visits, she had been confined to the common area. The stairs that came up from the entrance continued on to the upper levels of the tower, so Eva went over and mounted them once more. The upstairs was dark, untouched by daylight. After a moment's consideration, Eva went back to the common room. She spotted a candle and reached for it, already looking around for wherever witches might keep flint—did witches even use flint?—but when she closed her hand around the candlestick, the wick burst into flame.

She almost dropped it in her astonishment, but luckily maintained her grip. Eva stared at it in horror, wondering if she had been a witch all this time without realizing it, and set the candle back down on the table. As soon as she did, it went out. A long-standing spell that reacted to her flesh, then. Relieved, she held the candle aloft and went up the stairs to the second floor.

The second floor appeared to be the twins' bedroom. It was huge and round. The entire expanse of wall was lined with floor to ceiling bookshelves. A ring of workstations also made up the outer edge of the room. In the center were two mid-sized four-poster beds and a small sitting area. The bedspreads and rugs were lustrous and richly colored. Evadine nudged the corner of one rug with her toe and wrinkled her nose.

If there was anything of note in the bedroom, it was not recognizable to Eva. There were various instruments on the workstations, but none of them were familiar to her. She couldn't even begin to guess what they were for. The only thing she learned from this second floor of the tower was that the Maravilla twins were almost certainly not at home. She wondered whether they had enacted the first phase of whatever plan they'd hatched. If that first phase involved some kind of attack on Thiymen clan, they, like Alcander, must have believed that the coven of death was the biggest threat to Arido.

Eva went back to the stairs and climbed up to the third floor. As she neared the door—the third floor was the only floor closed off, it seemed, since the other entrances were open to the stairs—she noticed a strange, purplish kind of light. It seemed to pour down the stairs, dissipating three or four from the top into smoke-like wisps. When she was close enough, Eva leaned down cautiously and swept her hand through the hazy light. It felt cool, but otherwise harmless. She examined her hand close to the candle. It appeared to be undamaged by the purple aura, so she proceeded up the stairs and opened the door.

In the room, the purple light was ubiquitous but remained oddly dim. It emanated from the piles and piles of braided and twisted cloth which filled the room. She turned and examined the one nearest to her. It was perhaps two feet in length, made up of multiple thin strands of silk; these were braided, and then those braids were braided, and so on, and then the thick braid was wound and twisted upon itself into a kind of figure-eight knot.

She reached out to touch it. When she did, the hair on her arms stood on end and her breath caught in her throat. She gasped and pulled her hand back. Whatever the coils were, they contained great power—and the room was full of them. This must have been what the twins were working on. They were stockpiling magical energy. But where did it come from? Was it their own power, bound into the silk and tucked away for later use?

Whatever plans the twins had for this stored magic, they had left it unguarded, and Evadine was not the kind of woman who turned away from an opportunity. The coils made her deeply, instinctually unsettled, and were further proof against magic's inherent goodness. She went back down the stairs and out of the tower. When her guards saw her, they began to get back into formation, but Evadine held up her hand to indicate that they wait.

"One of you run back to the palace and bring a covered cart. No, two covered carts, and perhaps some more men if you can find them," she said. "We have some items which we need to transport back to the palace for the empress to inspect."

Hamish bowed quickly and disappeared into the crowd. Evadine pointed to two more guards and her herald.

"You three remain here," she said. "The rest of you, into the tower. I will show you these items, and then I want you to begin moving them down here for loading. Do you all have gloves on? Good."

They followed her back up to the storage room with the coils. The men could obviously feel the power coming from them, and they held back, squinting in the dim purple glow. Evadine glared at them.

"Go on, now, nothing to be scared of. Line up along the stairs and start handing them down. We'll pile them on the landing until the carts get here."

The men quickly moved to follow her orders. Evadine herself went into the twins' bedroom on the second floor. She picked up a book entitled *The History of Arido* and sat herself down on a sofa, leafing through the pages.

Perhaps an hour or more passed before Hamish came into the bedroom. He coughed to get Eva's attention, and she looked up from a rather intriguing section of Aridan history that she had somehow never learned.

"Yes? Is everything loaded?" she asked.

"Aye, Evadine-ami," Hamish said.

"And the carts are well covered?"

"Aye. The coils are quite hidden."

"Excellent," Eva said, snapping the book shut and getting up. "Then back to the palace we go. Hamish, run ahead again and request that Her Majesty meet us at the entrance. She will want to see these immediately."

The lad bowed and left the room. Evadine made to return the book, but thought better of it. She tucked it under her arm instead, exited the tower after Hamish, and signaled the men to pull the carts back to the palace. The return trip through the streets went slower; the carts, being loaded down, were heavy, and it was more difficult for the people still thronging the streets to make way for them. Though the coils were safely hidden from view, their effect on the people surrounding them was clear. The herald didn't need to blow his horn at all to signal their coming; the crowds parted instinctively as they approached. Evadine's understanding was that magic was natural and fundamentally neutral . . . yet whatever magic comprised the coils unnerved people, and they cringed to get away from it.

Guerline, Desmond, and Hamish were standing on the palace steps waiting for them. As the carts pulled up, Guerline descended the rest of the stairs. Evadine walked around to meet her.

"What is it, Eva? What have you found?" Guerline leaned forward, peering at the carts. Desmond frowned as he came down the steps behind her.

Eva pulled back the canvas covering one of the carts, exposing the coils. Guerline's eyes widened. She reached out to touch the nearest coil hesitantly, as Eva had in the Maravillas' tower. She drew her hand back before making contact and turned to Desmond. The tall, golden-hued man came forward and examined the coils closely. His frown deepened.

"Where did you find these?" he asked sharply.

Evadine winced at the accusation in his voice. Desmond Kavanagh had always found favor with Lina, but he and Eva were fundamentally at odds. He was, after all, an arrogant buffoon with little enough of direction or sense. And since his return to Del, he'd been colder toward her than ever, which she couldn't account for. She would have to be careful with what she said around him.

Guerline looked back and forth between them. "What are they, Desmond?"

"Energy coils," he replied. "Witches sometimes use them to set aside the magical power they will need for a large spell at a later date. My mother makes small ones for me occasionally, which I can then use to power simple spells. But these . . ."

He stared at them again and shook his head. Guerline put a hand on his arm and looked at him questioningly. Evadine kept her face neutral, trying to come up with something to say when he inevitably asked once more where the coils had come from. Should she tell the truth? Or some version of the truth? She could explain Alcander's conspiring with the Maravilla twins, but would they believe her?

She met Guerline's eyes and reached for her hand. As her fingers curled around Guerline's, warmth flooded her and Guerline smiled. Yes. Guerline would believe her. Eva glanced over at Desmond, who wore a suspicious glare. He stepped closer to Guerline, pressing against her from behind. Guerline twisted away from him and stepped to the other side of Evadine, facing the carts and taking Eva's other hand. Even as satisfaction settled comfortably in her chest, she guessed from Desmond's hard gaze that he would disbelieve her out of spite.

"What about these, Desmond? They feel . . . dark. Cold," Guerline said.

"This energy is dead," Desmond said gravely.

He reached into his pocket and pulled out something small and white. It was a miniature version of the purple coils. He held it out to them.

"Put your hands over it. Do you feel the difference?" he asked.

Guerline put her hand out, and after a moment she nodded. Evadine remained still. Desmond closed his hand around his coil and stared hard at Evadine.

"This energy has come from the world under the mountain," he said. "Now, you must tell us, Evadine. Where did you find it? Do you know who has gathered it?"

Guerline stepped closer to her and spoke quietly. "Please, Eva. Whoever has made these may be damaging the curtain between the worlds of the living and the dead. They are the ones responsible for the missing Thiymen witches. We must find out who they are."

Eva clenched her jaw. She turned and let go of Guerline's hand, slipping her arms around Guerline's waist instead.

"Let us get inside. I will tell you there." She glanced at Desmond, then back to Guerline. "Only you."

"I think not! Lina, please, let me speak to you first," Desmond said.

She looked at him, then looked at Eva. Guerline's face was neutral, and for a terrifying moment, Eva thought she might allow Desmond's usurpation. But she shook her head and put her hands on Eva's shoulders.

"Eva is my Chief Adviser. I will hear her, and then you, Desmond."

She looked at Desmond again, and Eva could see the slight glare narrowing her eyes.

"Obviously, whatever you need to tell me wasn't worth mentioning in our hours alone yesterday, so I'm sure it can wait a few more minutes," Guerline said.

Desmond opened his mouth, but was prevented from answering as screams rose from the palace green. Men began to appear around the corner of the wall that separated the green from the stone entrance yard, running full tilt. Townspeople raced out the palace gates, the castle staff through the palace doors. The guardsmen followed, some without their weapons or even pieces of their armor. All the while, the screaming in the distance got louder. Underneath the high keening sounds, there grew a low kind of roaring that sent chills down Evadine's spine.

"What is it? What's happening?" Desmond shouted, running forward and seizing the nearest man.

The man fought Desmond's hold, writhing in the northerner's big hands, his eyes wild with fear.

"The dead are coming! The dead are coming!" he screeched, clawing at Desmond's face.

Desmond let him go and the man fell backward, struggling to regain his balance. He twisted around and bolted toward the palace gates. Desmond watched him go, breathing heavily.

"What can he mean?" Guerline asked in a quiet, horrified voice, as though she already knew. "Eva, what can he mean?"

Eva did not need to answer, because, at that moment, the dead came into view.

CHAPTER TWENTY-TWO

THE DEAD FOLLOWED CLOSELY ON THE HEELS OF THE LIVING, moving surprisingly fast for all their stiffness. They were dirty, clearly just broken out of their shallow graves in answer to some unholy call. Some were still fresh, and were distinguishable from the living only by their jerking movements as they attempted to use dysfunctional joints. They stopped only when they fell upon a straggler. Desmond watched in horror as an older man tripped and was seized by two of the walking dead. They were joined by a third, and they set upon tearing the screaming man to pieces. They bit into his flesh, staining themselves with his blood, and pulled him in opposite directions until his bones broke and his flesh tore. The man didn't die right away, though. He continued screaming, eyes bugging, until one of the corpses finally severed his neck while pulling his head back to get at his throat.

Screams rose from the square outside the gate as well, and Desmond's head snapped toward the sound. There was still a steady flow of people into the entrance yard through the open gates. Ripples formed in the crowd as groups pushed this way and that.

"They're out there too," he said, his eyes wide. "There are people still bringing corpses. They must be all over in this section of town."

"Oh gods," Guerline said. "The guards. Where are the guards? They were all out on the green, digging graves!"

Desmond pointed. The retreating guards had formed lines at the edge of the entrance yard and the gate, and were attempting to hold the corpses back. They were failing miserably. Typically fatal blows did nothing to stop the corpses. They continued to press forward unless they were literally hacked limb from limb. The guards were not so fortunate.

"Guerline, Evadine, get back into the palace, now," Desmond said, turning back to the two women.

"But Desmond—" Guerline began.

"Don't argue now, Lina, please. Evadine, take her," he said.

He kissed Guerline on the cheek and turned away, running toward the guards.

"Someone get me a sword!" he shouted as he neared them.

Evadine's man, Hamish or some such, handed him a sword that had been dropped by another guard. Desmond accepted it and swung it experimentally. It was a little light for him, but it would do. He glanced back once to check on Guerline, and was pleased to see Evadine dragging the struggling empress up the palace steps. Evadine sent the door guards down to fight and pushed the doors shut herself. He was grateful. He didn't much care for Evadine, but she was a woman who could do whatever was needed in a given situation, even if it was difficult—even if it meant leaving someone you cared about behind. Guerline was not that sort of woman, and even though he usually liked that about her, it would only put her in danger.

He turned his thoughts away from Guerline. He was incredibly vulnerable, having not the slightest bit of armor. Hoping for inspiration, he looked around. If they attempted to stop the dead by simply dismembering all of them individually, it would take many hours and many lives. They needed some way to knock down several corpses at once. At the very least, they needed to create a barrier to keep them out of the entrance yard. They would still be free to massacre those outside the gates, which pained Desmond greatly, but it would give Desmond and the guardsmen a chance to regroup.

"Josen!" Desmond shouted. "Josen!"

The captain turned back from the fighting and stumbled over to Desmond. He had been bitten in multiple places, including his face. Part of his nose was missing and the hole left by it bled freely. Desmond reached into his pocket for the small white coil and held it up in front of Josen's face. He concentrated hard on the ragged edges of Josen's mangled nose. The bleeding slowed, then stopped. Desmond shoved the spent coil back into his pocket. Josen touched his nose experimentally. It was the merest of heal-ings. There was nothing Desmond could do to replace the nose, but at least he could use the magic his mother bound for him to do some good.

"Aye, Master Kavanagh! Thank you. Gods of the forest, please say that you have a plan," the man said.

"We have to seal off the entrance yard," Desmond said. "Start by closing the gate! Try to push them back and get the gates shut!"

Josen stared at him, his mouth open and his eyes wide.

"But there are still so many people out there," he said.

"I know, Josen, I know. But we won't be of much use to them if we're all dead. We must regroup and strategize," Desmond said.

Josen stared a moment longer, but in the end, his com-passion faltered before his military training. He nodded and made his way back to the front, shouting the orders. The guards gave him the same look he'd given Desmond, then started pulling the living roughly out of the hands of the dead and shoving them into the yard, trying to save as many as possible.

Out in the plaza, Bridget pulled her short sword from her belt and dashed through the crush of bodies, trying to get to the gate where her people were trapped. Her small size made her a difficult target, and she nimbly avoided the flail-ing of the living and the dead alike. In her mind, she cursed whatever magics were being used to reanimate the corpses. She wondered if it meant that Thiymen had come after all.

Were the black witches come to kill them? Wasn't that the tale on the streets?

She needed to find Desmond, tell him that Lady Malise was working with the twins. She wouldn't be surprised if the coils Eva had taken were what woke the dead. There was a strong, evil magic in them. Bridget felt it pulling on her power even now, though they were surely within the palace walls by this point.

"Orran!" she shouted, climbing on top of a large man standing dumbfounded in the plaza. He hardly even seemed to notice her on his back as she scanned the crowd for her second-in-command.

She spotted his tall sandy head before it ducked down, moving briskly away from the gate. Bridget hopped down from her human tower just as he was seized upon by one of the hungry corpses. She ignored his screaming as she too tucked her body down and ran in and out of the crowd.

"Bridget! There you are," Orran said as she approached them.

"How many did we lose?" she asked.

"Five dead, many more injured," he replied.

She glanced back down their strange little line of thieves on their hands and knees. It was difficult to tell who was injured because they were all covered in blood, both from the initial attack and from crawling. Yet it was better that they crawl. The dead were more focused on those who were running or remained standing than those on the ground.

"Good. Get the hell out of here," she said.

"What about you?"

"I've a message to deliver first."

She turned and tried to weave her way toward the palace. The crowd of bodies got thicker and thicker the closer she got to the gate, and she couldn't tell who was dead, who was undead, and who was still alive. She crawled and hacked off legs at the knees to get through until she couldn't even do that. She was close to the palace wall, and she tried to force her way to the top, climbing up the flesh around her. Then a surge came from behind her and she was pushed forward. Her head connected with the wall with a crack, and everything went black.

Desmond looked around the entrance yard again, searching for a solution to the second half of the problem: blocking the entrance to the palace green, which was inside the palace walls. Luckily, there was a wall encircling the whole palace and separating it from the green, and it was high enough that the corpses could not climb over. All they had to worry about was this one gap by which it could be entered. But what to barricade it with? The carts with Evadine's dead magic coils caught his eye, but because of their unsavory cargo, Desmond was loath to use them. He feared, if the coils weren't the reason for the waking of the dead, that they would only lend more power to the corpses and make them harder to defeat.

Desmond ran into the palace's stables through an arch to the left of the palace doors. He looked around and spotted some of the stable hands cowering in a stall.

"You there! Please. Is there anything in here we can use to make a barricade?"

The stable hands quailed in front of him, wailing quietly and covering their heads with their hands. One of them appeared to be praying, holding his hands flat in front of him and drawing them slowly across his face over and over again. Desmond went over to them and knelt. They shrank back with gasps of surprise and cried out when he shook them by the shoulders.

"Please! We have to block up the entrance so that they can't get through. You must help!" Desmond said.

It was no use. They were too in shock to even comprehend what he was saying. He stood up and turned away. When he did, he saw a small dark-skinned child of indeterminate gender standing at the door of the stall.

"Please, sir," ze said. "There are carriages. This way."

Desmond grinned and nodded. He followed the child to the far end of the stables, where the carriages were stored—just the sort of thing he needed. There was a black one, which Desmond spotted first, belonging to Evadine. Four were devoted to the empress's use, two of them large enough to seat eight. In addition to those, the palace housed five or six others belonging to the empress's councilors.

"Yes, this will be perfect," Desmond said, smiling. He turned to the child. Ze couldn't have been more than four. "What's your name, child?"

"Sonja."

"Can you be very brave now, Sonja, and run into the yard? Send back some guards to help me pull these out?"

The child nodded and ran off. Desmond put his sword down and went to Evadine's large black carriage. He positioned himself under the stay, bent his knees and put it as squarely across his shoulders as he could. He took a couple deep breaths, hooked his arms over the bar, dug his heels into the floor, and pushed off, throwing his weight forward. He straightened his legs, groaning and clenching his teeth with the effort. Desmond was a strong man, but Evadine's carriage was heavy. He continued to breathe deeply and maintained his pressure on the bar. Finally, he felt the carriage shift and he took a step forward. The carriage rolled with him, and he took another step.

He heard footsteps approaching, and a moment later, Sonja and four guardsmen rushed to take hold of the carriage on either side of him and help roll it out of its space. As they set it rolling, Desmond slipped out from under it.

"Go on, you three take it out and tip it over in front of the entrance to the palace green!" he said. "Crush some of the corpses with it if you can. Just block as much of the opening as possible."

He grabbed the shoulder of the fourth guardsman and pulled him away from the carriage.

"What's your name?" he asked.

"Barnet," the man said.

"Barnet? Excellent. You help me with the next one. We'll get it started," Desmond said.

The two of them went to the next carriage, one of the empress's eight-seaters. This time, Barnet pulled from up front and Desmond pushed from behind. This worked extremely well, since Desmond was able to brace his feet against the wall of the stable and achieve better leverage against the weighty carriage. As they heaved it down the center lane, the other three guardsmen came running back in, almost laughing.

"Did it work?" Desmond grunted as one man joined him at the back.

"Work! Oh aye, it worked. We crushed ten or so of the demons with that carriage when we pushed it over, and them devils actually hesitated before coming at it! They must have some instincts left to 'em, other than to attack people," the man said. He was practically giddy.

Don't get too excited. We'll still be able to hear those on the outside screaming.

Desmond used the anger welling up in him to power an extra thrust against the back of the carriage, which sent it rattling away down the lane and the guards running after it.

Once the carriage made it out into the entrance yard, more guards and townspeople fell upon it and practically carried it over to the gap in the wall. Desmond glanced over toward the gate. It was closed, but the corpses were pressed against it and reaching through the bars, swiping at anyone who came too close. They gnashed their already bloody teeth and groaned menacingly. At their feet was a mound of truly dead bodies. Some were wearing armor—clearly fallen guards. Some were the townspeople who had been seized before they could get through the gate. All were missing limbs and covered in blood, of which there was a great pool at the site of the thickest slaughter.

But the gate was closed. Desmond looked away. They would close the other entrance, and then they would find a way to stop the undead.

Desmond left it to the crowd to move the carriage and jogged around in front of it to try and direct it to the most effective place. Evadine's black carriage was on its side and blocked about half of the opening to the palace green.

There were guardsmen at the remaining opening, hacking at the undead still coming through. Desmond turned to the people moving the carriage.

"All right, lift it! Everyone heft it up, on my count! Three, two, one, lift!" he shouted.

As one, the people holding on to the carriage lifted. Desmond ran to the side facing the opening and tagged the people, gesturing for them to move around to one of the other sides. He jogged ahead again and motioned for them to bring the carriage forward.

"Fall back! Fall back!" he shouted to the guardsmen.

They moved out of the way and the undead began to surge forward. Desmond waved at the people holding the carriage.

"Now, now! Run forward with it!" he roared, running with them.

The people holding it roared battle cries and ran, gaining momentum slowly as they charged the walking dead with their rather ungainly weapon. Desmond whooped and cheered them on.

"All right, and tip it, tip it, tip it!"

The people stopped running and pushed the carriage away. It flew forward, crashing into the horde of corpses and knocking them to the ground. It skidded across the stones and grass, slowing down only when it collided with Evadine's carriage and the other side of the wall. The people in the entrance yard waited, heaving with exertion. They could hear the corpses banging against the other side of the carriages, but none came through. Cheers sounded from the entrance yard, and people began to jump up and down. Desmond grinned in relief and sank to his knees, as did many others.

But their happiness was cut short as the screams from the other side of the gate intensified. Desmond looked through the bars at the fountain square. It seemed that the corpses who had been trying to get in had given up and turned to easier prey.

Desmond got up from his knees again and ran into the center of the entrance yard. He shouted for people's attention, and they began to crowd around him. Before he could begin to address them, though, Guerline burst through the palace doors, arms laden with bandages. Behind her was a swarm of palace attendants and ladies-in-waiting, carrying bowls and pitchers of water and bags of medicine.

"Bring the wounded into the entrance hall!" she shouted. "This way, yes!"

She handed the bandages off to Evadine, who had co-operatively removed her silk overdress, and ran down to Desmond, tears streaming down her face. Her red-gold twists glinted in the sunlight as they bounced behind her. He opened his arms wide to her, and lifted her into his embrace just as he'd done when he arrived. He closed his arms tightly around her and spun with her momentum.

"Put me down now, Desmond. We have work to do!" she said.

He obliged and she ran to the nearest injured person, a little girl who had lost a chunk of her arm to a bite. Guerline hoisted the girl onto her ample hip. Desmond picked up a man lying nearby whose leg was torn off at the knee, and the two of them hurried toward the palace steps.

"We were watching through the guard slot, Eva and I," Guerline said. "I'd already ordered the staff to get water and bandages and everything ready. Excellent work with the carriages, Desmond, to block it off like that—although I can't say Eva's happy. You should have seen her face when you rolled her carriage out. I do believe it was only finished a month ago."

Desmond stifled a laugh as they deposited their charges into the hands of two volunteer nurses. The two of them trotted back down the stairs to help more of the wounded. Guerline paused as she stepped off the last stair and just looked around, her eyebrows furrowed and her lips pressed anxiously together. Desmond put a hand on her shoulder.

"What is it, Guerline?" he asked.

"So many dead so quickly. So many wounded," she said. "Why don't we have a Gwanen witch here at the palace? We only have the most basic of medicines, the ones they send."

"I . . . I don't know," Desmond said.

Guerline shook her head a little. "Never mind."

She started to walk again, but stopped when a shadow passed over them. They looked up at the sky, as did the people around them.

"What was that?" Guerline asked.

"Dragons!" Desmond said.

"What?"

He pointed. "Look!"

Indeed, there were three or four dragons circling above them in the sky. It was hard to tell exactly how many because they kept passing in front of the sun and swooping around the palace walls. One large red dragon came in low over the entrance yard, its jaws opened wide. The people in the yard began screaming and falling to the ground, but the dragon swept right over them. As it flew over the palace green, it let loose its flame, scorching the corpses still on the other side of the wall. An unearthly screeching rose up from beyond. The other dragons dove upon the green and breathed fire on it as well.

"Dragons! Perhaps this means that all is well with Thiymen," Guerline said, watching the dragons with wide, hopeful eyes.

"Yes, perhaps it does," Desmond said, feeling great relief, for he knew these dragons. The large red one was Silas, the dragon queen. Surely she would only have come if Fiona had sent her.

"But they can't breathe fire upon the square," Guerline said. "We still need to find a way to deal with those undead."

Desmond nodded and started looking around for Josen and the guardsmen, intending to summon them to the center of the yard. He was silenced by a rising blue light on the other side of the gate.

"Mother?" he said.

Guerline looked at him. He looked back at her in astonishment and then jogged over to the gate to get a better look at what was happening. She pointed to the stairs leading up to the battlements. Desmond nodded and ran up, Guerline close on his heels.

When they reached the top, Guerline gasped in shock at the scene below them. The square was doused with blood, and from their height, it was difficult to tell who was really alive and who was walking dead. The blue light came down from one of the streets that fed into the square, though whom or what it was coming from was still hidden from view. The blue was soon joined by flashes of red and green light as well, and Desmond whooped.

"It's Mother and my aunts!" he said. "It must be! But there's only three . . . where is Aunt Fiona?"

He looked up at Silas, wheeling through the sky, and back at the lights flashing beyond the buildings. His heart sank.

"Oh no," he said under his breath. Guerline took his hand and squeezed tightly.

The wind picked up suddenly, pulling at their hair and clothes. It seemed to sweep over the battlements where they stood and pour into the square below them, rushing across and funneling into the same side street from which the lights were emanating. There was a moment of lull in the air, and then the wind blasted back out into the square. It whipped around for a few seconds. Desmond and Guerline saw nothing, their arms over their eyes to protect themselves from debris.

When the wind stopped, they lowered their arms. Guerline gasped again, and Desmond peered down into the square. Nothing had changed, except—

"They're all dead," Guerline said.

Nothing moved now in the square. All the corpses, undead or otherwise, were still and silent on the ground. Desmond and Guerline turned to look at each other slowly, eyes wide in wonderment. They quickly descended the stairs and ran around to look through the gate. As they neared it, the wind flared up again and pushed them back. The gates were flung open; Desmond could hear the metal banging against the stone wall, though he was again blinded by the force of the gust. When it died down once more, he blinked the dryness from his eyes and stared.

"Desmond!"

"Mother!" Desmond said.

Olivia came into view and ran forward, arms spread. Desmond embraced his mother, and released her to find Morgana and Aradia also standing there. He embraced them as well, shocked to see them in spite of guessing their presence.

"Thank the gods you're here," Guerline said. "Today has been the strangest of days."

"It does appear that way," Morgana said, surveying the scene. The Adenen commander was nearly as tall as Desmond himself, with tanned skin and curly black hair plaited down her back. She wore her customary breeches and crimson tunic.

"I tried to contact you earlier, but my mirror was malfunctioning," Desmond said.

"All will be explained, my son," Olivia said gently.

"Yes, of course. And we have time, now that you've taken care of the undead," he replied. "Thank you."

Aradia, auburn-haired and brown-skinned, approached, her green gown flowing with each step. "Well . . . that wasn't us, Desmond."

He and Guerline exchanged surprised looks.

"Then who was it?" Desmond said warily.

At that moment, three people walked through the gates behind the Kavanagh sisters. There was a huge mountain of a man, brown-skinned and broad with white-blonde hair and an abundant beard. With him was a short, lithe woman with white skin and two long black braids. But ahead of them strode a fierce-looking woman with almond-shaped golden eyes, ebony skin, and short, spiky grey hair.

"The gods," Guerline said breathlessly.

CHAPTER TWENTY-THREE

"Don't be stupid, little queen. If we were gods, we would have long since abandoned this mess," Lisyne said.

Not gods? The ebony woman's voice was rough and shied away from the consonants, as if it were unused to the language she spoke. How long had it been since these three appeared in human form? Guerline looked away, looked anywhere but at Lisyne, and found Desmond's eyes.

"They're shapeshifters," he said. "Old and powerful, yes, but creatures of the earth just like any of us."

"Shapeshifters?" Evadine hissed. "But the—the Book of Skins—"

"All stories. Neria fabricated it all when Arido was founded, when the shapeshifters went into hiding," Olivia said.

"You may continue to think of us as gods, if it's a comfort to you," Seryne, the short white woman, said.

It was not a comfort to Guerline. It was just another lie. But there was no denying that the shapeshifters were the closest thing to gods they had, and the truth of their divinity was the least of her concerns. Everywhere she looked was riddled with human debris and doused in blood, even her own hands. The hem of her dress was heavy with what it had soaked up. This was the blood of her people. Four days into her reign, and hundreds had died on her doorstep.

"I would not want gods that slaughter those who could still be saved," Guerline said, her voice quivering like a taut bow string.

"It was the best way," Tirosyne said.

Guerline shook her head. "The quickest way. The simplest way. Not the right way."

"There were none worth saving," Lisyne said. "They would have all died of their wounds, slowly and painfully."

The shapeshifter stalked toward Guerline; her yellow eyes seemed to glow. Slowly, her mouth opened and the tip of her pink tongue ran over the inner rim of her lips. Guerline stood frozen, rooted in place by cold metal bars running through her bones and into the ground.

"You are the one it left alive. Was it for your compassion? Your *morality*?" Lisyne tilted her head to the side. "What is the point of your existence?"

"Do tell," Guerline said. She'd meant to sound angry, but the words came out as a whisper.

"Not *me*, silly queen. *The reason we are all here*," Lisyne said. "It killed your kin and left you living. I must know why. Put this—" She waved her hand at the scene. "—from your mind and come with me. We have much to discuss."

"It's here, Lisyne."

All heads snapped toward Seryne's voice. She stood at the corner of Evadine's covered carts, lifting one edge of the burlap to expose the coils beneath. Lisyne's golden eyes widened and the corners of her lips twitched into a tight smile. She looked at Morgana and Olivia and jerked her head toward the wagons.

"Bring those," she said. The two witches walked over with their hands outstretched and levitated the carts.

Lisyne brushed between Guerline and Desmond. The other two shapeshifters followed her, as did Morgana and Olivia, guiding the carts of dead magic. Aradia stopped in front of Guerline and took her shaking hands, gripping them tightly. Guerline looked down so she wouldn't have to meet the witch's eyes. She felt cold. All the warmth of her body was in her cheeks, and in the tears that burned in her eyes. They came unbidden, born not of any particular emotion but a tempest of all of them: rage, despair, fear.

"Let me take the edge off for you, child," Aradia said.

Guerline sniffed and lifted her gaze to Aradia's. "No."

Aradia glanced to the left, at Desmond; then nodded and let go of Guerline's hands. She stepped around the empress and followed the others. Guerline stared forward, not even looking down when Desmond grasped her abandoned hand.

"What are you thinking?" he asked.

"I'm thinking you were right," she said, addressing Evadine instead of Desmond. "We should be very, very afraid of magic."

Eva rushed forward and wrapped her arms around Guerline, who pulled her hand from Desmond's and returned the other woman's embrace. It felt so good to hold Eva; it steadied her. Feeling Eva's body against hers enabled her to breathe. Guerline was shaken to her core by Lisyne's display of violence and utter lack of remorse. Her words—*what is the point of you?*—still echoed in Guerline's ears. She slipped out of Evadine's arms and met the other woman's gaze, and finally, she understood.

"Magic is not always like this," Desmond whispered behind her.

She turned to face him, and a new wave of tears pricked her eyes as she took in his own pained, watery-eyed expression.

"I know. But when it is, we humans have no defense," she said.

"The witches—"

"Are following Lisyne's every order! They're terrified of her!" Eva said. "When the Kavanaghs cower, what are we to do?"

Desmond shook his head, slowly, mouth agape, but said nothing more. Guerline's mind spun with conflicting emotions. She still trusted the Kavanaghs, because she still trusted Desmond and the peace that had reigned since his family rose to power in the clans. But Lisyne and the shapeshifters were another matter entirely, and if the Kavanagh sisters could not fight her—

"Come along, humans. Lisyne wants you present," called the deep basso of Tirosyne.

Guerline took a deep breath, then turned and entered the palace with the others behind her, following Tirosyne into her own throne room. They had moved the council chairs down from the dais and set them up in a circle in the center of the room. Guerline sat stiffly on her relocated throne, her hands folded tightly in her lap. As she looked around the room, her pulse quickened. She was surrounded by six of the most powerful beings in the entire world. And she was a girl of nineteen who had ascended to the throne five days ago.

Wait. Six *of the most . . . ?*

"Where is Aunt Fiona?" Desmond looked at his mother, who sat on his right.

Olivia frowned and shook her head. She reached out and squeezed Desmond's free hand. His face fell and he looked around at his aunts.

"Fiona is dead," Lisyne said, staring at Guerline.

Guerline inhaled sharply, but quickly swallowed her shock. She took a deep breath and looked back at Lisyne with what she hoped was strength.

"How?" she asked.

"She placed a seal on the world under the mountain to stop a dark and evil thing from breaking free," Tirosyne said. "It required all that was left of her strength."

"What nonsense," Eva said under her breath.

Every head in the room snapped to her.

Lisyne growled. "What did you say?"

Evadine paled, but did not retract her statement.

"It's a lie," she said. "It must be. Fiona and Thiymen clan are responsible for everything that has been happening!"

"Eva!" Guerline hissed. *How can she become so angry so quickly?*

Morgana rose with her fists clenched. "What's your proof, Malise?"

"Think about it! All sides of the country have been beset by disaster, except the East. We've heard nothing from the East!" Eva shouted, rising herself. Her cheeks flushed red and her eyes grew wild. "And then the witches stopped showing up! Thiymen dropped all its duties to prepare for an attack on us. You all saw the dead rising and tearing the living limb from limb. Who controls the dead? Thiymen clan!"

As she spoke, her voice jumped to a high shriek. She stood in the center of their circle and spun around, staring at them all madly. She turned to Guerline and pointed at her. Guerline stood and held her hands in a gesture of surrender.

"Eva, please, this isn't you," she said. She recognized the mania she'd seen in court, when Eva snapped at her. Though her expression didn't change, tears filled Eva's eyes and broke Guerline's heart. It wasn't enough—loving each other wasn't enough to stop this fundamental opposition. Guerline felt more afraid of magic than ever, that was true . . . but still, she could not leap to the accusations now spewing from her lover's mouth. *Please*, she begged silently, over and over. But Eva's eyes dimmed, and she turned away from Guerline.

"And the dragons! You remember that man Brynn, who came and said the dragons were attacking Giarda? The dragons have gone wild! They flew here and attacked the palace grounds!" Eva said.

Desmond scoffed. "Eva, the dragons were attacking the *undead*—"

She spun again to face Guerline. "Do you remember your parents? Do you remember *how they died*, Lina?"

The room got very quiet. Evadine advanced. Guerline stood straight-backed in front of her throne, not flinching as Eva approached and bent down until they were practically nose to nose. Guerline fought her impulse to gather Eva into her arms for a moment, straining for decorum, then decided it was stupid to prioritize her imperial persona over the woman she loved. Eva's hand trembled so close to Guerline's that she could feel it. She grabbed that trembling hand in both of hers and held it tight, then opened her mouth to speak—

Alcander leaned out from behind Eva, and Guerline's words died on her tongue. He wrapped his one grey arm around Eva's shoulders, pressed his forearm against her throat. He seemed bigger than he had before, taller than Eva, as he hadn't been in life; he rested his chin on her head and his black, sludge-like blood dripped onto Eva's cheeks. She didn't seem to notice. Her wild grey eyes danced over Guerline's face.

"They *rotted* while they were still *alive*," Eva hissed.

The words sounded distant to Guerline's ears. Her focus was on Alcander, not on Eva. His arm slid across Eva's throat until his hand wrapped around it. His fingers applied gentle pressure, and Eva spoke again.

"Who else could possibly conceive of such a terrible curse than poor, mad, bitter Fiona?"

Guerline's eyes widened. Was Alcander . . . *controlling* Eva? Was he more than just a figment of her imagination?

Alcander grinned, as if he could tell what she was thinking. He reached for her. Guerline stepped back and opened her mouth to reveal his presence to the others, but before she could, Evadine disappeared before her eyes. Guerline blinked a few times and realized that Eva had been snatched up by Lisyne, who now held her aloft by the throat in the center of the circle. The claws of her left hand were extended and her bared teeth were elongated, and she was snarling up at Evadine with murder in her eyes. Eva went ash-pale and clutched at Lisyne's hand. She tore at it with her nails, and kicked fruitlessly in an attempt to get free.

Alcander was gone.

"No, wait!" Guerline ran over. She took hold of Lisyne's left arm. The shapeshifter turned to look and snarled at her, but Guerline held her ground. She swallowed her fear and looked directly into Lisyne's burning golden eyes.

"She's not herself. Her words mean nothing. She's been infected—"

"Her *words* have infected the country. Her words are the reason Fiona did not communicate with the crown, and why you have now been caught unaware by all of this," Lisyne said.

"The poor girl has been driven mad by her grief," Aradia said. "Please, Lisyne. You can hear it in her voice, and see it in her face. Have mercy on her."

"Grief?" Morgana sneered.

"For her lover, the dead prince," Desmond said.

"No! It is Alcander, but not like that!" Guerline said quickly. "He's here, he's—"

The shapeshifter barked a laugh.

"Damn it, listen to me! These words are Alcander's, not Eva's!" Guerline roared.

Lisyne paused for a moment, appearing to consider their words. She loosened her grip ever so slightly on Evadine's throat, and the young noblewoman gasped for air. Color flooded back into her face; her eyelashes fluttered as she teetered back from the edge of unconsciousness. Guerline held her own breath, waiting to see what the shapeshifter would decide. Her heart jumped when Lisyne lowered her arm.

"You are all fools," Lisyne said.

And she pulled back and threw Evadine across the room.

Eva hit high on the wall with a sickening thud that echoed against the stone, then crumpled in a heap on the floor. Guerline screamed and ran toward her until something solid caught her in the chest and knocked the wind out of her. She gasped for breath and realized that Lisyne was in front of her, holding her back.

"Let me go," Guerline wheezed.

Lisyne grinned at her. "Heart of Gwanen, does the lady live?" She twisted, and Guerline was able to see Aradia kneeling next to Eva. The witch stood and shook her head.

"I'm so sorry, Your Majesty," she said.

The empress stared at Eva's motionless form. No one spoke. Lisyne just continued to stare at Guerline, that amber gaze like a fire lapping at her cheek. Finally, the heat became too much to ignore and she looked back at the shifter.

"You . . . lunatic," Guerline breathed. Anger quivered in her limbs, the tension of it the only thing keeping her from collapsing there in front of all of them. Underneath that force, her insides were jelly, as though her bones were gone. Her nascent confidence shattered along with Eva's skull. How could she rule, how could she lord over the empire when she was so utterly incapable of matching the beings before her? When she couldn't even save her best friend and lover?

No doubt Lisyne would have found such a sentiment laughable; indeed, it seemed she could tell. She smirked at the empress, then leaned in and whispered in her ear:

"She knew he thought of you . . . and that he would come to you. She said nothing."

Cold sweat slid down her spine. Guerline looked back at her, mouth slack; then she turned and walked back to her seat. Desmond reached for her shaking hand when she sat down, but she waved him away. Her heart was completely detached from its place in her chest, and she was only just holding herself together. She could find no comfort in the hand of someone who simply stood by and watched.

"Perhaps you find me cruel, little empress," Lisyne said. "But I have done you a favor."

She too turned and walked back to her seat. She settled down in the chair and pulled her legs up, leaning one knee on the armrest and draping her other leg over the other. She rested her elbow against the propped-up knee and leaned her chin upon her hand.

"Now then," Lisyne began. Then she paused again, as though a thought had struck her. "What was all that she was saying about the dragons?"

Silence hung in the air as Guerline stared at Eva's body. Something wet dripped onto her breast; her trembling hands floated to her face and ineffectually wiped at the cascading tears.

Desmond leaned in and whispered. "Lina, please! There's nothing you can do for her now."

Aradia rose from her seat. "Perhaps we should take a short recess . . ."

Guerline shook her head to rouse herself and clear her thoughts. Her chest ached, and her mind spun with warring desires, one to retreat into herself and one to do whatever she could to put a swift end to all of this. A recess would mean having to come back after a few minutes, to these powerful people who had sat by and let Lisyne murder a girl. Guerline wanted nothing more than to be far away from all of them. At least if they said what they needed to say and were done with it, she would have the whole night before her. She made her decision, and looked away from Eva. *Just give me a few minutes, love.*

"We had . . . an emissary from Giarda come and say the dragons had been attacking villages across the mountains," she said.

"Strange. Is he still here?" Seryne asked.

"Yes," Guerline said.

"Have him fetched," Lisyne said.

Guerline nodded. She began to rise, but Desmond put a hand on hers and shook his head. He got up and crossed over to the throne room doors, poking his head out and passing the order on to the guards.

"Yes, right. As I was saying," Lisyne continued, "it seems to be about time we all shared our information. I think we're all fairly well briefed on the disasters of each region. Famine in the south, sandstorms in the west, hellhounds loose in the forests of the north, and so on. But it seems that some interesting things have been taking place in the capital. Would you care to enlighten us all, Empress?"

Guerline's upper lip curled ever so slightly. She couldn't tell whether or not she was being taunted. Not that it would serve her any purpose to wonder about it, since she was hardly in a position to demand respect from a four-thousand-year-old shapeshifter. So instead, she cleared her throat and addressed the room, doing her best to keep her voice steady.

"The first strange thing, other than the deaths of my family, was the Giardan emissary you've just heard about. After that, we learned that the Thiymen witches had stopped coming to collect the souls of the dead. People gathered outside the palace with the corpses of their loved ones. We buried them on the palace green until such time as we could get in touch with Thiymen and discover why they had abandoned their duties," she reported. Her voice came out in a sullen monotone.

"We can answer that," Olivia said. "Fiona first sealed the creature in the world under the mountain six days ago. In order to repair the damage done to the barrier, she forbade crossings. Therefore, the witches could not come to escort the souls."

Guerline glared at Olivia. "Well, that is good to know. It would have been better to know at the time that decision was made . . . but that is a discussion to have with the new Heart of Thiymen."

Any one of them could have sent her a message about the prohibited crossings. Hadn't it occurred to them that it was something of which the humans ought to be made aware?

Desmond coughed. "Today, before the dead rose, Eva-dine went out and came back with those carts loaded with coils of stored dead energy."

"Yes, let us talk about those carts!" Lisyne said.

"Where would she have gotten any dead energy, let alone two whole carts full?" Aradia asked.

"I believe it came from the Maravilla twins," Desmond explained. All three sisters nodded in recognition.

"So that's what they've been doing; that is still their goal," Olivia said. "They must have been traveling into the underworld and binding up the energy. That explains the tears Thiymen has been dealing with. But why would the twins risk such danger?"

"I think you mean, why are they so stupid? Dead energy is not workable," Morgana said. "It taints everything, and shortens the life of a spell."

"Perhaps they were trying to refine it," Aradia said.

Morgana scoffed. "For what? To increase their own power? They were always trying to speed their own growth. It's a wonder they haven't killed themselves with their ambi-tion."

"Was Evadine working with the twins?" Olivia asked.

"I don't know," Desmond said. He looked at Guer-line, who only stared back at him. "The undead attacked us before she could explain where or how she'd found the coils. And now, of course . . ."

They all looked rather reluctantly at Evadine's body.

"Sorry," Lisyne said, not sounding sorry at all.

"We'll find out where they were hiding. It can't be far from the palace. Evadine hates—hated the outer city," Guerline said.

"I believe I know that, as well. The old jail tower. I had . . . an associate investigating it," Desmond said.

Lisyne looked from Tirosyne to Seryne. The two shape-shifters nodded, rose, and left the room. Guerline watched them go with an ominous feeling. Had Evadine really been working against her? She couldn't believe it. She'd trusted Eva more than anyone, loved her more than anyone else, and Eva had trusted her. Eva had been ready to tell her about the coils when the dead came. She wouldn't have done that if she was involved in a plot against Guerline or the witches.

Yet—

She knew.

It was difficult to tamp down, even as she acknowl-edged the voice in the back of her mind telling her to be wary of reacting before she had proof. She took a deep breath and tried to push the thoughts of Evadine away. This impromptu council needed to get back on track, and con-demning the dead was not going to help them.

But their interruptions were not over. A guard entered and stood at attention.

"Your Majesty. The Giardan is nowhere to be found. We're searching the palace for him now," he said.

Stunned, Guerline stared for a moment. "Thank you. Excellent work." She dismissed him, and he bowed and left.

"My belief is that you will not find him," Lisyne said, watching the guard go. "Now please, continue. What hap-pened next?"

Guerline furrowed her eyebrows in confusion at Lisyne's comment, but brushed it aside. "After Evadine showed us the coils, the dead rose out of the earth and began attacking everyone . . . and that's where you came in. You, and the dragons," she said, looking to Lisyne.

"Speaking of the dragons, where have they gone?" Morgana asked.

"I told them to track down and dispose of any remaining undead," Lisyne said. She looked back at Guerline. "Thank you for telling us what's happened. I shall now share with you what I told the Kavanagh sisters before bringing them here."

She settled down into her chair and folded her hands over her chest.

"The world under the mountain did not form naturally. It was made. It was created to hold the chaos of the world," she said. "Four thousand years ago, a dark thing made itself known in the world. Death was always part of life, and we all knew that; but death came at the hands of predators. Death came at the end of long, long life. There was no sickness. There was no evil in it. There was only the obligation of prey to predator and to the earth that had brought us all forth.

"But then the dark thing came, and the babies grew sick and died, and the weak fell ill and died, and the strong went mad and died. All for no reason, for no purpose. They died neither to nourish a body nor to nourish the earth. Such pointless deaths are the worst evil." Lisyne snarled. "We, the shapeshifters, took it upon ourselves to expel it. We drew it out, and it took sentient form. But we could not destroy it. So we threw it deep, deep into the mountains and bound it there with all the magic we possessed."

A hush filled the room. Guerline thought of her parents rotting away while they still lived, dying with no explanation or justification—of Eva, murdered on a psychopath's whim. Guerline's fists clenched. Lisyne was right. Such deaths were truly evil. But what about Alcander? Alcander had been eaten by a wildcat. He died to nourish a body. Their parents' death must have been planned by this conscious, dark thing—that much seemed clear—but Guerline could only assume that Alcander's death was natural and right in the order of things, a simple matter of tragic timing rather than malicious design.

But then, why was he appearing in her nightmares? How had he manifested before her just a few minutes ago? How had he manipulated Evadine, forcing her to speak with a madness that got her killed?

"And this is what Aunt Fiona has been struggling with all this time? And Petra before her?" Desmond asked.

"Yes. Only Thiymen has ever been aware of its presence, and they are charged with keeping it bound," Lisyne said. "They escort human souls to the safe parts of the world we created, away from the thing, and they keep the boundary we made strong."

"That's why the actions of the Maravilla twins are so dangerous," Olivia said.

"The damage they're doing gave this thing the chance it had to push through and weaken the barrier," Morgana frowned.

"And it became too much for Fiona," Aradia said quietly. "We abandoned her, because we never knew what she was facing."

"It was always her nature not to ask for help," Olivia said.

Aradia nodded and took a deep breath to steady herself. Guerline watched, frowning. So much in the world was kept secret. There were things the witches didn't tell her, that she didn't tell the people, that the witches didn't tell each other, that the shapeshifters didn't tell the witches! How could they work together when they didn't all have the same information? How could they work together when one person or a group of people felt enough authority to decide that another person or group didn't deserve to know about something, or need to know, or wouldn't understand? This situation had come about because of one presumption after another. *Well. Never again. When this is over, our dialogue will be changed. There will be no more secrets.*

"Do you think the thing has broken free now that Fiona is dead?" Guerline asked.

"I do," Lisyne said. "I know. I felt the barrier fall. It happened right before the dead rose."

"So what must we do now?" Guerline asked her.

Lisyne did not answer. Instead, she cocked her head to one side and looked at Guerline.

"What do *you* think we should do, Empress?" she asked.

Guerline flushed red, both with embarrassment at being put on the spot and with anger that the shapeshifter was presuming to test her in the presence of so many who were older and wiser than she was. How was she supposed to know what needed to be done? She had never battled the personification of evil and illness before. She had only the most cursory knowledge of magic in the first place, and that only thanks to Desmond's spotty instruction on his visits over the years. She narrowed her eyes at Lisyne, who merely continued to stare at her with the slightest of half-smiles on her face.

Calm down now, Guerline. They were clearly entering into a war. If this thing had required all the power of all the shapeshifters to bind four thousand years ago, then they would surely require every witch in the empire to match that. This thing would likely expect such an action, so she very much doubted that it would come without an army of its own: hell-hounds, demons, probably every nightmarish creature she'd ever been told a story about. They would need to bring the standing human army as well. It made Guerline sick to think of sending her brave men and women out to engage such heinous creatures while the witches worked their magic, but how else could it be managed?

She looked around the room, blood pounding in her ears. Her face felt like it was on fire. She clenched the arms of her throne to keep from putting her hands on her cheeks. Desmond and the other Kavanaghs looked reassuringly at her. Morgana seemed to be trying to tell her what to say by waggling her eyebrows in ridiculous patterns. Aradia smiled warmly, nodding at her to go ahead and speak. Olivia simply looked at her and gave her a single nod. Desmond grinned broadly, which struck Guerline as inappropriate.

Guerline stood and let the cool-headed empress persona she'd been cultivating wash over her. With each deep breath she took, her emotions—her pain at Eva's loss, her fear of and anger at Lisyne—wrapped themselves tighter around her heart, giving this other Guerline room to overtake her body.

She addressed the Kavanagh sisters. "Return to your clans and prepare for battle. We will rally all our guardsmen. We muster just north of the city on the eastern bank of the River Acha. From there, we will march on the Zaide Mountains."

She turned and looked Lisyne in the eyes. The shape-shifter's expression had not changed, and she waited, eyes wide and mouth slightly open.

"You will lead the witches in resealing the gate while we engage whatever army the creature's brought on the ground," Guerline said.

Lisyne grinned.

CHAPTER TWENTY-FOUR

THE SHAPESHIFTERS AND THE KAVANAGHS FILED OUT OF THE throne room, off to make whatever preparations were required for the clans. Guerline watched them go. As soon as the door closed behind Aradia's green train, the empress let out a sob and ran to the crumpled body of her friend.

The back of Eva's head was flattened, and sticky with the blood and cerebral fluid oozing out under the sharp bits of skull that had pierced her scalp. Her face wet with tears, Guerline gingerly turned Eva over so that the wound was hidden, then took up her lover's cold hands and leaned forward until her forehead rested on Eva's still chest.

"What can I do?"

Guerline jerked her head up and twisted to look over her shoulder at Desmond. He stood a few paces behind her, hands limp at his sides. His brow was furrowed and his eyes filmy—but who were his tears for? A fresh wave of sobs rose in her throat as she thought of Eva's last few days. She had made many allies with her anti-magic talk, but would Pearce Iszolda weep for her? Would Lanyic Eoarn?

"Help me carry her," she said.

Desmond moved in immediately, nudging Guerline back with his shoulder as he scooped Eva into his arms and stood. Guerline struggled to her feet, hampered by her yards of dress, stiff with dried blood.

"Lead the way, Lina," Desmond said.

Nodding, she staggered over to the throne room doors, pushing one of the heavy bronze panels open. She led Desmond toward the rear of the palace, around the garden, to the Temple of the Shifter Gods. The doors were flung wide, and a thick line of people stretched back down the hall toward them. Guerline stopped short when she came upon it. No one had noticed her yet, and she was paralyzed. She couldn't face them, especially not when all she wanted to do was scream at them to get out so she could prepare Eva's body in peace. She would have to find somewhere else to go. She turned around and made for the garden's nearest entrance.

"Lina?" Desmond asked.

"What does it matter if she's prepared in the temple? The gods aren't real," she muttered.

She went to the fountain in the center of the garden, cutting through the labyrinthine paths with utter certainty. It seemed she did not get quite so lost in the garden as she'd always pretended.

The fountain was built of white marble, with three huge, ornately carved basins rising from the center. Clear, bright water bubbled from the very top and spilled over into each level, filling the several meters wide pool that formed the base. The water was perhaps two feet deep, so it would do well enough for a washing.

Guerline had removed her silk overdress during the undead's attack, and wore two layers of linen shifts over her undergarments. She unlaced and stepped out of the top one, a finer-woven lavender that was forever ruined by blood, then climbed over the short wall into the pool. The water was surprisingly warm and she let out a relieved sigh, then turned to face Desmond and held out her arms.

"I'll wash her here," she said.

He nodded and leaned over the fountain's wall, lowering Eva gently into the water. Guerline knelt and slipped her left arm under Eva's shoulders, holding her so that her face was still above the water. She brushed stray strands of dark hair back from Eva's face.

Something metal clinked and Guerline looked up. Desmond was removing his belt. Tears filled her eyes again as she guessed what he was doing. Two people were needed to wash a body and get it ready for a watch. But as she watched him set his belt on the ground, she realized that she didn't want him there. All she could think of was his silence in the throne room when Lisyne had Eva by the throat, when even his aunt Aradia, who had never met Eva before that hour, tried to defend her. All she could think was that, regardless of his opinion of Eva, he hadn't said a word to help Guerline persuade the shapeshifter to spare her closest friend.

The tears in her eyes spilled over and a sob escaped her throat, which stopped Desmond before he pulled his tunic off. He knelt on the fountain wall and reached for Guerline's face, brushed the tears from her cheeks.

"It's all right, Lina, I'm here," he said.

She shook her head, but couldn't speak right away. He leaned in to kiss her, and she froze.

"What's wrong?" he asked.

"I need . . . the soaps. And oils. And a fresh dress for her," she whispered.

Desmond hung in front of her for a moment. She looked down at the water, golden in the deep afternoon sun, lapping against the inner wall of the fountain. Then he exhaled and leaned back.

"Yes, of course. I'll be back as quickly as I can." He turned and began to walk away.

"Desmond!" she called.

He stopped and looked back. Guerline swallowed hard and took a deep breath, hoping to keep the tremor out of her voice.

"Can you find Theodor? I'd like him to help me."

She couldn't see his face clearly, between the distance and the blur of tears, but she felt the edge in his voice as he said, "Of course." He turned away again and disappeared from view. Guerline held her breath, but the sobs overcame her. She clutched Eva's body tightly and hung her head, coughing and gasping as she wept freely for several minutes; then she sucked air down in earnest, desperate to get control of herself.

More than anything, she wished that things had not been so tense between her and Eva for the last few days, the last few months, the last few years. She wished that she had been less afraid of her brother and her parents, that she'd demanded to participate and learned more about ruling. And she wished, above all, that Lisyne was wrong and that Eva had not known Alcander intended to rape her.

She *had* given Guerline the dagger. It had seemed such an odd birthday present . . .

"It doesn't matter now," she whispered, resting her cheek on Eva's forehead. Evadine was dead. Alcander was dead. Neither of them could break her heart anymore. She would wash Eva and prepare her for the watch, and then it would be over.

The watch. Guerline jerked her head up, eyes wide. The barrier between worlds had fallen. The Heart of Thiymen was dead. No witches had come for her dead people. No witch would come for Eva either. She would have to go in a shallow grave with all the others, assuming whatever sorcery it was that woke the dead did not strike again.

She squeezed Eva's body even tighter and looked up into the deepening blue sky, inappropriately clear for Guerline's dark musings. For the first time, she contemplated cremation. It was a grave dishonor for a body not to be given again to the earth, but better for her flesh to be reduced to ash than suffer the indignity of mindless reanimation. She closed her eyes and took another deep, bracing breath.

When she opened her eyes, a pale blonde girl in black stood before her. Guerline narrowed her eyes.

"I know you," she said.

"We've met," the girl said. Her lips were blood-red, her eyes dark as her dress.

Guerline remembered. The night her brother died. And . . . last night's terrible dream. "What is your name? Are you a Thiymen witch?"

"My name is Ianthe," the girl said. She looked down at Eva. "The wolf killed her."

The wolf. Lisyne. Guerline nodded, suddenly unable to speak. Ianthe walked forward until she pressed against the fountain's wall and Guerline had to crane her neck back to look her in the face. The girl knelt on the other side of the wall and rested her hands on the marble.

"I can take her soul to Ilys," Ianthe said.

Guerline's heart leapt. "But the barrier—" Her voice failed her. She didn't know what it really meant that the barrier had fallen. Was the underworld lost, or was it open? Had all the souls been let loose, or were those in Ilys still safe?

Ianthe's musical voice cut through her thoughts. "I will make it safe. It is within my power."

Part of Guerline told her she should be suspicious of this mysterious girl, but she was weak and weary of suspicion. She swallowed the lump in her throat and asked, "Why?"

After a pause, Ianthe said, "For the love you bear this girl, and for the hate I bear Lisyne."

Good enough for me. "She's not ready yet."

Ianthe laughed. "I care little for your sweet-smelling soaps. I will take her now, if you wish."

Guerline looked down at Eva and nodded. "What about her body? Will she be—if the dead rise again—"

"She will not wake."

She sighed in relief, nodded again, and held Eva out a little closer to the pool's wall. Ianthe reached down and laid a hand on Eva's chest. She lifted the hand, pulling with it the blue afterimage that was Eva's soul. Ianthe turned and, with her free hand, parted some curtain invisible to Guerline and guided Eva's soul through, singing over it in a language Guerline didn't recognize. Inch by inch, Eva's essence disappeared. Tears streamed down Guerline's face as she watched, and as the last of the light faded, Guerline closed her eyes.

"He told her that he'd kill you. If she warned you," Ianthe said.

If Guerline's heart continued to seize the way it had so many times over the last few days, she would surely die herself. She didn't even try to breathe through the pain in her chest as she met Ianthe's gaze, letting the tightness take her lungs until she was forced to gasp.

"What?"

Ianthe smiled sadly at her. "Lisyne did not tell you everything. Yes, Eva knew of Alcander's . . . intentions. And he swore to her that he'd kill you if she told."

Sobs wracked Guerline. "So she gave me the dagger." She shut her eyes again and curled around Eva's body, now soulless, now truly dead. Her own flesh felt numb, but she still noticed when Ianthe kissed the top of her head. She shot out a hand and grasped Ianthe by the wrist.

"Who are you? How do you know this; how do you know what Lisyne said in the throne room?" she demanded.

Ianthe looked down on her with eyes so black they made the night seem bright, so dark they reflected nothing. She twisted her hand so that she clasped Guerline's wrist in return, sat down on the fountain's edge, and leaned in close.

"Listen to me now, Guerline. Leave this place. Leave this land, which has taken everything from you. You owe nothing to Arido anymore," she said.

She pulled out of Guerline's grasp and walked away. Her steps hardly made a sound against the stone path.

"Ianthe," Guerline called.

She was almost surprised when the girl stopped and turned her head just enough for Guerline to see the rise of her cheekbone.

"If I tell Lisyne what you've said, what you've done . . . what will she say to me? What name will she give you?" Guerline asked.

Ianthe turned completely around and smiled at Guerline, a smirk that seemed familiar to her. A breeze swirled around them, meeting Guerline's damp skin, raising goosebumps all along her arms and lifting Ianthe's wispy blonde hair.

"Know this. Lisyne would have eaten your Eva whole, if it weren't for the witches. She still wants them to revere her, but even the Kavanaghs could not abide the mutilation the wolf would have wrought upon her flesh," Ianthe said.

When Guerline spoke, it was hardly more than a whisper. "Tell me who you are."

"You know already." Ianthe glanced down and laughed, a quiet, private laugh that Guerline almost could not hear. "And yet, you let me take her."

Guerline swallowed, a fresh wave of tears stinging the corners of her eyes; but she would not let them fall. She looked down at Eva, who could almost have been asleep had her skin not been so ashy, and folded the dead woman into a tight embrace. When she looked up, Ianthe was gone.

Instead, she saw Desmond returning with Theodor, jogging lightly down the path toward her. Theodor came to a stop a few feet from the edge of the fountain and immediately reached down, pulling off his boots and stockings. Desmond hung further back, his arms draped with a white dress, a blanket, and several small pots. Guerline watched them, exhaustion settling into her limbs like ropes tightening around her and holding her immobile. She saw the look on Desmond's face, a sweet attention that had never been there before, and felt utterly incapable of dealing with it. She wished he would just leave.

Her gaze met Theodor's; she saw there the steady calm she'd come to expect from him, and knew having him help her with Eva was the right decision. He nodded to her, a smile in his eyes if not on his lips, and turned away to gather the things they'd need from Desmond.

"Thank you, Desmond," Guerline said, her voice quieter than she'd intended.

"Please let me stay, Guerline. I don't want to leave you. I'll just sit over here," he said.

She shook her head, struggling to swallow the bile that rose in her throat. Theodor, silent and diligent, arranged the pots of oils and perfumes along the fountain's wall, then stepped into the water and knelt. He slipped his arms around Eva, taking the weight from Guerline. She rocked back and let her arms go loose, sighing as they sank slowly to her sides.

"At least tell me why, Lina! Why won't you let me—"

Guerline snapped her head up and gazed wide-eyed at Desmond. "Because you did *nothing* to help her. Because all you've done since you arrived is distrust her and, by extension, me. And because even now, all you can think about is your desire to insinuate yourself into my life, even as the woman I love lies dead in my arms!"

She stood, her legs tingling after kneeling for so long, water streaming down the sodden fabric that clung to her rolling form.

"You don't deserve to lay a hand on her. Not even to look at her. Now leave," she said.

Desmond stared at her, slack-faced with shock, and a cold flower of regret blossomed in her heart. She didn't want to cause him pain, but her heart was too overwhelmed, and if he stood there looking at her like that for a moment longer, it would shatter. She looked down and sank back into the water, her hand finding Eva's beneath the surface.

"I'm so sorry, Guerline. I didn't mean . . . please, tell me how I can best be of service to you."

Guerline glanced up and met Theodor's eyes instead of Desmond's. Her voice was caught somewhere behind her sternum. Theodor twisted his body and looked at Desmond over his shoulder.

"Perhaps you and Lord Marke might mobilize the Guild of Guards?" he suggested. "Have them join the muster in the Valley?"

Guerline kept her gaze trained on Theodor's shoulder and listened to Desmond respond.

"Yes. Of course."

His boot heels clicked against the stone where Ianthe had passed so silently mere minutes before. The sound faded until all she could hear was the gurgle of the fountain behind her. She let out a shuddering breath that had not fully escaped when her lungs contracted again and forced her to gasp.

"Thank you, Theodor," she whispered.

"Offer me no thanks, Guerline. I have done nothing more than be of service to my friend," he said softly.

She opened her mouth to thank him again, despite his words, but she could not summon up the energy to speak. Theodor reached out and put a hand on her shoulder. The pressure of his hand grounded her, brought her back to herself and gave her something to focus on other than the roiling knot in her stomach. She met his gaze, and he smiled at her, just the slightest upturn of his mouth's corners. She returned it, and nodded once.

He shifted his hold on Eva's body, splaying one hand under her neck and head and one in the small of her back, and lifted her so that she was nearly parallel to the fountain's floor. Guerline slowly and carefully unlaced Eva's linen shifts and pulled them off one at a time, leaving her naked in the water. Theodor moved his hands only to let Guerline maneuver the clothing, putting his hands back exactly where they'd been after she passed.

Guerline took the first pot and poured some of its contents, a sweet oil, into her hands. Theodor, who had been sitting back on his heels, rose up and lifted Eva out of the water. Guerline rubbed her hands over Eva's body, biting her lip until it bled in an effort to keep from weeping, her vision blurred by emotion and memories of their fifteen years together. She saw Eva crying when her parents left her behind at the palace, the collateral and payment for her merchant father's debts. She saw Eva leading the pack of hunters, tall and proud atop her great bay gelding. She saw

Eva, tangled in Guerline's own pale blue sheets, one naked, golden leg exposed, and remembered the way it felt when they were flesh to flesh together.

She and Theodor washed Eva down with the holy oils and soaps, and Guerline took as long as she could despite the utter pointlessness of it because every moment was another one before Eva was taken away from her forever. Every moment was one where she could pretend that this was someone else, and that Eva would arrive any moment carrying more rags for them.

But finally it was over, and Eva's cold, stiff form was washed and dressed in a white gown that once would have made her skin shine in contrast, and Theodor called in the servants to carry her away. Guerline sat on the edge of the fountain, her own dress still sodden, and Theodor knelt in front of her.

"Guerline. Where shall I send them?" he asked.

She shook her head to clear the fog. "What?"

"Where shall they take her?" His gaze flicked briefly toward the servants, holding Eva on a stretcher. "What of her soul?"

Guerline inhaled sharply. She pushed her shoulders back and looked at the servants, waiting expectantly.

"Take her to the mausoleum. Bury her as usual, the way it was before," she said.

The servants nodded and shuffled away. Guerline looked back down at Theodor, who sat still, with one ear tilted in the direction the servants had gone. When the sound of their footsteps could no longer be heard, he lifted his gaze to hers.

"Tell me," was all he said.

She put her hands in his and gave a slight tug. He took her cue and rose, repositioning himself next to her on the fountain's wall. She took a deep breath and shut her eyes. Immediately, she regretted doing so. Opening her eyes again felt impossible. She swayed, and felt a hand on her cheek—Theodor's, guiding her to lean her head upon his shoulder. She acquiesced.

"The world has upended itself, Theodor. The shifter gods walk among us, but they aren't gods. And what's more, they are murderers," she said.

She explained what he had missed, how the gods and the Kavanaghs had appeared, how the so-called Mother of Arido had killed Eva, and what Lisyne had told them about the evil that lay under the mountain. She rose from the fountain wall, tracing Ianthe's steps down the path.

"Lisyne called her the chaos of the world," Guerline said, "but she helped me. She made sure Eva's soul would be at rest."

"Ianthe, you mean. The form it used to come to you," Theodor said.

She whirled around. "No . . ." Her heart tightened. "Please, don't take this from me."

"Lina . . ." He stood too and walked to her, wrapping his arms around her and holding her tightly. She closed her eyes and pressed her face into his chest.

It had not been Ianthe she'd seen in the throne room, it was Alcander. Yet Ianthe had known what Lisyne said. Ianthe was no savior, no more than Lisyne herself. Ianthe was indeed the creature from under the mountain. Guerline remembered now all the glimpses she'd had of Ianthe, always showing up in her nightmares, overseeing the phantoms that stalked her—there for the blink of an eye, until Guerline spotted her and she retreated.

Guerline strongly suspected that Ianthe had killed her parents, had killed Alcander, and had sent the visions of them to haunt both her and Evadine. Ianthe had caused Eva's madness; Alcander was her puppet. Fiona Kavanagh was dead. The villain could be no one but Ianthe; no one else was powerful enough.

But Guerline could not deny that Ianthe had always been tender with her in their interactions. How could that be so, how could the evil under the mountain of which Lisyne spoke be the same as the beautiful woman who spoke so softly to her?

The Guard was already mobilizing; the Lords Paramount had flown back to their clans to gather their forces. Guerline had given the order to muster, and it did not feel like she could take it back. And what if Lisyne was right, what if Ianthe's behavior toward Guerline was a manipulation? Why *had* Ianthe left Guerline alive?

And while she sat here, her people were starving in the south, being hunted in the north, waiting for another disaster in the west. Guerline broke away from Theodor and rubbed furiously at her face.

"We go to war against the mountain," she said. "Ianthe—the creature—will be resealed in its prison, and things will go back to the way they were."

"Let me come with you," he said.

She faced him. "To what end?"

He reached for her hands, and she laced her fingers through his.

"You will always have my support, Lina," he said.

She closed her eyes again and sighed. As much as she wanted to say yes, to bring him with her, she couldn't. There was no one left for her to trust but Theodor. Evadine was dead. She was wary of Desmond, of the way he looked at her and his obliviousness to her pain. The gods were maniacs. The Kavanaghs were impotent. And the creature from under the mountain had given her a tiny, shining sliver of hope that was snuffed out by the truth.

"I need you here, Theodor," she said. She opened her eyes. "I need you to stay in Del."

He frowned, almost, just a slight downward twitch of his mouth; but then he sighed and nodded.

"Of course, Your Majesty," he said.

"Please, Theodor, I wish you wouldn't call me that. Not when it's just us," Guerline said.

He sighed again and squeezed her hand before letting go. "I know. But Guerline-basi, you *are* empress, no matter who you're with. Your father—"

"My father hardly set an example I wish to follow," Guerline whispered. After a moment, she asked, "Was he a good emperor? Really?"

"He was not loved . . . but he was respected. He was decisive and just."

Guerline sat down again on the fountain wall and traced her finger through the droplets of water on its surface.

"The thing is, Theodor, I don't *want* to be empress," she said. She laughed briefly, in relief at finally saying it out loud. "I never thought I'd have to be, and I was always grateful for that. You're so . . . exposed as a monarch. Visible. The measures my father took to create privacy for himself. . . . And half the time there's no correct way to do something, because you'll always be disappointing or angering someone. All you can really go by is your own sense of right and wrong, and it's so hard to be confident in that when everyone is telling you differently."

She looked up at him. "When they all died . . . you and Eva were the only ones who made me feel like I could handle this. And now that she's . . . you're the only one I trust to stay loyal to me when I'm gone."

"So you intend to ride with them," he whispered.

"What else can I do?" she asked.

He took up her hand and kissed it. "Then come. We must prepare you for the muster."

CHAPTER TWENTY-FIVE

DESMOND STALKED THROUGH THE GARDEN'S LABYRINTH, walking, walking, not minding at all the turns he took. When he was ready to get out, he'd vault the hedges; he was tall enough. For now, being able to simply move provided at least some outlet for his agitation. Spurned. She had spurned him, had sent him away in favor of *Theodor Warren*, as simpering a nobleman as Desmond had ever met. What of all their years of friendship? He had taken special pains to reach out to Guerline, to befriend her, because he had sensed how lonely she was. Did she have so many friends now that she could discard him?

It was only yesterday that she'd told him she was glad he was with her.

Evadine, again, had influenced Guerline—even in death, apparently, Evadine held sway over her. Evadine had not liked Desmond, and therefore Desmond was no longer permitted to be alone with Guerline. The memory of Evadine and Guerline kissing played over and over again in his mind's eye and he dissected it, drawing a different conclusion with each viewing. Was it a kiss of lifelong friends? Or were they really lovers? Jealousy squirmed like a snake in his belly, and he was instantly annoyed with himself. He had never been so possessive . . . but then, he had never truly loved a woman before Guerline. That was the only explanation that fitted all the circumstances; he was in love with Guerline, and that was why the thought of her being Evadine Malise's lover made him so uncomfortable.

Did it matter, though, what their relationship had been, now that Evadine was dead? Soon enough, Guerline would forget the strength of her feelings. The dead would fade and make room for the living.

He sank to the ground, leaning against the prickling hedges. He must be patient, that was all.

"Enjoying the mild night, witch-son?"

Desmond leapt to his feet and jerked toward the voice. Lisyne herself stood two horse-lengths from him, leaning casually against the hedges and smiling at him, white teeth with a hint of red gums visible in the still warm light of late afternoon. He took a deep breath and gave her a small bow. Her smile widened and she came closer.

"Enjoying may be the wrong word," she said.

He stiffened, and the pleasantry he'd been prepared to offer died on his tongue. Did she know what had passed at the fountain?

"Of course," she said with a scoff. "You're no fool, witch-son, you know your blood belongs to me."

"I don't know what you mean," he said.

She lifted her amber gaze to his, and though he truly didn't know what she meant, he felt that what she said was true. In the moment of their eye contact, every atom that made him up reached for her, sang to her, begged to be given instructions and to serve her will. The sensation frightened him, but he could not step back until she looked away; when she did, he staggered into the hedge behind him. She circled him, and he watched her, wariness and awe battling for dominance in his mind.

"Your great-grandmother betrayed me, witch-son, and I have taken the blood of the Kavanagh line as my repayment," Lisyne said. "Lirona, Seria . . . even your mother and aunts will be mine, one way or another. But you . . . your blood is mine twice over."

The shapeshifter moved with such precision it was almost uncanny to his human eyes, and awe won the war inside him. It was easy to believe that every stretch of sinew within her was handcrafted by magic, that she was in utter control of herself in a way that neither he nor even the witches could ever understand. She was nature itself, beautiful and impartial, servant to no one, master of all. Guerline, he knew, was frightened by Lisyne, and rightfully so; yet Desmond found that he felt no fear in her presence.

As if she knew his thoughts—which was foolish of him to even wonder; *of course* such a creature would know what his human mind could not hide—she smiled and said, "You must never fear me, Desmond Kavanagh. You are my miracle, the only creature of my blood in existence and the only one worthy of my love and loyalty."

"I still don't understand," he said.

Lisyne's form rippled, and when it stilled again, she was a male version of herself. Desmond blinked, and saw his mother in the arms of this male version of Lisyne, and understood.

"It's not possible. Lirona—"

"It is *possible*, Desmond. It is simply not the purview of witches to demand or decide," Lisyne said with a laugh.

Desmond sank to the ground again, his chest empty of air and organs and all except a single gaping question. "But why?"

"Many reasons, I'm sure," Lisyne replied, voice light and almost uninterested. "You needn't concern yourself much at this point in time. I tell you only to ensure you know that you can trust me, and should do so above all others, above even Olivia. I know your little empress fears me. She is wise to do so, but I fear her dislike of me will be the ruin of us all."

Guerline was afraid of Lisyne, but that didn't mean she would ignore the shapeshifter's counsel, did it? She had agreed that the thing under the mountain must be stopped, after all, and was mustering an army to support Lisyne in trapping the creature once more. Desmond frowned, torn between his fondness for Guerline and the certainty of his loyalty to Lisyne. He looked upon his newfound parent, once more in her female form, and sighed.

"Desmond, you must keep a close watch on the empress," Lisyne said. "Only she was left alive by this evil thing, and it must have some plan for her. It is possible that she has been spared only to become a trap for us."

He had not once wondered at Guerline surviving the massacre of her family, but now that he did, it seemed both unlikely and suspicious. Not on Guerline's part—she would never willingly truck with evil things—that, he was sure of; but Guerline had so little experience with magic, it would not be difficult for a powerful creature to trick her. He stood, filled with purpose. Lisyne's amber eyes gleamed proudly at him.

"You must not leave her side, Desmond," Lisyne said.

"She doesn't want to see me," he replied, remembering.

"Momentary ire over the girl's death," Lisyne said dismissively. "The reality of war is upon her, and she will need you for courage. Be moderate and respectful, and she will admit you."

"But if I must stay with her, I will not be able to join you on the field, to fight against the thing under the mountain."

Lisyne smiled. "Of course you will. Her Majesty will join us."

Desmond laughed and said, "I would be very surprised if she did."

"Morgana is sure of it, and has already departed with the intention of forging armor for her," the shapeshifter said.

Forging armor overnight? If there was anyone who could do it, it was his Aunt Morgana, but it still seemed a great risk to do so with battle so near at hand.

"The little basi doesn't know what Morgana intends to gift her; keep it that way," Lisyne said. "You must reestablish your friendship with her, and it is best that she be as unsure of herself as possible when you do so. Go now."

Desmond nodded and gave Lisyne another bow, then left the labyrinth, suddenly sure of his path even without jumping the hedges. His mind churned with all that had been revealed to him; he had not even asked if Olivia knew who had fathered him. Surely she would have recognized the shapeshifter's power, even if the form was not a commonly known one? And why else would she keep his parentage such a secret? She must have known; he would ask her before the battle, if he had a chance.

First, he must attend to Guerline. The thought of her being in thrall to the evil under the mountain made his heart ache. Hadn't she suffered enough in her life? The thing under the mountain was truly cruel to prey on the weakest of the imperial family in this way, to manipulate such a pure soul into possibly undermining everything she wished to accomplish. Guerline would be a good ruler, Desmond was sure of it, as long as *he* could ensure that she was completely in control of herself.

He made it back to the fountain and found only Theodor there, gathering up the materials from the washing. The Lord Engineer looked up in surprise.

"Master Kavanagh," he said. "I wanted to thank you," he added, before Desmond could say a thing.

"For what?" Desmond asked.

"For leaving," Theodor said. "I know Her Majesty was short with you, and I'm sorry for that, but letting her do the washing alone was a kindness she needed, and for that, I thank you."

Desmond snorted. "She wasn't alone. She was with *you*."

Theodor did not smile, only piled jars into his arms. "She wanted me here specifically because I can be unobtrusive, Master Kavanagh. I can diminish my presence in a room, and that is what I did here for her. She needed help physically, which I gave, but otherwise, she needed solitude. You could not have done that for her."

Desmond bristled even as he acknowledged the truth in what the councilor was saying, and the hidden compliment soothed him. Theodor was a meek man, to hide himself in such a way; Desmond was not, nor could he ever be such.

"My only wish is to help her," he said.

"I'm sure that's true," Theodor said evenly. "It is my hope that, from now on, you will help her in the way that is best for her, and not merely based on what you desire."

Desmond did not answer; even though he did not accept the rebuke, he didn't want to argue. After a few breaths, Theodor said, "She's gone to the armory. She means to ride into battle, and needs to be properly outfitted."

"Thank you, Lord Warren," Desmond said. He dipped his head and left.

The mail shirt was of good quality and fitted her well enough over the padded shirt and leathers, but finding a breastplate of the proper size was proving difficult. Guerline was as wide as a man, but shorter in the torso than most, and even with the layers and wrapping around her chest, her breasts gave her a shape that couldn't be matched by any of the unclaimed breastplates stored in the palace armory. The number of women in the Guardsmen's Guild had been increasing over recent decades, but most of them saw to their own armor, and the ones who had offered theirs to Guerline were, to a woman, taller and thinner than the empress.

"Never mind it," she said wearily to Josen, who was pulling off yet another breastplate that could not be buckled. "I'll wear no breastplate."

"Your Majesty, I cannot recommend you going into battle without one!" Josen said.

"Don't lie, Josen, you would not have me go into battle at all," Guerline said.

"That is true," he said without hesitation.

"I will go. No breastplate. We should be able to fit me for everything else."

With a sigh, Josen nodded, and the armory servants brought forth the remaining pieces they'd gathered. Pauldrons, vambraces, tassets, all were tried and discarded, along with many more pieces she didn't know the names of, until she was satisfactorily fitted with armor of middling quality.

"It's a shame we buried Alcander's armor," Josen muttered.

Guerline said nothing. They had held the funeral procession for him with his stuffed suit of armor as a stand-in for his body, and it was entombed with generations of royal corpses below the palace. She had no wish to ever see it again, nor anything of Alcander's. She certainly would not wear the armor of a man who hurt her into battle.

"Guerline-basi?"

Her heart leapt into her throat and she turned around. Desmond stood in the armory door. He smiled at her, even as his brow pinched in sorrow. Her guilt over sending him away welled up again, and forced her to give him a sad smile in return. She looked back at Josen and asked him to remove her armor and pack it up for the march.

So little time, she thought. They would leave at first light. The mustering fields were a day's ride north with a mix of walking and cantering, and even leaving at dawn, the infantry would not completely arrive until well into the night. Her stomach twisted hungrily, reminding her that she needed to eat and sleep. Well, eat, at least. No sleep would come to her this night, she knew that without a doubt, even as exhausted as she was. Her nightmare the night before had sapped the sleep she'd gotten of any of its restorative powers, and the day that followed had been the longest of her life. Still, sleep would elude her because of all the questions spinning in her mind. She wasn't sure she even wanted to try—she was torn between wanting to talk more with Ianthe, and being afraid of her.

"Desmond," she said, turning to him finally after her gorget was removed.

"Your Majesty," he replied. "I see you mean to ride out with us."

"I do. I don't know how much use I'll be, but if I'm sending my guards into a deathtrap, it's only fair that I go with them," she said.

She had intended it to sound brave and a little facetious, but Desmond hardly even cracked a smile. He folded his arms over his chest and said, "Would you like to spar? It's been awhile since we did any forms."

"I would like that," she said, smiling. Sparring would be just the thing to distract her through the long night ahead. She started to lift the shirt of chainmail off, but Desmond stopped her.

"I'd leave that on. Get used to moving with it," he said.

She nodded. Together, they turned and left the armory, went down the hall and into the gymnasium. She waited in the center of the sparring floor while Desmond retrieved two practice swords and handed her one. He swung his in a circle, rotating his wrist, and for a moment she thought he was going to rush her—then he came to her side and stood parallel to her.

"You remember the marks?" he asked. He demonstrated, stepping and swinging at the imaginary head, arms, legs, and chest of an opponent. Guerline followed him, multiple times, ignoring the ache that crept surprisingly quickly into her arm. How pathetic that she couldn't hold a wooden practice sword aloft for more than ten minutes! What was she thinking, to ride into battle?

"It's good of you to go," Desmond said suddenly. She blinked at him, shocked that he seemed to have read her mind, and then his lazy smile found its way to his mouth. "Your frustration's all over your face, Lina," he continued.

"It's foolish to be frustrated," she replied. "I know I'm no warrior."

"But you are empress, and it will give confidence to the soldiers that you're with them. That's what matters," he said.

She lifted her sword and frowned at it. "And who will give confidence to me?"

"I will. I won't leave your side; I'll—if you let me, I'll be with you every step of the way."

She heard the tenderness in his voice, and could not take her eyes off her sword. Why was Desmond so protective of her? They were friends, sure, but he had many all over the empire. As special as his friendship was to her, she knew he had no reason to feel the same about hers. What had she ever done to inspire such loyalty in him, or in Theodor, or even in Eva? She closed her eyes to stave off the tears that threatened. There was a reason she had so few friends; there was little in her worth loving.

"Lina?"

"I'm all right," she said.

"Tell me what you're thinking."

She laughed, mirthlessly. "Why? What's the purpose? We should all just be silent until this is over. We'll ride against the mountain, and we'll all die, and perhaps Arido will be . . ."

Safe. What did *safe* even mean? Safe from Ianthe and her rising corpses? Safe from the mad shapeshifters who cared nothing for human lives? She tried to be afraid of Ianthe, but when she summoned up that chill, it was Lisyne's face that snarled and snapped at her. For weeks, Guerline had fantasized about running away, and Ianthe had told her to do exactly that. *You owe nothing to Arido anymore*. She could see truth in that and felt cold in her chest at the thought. Just as clear was the sense that Ianthe meant to do harm to the empire and the people; she would have revenge for her long imprisonment. Guerline understood that desire but felt sick knowing that Ianthe's revenge would be taken on humans who were millennia removed from the wrong that had been done her. Where was the retribution in that? She couldn't let Ianthe do that, as much as she might wish that the creature could go free.

"Lina, please. Is something troubling you?" Desmond asked. "You can tell me anything. Or perhaps we should go to Lisyne—"

"No," Guerline said. She stepped into a fighting stance again. "I'm all right. Let us spar."

CHAPTER TWENTY-SIX

OLIVIA BURST THROUGH THE DOORS OF SITOSEN CASTLE, blue sail fluttering behind her. The witches in the great hall leapt up from their desks and ran toward her, clamoring to hear where she'd been and what she'd learned, whether her sisters were joining with her, and what their next step was. She tapped the shoulders of a few and whispered to them, ordering them to go through the rest of the castle and bring the entire clan to the hall for her announcements. They pushed their way through the crowd and dispersed into the different wings of their home. Olivia strode right up to her massive mahogany desk, raised up on a platform above the other desks lining the room. She sat down in her huge wingback chair and looked down at the witches gathered before her.

"Make room," she said. "Your sisters are coming, for you all must be present to hear what I have to say."

The witches pressed together and waited. Shortly more witches began to appear, all of them cramming into the center of the room and whispering amongst themselves. Olivia watched them patiently. Some looked fearful, others almost excited. Many simply waited silently, staring at Olivia, breath bated. There was an atmosphere of apprehension. They all knew that whatever was happening was once in a lifetime, even for those with such long lifetimes.

Finally, the hall was full. Several minutes went by where no more witches appeared. Satisfied that everyone had come, Olivia stood. The room instantly went quiet, and all eyes looked to her.

"My sisters of Sitosen, the time has come for us to go to war," she said.

Not a sound came from the gathered witches. Olivia could understand their confusion. Her clan was the clan of learning and knowledge, and while they of course were well-read in military history, strategy, weaponry, and the like, it was more theoretical than practical knowledge. That was not their function; it was Adenen clan's. Olivia stayed silent and watched the faces of her witches grow pale with the realization that whatever it was that needed fighting was too much for the Adenen witches alone. It didn't take long for them all to understand just how serious their situation was.

"We go to war against a thing of evil from legends that we have never even heard before," Olivia continued. "So arm yourselves, my sisters, with steel, with iron, with all your knowledge, and be brave."

She looked sadly over these witches that were hers to command, witches who had studied martial arts without ever thinking that they would one day use them, witches who were collectors rather than implementers of knowledge. She ached, seeing the resolute looks on their faces; they would fight, though they understood that many would die and that, though it was absolutely necessary, triumph was by no means certain. *My brave, brave witches. Let no one ever question the convictions of Sitosen clan.*

"The teachers will stay here at Sitosen castle with the students," Olivia said. "Every other able-bodied witch must go to the armory and prepare. Tesla, Carulina!"

The two witches made their way to the front. They bowed their heads, kissed their closed fists and raised them to Olivia.

"You will oversee the arming, and you will be my generals," Olivia said.

Tesla and Carulina nodded grimly. Then they turned, faced Sitosen clan, and began to direct them. Sitosen had enough weapons and armor for every witch in the castle. They were meticulously maintained, though they had not been used since the Thiymen Rebellion over nine hundred years earlier.

Olivia watched them leave, then ascended the stairs to her chambers. She went through her study into a very small room which she had not entered for almost a year. She raised her arms slowly; as she did, light came up in the dark room to reveal two sets of armor, two shields, two swords, and a bow and arrow. Her armor was a pale sky blue inlaid with silver, simple and sleek. There were wings on her shoulders and on either side of her helm, which featured a full cage mask over her nose, mouth, and chin.

The other set of armor was Desmond's, designed just like Olivia's except for a darker shade of blue. Her heart skipped a beat when she looked at it. Desmond would fight on the ground with Guerline. He would not be able to convince her to stay out of the fighting, so he would stay with her. Olivia reached up and put a hand on the expansive breastplate. She would pack it up and bring it along to the muster. Like all witch-armor, his was spelled for strength and protection against magic as well as weapons. He would need it in this battle.

Olivia turned away from her son's armor and stripped out of her gowns. She dressed herself in the simple tunic and trousers she wore under her armor and put on all her pads and leathers. Her fingers moved deftly over strings and straps, practiced despite how infrequently she had donned this garb. There were some things, it seemed, that one never forgot, and her grandmother Lirona had always impressed upon all of them the necessity of being ready for battle at all times, no matter what your clan. *We have not done the same*, Olivia thought regretfully. *My witches understand the concept of war. They understand what happens, and they understand why we fight. But will it be enough for them when the battle begins? Will they hold their ground?*

She stood before her armor, staring at it like it was another person. Then she lifted the breastplate.

I will hold my ground, and so will they.

Olivia put her armor on piece by piece, using magic to fasten straps and buckles she couldn't reach herself. The armor was not heavy; it was so light, in fact, that she hardly knew she was wearing it, except for the sounds it made when she moved and the different pieces touched each other. She almost wished that when she forged it, she had left some weight to it. Her assumption had been that it would be better to have lighter armor so that it didn't weigh her down or tire her unnecessarily during a battle, which she knew was still the case—but she had a desire to externalize the heaviness she felt in her heart, and had hoped to transfer that feeling to the weight of her armor.

She turned next to her sword. Lirona had made it for her, as a gift. Each of the sisters had gotten one when Lirona turned over control of the clans to them. The sword was called Silence, and silent it was. It was thinner than a typical longsword and made absolutely no sound, even when slashed through the air with full force. Olivia wondered whether it would make a sound when it hit armor or flesh or bone. She had never had to use it in a situation where she could find out, and had never thought to test it. She buckled the sheath around her waist, then lifted Silence from its bracket and slid it slowly into the leather.

The last piece of her ensemble was a very special shield: Neria's Shield. Olivia stood in front of it and stared, remembering twenty years ago when Arginine and Alanine Maravilla had snuck into her chambers while she was giving a lesson and tried to make off with the shield. She had caught them while they were still trying to unravel one of the first layers of enchantment on it, the one that prevented any but the current leader of Sitosen clan from touching it. They had never told her why they were trying to steal it, but Olivia had a fairly good guess. Neria's Shield had been made by Lirona for Neria, the first leader of Sitosen, for the specific circumstance of an attack from Thiymen clan. Petra had been a proud, bitter, and unforgiving witch, and though Lirona appointed her to rule Thiymen, Lirona did not trust her. Knowing that Sitosen was the closest and the easiest to approach from Thiymen, Lirona had forged for Neria a shield that would repel black magic. When Petra attacked with her necromancers and hoards of demons all shrouded in grave mist, Neria raised her shield and they were all thrown back.

Even then, it seemed, Arginine and Alanine were seeking to use the energy from the underworld, and had wanted the shield to protect themselves.

The energy from the underworld.

Had they ever found a way to purify it? Could it be used?

Olivia pointed at Desmond's armor and weapons. They leapt from the wall and began to pack themselves in a crate that was pushed against the edge of the wall. Olivia took Neria's Shield down and strapped it over her back. She then left the room and went down to the stables, the crate of armor floating behind her.

The witches of Gwanen shuddered with horror, and Aradia looked down at them from her high seat with tears in her eyes.

"I know, my darlings, I know! This thing is an abomination; it is the opposite of all the life and growth we hold so dear," she said. "That is precisely why we must go to war and stop it before it can ruin all that we have worked for."

Her followers looked up at her, and Aradia saw the fear and pain in their eyes. They were nurturers, not fighters. They gave life to things; they did not bring death. But that which they would have to fight was already dead, and she saw that they knew that. The witches looked up at her and they were afraid of this evil that brought blight to growing things, but they were more afraid of what would happen if they did not stop it. There was fear in their eyes, but there was no hesitation.

"Teachers and students shall remain. Jaela, Hewyna," Aradia said, looking down at them. "Lead everyone to the armory and get them ready. We leave within the hour."

Jaela and Hewyna nodded, kissed their fists, and bowed. They split the gathered witches and went to prepare.

Aradia, too, went away to prepare herself.

The sun poured into her chambers, which normally would have been a comfort to her. Now, though, her mind was clouded with fear and apprehension. She strode across the room to a wall of hanging vines. She placed her hands gently on them, and they drew apart, revealing a small room. There, Aradia's armor was displayed. It was made of leather rather than steel. She remembered Morgana's surprise when Aradia announced her decision to use boiled leather instead of metal to make her armor.

"Won't it bother you that you're wearing a dead animal?" Morgana asked.

"Do my clothes, made of dead plants, bother me?" Aradia asked with a slight laugh. "Death is part of life, but steel doesn't die, not in the same way that plants and animals do. I would rather be protected by something that used to be alive. I understand it better than I understand metal."

Morgana had laughed it off and Aradia had gone on to make her armor. It was hard and many-layered leather molded to her form. She had a coat of scale armor made from bone which she wore underneath the leather breastplate. She stared at the scales for a moment, thinking of the animals from which the bone had come and glancing over the uneven yellowing that decorated it. She reached out and touched the smooth, polished surfaces.

Protect me, she thought, *as you once protected the organs of your own body.*

She stripped and donned her armor. As she ran her hands over the breastplate, reaching around to fasten the straps, she felt the fine detailing on it. It had begun as a simple design, and the longer she'd worked at it, the more intricate it became: scenes of jungles and plants and animals hidden in a maze of delicate lines burnt into the leather. She looked up at her helm, a half-helm with nose and cheek guards. But she would wait to put that on. She turned next to her weapon.

Her sisters had each received swords from their grandmother Lirona, but Aradia had not. Instead, Lirona made Aradia a tall and exquisite scythe which she named Mercy. It was hung on the wall, its curved wooden handle cradled by the vines that held it steady. The blade was a brilliant shining silver, etched with ivy leaves on the forte. Aradia ran her fingers over the handle and the vines which clung to it released their grip. Mercy fell gently into Aradia's hands. Lirona had chosen this weapon for her because of her comments about steel when making her armor.

"I thought you'd prefer the wooden handle," Lirona had said.

And so she did.

When Morgana arrived back at Fortress Adenen, she needed only to look at Aalish to set the gears of war in motion. Her Hand sent witches running with messages for the six lieutenants, ordering them to prepare their battalions. Each battalion was made up of one hundred mounted witches and each could be ready to march in half an hour. Aalish also sent word to the trainers to assemble any battle-ready students and others who had not yet been promoted to mounted battalion into an infantry column. It was all undertaken very quickly. Adenen spent much of their time training and running drills for this very thing. They had it perfectly timed.

While Aalish took care of rallying the troops—who needed no speeches about why they went to war and what they were fighting for; such things were saved for the battlefield—Morgana went to her private forge in the belly of the fortress. She had seen the look in young Guerline's eyes. The empress meant to fight in this war. They were too pressed for time to either convince her otherwise or to train her properly, Morgana recognized that, but there was another way in which she could offer aid to her brave young liege lord.

The empress needed a set of armor, and a sword.

The fire blazed up in the furnace when Morgana entered. She smiled, then took a deep breath and closed her eyes. She centered all her strength and held it there. She visualized Guerline's height, weight, and shape, memorizing every detail and designing the armor in her mind. Slowly, slowly, she let her power flood through her whole body once more.

She opened her eyes, and burst forth into the room.

She moved almost too fast to see, gathering materials sometimes with her hands and sometimes by summoning them to her from across the room. She lay flat sheets of metal out on the ground and cut the pattern, then took up a piece and began to hammer the edges out upon a sinking die with her rounded hammer. She worked quickly, moving from piece to piece, hammer to hammer, anvil to anvil as she molded the metal. She fed magic into it the entire time she worked: spells of protection and power and courage. She wanted to give Guerline armor that would support her as much as possible, as well as keep her safe. The rest would come down to Guerline's own strength.

Morgana kept the design simple, since she was so pressed for time, but she did add a slight hint of color to the steel. She chose a lovely, rich shade of purple, the color which represented the royal house. She was also able to add some small flourishes to the shoulder articulations. Her only other adornment to the armor was the crown which she worked onto the helm, bright silver against the purple so that everyone on the battlefield would know that the wearer was the empress.

Morgana moved on to the sword. The fire in the forge flared up once more and swirled with magic. The sword would end up being almost all magic-forged. It would use up a great deal of Morgana's strength, but she could rest on the march in a wagon designed for that very purpose. Aalish would lead. She took a deep breath and thrust the metal into the furnace, turning it slowly and feeding power down through her tongs.

Two hours later, the sword was laid out on her workbench and she held her hands over it, finishing the spells. It was thin and light, like her sister Olivia's sword, Silence. Morgana thought that would suit the young empress. The sword pulsed under her fingers and she whispered soothingly to it. It wanted to be held, and swung, and named.

Wait a little while longer, and you'll meet her, Morgana told it.

She lowered her hands just as Aalish came in.

"Commander, everything is ready. We await your order," she said. She paused as she took in the scene and realized that Morgana was not suited up in her armor. "Are you—"

"Pack my armor, and Honor and Duty," Morgana said, referring to her double blades. "I will don them at the muster. I must rest on our march."

Aalish's gaze fell on the armor and the sword on the table.

"Yes, pack these as well," Morgana said.

Aalish nodded. She went to Morgana and placed a hand on her shoulder. Morgana felt warmth seep through her body as Aalish transferred a little bit of power to her. Smiling, Morgana clasped Aalish's hand, and then the two broke apart. Morgana left the forge to go and make sure her cart was ready, and Aalish began to pack the gifts for Guerline.

Morgana was on her way to the stables to hitch up the cart to her destrier, Seamus, and trying to figure out a way to pacify him enough to get him to wear the thing when a figure stepped out from the side of the yard and grabbed her

arm. She turned to see Aasim standing there in his full cer-
emonial robes. The expression on his face was a difficult one
to read. It seemed to shift back and forth between anger and
concern. She realized that it must have been very strange for
him to have her snatched by a huge wolf in the middle of
the night and then not to hear from her upon her return.
To be honest, she had forgotten about him, what with the
undead and the personification of sickness and evil they
were preparing to fight. But Aradia would tell her that was
no excuse. She owed Aasim an apology.

"I . . . am sorry, Aasim," she said painfully. "I should
have told you I was back."

"I tried to raise your clan to find you when you were
taken," Aasim said, his voice carefully restrained. "But
Captain Aalish did not seem concerned. Surprised, but not
concerned."

"That's because the wolf who took me is a shapeshifter
named Lisyne. She's . . . she's rather a legend around here,"
Morgana said, struggling to find an explanation that would
make sense to a foreigner. "She's been in hiding for one thousand years, which is why I was so shocked when I saw her.
But she was the one who trained the first witches, and so we
all know her history—at least from before she disappeared."

"So Aalish . . ."

"Would have known who took me, and that there was
nothing she could do about it," Morgana finished. "It's all
right."

"And now, you are going to war. Is this because of
something the shapeshifter told you?" he asked.

"It is. She told us what is behind the disasters, and that is what we are going to fight. We are going to bind it up and imprison it again."

Aasim stared at her, his jaw clenched, his eyebrows knitting and unknitting. He seemed to be deciding whether or not her explanation was enough to justify the damage to his pride, the embarrassment he must have felt after going to Aalish and having his fear for Morgana's life met with dismissal. *Aalish is too much like me*, Morgana thought. *We must learn how to communicate in a kinder fashion.*

"This thing has affected the Atithi as well," he said finally. "Fazl, Daleel, and I will go to war with you."

"Excellent," Morgana said, smiling. "You can join my brigade."

Aasim relaxed a little himself and held his arm out to her. She reached out and gripped his forearm; his hand closed around hers. They squeezed each other once, tight and brief, before breaking away, Aasim to get his horses and Morgana to finish getting her cart ready.

She pulled Seamus out of his stall and told him to stand and wait while she went to get the cart. When she pulled it toward him, he snorted and stamped one of his hooves. Morgana rolled her eyes and put the harness on him. The cart was just a little thing, covered on the inside with pillows and blankets, with doors at front and back. They had a number of larger ones for long marches so that those who needed it could rest; she was the only one who had a private wagon.

Once she'd finished hitching the cart, she led Seamus out and past the rows upon rows of mounted witches waiting outside Adenen's walls for the order to march. She went to the front of the column, where she found Aalish and the wizards waiting for her. She led Seamus into place, then opened the back doors to her cart.

"Aalish, forward march," she said, and climbed in.

CHAPTER TWENTY-SEVEN

MORNING LIGHT GLINTED OFF DEWY CANVAS AS GUERLINE rode aimlessly through the quiet camp on her gelding. With the exception of a small force left to guard the city, the entire Capital Guild had ridden forth to join the muster in the Achazia Valley. Guerline had also sent messages by horse and bird and spell to the major cities, drafting their forces too. She and the rest of the capital contingent had arrived with the sunset the day before yesterday, and soldiers were still streaming in from all directions. She'd tried to catch the officers as they appeared, with mild success. There would have to be a more official conference once everyone had arrived, either that night or early the next morning.

If Ianthe gives us that much time.

She shook her head. She had to stop thinking of the thing under the mountain as the woman who had shown mercy to Eva and remember that Ianthe was as complicit in Eva's death as Lisyne. Ianthe had sent Eva's madness.

Desmond rode behind her on his bay, Keno, carrying her standard. Guerline had been confined to the palace growing up, barely allowed into the First Neighborhood of Del, never mind the rest of the empire, and excluded from all but the most important festivals. The valley nobles and officers may have seen portraits of her, but portraits as a rule hardly looked anything like the people they were supposed to be depicting. So Desmond followed with Guerline's banner, the bright silver starburst on a rich purple field. She wore her hair braided in a crest along her head, her delicate crown-combs in place on either side.

Guards dropped to their knees and jumped out of the way as they rode through. Guerline waved to them on each side, acknowledging them as they called out to her. Some, especially those who had not been present for the undead fiasco, seemed confused and unsure whether they ought to be reporting to her. Some gave her such a clear expression of amazement that she caught herself wondering, as they were, what she was doing there.

But as strange as it felt to be amidst the clanging of steel and the stomping of horses, there was a part of Guerline that felt at home in the camp. She was afraid, yes, of what they were gathering for, but it was a relief to her to see that so many had come. She was comforted by their presence. They came to take up arms against something more dark and terrible than anything they had ever known, but they had all come, and they were all prepared to go into battle together.

There was such a camaraderie amongst the guards. It made her smile, especially when they hailed her and made her part of it. This happened more with the capital guards than those from the outer cities, but the word spread quickly around the camp that the young empress was among them and would command them. The men and women seemed to be heartened by that knowledge, and her presence, as much as Guerline was heartened by them.

She and Desmond rode back toward the center of the camp, where her massive tent stood bright and white against the sea of smaller, vaguely grey and yellowing tents of her soldiers. She'd resisted having such a grand tent at first. It hardly seemed necessary, since she didn't need to bring anything with her except a pallet to sleep on, but Desmond and her council had explained to her that it wasn't just a tent for her to sleep in; it was also where the commanders would meet, where they would discuss their plan of attack. It needed to be tall and grand so that it could be easily found. It also wouldn't hurt to show herself off to the four regional High Commanders, who might perhaps be more skeptical of her abilities than the guards in Del and the center cities, and who had not been privy to her savvy command of late. It was important for her to seem in control and prepared.

Even if she wasn't.

Guerline dismounted in front of her tent and tied her horse up at the post. She took the standard and staked it into the ground while Desmond dismounted and tied Keno up. They took the saddles off their horses and put them to the side on a waiting rack. Guerline rubbed her horse down briefly and then went into the tent, Desmond behind her.

The tent was sparsely furnished. Though her council told her that sovereigns typically brought tapestries and rugs and all other manner of decoration along with them, Guerline struck down that idea. She allowed only her pallet, an ornately carved chair to serve as a throne, a large desk upon which were spread maps and hastily scrawled notes about the situation, and many, many candelabras to light the space. To one side stood the suit of armor they'd scrounged up for her from the armory, as well as an old sword that seemed to fit her arm.

She looked dismally at the set, piecemeal and mostly antique. She was certainly glad they had found something for her, but she couldn't help but think the simple, dark grey armor would not help her inspire confidence on the field. Whether the rusted plates would protect her from unearthly blows was also doubtful.

Desmond waited for her to speak. When she didn't, he took a step forward and cleared his throat.

"Would you like to spar some more, Guerline?" he asked.

Their hasty review of basic sword techniques before leaving Del had not helped her remember so much as remind her of everything she had forgotten; but they'd kept at it until the last moment, and her confidence had increased a very small amount. She knew she ought to practice more, but another part of her felt it was too little too late. She would not become an accomplished swordswoman before the battle broke upon them. She knew that. She did not hope to be the deadliest soldier on the field, she only sought to be present on it. She would have Desmond to protect her, and Josen and a group of guards assigned to her specifically. It was more than her other guardsmen would have, and it was enough to her. To take up her sword again at this point would only dishearten her. So she turned to Desmond and smiled.

"No, I don't think so. Perhaps later. Now I would like to rest," she said.

He nodded and reached out to her. She stepped into his arms slowly, resting her head against his broad chest. She could hear his heartbeat, and she closed her eyes, focusing on the sound. It was even and steady, and she timed her breathing to match. True to his word, he had hardly left her side; yet Desmond had been formal with her since she'd sent him away from Eva's washing, keeping his distance and trying not to touch her even as they sparred. She was grateful for the space, and even for this chaste embrace; it helped to ease some of her guilt. She was frustrated and angry with Desmond, but much of it had to do with her expectations of him as a friend and how his actions with regard to Eva had felt like betrayal. But under all of that, she did still consider him a close friend, and it pained her to feel such conflicting emotions toward him. And, despite how much she might wish to, she could not yet put all her feelings to words, could summon up neither apology nor admonition.

So she stayed silent. She squeezed Desmond tightly and then released him, slithering out of his arms. She went over to her temporary throne and sat down. Desmond sat on the bench next to her desk and leaned back against the tabletop. Guerline rested an elbow on the arm of her chair, leaning her head upon her fist, and watched him. Though she relied on her own strength as much as the support she got from him, she valued his dedication to helping her. The guards may look questioningly at Guerline, human and womanly as she was, but they needed only to see Desmond standing behind her to give her a second look and an attentive ear.

Soon, I will prove myself to them on my own merit. They must respect her for going afield and being among them despite her lack of martial skill. This was her hope, anyway.

She closed her eyes, hoping for a chance to doze briefly. Hooves pounded and shouts went up from outside her tent. Desmond sat up at attention. So did Guerline. They remained as still as possible, and strained their ears to catch the words in the shouting.

The hoofbeats grew louder and Guerline and Desmond got up, going to the door of the tent and looking out. They saw a stout black pony galloping toward them. On its back was a woman in jet black armor and a flowing black cloak. Her helm had a tail of black horsehair and a full mask, so they couldn't see her face. She looked strange, riding on the pony in her armor; though the pony was large, as ponies go, it appeared smaller than it was amongst the Adenen warhorses of the guards. Guerline stared at the approaching figure. She had to be a witch, to have armor so fine, and it being black seemed to indicate Thiymen clan. With any luck, Thiymen was finally contacting them and joining the fight.

Guerline turned to Desmond to get his opinion, but the look on his face stopped her. His jaw was slack, and his eyes were wide as he stared at the woman riding toward them.

"Desmond? What is it?" she asked.

"Aunt Fiona," he said.

"What?" Guerline snapped back to look. There was no way—Lisyne herself had told them of Fiona's death, and despite the monster that she was, Guerline didn't think it was something she would lie about. But she herself had guessed that the rider was a Thiymen witch.

The rider reined up and skidded to a stop just in front of Guerline's tent. Guerline waited, as was proper, for the rider to announce herself; but Desmond could not wait. He ran right up to her.

"Aunt Fiona! Is that you?"

"Oh, Desmond. I wish for that as much as you," said the woman.

She removed her helm. She was young and beautiful, with smooth white skin and light brown eyes, like diluted molasses. Her face was flushed red with riding and the heat of her armor. Her tightly curled black hair was braided and wound many times around her head. She looked down at Desmond with anguish in her eyes and sadness in her mouth. Guerline felt a rush of warmth and a sudden urge to embrace this woman.

"Kanika," Desmond said.

He reached up and offered her a hand. She took it and swung herself down from the pony, then turned and knelt before Guerline.

"Guerline-basi, may I present Kanika Asenath, the new Heart of Thiymen," Desmond said. "Am I right, Kanika?"

"You are, Desmond, to my everlasting regret," Kanika said. "I have come now to offer what assistance I can."

"Then by all means rise," Guerline said. "We welcome you whole-heartedly. Please come in."

Guerline led them inside the tent and they each took a seat, Guerline on her throne and Kanika and Desmond on the bench.

"We are very glad that you've come, Kanika-lami. We all are. Lisyne has told us all about the thing under the mountain, but it is a comfort to have Thiymen with us as well. You are so much more intimately connected to it than the rest of us. How many of your clan have come?" Guerline asked.

Kanika grimaced. "None, Your Majesty."

Guerline blinked. "I–I'm sorry. None?"

"None. I only just escaped the Citadel myself," Kanika said.

"What happened?" Desmond asked.

Kanika took a deep breath. It was difficult to tell because of her armor, but her body seemed to be slumped, supported only by the metal. She looked up, her weariness now overpowering her expression.

"When my lady Fiona died, we—we immediately held her funeral. We entombed her in the catacombs where all Thiymen witches are laid to rest. Moira Emile, Hand of Thiymen and Captain of the Thiymen Guard, was supposed to then be recognized as the new leader of the clan, but she was severely weakened by the Guard's last attempt to push the thing under the mountain back. We waited for hours, all standing round her and feeding her power, but it wasn't enough. She too died, and leadership fell to me.

"But other than a handful of us, much of the clan seemed to have lost their minds. It is difficult to convey how much Fiona meant to us, but she was truly the backbone of our coven," Kanika said. Tears formed in her eyes. "She never let us forget how important our task was, and said that it was better to keep Arido safe and be hated, than to fail our people and be loved. It was a comfort to many of us who were sensitive to the fear humans felt of us, because we believed her. So, when she died . . . we lost the rock upon which we leaned, the pillar which held us up. It is only in the wake of her loss that we have learned how weak we truly are."

She took another deep breath and looked down at her gloved hands. Guerline waited patiently for her to begin speaking again, giving Desmond a pained look. She felt sorrow and sympathy for Kanika and the other witches of Thiymen, to have lost their beloved leader, but she also felt great disappointment to learn that Thiymen clan would not be joining their fight. But then, what were they doing? Were they still in the east?

"I see your thoughts in your face. It gets worse, Majesty," Kanika said. "I was in Fiona's rooms, preparing messages to send out to you and the other clan leaders informing them of what had happened, when great rumblings shook the citadel. I ran out and joined a crowd of my sisters, all rushing to the gate of the underworld, from whence we knew the shocks must be coming. When we got there, we saw that the gate had collapsed. The chamber was full of smoke, and down where the gate had been, there stood two witches. They were dressed in black, but I didn't recognize them. We demanded they identify themselves. Instead, they attacked us.

"They were powerful, very powerful. Though we all fought them as one, they didn't seem to tire or weaken. They just continued to repel us. But as we fought them, a strange thing happened. The smoke surrounded us, and gradually, some of my Thiymen witches ceased to battle the intruders and instead began to attack the rest of us. Breathing in the smoke was infecting them and causing them to become possessed by it. I believe it came from the thing under the mountain. I did the only thing I could think to do. I shouted an order for retreat, and we fled."

She sighed and blinked back the tears threatening the edges of her eyes again.

"The smoke chased us, claiming more as it did. I managed to make it back to Fiona's rooms and shut the door. I donned her armor, which has spells upon it to repel almost any kind of dark magic, took up her sail, and leapt from the window. The possessed witches followed me and shot spells at me. One ripped my sail, and I fell to the ground, but after that they did not chase me. I was given the pony by a farmer near Petra's Bay, and I have been riding to meet you ever since."

Guerline sat in silence for a few moments, taking in Kanika's story. She felt a sick, heavy knot in her stomach. She had hoped to have the power of all four clans on hand to remake the spell that had kept Ianthe bound. She had no sense of how the power or numbers of the shapeshifters four thousand years ago compared to the several hundred witches of each clan now, but she would rather have had more power at her disposal than less. The idea that not only would she lack the power of Thiymen clan, but that the witches of Thiymen would in fact be members of the thing's army, was almost enough to take away her hope. Desmond, too, looked grim.

"Are you the only one who escaped the smoke?" Desmond asked.

"The only one that I know of," Kanika said. "There may have been others who are in hiding."

"We thank you for coming to join us," Guerline said.

She stood and walked over to Kanika, placing her hands on the witch's shoulders. Kanika looked up at her, and with her gaze, Guerline tried to convey all her condolences and all her gratitude. But there was work to be done. There would be time to grieve later—that was what she kept telling herself, at least.

"Desmond, please escort Lady Kanika to the mess hall and get her something to eat." Guerline turned away and went back to her throne. She smiled at Kanika. "You must be famished and exhausted. Please, take your ease. We will let you know as soon as the other clan leaders arrive. Then we will discuss our next move."

Kanika rose. "Thank you, Your Majesty. I hope I may be of service."

"We have no doubt that you will," Guerline said.

She gestured toward the door. Kanika nodded and left. Desmond went over to Guerline, took her hand in his, and kissed it. She squeezed his hand, then he turned and followed Kanika out. Guerline waited a few minutes to give them time to get away from the tent, and then she too rose. She poked her head out of the flap and looked at her guards.

"Hamish, Frida," she said. "I am not to be disturbed until the Kavanaghs or the shifter gods arrive. At that time, please wake me and have them brought to me."

They nodded to her, and she retreated back into the tent. She went to the pallet that served as a makeshift bed and removed her crown, setting it on the crate next to her. Then she laid herself down, resting her head on the small pillow. During their sparring sessions, Desmond had told her that the first rule of war was to never turn down an opportunity to eat, sleep, or relieve oneself. Guerline felt that now was a good time to employ that rule, and try to get at least a little bit of rest before the storm.

CHAPTER TWENTY-EIGHT

"THERE NOW. ALL FINISHED," DESMOND SAID, SMOOTHING the canvas.

He and Kanika had eaten a quick meal in the mess tent and had just finished setting a tent of her own up right next to his, on the left side of Guerline's. He stepped inside. Kanika sat on her pallet, removing the last of her armor. Her tunic and leathers were all black as well. She finished unfastening the vambrace and laid it down on a cloth with the rest, gently. She brushed her fingers over it.

"It must feel strange, wearing her armor," he said quietly.

"It's completely unreal," Kanika said. "I mostly feel like I'm dreaming, like I've dreamed this whole thing, and any moment now I'll wake up and Fiona will be telling me some new, better way she's devised to ward the tears we make when we cross."

Desmond sat next to her. "If only this were a dream."

"But it's not, and so we must not wish it is," the witch said, sitting up straighter. She looked at Desmond and smiled. "This new empress is more composed than I expected to find her. I thought she was not given any lessons on leadership."

"She's just a natural," Desmond said. "I wish she could see herself."

"She's doing remarkably well, from what you have told me," Kanika said.

"Yes. She's brilliant. And she doesn't even realize how handily she's taken care of everything that's been thrown at her so far." He smiled bemusedly at Kanika. "I think she'll be absolutely amazing as empress."

"Yes, I thought you'd say that," she said, winking at him.

Desmond stared. He felt heat rising in his face. The memory of Guerline glaring as she stood in the fountain consumed him and for a moment, he felt dizzy. Remembering her expression and her words sent a stab of pain through his heart every time, because she'd been right. His desire to help and comfort her had had everything to do with her, not Eva, and it had made him insensitive to the kind of comfort Guerline truly needed. He only hoped the damage done to their friendship was something he could be redeemed of.

He had tried to push it all from his mind, tried to rein in his improper physical attentions to Guerline—but Kanika had still noticed something. Were his feelings still influencing his behavior, and making him too familiar in Guerline's presence?

He decided to feign ignorance. "Whatever can you mean, Kanika-lami?"

"Don't be dull, Desmond! I may be exhausted, but you can't fool me." She laughed.

"I haven't the slightest idea what you're talking about," he whispered.

Kanika frowned and leaned in toward him, tucking her chin and looking up at him through her eyelashes.

Before she could speak, though, several horns sounded across the camp. Desmond jumped up, grateful for the interruption. He really did not want to discuss his feelings for Guerline with anyone else before he had a chance to talk about them with the woman herself. Kanika was one of his many "older sisters" in the clans, but this was really an affair he would prefer to keep private until he knew what was going to happen. He didn't want to jeopardize any small hope he may have—and more than that, he couldn't afford to make a mistake and be banished from her side once more, not when the thing under the mountain might still have its hooks in her.

Kanika stood up next to him, her teasing manner gone.

"The clans have arrived," she said.

They left Kanika's tent and jogged across the green to Guerline's. Only one guard stood at the door as they approached, but a moment later, the other one emerged and jogged off toward the south. Kanika and Desmond entered the tent to find Guerline lighting candles. She finished one set and moved on to the next, stifling a yawn and rubbing sleep from her eyes.

"Oh good, you've come. Are you feeling better, Kani-ka-lami?" Guerline asked when she noticed them.

"Much, Your Majesty, I thank you."

"Desmond, could you and Frida bring the chairs in?" Guerline said.

"Of course, Your Majesty," Desmond said.

Guerline stared at him for the briefest of moments. What was going through her mind? It was impossible to tell. She nodded to him. He bowed and went outside the tent to where the chairs were stacked. Desmond wasn't sure how many they would need, so he and Frida just decided to bring them all. It took them two trips to carry them in, stacked as they were. Kanika and Guerline helped to lift and arrange them in a circle in the center of the tent, wide enough to include Guerline's throne.

"I'm not sure who all to expect," Guerline said, half to herself. "The northern legion has all arrived, as well as most of the East. We may still be waiting on some from the South, but I think the regional commanders are all here. I've sent Hamish to go and summon them. Please, be seated in the meantime."

She went back to lighting the candles and lamps. Desmond crossed to her and closed a hand over the one of hers that held the wick. Her skin was soft and warm, and the light flickered in her red-gold hair. She looked up at him, and he smiled down at her.

"I'll light the rest for you," he said. He reached up to run his hand over her hair, but caught himself. "You're missing something."

Guerline smiled back at him, nodded, and held the wick up. Desmond took it lightly from her hand and watched her walk to the other side of the tent. She picked her crown up from the crate by her pallet and slowly placed the combs into her hair, then she went to her throne and sat down. Her simple linen gown was slightly rumpled from her brief respite, but other than that, she was as lovely and well-kempt as ever. Kanika made a small coughing sound in her throat. Desmond jumped and turned away to light the candles.

He had just finished when all three of the Kavanagh sisters entered the tent. Olivia led in her sky-blue armor, followed by Aradia in her leathers. Morgana brought up the rear. She was not in her armor yet, and her hair was mussed. It looked as though she had slept on the way to the muster, following one of the rules she'd always impressed upon him: never turn down an opportunity to sleep. Behind Morgana floated a large wooden crate.

The three witches all bowed before Guerline, who sat straight now on her throne, her hair thrown behind her shoulder. She nodded to each of them and swept her hand toward the chairs they'd arranged, indicating that the Kavanaghs could take their pick. Each of them passed by Kanika and took her hand, welcoming her to the fold of command, and sat down. Morgana was the last to pass, then she guided the crate and set it down next to her chair.

"Welcome, Lords Paramount," Guerline said.

"Thank you, Your Majesty," Olivia said. "We have each of us brought the full strength of our clans to join in battle against the thing under the mountain."

Some of the tightness in Guerline's face relaxed. "Excellent. We are well pleased to hear it."

"You've gathered a sizable host here yourself, Majesty," Morgana said. "It was well and rapidly done."

"And for that, we commend our swift messengers and our well-trained guardsmen." Guerline smiled at Morgana, for it was she who had trained them. "They have not forgotten their drills, nor their loyalty. They have all come with hardly an explanation as to why, and none have questioned us so far."

Morgana laughed. "That is well. An army that does not trust their commander is practically worthless."

She glanced around the tent and caught sight of Guerline's impromptu set of armor. She laughed anew and examined it, tutting and shaking her head. Desmond glanced to Guerline and saw her mouth tighten as she struggled to hide her embarrassment. Desmond himself felt a small wave of anger rise at his aunt's lack of consideration, even though he knew what she'd brought for Guerline. Morgana was usually not one for social niceties, but this was beyond her usual absent decorum.

He stopped himself from glancing at the crate and said, "Aunt Morgana, why do you laugh so? It was the best we could find to fit her."

His aunt turned to look at him, her eyes wide and bright.

"Desmond, my dear boy. I am laughing in *relief*. I should have been very concerned for you indeed, Empress, if you went afield in such steel," Morgana said.

Desmond and Guerline exchanged looks, and even Aradia and Olivia raised their eyebrows. Morgana grinned, excitement apparently building in her, and dragged the crate into the center of the circle.

"Fear not, dear Guerline-basi. I have brought you a gift," she said.

She stood over the crate and lifted her hands. The top of the lid came off and the straw packing swirled up. Morgana twisted and turned her hands and began to arrange the something that rose out of the crate. All present leaned forward with interest, trying to make it out in the ubiquitous but flickering candlelight.

At last, the thing ceased to move, and Morgana allowed the straw to fall back down to the ground. Guerline gasped. A suit of armor was revealed, exactly Guerline's size. It was tinted a rich purple and edged with simple silver flourishes on the articulations. The full helm was topped by two rows of crystals exactly like the crown Guerline wore now. The steel plates were all arranged over a glistening coat of ringmail.

Guerline rose from her chair and went toward it. She reached out and plucked the helm out of the air, running her fingers over it. She looked up at Morgana and smiled.

"Thank you, Morgana-lami," she said. "This is exactly what I needed."

"I thought so," the witch replied. "Tomorrow, Desmond and I can show you how to get into it, and I can make any minor changes necessary. But wait, that's not all!"

She allowed the rest of the armor to descend back into the crate, but not before she plucked something quickly out of the bottom. Guerline reluctantly put her helm in with the rest and then looked with interest at what Morgana presented to her now. She gasped once more when she realized that Morgana was holding a sheathed sword out to her.

Morgana grinned. "This is why clan Adenen was delayed, and why I have not arrived in splendor like my sisters. I knew your intentions, and I knew that you were not equipped to fulfill them, so I decided to do what I could for you. I made your armor, and then I forged this—in record time, I might add."

The other Kavanaghs chuckled. Morgana shot them all a glare that only made Desmond smile wider. He could see the change the armor wrought in Guerline. She stood straighter, and she seemed to be less worried than she had been a moment before. She reached for the sheath which Morgana held out to her and took it in both hands, then looked back up at Morgana, as though wondering what to do with it.

Desmond walked over to her. "Take the handle. Draw your sword."

Guerline grinned at him and wrapped her hand around the sword's grip, finger by finger. Then she pulled the sword out of the sheath and held it aloft. It shone even in the dim light, and Desmond could feel the magic coming off of it. Morgana must have poured a great deal of her energy into the forging of this sword, both to accomplish it in time and to create the number of spells worked into the metal. Guerline gazed up at it in awe, eyes wide with wonder.

"Do you like her?" Morgana asked breathlessly.

"She is perfection," Guerline said.

She stepped back and gave it a few tight practice swings before straightening again and grinning wider than ever. Desmond too, smiled, as he saw that her technique was surer and less hesitant.

"I shall name her Order," Guerline announced.

"Ah, an excellent name," Olivia said. "May she ever be the champion of what is right and proper."

"And may you make Order from chaos," said a voice from the entrance.

All eyes turned toward the noise. Lisyne entered the tent, followed by Tirosyne and Seryne. Behind her also came a tall, dark-skinned woman whom Desmond recognized as Silas, the reclusive queen of the dragons. When Desmond was younger, he had always wondered at what a massive woman she was. Now, of course, Desmond was quite as large as Silas. The dragon queen stood respectfully behind Lisyne, her face stern and sharp.

The shapeshifters and the dragon queen stopped right in front of Guerline, in the center of the circle of chairs. They bowed to her. Guerline nodded back to them and sheathed Order. Rather than put it back in the crate with her armor, she held open the belt loop and hung it on the back of her throne. Morgana moved the crate behind the line of chairs, back to the corner of the tent where Guerline's makeshift armor stood, looking more forlorn than ever.

"We have been watching the progress of the muster from above," Lisyne said. She stepped aside and gestured to Silas. "I present Silas of Purvaja, the Dragon Queen."

Guerline nodded to her. "It is an honor to meet you, Your Grace."

"I need no great titles, Your Majesty," Silas said in her deep, rough voice. "I know my kingdom is a small one given me by your grace and the grace of Thiymen clan."

"Still, you are great." Guerline smiled at her. "We shall forever be grateful for your assistance in dispatching the hordes of undead in Del. Your actions saved many lives."

"I shall always work to rid the world of that which is evil and unnatural," Silas said, bowing again.

"So will we all," Guerline said. "Please, be seated. We are only waiting now for the high commanders of the Guild of Guardsmen, and then we may begin to address the situation at hand in more detail."

As if summoned, Hamish entered the tent, followed by three men and one woman, all in silver armor.

"Your Majesty, the High Commanders of the Guild: Bertrand Altec of the North, Tragar Madacy of the West, Yana Lot of the South, and Maddox Bolva of the East," he said, bowing and stepping out of the way.

The four commanders stepped forward, removed their helms, and bowed. Sir Bertrand was a tall, wide man of typical northern stock, with fair hair and skin. He had an elk, the symbol of his house, engraved upon his breastplate. Sir Tragar was a tall man as well, though shorter than Sir Bertrand, and only half as wide. He was a rider of great repute, and the youngest of the high commanders. He smiled broadly at Guerline, and it was pleasing enough on his handsome brown face that the young empress seemed to blush a little. Desmond crossed his arms and narrowed his eyes at Sir Tragar.

Sir Yana was a petite woman with quick green eyes and dark hair, streaked with grey and plaited. Her white bone-bow was slung over her back, and Desmond peered at it with interest. It was a well-known artifact from the early days of Arido, the weapon of choice for Dalia, the first leader of Gwanen. The story was that the heavily-spelled bow had been gifted to Tevan of the Loti, Dalia's favorite lover and Yana's ancestor. She caught him staring and winked at him. The last was Sir Maddox, a slight-framed, mountain-dwelling man with shaggy brown hair and hollow cheekbones almost hidden by his long beard. He was the oldest of them, his hair and beard streaked through with grey, and wrinkles forming webs around his eyes; but those eyes were quick, dark, and alert. Though his appearance was by far the most discomforting, especially next to the shining and healthy bodies of the others, Desmond strangely felt that Sir Maddox was the most trustworthy of them, and perhaps the shrewdest as well.

"Welcome, High Commanders," Guerline said, rising and dipping her head to them. "We cannot thank you enough for coming on such short notice and short information."

"I go where my empress directs me." Sir Tragar smiled again. Desmond thought he detected a slight rolling of the eyes from Sir Bertrand.

Guerline returned the smile hesitantly. "Thank you, Sir Tragar."

"Yes, we have come, and we are ready to do your bidding, as soon as we know what it is," Sir Yana said.

"Of course. Be seated, please, and we shall explain all."

Each of them turned and settled themselves in the remaining chairs. It appeared that everyone had naturally grouped themselves. Desmond sat on Guerline's right hand, with his mother, aunts, and Kanika all next to him; then came Lisyne, the shapeshifters, and Silas; and on Guerline's left side, the high commanders. Desmond noted with displeasure that Sir Tragar had jostled for a seat immediately next to Guerline. The witch's son glared across Guerline's lap at him. Tragar noticed his expression and winked.

Desmond decided in that moment that he was not well-disposed to this western flirt.

"So, we are all gathered . . . but where is Lady Fiona?" Sir Bertrand asked, staring at Kanika. Sir Bertrand had likely never met Fiona, but he seemed to know enough about Thiymen witches to realize that dark-haired Kanika was too young to have been leading the clan for six hundred years.

"Fiona-lami is dead," said Sir Maddox, his raspy voice cutting across the room.

"What? How can this be?" Sir Tragar asked, his smirk knocked from his face by his shock.

"Don't be a fool, boy. Can't you see that's why we're here? Because Fiona is dead and whatever killed her is coming for us all?"

Yes. Desmond was definitely convinced that Sir Maddox was his favorite.

"Is this true, Your Majesty?" Sir Bertrand asked, looking to Guerline.

"We are afraid it is," Guerline said. "The shapeshifters—"

Sir Yana noticed the shapeshifters first. "Good god! I mean, gods!" She and Sir Bertrand immediately fell out of their chairs and onto their knees, their armor clanking loudly, and bowed in the direction of Lisyne and the others. Sir Tragar only gaped, and Sir Maddox didn't move. Desmond resisted the urge to shake his head. He must remember that not everyone knew the truth. For many, the shifter gods were real, and it would be a shock to see them; but for just as many, the shifter gods were *not* real, making it a possibly greater shock to see them than it would have been for a believer. Sir Bertrand, Desmond pegged as a believer, but he could not be sure about Sir Yana.

Guerline snapped to get the attention of her commanders and gestured impatiently for them to get back up.

"Yes, the shifter gods have come down to join us," she said. "They have told us what we face."

"And what is that?" Sir Maddox asked.

"Chaos and atrophy," Lisyne said. "The opposite of all that is good and natural."

"Oh. That's all very well, then," Sir Tragar said.

"Peace, Sir Tragar," Guerline said. "Lisyne, in your flights, did you happen to observe the Zaide Mountains?"

Lisyne smirked. "Of course, Your Majesty. We observed great billows of smoke surrounding the Thiymen Citadel. There was a powerful pull coming from the mountain. The thing has thrown the gates open wide and is rallying an army of the underworld to it."

"What manner of creature may we expect to fight?" Sir Maddox asked.

"I imagine that the thing will hold nothing back," Kanika said grimly. "It has been imprisoned for four thousand years. Not only will it have the demons and monsters of hell to command, it has also taken possession of the whole of Thiymen clan."

"You mean, we'll be fighting your own witches?" Sir Yana gasped.

"You let us worry about the witches," Morgana said.

"And what are we to worry about?" Sir Bertrand asked. "Are we to fight the demons and the monsters?"

"That's exactly what we will do, Sir Bertrand," Guerline said. She stood. "This will be unlike any battle you have ever fought, and the stakes will be much higher. The only way we can succeed and defeat this thing is by resealing it and trapping it even deeper under the mountain than it was before. The shapeshifters and the witches will work to create this seal while the Guild handles whatever army the thing commands."

"But Your Majesty, how are we to fight that which we do not understand?" Sir Tragar asked.

"The monsters of the underworld are unimpressive foes, if you know how to handle them," Kanika said. "The hell-hounds, the devil-cats, they are nothing more than unfeeling bodies. Their greatest strength is their stamina, which they have in droves because their bodies are dead and do not tire. However, they may be easily stopped by dismemberment or the strategic severing of the muscles necessary for move-ment. A slash under the jaw prevents them from biting, cut-ting a deltoid stops them moving, and then all it may do is lay on the ground and gnash hopelessly at you. It will then be harmless, provided you don't step onto its teeth."

This information seemed to comfort the human com-manders, and they relaxed by the slightest degree.

"But what about the demons?" Sir Tragar pressed.

"The demons will be trickier, but there will be fewer of them. The best way to kill a demon is to cut off its head, or at least its horns. If you cut off a demon's horns, its strength will be greatly decreased, because that is how they gather their power," Kanika explained. "The hardest part about killing a demon is getting to it through its hordes of undead monsters."

The new Heart of Thiymen turned to Guerline.

"I think, Your Majesty, that it would be best if I joined you in the battle. My knowledge of these creatures will be indispensable," she said.

"We agree. We should be very glad to have you by our side." Guerline turned to her four commanders. "You have been given valuable advice for the battle. Be sure to spread it among the soldiers under your command."

They nodded vigorously. Desmond could see they were much more nervous than when they entered the tent, but their loyalty had not wavered. Sir Maddox, in fact, hardly even looked surprised at the news that they'd be battling creatures from the underworld—but that was typical of an easterlander. The only exception was Sir Tragar, whose smooth upper lip had a barely discernible sheen of sweat upon it. If anyone was going to break and run, it was going to be him. Desmond made a mental note to tell Guerline to keep Tragar in the main force. Though excellent riders typically made up the vanguard, Desmond did not trust Sir Tragar in that honored position. Better to have him in the main company, under the eyes of Guerline herself, so that if he turned and ran, the whole Guild would know his shame.

"Lisyne, have you an idea of our timeline? Do you believe the thing will march?" Guerline asked.

"It would be a poor move on his part," Sir Maddox said. "There are fewer more easily defensible places than the Zaide Mountains."

"True, very true. We can only hope that its eagerness for revenge and conquest overwhelms any good sense it has," Kanika said.

"I do not believe the thing will come down to us without enticement," Lisyne said, "but that is really all for the best. It will be easier to seal it if it stays in the mountain, but I do not believe it will do this either. It will slink out slowly during the battle. It knows we will try to seal it, but we must hide from it just how much power will be behind the seal. Therefore, the witches must appear to join in the fighting on the ground."

Everyone nodded. That much made sense; the element of surprise was an essential tactic in a battle such as this, and it was better to allow the enemy to underestimate them for a time. While the ruse would put pressure on the human army, it would hopefully give the witches enough time to prepare and allow them to end the battle quickly and decisively.

"Another thing, Empress," Morgana said. "If it can be managed, we must avoid fighting this battle during the night. That will be the thing's preference, but we cannot allow it. I suggest we march during the night so that we get to the mountains by daybreak, and then we will draw it out."

"But how will we do that if it loathes to fight in the daylight?" Guerline asked.

"That's simple. We start the seal," Lisyne said.

CHAPTER TWENTY-NINE

THEY LAID OUT A PLAN OF ATTACK THAT MOST EVERYONE agreed with. The pass leading up to Thiymen Citadel was flanked by a jut of smaller peaks on one side and Petra's Bay on the other. Creatures of the underworld were weakened by flowing water, so the goal was to push the hordes toward the water. Sir Maddox would lead the vanguard through a gap in the jut between Mon Zeferin and Mon Jarga and drive south, while Sir Yana and her archers defended from the top of Mon Zeferin. Once they were in the foothills of the mountains, Lisyne, the shapeshifters, and the Kavanaghs would form their circle and start the spells for the seal. With any luck, that would induce the thing under the mountain to attack, and leave the safety of the underworld.

Empress Guerline, Sir Tragar, and Sir Bertrand would lead the main force. The witch clans would follow them, alternating groups of Sitosen and Gwanen witches among the six Adenen battalions. The role of the dragons was hotly contested. The human commanders wanted to make full use of them, no doubt feeling that it would increase their chances substantially. Guerline quickly rejected that measure.

"Next to the shapeshifters, the dragons are indeed our most powerful asset. That is precisely why they must stay hidden until absolutely necessary," she said firmly. "We cannot reveal our full strength to the thing until the last moment. Doing so any earlier would negate the advantage of surprise."

Their numbers were at least three thousand warriors total, all of them made of flesh and blood and all subject to weariness and injury. Yet Kanika was hopeful. Hell-hounds and devil-cats were all frightening to look upon, but their bodies were held together almost completely by magic and were vulnerable if you knew how to attack them. Shooting arrows was pointless, unless one had such power and accuracy as to split muscle from bone at a distance. Spears may stick the things and hold them at bay, but they would eventually just push their way down the spear toward the attacker. Swords and axes were best, and decapitation was the most effective way to stop such a beast.

Tomorrow, Guerline would ride through the camp with Lisyne and Kanika. It was Guerline's hope that seeing Lisyne would give courage to the guards. Kanika believed that it would. She was not so sure about her presence. She realized that it was strange for her to be the only Thiymen witch in the camp, especially when the army was planning to march on the seat of Thiymen. But Guerline convinced her that riding with the empress and Lisyne would increase her credibility, and that she was best suited to answering any questions about their foes the soldiers might have.

Kanika went back into her tent and sank down onto her pallet. She was still recovering from the exorcism and healing of Jerica. She and the others who came down had thrown every cleansing charm they knew at the cursed people, and it had taken all of them to finally stop the rotting of living flesh. Even with that, many of the Jericans had died. Though she knew she should feel grieved, she was still too consumed with relief that Feoras and Lorand had survived.

Before she left the city, her son had looked up at her and very calmly told her to kill the thing that hurt his papa. She'd promised solemnly that she would.

She looked at her armor, remembering the last time Fiona had worn it, almost three hundred years ago. Kanika had been just a child, newly arrived at the Citadel. Fiona had decided it was time for her to test her armor once more, so she'd donned it and held a massive sparring match in the main hall of the Citadel. She invited any witch who dared to come forth and fight her. The black armor had glinted in the magical light that illuminated the cave, and her black sword had been so difficult to see—just flashes of light when it caught the candles—but Fiona had wielded it so masterfully that those moments were too brief to make out her moves.

The new Heart of Thiymen unbuckled that same sword's belt from her waist. She held the sheath in her hands and slowly pulled the sword free. It was black as night and felt satisfyingly heavy in her hands. The sword's name was Sacrifice. Kanika looked at it sadly, turning it back and forth. *That was always going to be your legacy, wasn't it, Fiona? You never intended to die any other way.*

"She always meant for it to be you," said a voice from the door.

Kanika whirled around, her grip on Sacrifice tight and ready; but it was only Silas. She smiled at the blade. Kanika laughed nervously and sheathed it, setting it down with her armor.

"Silas," she said. "What do you mean?"

"Fiona always meant for you to succeed her," Silas said, coming in and sitting down on Kanika's pallet. Kanika stared at her, crossing her arms over her chest.

"But Moira—"

"Moira was next in line, yes, but Moira was older than Fiona by a century. Fiona knew her Hand would not outlive her. Rather than promote you to Hand and oust Moira, she simply decided to wait until Moira died. Though I'm sure she did not expect to die in the same day as Moira," Silas said.

"No, certainly not," Kanika said.

She went and sat down next to Silas, staring at her hands. Her skin was white, very white. She couldn't remember what it had looked like before, when she was a child. She had vague memories of living in the South, being on boats and poling through shallow rivers under thick canopies of green leaves. They were like dreams, totally foreign to her for all their familiarity. Had she been a river rat once upon a time, living in the swamps of the peninsula? Had her skin once been dark like Silas's? How many years would it be before she looked like Fiona, all white skin, white hair, white eyelashes?

"Do not lead the way Fiona did," Silas said.

"What?" Kanika gasped. "But we all loved Fiona."

"Yes, and the rest of the world hated her. She did not want that for you. You must be more present in the world, Kanika. Fiona had hoped to spend time with you, teaching you the lessons she learned from her mistakes. Obviously, we do not have that chance. But she told me everything, and I mean to use this to help you," she said.

"Thank you, Silas," Kanika said. "I am grateful. But before we talk about how I am to lead, we first have to see how much of a clan there is left for me to be leader of."

They both sat in silence for a moment, thinking of all the witches they'd left behind. Kanika had blocked the feelings she'd experienced as she watched her sisters turn on her one by one, but they could not be ignored for much longer. She knew many of her fellow clan members would die in this battle, beset by the humans, the dragons, the other witches. It was a mire of a situation, because they were not in their right minds. They had not willingly gone into the service of this evil thing. But how to save them, while they were trying to kill all these allies of nature? Kanika imagined that whatever hold the thing under the mountain had on them would be broken once the thing was resealed, but what to do until that time? They couldn't just be ignored, because they would be on the attack. Too many lives would be lost by trying to capture and contain them.

"We will not forget them, Kanika," Silas said, as if she was reading her thoughts. Kanika gave a small laugh and dabbed at the edges of her eyes. She supposed Silas had had centuries of practice understanding what Fiona was thinking when she would not speak, so Kanika's expressive face must have been very easy for her.

"No, no we will not. We'll just have to win the day as fast as possible if we hope to save them," she said. She rubbed her forehead. "Oh, I only hope that we have enough power."

"I think our odds are favorable," Silas said.

Kanika raised an eyebrow at her. She smirked.

"Really, I do. We have almost two thousand witches, some of whom are very powerful indeed; we have three very old, very strong shapeshifters. The greatest impediment to their success is distraction by attacking hell-monsters—and on that account, we have one brave young empress, whom I am beginning to find very inspiring," she said.

"Yes, a brave ruler and a loyal army may accomplish much," Kanika agreed. "But you must not forget one of our most important advantages."

"And what might that be?" Silas asked.

Kanika smiled. "We have an incredibly formidable pack of dragons, with a brave leader of their own."

Silas smiled back. "I thank you, Lady Kanika." She stood and bowed. "And speaking of that pack, it is about time I got back to them. Farewell for now. We will see each other again on the morrow."

"Yes. Goodnight, Silas," Kanika said.

She nodded and left the tent. Kanika stretched and rolled over to lay down on her pallet, exhausted from the day and fully prepared for a good night's sleep—though not too good, so she would be able to nap tomorrow before the night march—but then she heard a noise shuffling out across the grass. It was faint, almost faint enough to be wind except for the way it moved. It was making a definite circle of her tent. Kanika lay absolutely still and thought she heard a sniffing sound as well. It was difficult to tell with all the noises of the camp settling down.

Her suspicions aroused, she sat up and swung her legs off the bed, moving as quietly as she could. She slipped out under the flap of her tent and took a few steps around it, listening carefully. The shuffling became rapid and Kanika looked around wildly, but she couldn't see anything that would be making it. It stopped in the vague direction of a storage crate. Kanika narrowed her eyes at the box, and then allowed her eyelids to flutter shut. She muttered a simple spell to alter her vision. If her instincts were correct, there was a spy in their midst—one who was not of this world. She needed otherworldly eyes to see it.

When she opened her eyes, they were fully yellow and glowing. A nearby guard jumped in alarm, but Kanika ignored him. She could see her quarry now. It believed itself safe from her notice and crept toward the entrance to Guerline's tent. It looked like an oversized gopher, long and white of fur. Kanika slowly drew her left arm up and curled her fingers around the bow she imagined in her hand. She reached forward with her right hand and pulled back the magical string and arrow, aiming for the crawling, slinking thing. She took a deep breath, waiting for her shot—the arrow would set fire to Guerline's tent if she missed—but she waited too long. The thing shuffled quickly into the empress's tent. Kanika cursed, dispersed the magical bow, and ran into the tent, knife drawn. Before she acknowledged any reactions, she dove on the creature and drove her knife through its spine.

"Kanika? What's going on?" Guerline asked.

Kanika's eyes fluttered as she dropped the seeing spell and her eyes returned to normal. She held the creature up by her knife handle, protruding just below the skull. Its invisibility was stripped from it now that its neck was broken and the magic was fled. Now, it was just a pile of dead pieces covered in a white pelt.

"A visitor from our enemy," Kanika said. She turned it around and inspected its mouth. "A somnalius. They come to steal souls while people sleep. You see the teeth? For latching onto your face and sucking your soul out through your mouth."

Guerline paled.

"Thank you very much for saving my life, Kanika," she said shakily.

"It is my pleasure, Majesty," Kanika said. "Fear not. I'll burn this thing, and set some wards up on your tent to keep further intruders out."

Kanika left the tent and carried the somnalius over to the nearest fire, positioned across the footpath from the empress's tent. She laid the sack of flesh on the ground and pulled her knife from its head. With five deft cuts, she dismembered the creature and tossed it piece by piece into the fire. The flames glowed purple for a few minutes, and several guards stopped and stared.

"Dismember and burn, gentlemen," she said to them, staring into the fire.

They jerked their eyes away from the purple flames.

"Pardon, my lady?" one asked.

"Creatures from under the mountain," Kanika said, turning to look at them. "Dismember them, and burn them, and they will stay dead."

The Citadel was in ruins.

Cave-ins closed many of the tunnels that made up the majority of the structure. The few that remained all led to the gate chamber. There was a steady flow of traffic from the underworld into the upperworld as the enthralled Thiymen witches bewitched demons and summoned hordes of undead creatures. The hell-hounds and devil-cats were joined by gigantic serpents, spiders, and all manner of nightmarish creatures. The witches made more of them, venturing down into the mountain towns. The towns had been abandoned after the display put on by the dragons when Fiona died, so there was no ripe flesh; but they made do with digging up graves and scrounging for animal bones. The witches cobbled together monsters out of their own imaginations and shrieked with glee and terror when they were finished.

The twins walked arm in arm throughout the Citadel, the wind rushing through holes in the outer walls to tug at their hair and clothes. They had switched back to their yellow dresses, having no longer any need to hide their presence; in fact, their dresses identified them to their subordinates. They reveled in the sight of Thiymen witches bowing to them, their twenty-year exile ended and they returned to glory. There was no one closer to the queen than the twins.

Their stroll halted as they suddenly felt an icy shiver down their spines. He was there behind them. They could feel his hollow stare on the back of their heads, boring into them. They felt fingers in their hair and trembled again as the strands were lifted and combed, allowed to fall again like spiders alighting on their necks. Then he was gone, past them, walking down the tunnel to where the queen stood at the edge of the rubble in one of its human forms.

There was no one closer to the queen than the twins . . . except for the general.

The twins changed course and headed back into the mountain, down to the gate to oversee the other witches.

"Let me go to her," the thing that had once been Alcander demanded.

"No," the one from under the mountain said, knowing whom he spoke of. "I will deal with her."

"She is mine!" Alcander said. There was the slight edge of a growl to his voice, as much as he could allow himself in her presence. "You promised."

"Only because that was what was in your heart," Ianthe said. "I have changed my mind, and there is nothing you can do to sway me. Do not be a child."

Wisely, he was silent. Ianthe looked down the mountainside to the scree below and counted the ways Alcander had disappointed her. Perhaps it was not his fault. It must be said that, perhaps, she had miscalculated what she would require. How could she have watched the Hevya family for so long, only to be as ignorant as the rest in the end? She had overlooked Guerline as everyone else had, and had claimed the wrong heir for herself.

"Do you wonder why I chose you?" she asked.

Alcander scoffed. "Who else can do what is required?"

"And what exactly is that?" Ianthe asked. She looked her general up and down, lips slightly parted.

"I will destroy the Kavanaghs. I am the only one who can. It's my destiny."

The one from under the mountain smiled as she considered this. Alcander smirked and swung his sword with his one good hand. She felt his pleasure as if it was her own. Though death was not something he had particularly wanted, it had turned out rather well for him so far. He had been elevated to a seat of power not unlike his previous one, given an army to command—and the strength he possessed! It was like nothing he'd known in life. Now, he knew that he could accomplish his goal and eliminate the Kavanagh sisters.

"I am amazed," Ianthe said with a smile, "that you consider yourself so significant."

She smirked at her puppet and walked away, back into the mountain and to the chambers of its former warden. Fiona's rooms were as dull and cold as the witch herself had been, but it gave Ianthe great satisfaction to lay in her bed and take ownership of her possessions. She curled up in the silky black bed coverings with a grin on her face. As a mere witchling, Fiona had bested her, and she had stewed in that bitterness for years . . . but what joy had she felt when Fiona found her again, bound in the tree at the core of the mountain? How many centuries had she spent pleading with the witch to free her? Four hundred years of refusal and rejection . . . finally at an end.

"Don't get comfortable, beast."

She looked up. Standing over her was the wolf, hiding in woman's form, with slanting eyes and short grey hair. Ianthe continued to smile and rolled over onto her back.

"I cannot help it, Mother of Arido. Lambswool is so much softer than hellrock."

"I promise I shall trap you forever this time, foul thing," Lisyne said.

Ianthe rose up onto her knees so that her face was level with the shapeshifter's, and she planted the lightest of kisses on Lisyne's lips.

"Do it. And then I shall promise to see you in another four thousand years."

CHAPTER THIRTY

GUERLINE SAT STRAIGHT ON HER HORSE'S BACK AT THE EDGE of the camp, staring at the Zaide Mountains. Morning light washed over the grassy hills of the valley, but the sun didn't seem to make it to that foreboding range. Clouds gathered over it and hid the highest of the peaks from view. Guerline marveled at them. She had never been to the East, had never seen those mountains up close. They had always been just a black line on the distant horizon, as far from her mind as they were from her person. Now, those black slopes could be the witness of her ruin.

Last night's incident had rattled her more than she wanted to admit. The somnalius had been completely invisible to her until Kanika broke its neck. How many more enemies surrounded her, possibly even now? Whether they were truly there or not, the thought of them haunted her. Guerline had never fought even a human foe, and now she faced something she understood even less. She was grateful in every bone for Kanika's sharp senses and quick reflexes, and she was grateful that Kanika would be by her side in the battle to come.

Would that I were a witch. She would have felt much more confident about her own chances.

There was a sick, sinking feeling in her stomach as she envisioned, yet again, the battle that would take place. She saw their lines overwhelmed by evil creatures and unseen ghouls, tackled by rotting flesh and dragged down by invisible hands. She saw witch fighting against witch. She saw her fallen soldiers rising up again to turn against their comrades.

A cold tear ran down her cheek. She reached up and wiped it away, frowning. She was afraid, so afraid. The fear nauseated her, and it drained the feeling from her fingers. But she must not let it paralyze her. She gripped the reins tightly, leather cutting into her trembling hands, and glared at the mountains in the distance. She would let the sickness of her fear turn to disgust and hatred of her enemy, and use that to carry her through the battle. If she could only keep Ianthe's lovely face from her mind, she could prevail.

She pulled back on the right rein to wheel around and ride back into the camp, but came up short when she realized she had an audience. Dozens and dozens of guardsmen stood behind her, watching her. Her eyes widened as she took in the sight of them. They looked back at her with a variety of expressions. Some seemed dour and unimpressed, others studiously impassive. Some smiled; some looked afraid. Guerline sat up straighter in her saddle. Though she felt quite as apprehensive as most of her soldiers, she must appear strong for them. So she smiled, and walked her horse forward.

"We march tonight, Your Majesty?" one young man asked her as she approached.

She nodded. "Yes. We march tonight."

The young man thrust his hand out toward her. Without thinking, Guerline reached down and brushed his fingers with hers. All of them started to reach for her, putting their hands into the air. As she rode through them, she held her hands out to the sides and let her horse walk where he would while she touched the tips of her fingers to those of her soldiers. The crowd continued even after she got back into the maze of tents. The men and women heard the empress was on the edge of the camp, facing their destination, and they came to see what it meant—whether she was afraid, or whether she was defiant, or whether she was resigned.

She rode through the crowds seeing those questioning expressions and she had no answers for them, so she merely smiled and touched their hands.

When Guerline got back to her tent, she found Morgana and Desmond there waiting for her. They stood upon her entrance and smiled at her. She smiled in return.

"It is time, Guerline-basi," Morgana said. She gestured at the crate with Guerline's armor, which Morgana and Desmond had brought into the center of the tent.

Guerline nodded. She removed her overdress and reached behind her to unlace the back of her gown. Morgana coughed and Guerline stopped, looking up at the witch questioningly. Morgana waggled her eyebrows at Desmond, who had been simply standing at the head of the crate waiting to pull the armor out. He jerked to attention when he realized that both Morgana and Guerline were staring at him. He blushed.

"Oh! Yes. Right." Desmond met Guerline's eyes, his mouth slightly open. Then he turned and left the tent.

"He'll just wait outside," Morgana said, her amusement only just noticeable.

Guerline turned back to her with a wry grimace and reached behind her back again to loosen her gown.

Morgana helped her out of the gown and her other undergarments, then helped her dress in the ones she would wear under her armor. Guerline dressed in the linen shirt and leggings, with wool stockings cinched under her knees by a leather band. Over this she wore the arming suit, a padded tunic and trouser set. Over this went a leather jerkin, then the ringmail, and over that went her fabulous purple armor. She donned everything except for the helm, and she kept her mail hood down for the time being. Desmond wandered back into the tent at some point during the arming suit, and he now sat and quietly watched while Morgana worked Guerline's twists into a larger braid and wound it around her head so it would fit under the helm.

"Everything fits perfectly, Morgana-lami," Guerline said, sitting on a bench and marveling at how comfortable she felt. The armor was thoroughly articulated. She lifted her arms and bent them at the elbow, testing her range of motion.

"Of course it does," Morgana replied. "I made it, didn't I?"

Desmond laughed. "You are the picture of humility, Aunt."

"And you are a cheeky prat," Morgana said.

Guerline smiled. The banter almost made this feel like a regular fitting, for a gown or some other perfectly unwarlike thing, instead of a preparation for battle with something powerful enough to draw out the dormant shifter gods. The momentary lightheartedness faded and Guerline stood. Morgana and Desmond stopped teasing each other and looked at her expectantly, waiting for orders.

"Signal for the evening meal, and use the opportunity to give the guards a final briefing," she said. "We eat, then we break camp and head east."

Morgana nodded, gave Guerline a slight bow, and left the tent. Desmond stood up and took a step toward her.

"You look . . ."

"What?"

"Intimidating." He chuckled.

She frowned. "You don't sound very intimidated."

"I laugh, only to keep from trembling," Desmond said. He smiled and stroked her cheek. "Truly, you look awe-inspiring. Lina—"

She twisted away from him. "Let us hope it works on the thing from under the mountain as much as it works on you," she said.

A few hours later, Guerline rode again to the edge of the camp. This time, she faced the river and looked out over the sea of tents. It was vast and stretched beyond the furthest reaches of her vision, dissolving into the shimmering waters of the River Acha in the west and the whispering grasses of the valley in the north. This was her host, her country, her only hope. As the sun set before her, it cast a red glow over the tents, which rippled and billowed as they were taken apart and packed. The effect was unsettling—like an ocean of blood—and Guerline cast down her eyes.

The sun had almost completely disappeared by the time the legion was aligned before her in two columns. Desmond, the Kavanaghs, and Kanika trotted up to join Guerline at the head. She smiled at each of them, but dared not lift her hand to them lest they see how she trembled. She took a deep breath to steady herself.

She felt pressure on her leg and glanced down. Lisyne was there in wolf form, absolutely massive. Guerline could have held her arm out straight from her shoulder and put her hand on Lisyne's neck. She hadn't even noticed the wolf approach. How could such a beast move so quietly? Perhaps Lisyne really was a god after all. What were the qualifications for being a god anyway?

Focus, Guerline, she told herself. Lisyne was looking at her with expectant yellow eyes. Guerline held her gaze and worked to keep her face blank. Finally, she looked away and unbuckled an ornate horn from her saddle. It was black and inlaid with silver, tiny intricate scenes of battle and conquest that Guerline had memorized during her fascination with it as a child. It was a family heirloom on her mother's side, one of the few that her small house possessed. It was made of some foreign creature's horn by commission for Guerline's great-great-grandfather, a merchant who ventured far into the southeast.

She doubted the horn, with its aspirations to glory, had ever before been carried into battle.

Guerline raised it now to her lips and blew as she'd been taught. A warm and resonant note filled the air, and the columns cheered. Guerline sounded the horn again to more cheers and shouts. She buckled the horn back in its place, brought her horse around, and with that, the march began.

When the sun's light faded into heavy grey dusk, the witches conjured floating torches to surround the columns and light their way.

"Won't that draw enemies to us?" Guerline asked warily.

"Human enemies, yes," Morgana answered. "Underworld beasts fear all light."

"Let us hope they are still willing to fight us by the light of day," Desmond said.

"If their master orders it, they will fight," Kanika said.

Silence fell again and Guerline bit her lip. She wasn't sure whether to be grateful for the dead creatures' loyalty or not. Fighting during the day would be their most important, if not only, advantage.

The young empress dozed off a number of times, but each time, she woke with a start only to find that she had not veered off course. Indeed, her horse did not seem to need direction from her at all.

"The shapeshifters are leading them," Desmond said after observing her confusion.

"Why aren't the horses afraid?" Guerline asked. She'd expected them to shy from the massive predators.

Desmond shrugged. "Animals recognize authority. They also recognize danger. There is no danger, so they are not afraid."

After that, Guerline felt freer to drift to sleep. She had rested most of the day in preparation for the night march, but her anxiety was sapping her strength. Better to take the opportunity to sleep, and sleep she did.

They stopped at morning light. Guerline swung herself down from her horse's back and winced at the stiffness in her legs. She wasn't used to riding so long, nor to riding in armor. Beside her, Desmond stretched and groaned with satisfaction. He beamed at her, his grin crinkling his golden skin.

"Doing all right, Empress?" he asked.

"Cease your smirking before I have you beheaded."

Desmond laughed, and Guerline allowed herself a small smile.

"Where are we?" she said.

"We're just shy of the Dragon Road. See that town over there? That's Ravinea."

"But that . . . that's not possible. That means we're halfway there. There's no way we could have traveled that distance in a single night!"

"No way without magic," Desmond said.

Guerline raised an eyebrow at him. "Wouldn't we have . . . noticed?"

He grinned. "Well, not you. You slept all night."

She laughed and shoved him. He chuckled, then nodded to the three shapeshifters. They were in their massive animal forms, sitting quietly and watching the humans and witches. Occasionally, they glanced at each other, as if they were having a conversation. Desmond's point was made. Witch magic she might notice working; but the magic of the shapeshifters was a strange new thing. She might not notice something so strong after all, not if they didn't want her to.

"We're a day and a half's ride from the mountains now," Desmond said. "We'll continue unaided from here, so we can get there at daybreak tomorrow."

"Yes, of course."

A few hours' rest, then on to our deaths.

When Guerline woke in her saddle the next morning, the sun was bright in the sky and the Zaide Mountains were so close she had to crane her head back to see where the peaks disappeared into the clouds. She could see Petra's Bay on their right and knew that it was time. She brought out the horn once more and signaled for a halt. Three more short blasts and the columns broke apart as the witches and guardsmen rearranged themselves for battle.

Guerline looked up at the sky, though she knew she would not see the dragons. They had flown ahead in the night and were already hidden among the crags. They were to be the reserve force, to come out if things began to go badly for the crown. With any luck, the dragons would not need to get involved; but Guerline was not so optimistic.

An impatient growl pulled her back to the ground.

"We must go and begin the spell now," said Lisyne, human for the time being.

Olivia trotted over to Desmond and leaned half out of her saddle to embrace him. Guerline saw the tension and twitching in Desmond's hands as he held his mother and, like a blow to the gut, she realized that mother and son did not expect to see each other again in this life. Morgana and Aradia similarly clasped hands, making their goodbyes now.

You fool, Guerline. Of course she had known that they might die, but she had not connected that knowledge to these people. These people were eternal to her. Aside from Desmond, they had lived dozens of lifetimes before she was born, before her parents were born. How could such people die?

Lost in these thoughts, she didn't notice the movements of the others until she was lifted from her saddle and passed into the arms of the Kavanagh sisters. Their armor clinked together as the three of them surrounded her and embraced her. Though she couldn't feel the warmth of their skin, she felt their love and their support like a wave sweeping over her. It was too much to bear. Guerline wept and clutched at them, her gauntleted fingers slipping over their armor.

They said nothing, and when they released her, Desmond helped her back onto her horse. Tirosyne and Seryne, still tiger and fox, came and pressed her hand with their snouts. Then Lisyne led the shapeshifters and the sisters off to the cairn where they would begin the spell.

Her face wet with tears, Guerline took her standard from its bearer and raised it. Desmond handed her a small white energy coil and spoke a word she didn't recognize over it. Whatever it was, she tucked it into her gorget and rode to the end of the line, showing her standard. She spoke as she rode back, and her voice carried across the field:

"My friends, we ride against an evil so terrible that it has no name. Yes, we tremble with fear—but we also tremble with fury. We tremble with rage at what this thing has done. Our hands and hearts ache to destroy it. My people, the time has come! Today will be the end of evil, and our purpose will be fulfilled! Ride!" She rode back to the center, handed her standard off and drew her sword.

"Ride!" she said again.

"We ride!" the legion roared behind her.

"Ride!" she said once more, spurring her horse forward. And they rode.

"Quickly now," Lisyne said over the shouts of the soldiers behind them.

The six of them formed a circle at the crest of the hill, alternating shapeshifter and witch. Lisyne took her stance and looked each witch in the eye.

"Your chant is this:

Dark, dark, into the pit
Seal it away, seal it away
Dark, dark, bury it deep
Seal it away, seal it away

"We will be saying something different. Do not mind it," Lisyne said. "Stand still and do not move, but let your energy flow freely."

The Kavanaghs nodded, closed their eyes, and held their palms face up. They began to chant slowly. Light crackled in their palms: blue, green, and red. Lisyne watched, then met the eyes of Tirosyne and Seryne, now human. As one, they stepped out and began to dance. They chanted in a language unknown in Arido for a thousand years—guttural, brief, and consonant. They wheeled their arms and stomped their feet and flung their torsos from side to side. This was a traditional shapeshifter casting, and they danced around the witches.

A ball of light crackled into life in the center of the circle. It pulled from the witches' light and grew bigger as the shifters danced. The chanting grew faster and the light roared into a column, shooting into the sky.

Now, it will come, thought Lisyne.

CHAPTER THIRTY-ONE

AFTER GUERLINE'S SPEECH AND SUBSEQUENT RIDE INTO THE
pass, it was difficult to stop, hold the line, and actually *wait*
for the enemy. Desmond could feel the tension in the line
and in himself, and he was anxious to relieve it. Guerline
was immovable. Something had changed in her during her
goodbye with his mother and aunts. It was almost as if
she'd decided to shut everyone out until after the battle,
when she would welcome back anyone who was still alive
with open arms.

Perhaps that was the best way.

A roar and a great light rose up behind him, but he
didn't look back. He knew it meant the spell had begun,

and soon the enemy would be pouring out of the Citadel looming over them. Instead, he looked at the lower gate of the black Thiymen castle. Something flashed to his left and he saw Kanika on the other side of Guerline. Her palms were face up, her eyes closed, and she was chanting. White light bounced between her hands, writhing and shifting and growing in size. Finally, she uttered the finishing word and pushed the light out from her. It swept across the empty field. Desmond squinted at the brightness. When it faded, he saw that the field was not so empty after all. Here and there dead monsters crept slowly toward them. They did not seem to realize they were no longer invisible.

"Guerline," Desmond said, keeping his eyes on the creatures. "I must tell you. I—"

"No," she said quietly. "Tell me when this is over."

He nodded and blinked the tears from his eyes.

"Draw!" Guerline roared.

Those soldiers who had not yet drawn their swords did so and the mountains echoed with the scrape of steel on scabbard.

"Remember your anatomy," Kanika said softly. "Cut under the jaw and above the shoulder, and you will render the beasts helpless."

With the swords and shields now glinting in the sunlight, the creatures hesitated. The mountain rumbled. In answer, the hell-hounds and devil-cats began to scream.

Then they charged.

Desmond spurred Keno to jump in front of Guerline and her horse. She was quicker to react than he and they almost collided. He heard her shout his name in indignation, but he didn't really care. Monsters poured out of hidden places in the rock to join their comrades in the pass. There were more hell-hounds, more devil-cats, and many other kinds of horrors. Some were simply larger versions of normal menaces, like snakes and spiders; others were terrible blendings of many creatures. There was a thing with the head of a boar and the body of a horse. Another had wings like an eagle and a long, serpentine body with thousands of scaly legs. He couldn't tell where its eyes were, but he hacked at it wherever he could reach it.

Their magical armaments seemed to give the creatures pause, and for that Desmond was grateful. Even the human soldiers who did not have spelled armor were holding their own, and Desmond wondered if someone was casting protection spells on them. He felled a devil-cat and took the moment to glance behind him, where indeed he saw a group of Sitosen witches far behind the line with their palms spread wide.

The line moved steadily forward, hacking and slashing at the evil things. Yana and her archers used flaming arrows to blast through the rotting wings of those creatures that had them, sending them crashing into their comrades on the ground and igniting them. Maddox and the vanguard came barreling down the hill to the left, and Sir Bertrand swung his flank to meet that line. The beasts were slowly being driven to the water.

A series of twangs, as from bow strings, sounded behind him. He heard shouts of pain from the back, and then screams from the front. He looked back. The Sitosen witches who were warding had been shot down with arrows. The men and women at the front were now vulnerable to the beasts.

"Witches!" he shouted, scanning the sky frantically. "Thiymen is in the sky! Archers!"

But he looked up on Mon Zeferin and saw that half of Sir Yana's force had already been shot down. The remaining archers were no longer shooting. They crouched and held their shields over their heads.

"Kanika!" Guerline cried.

But Sitosen had already tied their sails to their hands and launched into the sky. Though the Thiymen witches were invisible to Desmond and the other humans, it seemed the Sitosen witches could see them. They didn't hesitate to loose their arrows. Black-clad witches fluttered into visibility as they toppled from the sky.

There was a huge thunder clap and a crack of lightning. Desmond hacked once, twice, three times at the neck of a hell-hound until the head fell off with a sickening splintering sound. He looked up and saw black clouds coming from the Citadel, pouring over them and dimming the sunlight.

"There are demons on the battlements! They're casting the clouds!" Kanika screamed.

"Can we reach them?" Guerline demanded.

Desmond glanced at her and did a double take. The action of the battle seemed to slow down around him as he took her in: mounted on her horse, glittering sword in hand, her purple armor half covered in rotted black blood and pieces of dead flesh. She had a scratch on her cheek that was bleeding freely and her eyes were wide—but not with fear. She looked almost crazed, eyes flicking this way and that as she looked for another enemy.

Who is this woman? Can this really be Guerline?

"Not with arrows!" Kanika shouted, pulling Desmond out of his thoughts.

Guerline wheeled her horse around. "Aalish!"

She rode back through the line to where the Adenen captain was, overseeing the battalions as half of them lent energy to the spellcasters on the seal and the other half prepared magical catapults to launch stones at the undead beasts. Desmond couldn't hear what she said, but saw a hundred Adenen witches take to the sky and surround the battlements. The ominous dark clouds began to disperse as the demons' casting was interrupted by the attack. The sun beat down again.

The monsters of the underworld continued to crawl out of the mountains. Some were small and able to sneak through the legs of the soldiers and make their way into the ranks, chewing off legs and dragging men and women down. Others were huge, slapping guards from their horses and crushing them beneath massive feet. More than one soldier lost their weapon, stuck in the calcified bone of some hell-hound. Desmond hauled one such man up from the ground and pushed him toward the back of the line.

"Go, go, get out of here!" he shouted at the stunned man.

He looked back to the front and realized that he was far behind the line himself. Guerline was at the very front, small at this distance. Her silver crown caught the sunlight and the light from the roaring column of magic behind them. Her sword flashed as she brought it down on the arm of the hairy humanoid thing that was reaching for her. Her horse twisted away from the creature and brought Guerline in a circle. Desmond spurred Keno and tried to push forward, though it was difficult to get through the mass of bodies between him and the empress.

"Hurry, Keno. I must get back to her!" Desmond said.

Keno screamed and a path slowly opened up for him through the ranks. They began to move forward, Desmond never taking his eyes off Guerline. He was watching when her horse reared. It seemed like Guerline would be able to hang on—

Until something behind her pulled her down from her horse's back.

"Guerline!" Desmond shouted.

Guerline felt deaf. The sounds of battle grew and grew until they were too loud, too close for her to register and she simply shut them out. Her ears rang with empty noise. She felt herself shouting and screaming at her enemy, watched as the beasts shrieked back at her, saw her sword cut through bone and sinew, but heard no sound. Where was Desmond? Where was Kanika? Her guard had dissolved, but she hardly took notice. There was a devil-cat in front of her, and she needed to kill it.

The beasts recoiled from her at first, and she knew it was because of the magic in her armor. They screamed with fury when they could not approach her. They surrounded her but couldn't overwhelm her, couldn't come too close for too long. All they could manage were desperate swipes, and she was well prepared to strike back at them. Her entire world was the enemy and her sword arm.

She cut off an arm without looking to see what creature it belonged to. Her horse screamed and wheeled around. She cursed as she tried to get him back under control. He reared up and she gripped him with her knees, scrambling to gain a better hold on the reins.

Then something pulled her from behind.

She fell to the ground and wheezed, the breath knocked out of her by the fall. She blinked furiously as her horse kicked up dust around her, and something wet seeped through her armor at the elbow. She looked down and realized that she had landed in a pool of blood—fresh, red blood. It was the blood of her people, not the blood of the enemy. She snarled and pushed herself up, holding her sword before her with both hands and looking wildly for something to kill.

"Gods, look at you. You're like an animal."

Guerline whirled around and brought her sword down on whatever was behind her. Her blow was blocked by another sword, which was the first thing that gave her pause. The beasts of the underworld didn't carry swords. Was this a demon? Her eyes slowly came into focus on the enemy she faced, and when they did, she gasped.

"Alcander," she said, her voice hoarse.

"Are you surprised? I must admit that I was," Alcander said.

He parried her sword and pushed it away, taking a few steps back. He seemed larger than he had been when he was alive. He was bare-chested, dressed only in a pair of trousers. He wasn't even wearing boots, but then, Guerline supposed the dead didn't need boots. For he was most certainly dead. His skin had a sallow yellowish-green tinge, mottled here and there with dark purple bruises. The whites of his eyes were yellow and dried blood was caked around his mouth. His red-gold hair, the same color as hers, was loose and long, matted with what looked like dirt and more blood into an outrageous mane around his head. His throat was torn open, skin and muscle hanging in ragged strips around his exposed spine. And there, at his left shoulder . . .they'd found the arm that should have been there in the Orchid Vale, where he died. It was all that was left of him. Around the empty socket were strange rocky growths, spiking out from his flesh. He lifted his sword, a great black thing, and grinned at her.

"Well? Come and kill me, little sister."

"You're real now," she whispered.

He tilted an ear toward her. "What was that? What did you say?"

She rushed at him and swung on his left for the neck, hoping to decapitate him in a single blow. He dropped his left shoulder back and parried rapidly, then backhanded her in the face. She stumbled backward, head ringing. She shook her head to clear it and charged him again, feinting a blow to the head and stabbing him in the gut when he went to block the high swing. She pushed her sword in to the hilt and twisted it, but Alcander only laughed—a high, grating sound that chilled her blood. He struck her on the top of the head with the end of his sword and shoved her away from him. She fell, but clung desperately to her sword. He brought his knee up and struck her under the chin. Blood filled her mouth as she bit her tongue on impact and she finally let go of the sword. Alcander kicked her and she rolled away from him.

"Empress!" screamed a nearby soldier. The woman threw herself at Alcander, who swung his sword almost lazily and cut her in half.

"No!" Guerline cried.

"Yes!" Alcander said. "What *have* you been doing since I left? They're willing to lay down their lives for you. That's quite good, Lina. You may be worth something after all. Or you might have been."

Guerline coughed painfully. Her vision was swimming. She spat out blood and struggled to get up.

"No, no, stay down, Lina. This is not playtime," Alcander said.

He kicked her in the jaw and her helm flew off. He reached down and put his sword in the ground, then pulled her mail hood back. He ran a swollen finger down her cheek.

"There we are. I almost didn't recognize you in all this armor. This is my lovely sister, here." His voice was almost gentle.

"Don't touch me." Her voice trembled. She spat more blood into his face.

He laughed again, apparently unfazed. Straddling her, he forced his hand into her hair and yanked her head back, staring wildly into her eyes.

"Stop me! I have power you have never dreamed of. I feel no pain. I have no weakness. I have conquered death. I am a god," he said, breathing heavily. He lowered his hips onto her and pressed against her hard, cold armor. Her blood drained out of her limbs, sucked back into her heart and set on fire by the anger and revulsion boiling there. Hot rage shot through her body and strengthened her.

She kneed him in the backside, hooking her left hand under his remaining arm to fling him off of her. With her free hand, she pulled her sword from his gut and scrambled away from him. A rancid smell wafted over her as fluids and organs burst from the hole she had made in his stomach. Bile rose in her throat, but she choked it down. Alcander did not even seem to notice the damage to his body.

"I have met gods, Alcander, and you are not one of them." She got to her feet. He seemed content enough to let her.

"So the unworthy always say," Alcander replied. "But I was specially chosen."

"Is that what the thing under the mountain told you, to make you forgive it for killing you?" she asked.

"It gave me immortality!" the dead prince shrieked.

"It gave you rot!" Guerline shouted back. "Look at yourself! You are vile. You could have been an emperor, a great ruler, and this thing has taken it from you and made you into a one-armed sack of gross flesh!"

Alcander roared and charged her. She dodged and slashed at him as he ran past. Her sword split the skin of his back.

"You're nothing now, Alcander. You are just a murderous puppet. But I am the leader of a great army! This legion is under my command! I have brought them together, and they fight for me, for what is good and natural. You will never know what that means," Guerline said. Tears welled up in her eyes and spilled onto her cheeks, streaking through the blood that stained her face and blurring her vision.

"I don't think you ever did," she said.

Alcander's face twisted up in fury and he glared at her. "How dare you speak to me that way? You are worth nothing! You are the second child, a daughter, human and worthless! I am the right hand of a great and terrible power! You were not even important enough for my master to kill! You will not say such things to me!"

They rushed at each other and traded blows, the sounds of their battle echoing off the mountains. Guerline cut him many times, but he was too fast, and she could not find enough purchase to seriously damage him. He was stronger than her physically and had unearthly stamina. Her armor was strong, and his blows did not cut her, but she felt each one shudder through her body and rattle her bones.

He struck her to the ground again, and she clambered to her hands and knees, coughing. Her hair was coming loose from its braids and sticking to the blood on her face. Though she stared at the ground, she felt him approach and kneel next to her. She looked at his feet under her arm. He stuck his sword in the ground again; she realized why when she felt his fingers in her hair. He pulled her head back, but she kept her eyes on the ground.

"Look at me, sister."

She didn't move. He shook her head violently.

"Look at me!"

Guerline took a deep breath. Then, with all her remaining strength, she surged up, twisted her body, and swung her sword. The handle grew hot with magic, so hot she felt it even through her gloves. It sliced through Alcander's neck without a sound. His body remained still for a moment, then slowly began to fall. Guerline frantically stumbled away from him. She stared in horror, mouth agape, at the headless body. His head was facing her, his eyes glazed over, his own mouth open. She went to it and rolled it over with her foot so that it looked away from her.

"I will not remember you this way, brother," she said softly.

And then she vomited.

CHAPTER THIRTY-TWO

BEFORE **G**UERLINE COULD COUGH THE LAST OF THE VOMIT from her throat, something grabbed her by the neck and lifted her off the ground. She kicked and screamed, twisted her body, but her captor didn't release her. She could feel fingers, human fingers, in a grip that was firm but not deadly. It wasn't trying to kill her.

That was its first mistake.

She gripped her sword in both hands and stabbed upward. She had to get it to let go of her before they got too high, or she wouldn't survive the fall. If it wasn't killing her, it was taking her somewhere. All experience told her she didn't want to go there, wherever it was.

Her sword wasn't hitting anything—or if it was, her victim wasn't reacting at all. She tried to look up and get it in view, but its grip on her neck was too restricting. Her feet started to go numb.

Color flashed around her and wind burned her cheeks. They were moving fast. What carried her? A witch, or some other hell-beast? The blue sky disappeared and she was surrounded by black. The air rushing past her got colder. Her heart sank to her tingling toes as she realized she was being taken under the mountain. She renewed her struggle to get free, jabbed her sword back, and swung her body around.

The blade stuck in something and a shriek echoed in the blackness. The fingers around Guerline's throat slipped away. Guerline screamed as she fell, every muscle in her body tense.

The ground rose up quickly to meet her and her cry was cut short by the bright thud of her armor against rock. She pushed up onto her hands and knees, coughing and wheezing, trying to get air back in her lungs. If it weren't for the pain in her chest, she might have been convinced that this entire adventure was a nightmare. There was no end in sight, and there never would be. Even if she survived this, she still had to rule Arido, and that meant that every grievance in the country would become hers. She'd never have peace. Even if her land flourished, she herself would never be able to rest. A moment's rest for the empress could mean disaster for her country.

"Shh, now, little queen. I'm here. I'll help you."

She caught a whiff of her mother's perfume. She breathed it in deep and sighed, then sat back on her heels.

"You should have chosen another guise. My mother and I were never close," Guerline said.

She stood and held her sword ready, though she still couldn't see anything in the blackness that surrounded her. Slowly, the darkness lifted and an expansive chamber came into view, illuminated by rolling luminescent smoke. A pale blonde girl with red lips and black eyes strode toward her out of the mist, smiling. *Ianthe.* Guerline did not lower her sword.

"Does this one please you?" the girl asked.

Guerline stayed silent. She mustn't engage with the thing. If she gave it an opening, some way to get at her, she was done for. Her one comfort was that her survival didn't mean much. As long as Lisyne and the others could complete the seal, it didn't matter whether Guerline herself lived or died. Now, perhaps, she at least had an opportunity to distract the thing and give them more time.

"Do you want to know why I brought you here?"

The girl-thing smiled when Guerline gave no response.

"I know you do, so I'll tell you even though you do not ask me. I brought you here because I wanted to see you. You have managed to exceed all my expectations of you."

"Your talent for flattery is truly astounding," Guerline snapped before she could stop herself. Her cheeks flushed and the girl-thing laughed.

"Truly, if I had any inkling you would have risen to the occasion with such fervor, I would have killed you much sooner," Ianthe said. "When I first came to you, you were so obviously weak, such a victim of your family, I thought it would be cruel for you to never know freedom. I am not without compassion. But when I visited your court, how changed you were!"

Guerline frowned. "At court?"

"Aye, Lina. I came to you as a man," Ianthe said.

The Giardan. Guerline glared at the thing and tried to bury her fear. "How were you able to get through before the gate fell?" she asked.

"I have always been able to get through Fiona's curtain, in small ways," Ianthe said. "Do not be so alarmed. I have patiently waited for this moment; it would hardly have served my purpose to wreak havoc before the proper time."

Guerline bit the inside of her lip to keep from screaming at the creature and tightened her grip on her sword. Ianthe spotted the movement and stared at Guerline's hand, then lifted her black gaze to Guerline's face.

"You see Lisyne for the monster she truly is, I know you do. Yet you band with her to destroy me, when it was I who liberated you from your family? I who carried the soul of your lover into Ilys?" Ianthe whispered. "I'm merely trying to restore balance, Guerline. I am a natural part of this world, as much as Lisyne or Lirona or even you yourself! This world birthed me as well! Do I not deserve a place in it?"

The creature's voice swelled in volume until Guerline's ears burned. She put a hand over her ears and cried out until the pressure ceased. Her shaking glove came away bloody.

Fingers caressed her sweaty cheek and she looked up. Ianthe was right in front of her now, her hand resting lightly on Guerline's skin, her wholly black eyes locked onto Guerline's.

"I think you understand me, Guerline second-daughter, chattel-child," she said.

She leaned in. Guerline's fingers flexed around her sword handle, but her arms felt leaden and she couldn't lift them. She couldn't move as Ianthe kissed her lips. She braced herself, but the kiss was unexpectedly soft, gentle even. Warmth flooded her body, but panic rose in her chest. It was a lie; it was false. The thing was putting her under a spell. She summoned her strength and pushed away from the girl-thing, stumbled backward until she gained her feet again.

Ianthe was frozen with an expression almost like surprise for a moment, and then she slowly dropped the hand that had hung in the air.

The thing looked human to her in that moment, crestfallen. Guerline was seized with a hot lance of pity, a spike in her heart. Deep down, she did understand. Lisyne had called Ianthe the opposite of nature, but how had she come into being if not *through* nature? Would it be different if the thing hadn't been trapped for so long? Would she be less vengeful? Would the Aridans even think of her as bad, or would she simply be the other side of the coin of fate?

Had Lisyne ruined everything four thousand years ago?

Guerline lowered her sword, slowly. "Why didn't you kill me, after you saw how I'd changed? You killed my parents, Alcander, why not me?"

The thing was silent for a moment. Guerline held her breath. Her panic returned, flushing out the pity like snowmelt rushing down a river. She should never have asked that question. That was exactly the kind of opening the thing wanted.

"Can you not guess, little queen?" she asked.

Don't answer. Don't say a word.

"It's because I wanted you alive."

Ianthe walked toward her again. Guerline lifted her sword and held it in front of her. The girl kept walking, eyes wide and manic. Guerline swung at her, but she caught her blade in her hand and stopped it flat. Ianthe stepped in close to her.

"I like my women with a lot of *flesh*."

The last word dissolved into an echoing hiss that sent shivers up and down Guerline's spine. She pushed her weight against the sword and watched it slice through the pale, stretched skin on the thing's hand. The thing didn't react at all—didn't bleed, didn't wince, didn't let go.

Guerline felt faint, but she wouldn't let herself pass out yet. She jumped back, yanking her sword from the Ianthe's grip, and raised it high. She charged forward and struck at the thing's head.

Before she made contact, the thing screamed and turned to look out at the far end of the cavern. Roaring filled the space and made Guerline's head pound. She squinted at the girl-thing in the rising wind, but she—it—ignored her now. It burst into black smoke and whipped out of the cavern, taking the wind and everything else along with it. Guerline was plunged into blackness and silence again.

She waited a few moments and caught her breath before stumbling in what she thought was the direction of the exit. Luck was with her. She found a wall and kept her hand flat against it as she picked up her pace and tried to find her way out of the mountain. She wasn't sure what was happening, but she had to get back to the fight, even if she could hardly see through the tears in her eyes.

Lisyne leapt into the air, panting heavily. Their spell steadily gathered strength, the column of white light spinning with great force. It was impossible for her to tell how the battle in the pass went. All her energy was focused on this one thing. She could feel the anxiety of the Kavanagh sisters, though. They were weakening the spell as they tried to cast out lines of awareness down to the field. Angrily, she dragged them back and demanded that they focus. Guerline, Desmond, and the others in the pass only had a chance of survival if those on the hill completed the seal.

The witches doubled down on the spell. They had all stopped chanting. The spell was in them and around them now, gathering power and waiting to be launched upon the enemy. They couldn't hold it too long or it would sap them all of their strength, but Lisyne was loath to cast the spell before she got a glimpse of the thing. There were places in the mountain where it could hide, or it could slip into some other part of the world under the mountain, and avoid getting hit. If she could hit it squarely and wrap it up in the spell, it would be easier to bring it down.

Something struck her on the back of the neck, searing her skin. She growled and turned out of the circle, one hand stretched toward the column to maintain her connection with it. Two blonde women in yellow gowns were flying around them, firing blasts of purplish-black energy down at the spellcasters.

"The Maravilla twins!" Olivia shouted.

Lisyne growled again and broke her connection. She bent her knees, preparing to launch herself into the air to eviscerate these miserable excuses for witches. The Kavanaghs cried out, though, and Lisyne glanced back to see the column wavering out of control. Cursing, she leapt back into the spell, immediately stabilizing it.

Damn it. She couldn't leave the spell. She was the strongest of them, and the others couldn't hold it without her. Tirosyne and Seryne, too, would have to keep their hold. It was up to the Kavanaghs to dispatch the twins, and quickly, without using too much of their own power. That power was needed for the seal.

Olivia pulled herself out of the spell and swept her arm through the air. A strong wind knocked the twins out of the sky; while they stumbled to their feet, Olivia danced through them and sliced their yellow sails, grounding them. Lisyne held the spell with one hand, watching the battle intently. The Maravillas each drew double short swords and advanced on Olivia. Four blades to one were not good odds, but Olivia also had Neria's Shield. She swung the shield off her back and onto her arm just in time to block one of the twins' attack. The three witches traded blows too fast for a human eye to see, magic sent to their limbs to increase speed and strength. Olivia's sword made no sound, not even when glancing off armor, so the first twin did not even notice that she had been stabbed until she saw the blood on Olivia's withdrawn blade. Olivia raised Silence for the killing blow, but it never landed.

The second twin drove both swords into Olivia's back.

They hung there, the second twin holding herself aloft with her sword hilts sticking out of Olivia's shoulders. They had sliced through the straps that held the breast and back plates together and slid through her mail into her flesh. Olivia fell to her knees, her sword falling from her hand. The twin put her foot in the center of Olivia's back and pushed her to the ground, pulling her swords out in the process. Lisyne didn't move, but she was vaguely aware of Aradia sobbing.

Olivia lifted one hand weakly, reaching toward the spell column. Blue light gathered at her fingertips and shot into the column. The column swelled. Then Olivia's hand fell, and she was dead.

With a roar, Morgana ripped herself from the spell and drew her own double sabers. She fell upon the twins, blades flashing. The first twin was weakened by the wound Olivia had given her, and Morgana assaulted her without mercy. She knocked both short swords from the rogue witch's hands and drove her backwards, finally cutting her throat and her gut open with two quick slashes. Morgana whirled around to find the second twin charging her and thrust both of her sabers through the twin's chest. The war-witch growled and flung the body of the twin through the air, watching as it rolled down the hill. Lisyne watched as Morgana turned, dropped her swords unceremoniously, and came back into the spell. Her face was wet with tears.

Though it was hard to hear over the roaring of the seal, Lisyne thought she heard a rumble coming from the mountain. She looked toward the Citadel, and indeed, she saw black clouds gathering near the top.

"Get ready! It comes!" she shouted.

Her compatriots turned toward the mountain and the column flared up. The black clouds gathered themselves into a funnel shape, with long tendrils snaking out like arms. Lisyne watched those arms touch down indiscriminately on the field as the black thing slunk toward them and imagined all the creatures it was crushing and swallowing in darkness. Her upper lip curled in an unvoiced snarl.

As it neared, the black thing lashed out with a smoky tendril and surrounded Aradia. She screamed, and green light flared up around her as she tried to fend off the attack. Her connection to the spell was severed as she turned all her attention toward survival.

"No, Aradia, no! The seal, give it to the seal!" Lisyne bellowed.

The gentle witch turned back to the column, agony on her face. She gathered the green light into herself, and then launched it into the column. The column flared again, and Aradia went limp. When it realized she was dead, the smoke released her and moved on to Seryne, who was next in line. The little woman with long black braids growled and slashed at the air with her claws. Three bright blades of white light rushed the black thing and it recoiled, but only for a moment. It roared back and sent smoke rushing forward to surround all of them. Tirosyne and Seryne disappeared, but the column flared up twice, and Lisyne knew what they had done. She glanced to her left and stared through the smoke at Morgana, who was still trembling from her battle with the twins. The witch nodded, then dropped her arms and closed her eyes. A bolt of red light shot into the column, which swelled to its greatest size yet.

The black cloud-thing rumbled angrily.

"Why, Lisyne?" it roared at her. "Four thousand years of wondering and I've never figured out why you persecute me this way!"

"Because you are evil," Lisyne shouted back. "You know that to be true."

It roared again, and Lisyne turned to face it square on. She panted with the effort of restraining the spell, which was now practically wild with power. She pulled it back as much as possible, pouring the last of her strength into it.

This ends now, Ianthe.

With a great howl, Lisyne launched the spell into the churning mass of black smoke. The rumble of laughter turned into a high wail and the wind picked up around them. Lisyne screamed and ran toward the thing, pushing it back with the swirling tornado of light that was more now than just their only hope. It was her friends and her family, it was herself entirely. It was the indomitable spirit of nature.

Light will always overwhelm the darkness.

And so it did. The black smoke retreated to the Citadel. Lisyne followed it down the hill and then released the spell to pursue its quarry. The wake of the spell swept everything dead up with it and carried it down into the bowels of the world, out of sight and locked away for what Lisyne hoped was forever.

CHAPTER THIRTY-THREE

GUERLINE LEFT THE BLACKNESS OF THE MOUNTAIN AND staggered down the rocky slope to the battlefield below. She'd barely touched the grass with her boots when shadows fell, as if the dark had followed her. For a few long, terrible minutes Guerline was afraid they had lost and the end was upon them. She heard the growling of hell-beasts all around her and slashed at the darkness, led only by sound and the soft glow of her blade.

"Desmond!" she screamed, suddenly afraid.

She thought she heard him shouting for her, but the noise sounded muffled and distant. She struggled toward it and tripped over something, splashing into a pool of what she knew was warm, sticky blood.

"*Desmond!*" she screamed again.

"Guerline!" someone shouted.

It wasn't Desmond, but Guerline was comforted nonetheless. It was Kanika. Guerline felt hands on her arms, lifting her up. Light appeared, streaking through the murky darkness. Kanika unhooked her mask and pulled it open, staring at Guerline.

"What's happening?" Guerline asked.

Kanika only shook her head. It was impossible to tell. Screams filtered through the blackness and Guerline wondered how many had given up hope and abandoned their fight. Would she see them all running when the blackness lifted? *Would* the blackness lift? Guerline felt her strength waver, and her knees buckled. Kanika held her up.

Suddenly, the wind picked up and almost toppled them. It rushed back toward the mountain and carried the thick black smoke with it. As the smoke receded, a bright light appeared on the horizon; it grew stronger and stronger until Guerline couldn't bear to look at it.

"The seal!" Kanika cried, her voice breaking. "It's the seal! They've cast it!"

The roaring wind became too loud to speak then. Kanika and Guerline ducked their heads and squeezed their eyes shut against the pounding gusts. After a few agonizing minutes, the wind calmed and they lifted their heads. The sun shone down on the pass, which was now empty of demons and possessed corpses. Those that had been hacked to pieces remained, harmless chunks of rotting flesh with no more magic in them. Soldiers stumbled around the pass in shock and confusion. Slowly, a cheer rose up as they realized that the world had not ended, and that the battle was over.

"Guerline!"

Her gaze snapped toward the sound and there he was, whole and alive. Guerline sheathed her sword and ran to him. They seized each other and fell to their knees together. They were covered in blood and sweat and gore and did not care at all. They were alive, and that was what mattered most to them in that moment.

"I love you," Desmond said. He said it over and over again, and Guerline could only nod, half laughing, half weeping. She could not bring herself to push him away. He tried to hold her close, but their breastplates made it awkward to embrace. Desmond laughed, almost hysterically.

"Damn this armor!" he gasped.

"No, don't! This armor has preserved us. I will be grateful for it forever," Guerline said.

Desmond kissed the top of her head. "Your strength has preserved us."

"No," Guerline said, remembering. "The seal has preserved us."

She rose to her feet, and Desmond rose with her.

"The seal," he said.

They turned to look at Kanika, who nodded. The three of them grabbed the nearest horses and swung into the saddles, spurring them toward the hill where the spell had been cast.

When they arrived, they saw a deep chasm in the earth on the center of the hill. The grass around the hole was singed, and the rocks melted. Guerline looked around. Where were the shapeshifters and the Kavanagh sisters?

She glanced to the sky, where the dragons now circled. Had they flown away? Why would they have done that? She was beginning to fear the worst when she heard Desmond sob and her fears were confirmed.

She dismounted and looked to the ground. There were five bodies: Olivia, Morgana, Aradia, and two blonde women so identical in appearance Guerline knew they must be the Maravilla twins. Olivia and the twins had discernible wounds. Morgana and Aradia appeared un-touched. Desmond knelt next to his mother's body with his head in his hands. Kanika walked slowly among them, examining the bodies.

"Olivia battled the twins. She was killed by one of them . . . and then Morgana was the one to kill the twins. These wounds were made by sabers," Kanika said.

"And Morgana and Aradia? How did they die?" Guer-line asked.

"They must have given themselves to the spell," Kanika replied. "They came to the end of their strength, and in-stead of stopping, they slipped into the magic."

"How do you know?" Guerline pressed.

"Their souls are gone. All of them. My guess is that the twins lost their souls in the service of the thing under the mountain."

"What does that mean? Will they find rest?" Desmond demanded, lifting his head.

Kanika went to him and put her hands on his shoul-ders. "Yes, of course." She looked up at the mountain. "I think they are in the world under the mountain. They must be part of the seal on the underworld now. They will help to protect it."

He stared blankly at her, his grief too strong for him to either accept or deny her statement. Guerline took a shaky breath and surveyed the scene again, the bodies of the Kavanaghs and those in the basin. So many dead so that Ianthe might be trapped once more. Guerline sank to her knees as the heavy weight of failure settled on her shoulders. She should have asked Ianthe to stop. Perhaps she and Lisyne could have . . .

"The shapeshifters. Where are the shapeshifters?" she asked.

Kanika and Desmond looked around too.

"There," Desmond said, pointing into the distance toward the north.

Far off toward the horizon, barely visible, was a massive wolf. It stopped and looked back at them, then turned and limped away.

Desmond, Kanika, and Guerline rode slowly back to the field. Soldiers wandered around, trying to find their lines and waiting for someone to tell them what to do. Sir Bertrand had raised his standard, and people gravitated toward it. Guerline rode ahead to help her soldiers.

Bodies—humans, witches, horses, monsters—littered the ground. Desmond and Kanika joined those Gwanen witches who still had their senses and went among their fallen sisters, checking for signs of life. A tent was erected to protect the sick. Some witches were taken there; others were lined up and covered with tents, cloaks, and blankets, whatever was on hand.

Desmond spotted Aradia's Hand. "Jaela!"

"Desmond, thank Lisyne!" She stumbled toward him wearily, her arms laden with saddlebags full of medicines. Other than a nasty scrape on her brow, she seemed unhurt. Desmond embraced her and took one set of bags from her. The three of them set off to the medic tent.

"How is it with the clans, Jaela? What can you tell?" Desmond asked.

Jaela frowned. "We have given much, Desmond. Many are dead, and many others are at the last of their strength. We held back from the main battle in order to lend our strength to the seal, and it has consumed the souls of many. They will now live forever as wards of the underworld."

"And Thiymen? What of Thiymen?" Kanika asked anxiously.

Jaela turned to her, her brown face twisted with sorrow. "Many of them disappeared into the smoke. I have not found any alive on the ground. Yet," she added hastily, as Kanika's face turned ashen.

Kanika turned and looked to Desmond.

"Go," he said. "Find them, if you can."

And then she was gone. Desmond watched her disappear. His heart felt heavy in his chest, and he remained still as Jaela turned away to attend the sick that had been brought to her. From here, he could see the whole field. He could see Sir Yana, clutching her bow arm as she led her archers down from Mon Zeferin. Sir Maddox and his troop seemed to have fared the best. Many of them were still mounted; they rode through the field, stopping now and then to heave an injured man or woman across their saddle and bear them to the sick-tent. Sir Bertrand still stood by his standard, leaning heavily upon another soldier. Desmond could not see Sir Tragar.

Guerline sat on her borrowed horse and directed the able-bodied to gather the necrotic corpses into huge piles. One by one, fires were set, and the bodies of the enemy slowly turned to ash. Desmond stared, not at the fires, but at Guerline. Her massive twist of braids was coming loose. Her face was streaked with blood. Her armor was half-black with the rot of the enemy caked on it. And she had never looked more glorious or more regal.

"Master Kavanagh," said a weak voice next to him.

He looked down and saw a Sitosen witch he did not recognize hobbling toward him. He went to her and scooped her up in his arms, and then carried her into the tent to find some kind of bed.

"Who leads us now? My lady is dead. I feel it. She is gone," the witch muttered.

Desmond clenched his jaw but did not answer. His mother, all his family, was dead. Though he was still in shock, he felt the grief growing in his stomach like a sickness. Yet it was not his grief alone. The clans, too, had lost their mothers. There were few in the clans who surpassed his aunts in age; for many, this would be the first time leadership had changed. Though there were procedures in place, these things were so much different in practice than they were in theory. The witches, however many were left, would be looking as much to him as to their new leaders. He realized this now. He was their last link to the Kavanagh sisters.

The Hands. I must find the Hands.

Jaela, he had already found; she would be the new Heart of Gwanen, that much was clear. Thiymen too had its leader, if there were still any Thiymen witches left. Sitosen would fall to Tesla, and Adenen to Aalish, if Desmond could find them alive and well.

He found them as the sun began to set on the far western horizon, turning the black mountains above them red. They were together, rousing what witches they could find. Tesla had a broken arm. Aalish was missing her left leg from the knee down, and was using a broken lance as a crutch.

"Aalish, what are you doing? Go see Gwanen!" Desmond said as he ran to them.

"Nonsense," she replied, her voice hoarse with pain. "Tis but a scratch. Besides, none of us have enough magic to heal something like this."

She gestured to the bloody stump of her leg, then smiled grimly at Desmond.

"Gods, Desmond. I've never felt so weak in my life," she said.

He could tell by the look on Tesla's face that she echoed the sentiment. "The seal—"

"We've given it everything," Tesla said. "Only time will tell how much of it comes back to us."

This was something Desmond had not considered. Olivia had had her theories that the magic of the witches was finite, that the way they used it was not sustainable like it was for the shapeshifters. It was these musings that had inspired the Maravilla twins' rebellion, after they realized that their approach to solving the problem—the use of dead energy—was not what Olivia had in mind. But Olivia's projections for the extinguishing of magic had been much, much further in the future. She had not anticipated the seal. Was it possible that, in order to seal away the thing under the mountain, the witches had used all of the magic that remained to them?

If that was so, then despite their victory, Arido was a much weaker country than she had been.

Their remaining forces marched for Del early the next morning. Guerline rode at the head, wearing only her linen underclothes and her leather jerkin. Her armor had been cleaned extensively last night, the victim of her insomnia. She supposed she ought to return to Del gloriously arrayed, as befitted a victorious empress, but the thought left a bad taste in her mouth. No, she would return as she was, victorious but deeply humbled. Her commanders followed her example, and rode beside her dressed likewise.

Their losses had been grave. Half of the guardsmen fell to the jaws of the hell-hounds, devil-cats, and other monsters. The remains of their bodies had been washed in Petra's Bay. Others had simply disappeared in the smoke, and Guerline feared the fate to which they were lost. Sir Yana's archers had been decimated by the possessed Thiymen witches; only twenty of them escaped without severe injury, and only sixty some survived at all. Sir Bertrand made it through the battle but succumbed to his grievous injury during the night. Sir Tragar was still unconscious; he was in the Adenen rest-wagons with the other wounded. Sir Maddox and his ilk fared best, so they now guarded those who remained.

The witches were greatly weakened as well. Many died, and many more were comatose. Jaela could not say whether they would wake again or no. Each clan had perhaps two hundred witches left, out of the many more hundreds with which they'd begun. Thiymen suffered the most. Kanika found fifty witches able to be roused. Seventy more were in deep sleep. The rest had simply vanished.

Late last night, Guerline met with Desmond, her high commanders, and the four new Hearts of the clans. Her heart was heavy with the new blow that magic was virtually gone from Arido. Tesla was optimistic that it may return, but the situation was unprecedented, and she had nothing to support her hopes. The only one who could have explained this situation to them, Lisyne, had disappeared. Guerline knew that the wolf they had seen was the shapeshifter, and she knew that Lisyne would help them no more.

"What will we do now?" Aalish had asked Guerline last night.

It was then that Guerline understood the real shift in power that had occurred. The Kavanaghs had respected her, yes, and let her command them; but they had not really looked to her for answers. She remembered the impromptu war council in her throne room, the parental smiles she'd received from each of them as she'd struggled to answer Lisyne's challenge. Now, the Kavanaghs were gone, and their replacements were all looking at her for direction. The clans deferred to her, just as Eva always wished they would.

"We will go home. We will tell this story. We will adjust," Guerline replied.

She had no idea what they were going home to. She'd promised the people of Del that their loved ones' souls would be taken to Ilys, but as she and Kanika had discussed privately, that may no longer be an option.

"Even if I had the witchpower for such a task, I do not understand this new gate," Kanika said last night after everyone else had gone. "It has a life of its own. I will need time to learn more about it."

What would Guerline tell her subjects: that she must break her first promise to them? There were so many other questions weighing on her. How long would the magic be gone? What if it never came back? In one thousand years, Arido had never been without the power of the witches. Much would change. Desmond had said her rule would be different from her parents', but he could not have guessed how much.

The column arrived at the edge of the Orchid Vale with the setting of the sun two days later. Guerline gave the order to make camp and spread the word that the next morning, they would bury their dead at the forest's edge.

Desmond came to her that night, and they held each other and wept for the first time since the battle. She couldn't say what Desmond wept for. Guerline wept for the dead, and the lost, and for those who remained; but she wept for herself the most. She felt dead and cold inside, though she knew she was still alive, and she didn't know how to make that feeling go away. Even as she curled against Desmond's warm, broad chest, she ached with loneliness.

The dawn came with an unusual chill, though Guerline couldn't determine whether it was the air or her own body. Since magic was lacking, every able body manually dug the great barrow. No one objected to the mass grave, and witches and humans were laid in it side by side. It was dark again by the time they finished. When at last the barrow was built, Jaela and the remaining Gwanen witches stepped forward. They held out their hands. Light shone forth, and a huge silver tree burst from the top of the barrow. Its roots slithered down to the base of it, enveloping it all, while branches shot into the sky high above the other trees of the Vale.

Tears pricked Guerline's eyes, and she put a hand on her heart as some of the coldness receded from her. She knew that Jaela and Gwanen had just given the remainder of their magic to create this monument. Knowing this place would be marked by such a glorious symbol of life and death comforted her.

"It is a beautiful barrow tree, Jaela-lami. Thank you," Guerline said.

Jaela only nodded, too choked with sorrow to speak.

They camped one more night under the soft glow of the barrow tree, and in the morning, they set off finally for the city of Del.

CHAPTER THIRTY-FOUR

THERE WAS CHEERING.

The column entered from the East Gate and was immediately met by a joyous throng. Guerline halted the march and stared in disbelief as people rushed forward, hands outstretched. Laughter and singing rang from the stone walls of the buildings that lined the road. Hands grasped at her horse's reins and led it forward as the crowd parted, turned, and began to walk toward the palace. One of her guides, a tiny blonde woman with a bandaged head, grinned up at her. Guerline turned to look at Desmond, eyes wide and mouth agape. He looked quite as shocked as she was, and shrugged. She heard her name chanted in the streets in front of her, and soon behind as the soldiers took up the call. Though she left her standard on the battlefield, she saw makeshift flags being raised by the Dellians, her silver starburst crudely sewn onto splotchy purple burlaps and tied to long poles.

Everywhere there were people. Huswifes and children went along the column with food and water. Flowers rained down on them. Guerline saw all this and was overwhelmed. Such a welcome dispelled her worst fears and apprehensions. She held her hands aloft and tears covered her cheeks. This time, her tears were not sorrowful. She smiled and felt the cool breeze on her wet skin, and knew that the darkness had passed. The road ahead was long and fraught with hardship, but at last she had hope.

They were escorted through the streets straight to the palace courtyard. The people lifted Guerline from her horse and set her on the ground. The gates opened and her council of advisers came rushing out, led by Lord Engineer Theodor Warren.

"Guerline! Thank the gods, Guerline!" He ran toward her and fell to his knees. "We knew that you had triumphed when the souls broke free, but we could not know how many had survived. We saw such things; black clouds, and great towers of light—" He looked at her with clear blue eyes. "What a battle it must have been."

"Yes, such a battle as I should never wish to have again," Guerline said wearily. "Come, let us go inside. You must tell me how it has gone here, and we will tell you how it was with us."

So they went into the throne room and the council presented her with all that had passed in the city since she left to muster an army. They had attempted to hold court as usual, but since there were still people holding vigil in the entrance yard, they'd had very few supplicants. Everyone was too scared, too apprehensive, to attend to their daily wants. Refugees from nearby cities flooded in. They came with ashen faces and grievous wounds, and they'd muttered absently that the dead had come alive and attacked them. The councilors deduced that across the country, all of the deceased to whom Thiymen had not come had been reanimated with murderous intent. They tried to arrange for aid to be sent to the other cities, but Del could not be mustered. The whole city had come to a standstill.

Then they saw the column of white light and the gathering black on the fifth day. That day, the wispy blue souls of those who had stayed buried on the palace green erupted from the ground and sped away to the east. For a few hours, there was terror, since no one understood what it meant that the souls had gone away; then the light won out, and the clouds disappeared, and gradually people understood that the horror had passed and that they were safe. After that, they'd prepared eagerly for the return of the empress and her troops.

Guerline listened to all of this with relief. She hadn't even thought about what would happen in the city, and she was extremely glad to hear that her oversight had not led to any damage. So, with her anxiety quieted, she told her councilors about the battle. Desmond, the witches, and the high commanders filled in where necessary, but it was mostly left to Guerline to tell the tale. They could only guess what had taken place on the old cairn where the seal had been cast.

"There was a general among them, who came to me directly," she said slowly. She was still unsure whether or not she wanted to speak of her battle with Alcander, but she felt that she must disclose everything, at least to these people. She took a deep breath to steady herself.

"It was my brother, Alcander," she said finally, and looked sternly around the room. "This part must be left from the public record of the battle at all costs! But it was him, at least in form. He was dead, and missing the arm we discovered."

"Gods. Guerline," Desmond said.

He reached out for her hand and she gave it to him, smiling sadly.

"It must have been a devil-cat that took him, not a regular wildcat," Kanika said. "Some demon used necromancy to give him life again."

"He was not himself, that much was clear. Whatever inhabited him was not my brother, it had simply assumed his likeness," Guerline said unconvincingly. In truth, he had been exactly the same: cruel and arrogant, his native traits exacerbated by the power he'd gained. "In any case, I killed him."

There was a moment of silence, and then Desmond resumed the tale of the battle. Guerline kept her encounter with Ianthe secret, envisioned it as a small thing clasped between her hand and her chest. That had been her chance to stop it, and she had squandered it, and now they were left without magic, without the Kavanaghs . . . weak.

Desmond's words were indistinct to her, but the rise and fall of his voice lulled her to a calm. At least she still had him.

"There's still so much to do," Guerline said quietly, staring out her window. "We'll have to ride out again, visit the borderlands. The Lord Merchant told me that there is still rioting in the west. We have to deal with that. The damage must be assessed. Aid must be sent out. And . . . what else? I'm forgetting something."

She glanced back at Theodor. Her chambers were just as she'd left them, that day which felt like an age ago. It felt strange to be back in them, strange to be back to palace life. She had gone away from the only place she'd ever been and come back a completely different person. Everything here was the same, at least on the surface. But Guerline knew that the carts full of dead energy, the last vestiges of magic, were in the dungeon, waiting to be dealt with. And Evadine was dead.

A small sob escaped Guerline as memories of her friend, pushed away by the battle, flooded back to her. She had missed something. Eva had lied to her. Eva had conspired with enemies of the empire. When had Eva changed? Had it been Guerline's fault? She couldn't believe that Eva had truly had any voluntary involvement with the Maravillas or Ianthe. She had so many questions, and the only three people who knew the answers—Eva and the Maravillas—were dead. She would never know the extent or motive of Evadine's apparent betrayal, but that didn't stop her from all kinds of wild imaginings.

"So much to do," she repeated. "And Eva—"

"Oh, Lina," Theodor said. "Lina, Evadine is gone, and her schemes have ended with her. We must focus on those who are alive and need us. You're not alone in this," he said. "Jaela, Tesla, Aalish, and Kanika will return to their strongholds tomorrow. Once the witches are settled, those four will return, and we will find the right path for Arido's future together."

"I know," Guerline said. "I know this. Theodor?"

"Yes?"

"Do you think the magic will ever come back?"

He sighed. "That I do not know. But whether it does or not, I have faith in Arido. And I have faith in you."

EPILOGUE

LISYNE WAITED UNTIL AFTER THE HUMANS AND WITCHES HAD left before she returned to the battlefield. She treaded slowly through the pass, where the ground was still black and the wind carried ashes from the burnt pile of corpses. She stood still and closed her eyes, breathing deep and feeling the anguish of the earth. There was still the feeling of deadness everywhere.

Though she herself had not lost her magic, she felt the change in the earth's energy. It felt like the old time, before the humans had gained their magic, before they had even come to this place from across the mountains. Lisyne sat down, raised her nose to the sky, and howled.

She was surprised to receive an answer. It was not quite sound, and yet she heard it with her ears, which pricked forward with interest. It was coming from the place where they'd cast the seal, where she'd lost all her earthly companions. Slowly, she trotted over. Their tower of light had burrowed into the ground, it seemed, and left a great pit. She toed the edge and peered down into the blackness. She could see nothing, so she circled once and changed into a great owl. She flew one circle over the pit and then alighted down into it.

At the bottom there was a great stone slab, and on it rested the thing that had made the noise-which-was-not-noise.

It looked like a human infant, but its eyes were golden like hers, and its ears were pointed. Its skin rippled every now and then like a shapeshifter's did during a change, and yet it stayed the same. This was not human, but it was not a shapeshifter either. Lisyne sniffed at it, and its noise came to her ears again. This time, it was light and modulated, like laughter. It reached for her with its tiny, five-fingered hands.

Lisyne ruffled her feathers and changed again into a griffin. She gathered the infant in her front claws and clutched it close to her chest, then spread her wings and took flight.

ARIDO AT A GLANCE

Arido was founded one thousand years ago by the witch Lirona Kavanagh. It is, for the most part, economically isolated, exporting selectively and importing mainly luxuries and foreign novelties, except in times of need which are few and far between. It is culturally isolated as well; though attractive to immigrants, its citizenship process is long and expensive, and its borders well policed. Foreign visitors tend to be only dignitaries or entrepreneurial merchants, who must lobby for years to earn space in Aridan markets. Aridans rarely travel outside the empire, indeed, they barely travel outside their own regions. Loyalty to old clans is fierce, but tends to only flare up when an insult is perceived.

The country has self-arranged into rings. In the center is Del, the capital city, surrounded by smaller "cities" made up of the modest estates of lesser nobles, wealthy merchants, and the villages of those who serve those houses. These cities are collectively called the center cities or, sometimes, the lake cities, since they surround Lake Duveau.

Beyond these cities are the middle plains, also called the valley lands, which is mainly composed of ranches and farms owned by nobles and worked by people who live in villages attached to the nobles' estate. These nobles are both landlord and overseer, businesspeople who are well-educated. There are some ranches and farms experimenting with a more egalitarian hierarchy than noble-owner and tenant-worker; several in the South have established democratic councils that make decisions regarding the farm together.

There are towns and cities in the middle plains that are not a working part of a noble estate; these have generally grown out of trading centers between estates, and are places where an independent artisan might establish themselves. Olsrec and Seul are two such towns. Less frequent are towns like Larame, insular subsistence communities which are probably the result of people leaving their liege lord's estate and establishing a permanent camp.

The last ring is the borderlands, where true cities develop again, run by crown-appointed governors rather than landed families, who are beholden to the witch clans, whose leaders are Lords Paramount of the region.

Government

The apex of government is the Emperor or Empress, currently House Hevya. Below the Empress is the imperial council:

Chief Adviser, who speaks with the Empress's voice in her absence
Lord Treasurer, manages the kingdom's currency, expenses and revenue
Lord Justice, commands all guardsmen in the country
Lord Legislator, responsible for drafting new laws and
reviewing old ones for relevance
Lord Merchant, deals with issues of trade and
goods distribution and matters of the economy
Lord Engineer, handles the construction and
repair of buildings, bridges, ships, etc.
Lord Historian, the loremaster, who keeps the histories and
scrolls of the kingdom

Equal to the councilors are the Lords Paramount (referred to by witches as the Heart of the Clan). The Lords Paramount command the witch clans and represent the crown as high arbiter in the borderlands, protecting each region and addressing the needs of the people.

Morgana Kavanagh of Adenen in the west
Olivia Kavanagh of Sitosen in the north
Fiona Kavanagh of Thiymen in the east
Aradia Kavanagh of Gwanen in the south

Below the imperial council and the Lords Paramount are the governors, appointed by the crown in the major cities which exist independent of a noble family. These governors are often the non-heir children of those landed families. These governors may appoint mayors to manage smaller towns or villages orbiting the city; they may also have a staff of officers to assist in city management. Often in small villages without an appointed mayor, the head of the village will use the title "Governor" whether or not they are crown-appointed.

The Guild of Guards (sometimes the Guild of Guardsmen or Guardsmen's Guild) is trained by Adenen and stationed in densely populated areas. The chief guard of the chief precinct in a city serves as magistrate in conjunction with the governor.

The First Families (Branwyr, Pental, Croy, Masa, and Arden) have no legal power in Aridan government, but are nonetheless very influential. These families not only own the most private land in Arido, encompassing much of the population, but their land and enterprises are crucial to the empire's existence.

Gender

Children are addressed by the ze/zim/zir pronouns unless or until such time as they claim another set, usually between the ages of five and seven. Most children choose either male or female designations and, if desired, undergo a spell to align them physically with the typical reproductive aspect. While many children are named at birth, some families allow children to name or re-name themselves when they declare their gender. Lower class families often do not name their children at all, allowing the child to choose their own name.

Education

The first school in Arido was established in 190 YM by Empress Mona Sanier Altec. It was run by Sitosen witches, with some human teachers on staff, and taught human children reading, writing, and more, from the age of five to the age of twelve. There was a fee for those who could afford it, and scholarships for those who could not, awarded at the Empress's discretion.

In modern times, children attend crown-run and crown-funded schools from the age of five until the age of sixteen. After this point, the children either apprentice to some trade, or are given private tutelage paid for by their parents. Schools are now fully run and staffed by humans, except on the northern border, where Sitosen witches still serve as administrators.

It was once common practice for noble families to secure witch tutors for their graduated children, but this practice has nearly disappeared, in favor of human tutors.

REGARDING WITCHES

According to the Book of Skins, Arido's dominant religious text, Lisyne the Mother Wolf created the witches to serve and protect her human children. In the early days of Arido, the witches did not all live in their citadels, as is the practice today. Instead, only students and teachers tended to reside at the base, while most fully-fledged witches traveled the country in mixed bands.

This practice ebbed slightly in the lead-up to the Thiymen Rebellion in 64 YM, and following the rebellion Thiymen withdrew completely from the communal bands, choosing to leave their Citadel only to investigate underworld breaches or to oversee the funerals of major chieftains. When Fiona took over Thiymen in 410 YM, she began the practice of having Thiymen witches serve as escorts for dead souls—an unnecessary practice, but one that made the dark witches indispensable to the empire in the eyes of the humans. Today, Thiymen witches stay within the Zaide Mountains except when collecting souls.

The witches of the other clans began to retreat between 480 and 520 YM. The last roaming witch band came home in 521 YM. Since then, the witches have kept to the borderlands, where witches and humans interact regularly and tend to be on very good terms. In the middle plains and the center cities, though, humans rarely if ever see non-Thiymen witches. Thanks to their lack of experience with witches, most Aridan citizens are, at best, indifferent to their distant protectors.

In the past, girls were tested at age nine for magical ability. A male-identified Aridan has never exhibited magical power. Girls exhibiting magical ability decreased sharply in the 8th century, and so Sitosen stopped sending envoys out to test children in 876 YM.

Witches live several hundred years on average (Aradia, the oldest living witch, is nearly nine hundred years old). Because of this, they often have dozens of lovers over the course of their life, and their relationships are varied and fluid. When they take human lovers, they often choose those with strong magical energy, particularly if the witch is looking to reproduce. Witch-born children reside with their mothers until their gender is claimed. Because male-identified children tend not to develop magical ability, once a witch-born child claims the male gender, the mother typically recuses herself from the boy's life, and he's sent back to the father or to a suitable family. Witch-daughters who don't develop magic sometimes stay with their mothers, but more often ask to rejoin any human relations.

MAGIC

The common areas of witchcraft include charms and transformations, martial magic, organic magic, elemental magic, healing, divination, and necromancy; these can take the form of spells, potions, or enchantments attached to objects. Witches of all clans are schooled in all forms of magic, with the exception of necromancy which is practiced exclusively by Thiymen; but each clan specializes in certain types, and each witch tends to specialize further over the course of her life.

Magic exists as part of the landscape in Arido, and witches are able to draw it from the world into themselves, then reshape and expel it in several forms. Like all conduits, there is variety in capacity, and witches range widely in power and skill. The biggest limit on a witch's magic is her own level of energy; her personal energy protects her body while channeling magic. A being's personal energy grows with age, accumulated over the course of a life, and so old witches are very powerful. A witch's capacity for channeling magic can be increased over its natural limit with some exercise, but this is a dangerous practice. If a witch exceeds her capacity, her personal energy is pulled into the spell and she runs the risk of exhausting or even killing herself in the process.

Witches typically come into their full power between one and two hundred years of age. Witches who become extremely powerful extremely young—that is, whose conduits open fully sooner than others—rarely live as long as their more paced peers. The prevailing theory is that youthful missteps in accessing such amounts of power take an early and serious toll on the witch's body, leading her to weaken and age sooner. Young witches who display great power are assigned a mentor who is with them constantly during their training to teach them how to manage their access to magic; with discipline, abnormally powerful witches often live between five and six hundred years.

THE CLANS

The witch clans are sisterhoods dedicated to the study of magic and the service of the empire and land of Arido. Each clan is stationed at the point of a compass, and specializes in particular areas of magic. The clans are individually ruled by a triumvirate of the Heart, the Hand, and the Memory, with the oldest Heart ruling over all clans as the Head of Witches.

Adenen

Adenen is a coven that values loyalty, strength and discipline above all else. Their witches are trained as an army, skilled in various kinds of combat. They are also master craftswomen, specializing in leather and metal. Adenen is renowned for its horsemanship, and horses bred by Adenen are the most coveted in the realm.

Sitosen

Sitosen clan is revered as the source of the realm's knowledge. Through their research and efforts, the country is kept on the forefront of innovation. They keep the histories, not just of Arido, but of neighboring countries and of a time before the empire. They are not just bookish, though. Sitosen is home to some of the most highly trained engineers in Arido.

Gwanen

Gwanen is widely regarded as the gentlest of the clans, largely due to its kind-hearted leader, Aradia. They believe in hard work, dedication, and simple rewards. Their expertise and innovation in agriculture keeps the realm well-fed, and their healers are famously skilled.

Thiymen

Thiymen clan is charged with guarding the boundary between life and death, and with escorting human souls to the appropriate realm of the underworld. Their use of black magic in this task, and the threat of the Judges who decide where in the underworld a human soul deserves to go, make them perhaps the most feared and misunderstood of the four clans.

MAGICAL CREATURES

Shapeshifters

True shapeshifters, even the weakest, are far more powerful magically than any witch. There is no limit to the amount of magic they can channel. Shapeshifters can transform into anyone or anything, but most of them tend to favor one or two forms. The shapeshifters were once the dominant creatures in Arido, until Lirona Kavanagh came into power. Slighted as a lover, jealous of their power and the respect they held (witches were still viewed as something of a nuisance), she led the witches in a march against all shapeshifters. Only a few survived, and retreated far into the North, outside Arido. Since then, the shapeshifters in Arido have been reframed as deities, the shifter gods.

Dragons

True dragons were once a powerful force on the continent, but they left in the early days of human migration into the Aridan valley.

The Purvaja dragons were a human tribe that resisted Thiymen rule in the early days of the Kingdom. As punishment, the first Heart of Thiymen, Petra, cursed them. Though they gained the long life of the witches, they became the slaves of Thiymen, living in caves in the mountains and forced to transform into scaly monsters at the witches' bidding. In the war days at the formation of the country, the dragons had been Thiymen war-mounts; later, they had served to police the Thiymen territories. In modern times, the dragons are hunters and scouts. Under Fiona, the tribe has been given more privileges, such as the ability to transform at will and travel freely in the East. Sights of them soaring over the countryside tend to frighten non-easterners, making the east a shunned region to most of Arido.

Giants

Tall, stocky, and more clever than one might think, the giants live in the remote forests of Lisyne's Range, the northernmost tip of Neria Forest. How many remain is unknown, since even the witches venture that far north only rarely.

Goblins

Like many nasty things, goblins live in the caves of the Zaide Mountains. They are short, stunted creatures with moon-pale skin and large eyes. They can go for weeks, sometimes months, without eating, but they are always hungry for flesh. In the time before magic, they often raided human villages in the night, but Thiymen has since put wards on the mountain passes that prevent them from coming down. These days, they stay deep in the mountain, lest they become sport for the Purvaja dragons.

Griffins

Griffins are majestic creatures with the head, wings and talons of an eagle, the body of a horse, and the tail of a lion. They roost in the ledges and crannies of the Latanya Cliff face in the West, but spend much of their lives in the Wastes of Aadi. It is said that in the War on the Shapeshifters, Lirona rode a griffin into battle, and since then many witches have tried and failed to do the same.

ACKNOWLEDGEMENTS

I started writing *From Under the Mountain* when I was fifteen. Back then, it was called *A Witch's Way* and was little more than a mash-up of Harry Potter and Lord of the Rings developed for a forum RPG. Since it's been eleven years and innumerable revisions since then, I hope my friends and family will forgive me if I miss anyone by name—rest assured, you have my thanks.

Thank you to my parents, my father for being a dreamer, and my mother for encouraging me to dream big (and helping me figure out the *2007 Writer's Market*). Thank you also to my in-laws, Paul and Kathleen, who have been all-in supporting me in this since Matt and I started dating. It's so, so appreciated.

Thank you to my husband Matt, for everything you've done to ensure I have the freedom and ability to pursue a career in publishing, for encouraging me not to stop when things seemed bleak, for doing whatever you can to help me succeed. I love you.

Thank you to my roleplaying friends, who suffered through two versions of this world before I started to figure it out—especially to Lanette, Ashlynn, and Caroline. Further thanks must go to Ashlynn for being my first real editor, who convinced me there was something to move forward with in this story...by utterly destroying my ideas, in a showing of true friendship. Thank you for continuing to encourage me through drafting, revising, querying, and publishing, for all these years.

I made the decision to seriously publish *From Under the Mountain* in 2012; thank you so much to the early beta readers whose feedback helped clarify the direction of the novel and its graduation from YA to NA. Thanks especially to Zac Anger, who not only read and provided feedback on the early manuscript, but wrote a whole album for the novel when I asked him for one song.

Thank you to Kisa Whipkey, who listened to me prattle on about this novel for more than a year before it finally signed to REUTS. I always knew *Mountain* would be in good hands with you as its editor. To Ashley Ruggirello, thank you for taking on this book, for the beautiful cover, for your input and assistance on other related materials.

I undertook a pretty ambitious plan to host a fashion show for the book launch, and in order to pull it off I launched an IndieGoGo campaign to raise money, get the book's name out, and give away swag. A huge, huge thank you to all the donors, but especially: Terence W. Cudney, Christopher M. Bruneau, Yvonne Lopez, Leslie K. Inman, Laura Spivey, James G. Kratovil IV, Liz Kuzmer Sandin, my mother Pamela Snurr, my father Mark Spivey, my in-laws Paul and Kathleen Inman, Robert Frankland, and Kathryn Scott.

I'm grateful for the wealth of fantasy authors out there, old and new, who demonstrate the versatility of the genre with every new work and continually inspire me. I'm also grateful for the online community of writers, particularly my friends on Twitter, who are supportive and enthusiastic and reassuring. And I'm very grateful for the Portland literary community, and for the interest they've shown in my work and the opportunities for outreach that have been provided for me. #keepportlandreading

Thank you to everyone who has ever said "That sounds cool" when I tell them about the book, and thank you, reader, for reading it. You're the ones who make this worthwhile.

Happy reading.

CPSIA information can be obtained
at www.ICGtesting.com
Printed in the USA
LVHW01s2224120218
566243LV00003B/646/P

9 781942 111399

ML   FEB   2018